Drawing Simplified

This edition published 2025

By Living Book Press

ISBN: 978-1-76153-447-8 (softcover)

       978-1-76153-446-1 (hardcover)

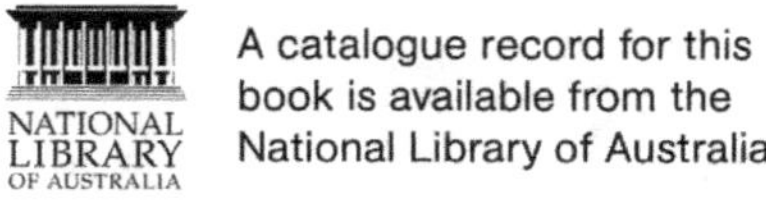
A catalogue record for this book is available from the National Library of Australia

Drawing Simplified

PREFACE.

The entire system of DRAWING SIMPLIFIED is divided into two books:

(1) "Drawing Simplified."

(2) "Elementary Drawing Simplified."

DRAWING SIMPLIFIED is a regular and complete course in *Representative Drawing* adapted for the intermediate and grammar grades. and for the self-instruction of teachers.

This book is divided into four parts, each part representing one year of work in the common schools.

They are:

Part I. The Cube and its applications.

Part II. The Cylinder and its applications.

Part III. The Triangular Prism and its applications.

Part IV. Light, Shade, Shadow and Reflections.

These parts go into the hands of the pupil as a text-book to be studied and lessons learned after the same manner as lessons in arithmetic.

The four parts are bound together in one volume for the use of teachers.

ELEMENTARY DRAWING SIMPLIFIED is a teacher's hand-book fox Primary Drawing. It is designed to show teachers how to teach drawing in the primary grades. Each step is fully illustrated and carefully graded. It does not go into the hands of the pupil at all, but guides the teacher step by step through the first four grades.

A knowledge of "Drawing Simplified" is necessary for successful work in "Elementary Drawing Simplified."

The same general plan is pursued through both books, and the same principles followed and used over and over in all of their applications.

The whole system is based on three type forms:— The cube, the cylinder, and the triangular prism, which are made the basis of all forms.

SUGGESTIONS TO TEACHERS.

MATERIALS. - The materials necessary for work are: (1) A model for each pupil and one for the teacher, (2) a medium soft pencil, (3) a rubber eraser, and (4) paper.

MODELS. - Models may be made out of card or pasteboard, cut out of plaster of Paris, paraffin, chalk, or clay, or whittled from wood. These models should be used continually in the class, and all questions referred to it. There will be a strong tendency to neglect the use of the model. This must be overcome. The pupil should be led to acquire the habit of seeking the model to help him out of difficulties, especially those involving principles. If this is done, the understanding will be clearer and the work thorough.

TEXT-BOOK. - Each pupil should have a textbook of his own as soon as he is able to understand one. Some teachers take the place of the textbook themselves and impart to the class all they know of the subject. This is right in the primary grades and may work fairly well with teachers of marked ability in the upper grades, but at the best, the knowledge will be fragmentary and the work unsatisfactory.

PLAN OF WORK. - (1) Point out and explain to the class the principle from the model. (2) Illustrate the principle on the blackboard by means of drawings. This may be reversed, with the principle explained first from the drawings on the blackboard and then verified by the model. (3) The pupil should explain the same principle from the model and illustrate it on the blackboard by drawings. (4) The principle should then be used to draw objects similar to the model.

PROBLEMS. - A clear understanding of the problems is the basis of thorough work in drawing. *Do not hasten to picture-making.* Use the greater part of the time with drill work in the problems. Draw each problem in at least four positions and often in the whole nine. You cannot fail if you do this.

COPYING. - Do not tolerate copying without understanding. It is time wasted. Teach your pupils to work independently from the principle. Then drawing will mean something to them and be a pleasure; otherwise, it is drudgery and a waste of time.

STRAIGHT EDGE. - Do not allow the use of the ruler or straight edge. Let each pupil depend on his unaided hand and eye. After control over the hand has been gained so that the execution is accurate and correct, then there will be time enough to teach the use of the ruler and straight edge.

THE BLACKBOARD. - Much of the classwork should be at the blackboard. No work will show to the teacher the pupil's knowledge so plainly or accurately or give the pupil greater confidence and independence than work at the blackboard before the class.

DRAWING FROM THE OBJECT. - It is of little use for the pupil to draw from nature or the real object until he has some knowledge to draw with, some principles that will aid him to draw intelligently. Nature's laws are so subtle that a pupil cannot understand them by copying; they must be explained and carefully verified first. Blindly copying from nature is but a step higher than blindly copying from a picture. Neither will alone teach the pupil to draw intelligently. By such methods, the pupil, through repeated failure, soon dislikes drawing. The method also requires too much time. A better plan is to commence with the idea of principle and always keep the idea behind the drawing as a propelling force. This may be done by using the type form or model and the blackboard together, using one to explain the other and then applying the knowledge to similar forms.

THE FOUNDATION. - Four studies are the foundation of all other branches; they are number, language, drawing, and music. These studies take more time to master because they are the basis of whole departments. They are not like algebra, geography, physiology, etc., but are the basis of these studies. *For this reason, the drawing class should meet every day.* In proportion as a thorough knowledge of the fundamentals is acquired, the time for the mastery of all the other branches may be shortened.

SIZE OF DRAWING. - In general, the size of the paper determines the size of the drawing. This is not arbitrary, however. A drawing with a lead pencil should be at least two by three inches for a single object and eight by ten inches on the blackboard. The habit of making very small drawings should be discouraged.

WHAT A PUPIL SHOULD KNOW IN DRAWING. - A pupil should not only know how to draw objects placed before him but *his own thoughts as well*. He should (1) be able to draw the object as placed before him, (2) draw from memory, and (3) draw from the imagination.

FORM STUDY AND DRAWING.

THE CUBE.

THE CUBE is the basis of forms having straight lines and square corners.

The *top face* of the cube is the basis of all square or rectangular *horizontal surfaces*, such as fields, floors, streets, etc.

The *side face* of the cube is the basis of all square or rectangular *vertical surfaces*, such as walls, sides of buildings, etc.

The *inside* of a hollow cube or box is the basis of all enclosed cubical or rectangular spaces, such as rooms, halls, tunnels, etc.

The *square or rectangle* is the most prominent figure.

The first difficulty the beginning student of drawing meets is to *represent distance away on a flat surface*, to represent apparent thickness where there is no *real* thickness. For example, there is no trouble to represent the square face, ABCD (Fig. 1). The difficulty begins when the attempt is made to represent the receding faces DEFC and ADEG. This difficulty must be overcome before much progress in drawing can be made, and to accomplish this end is the first object of the following problems.

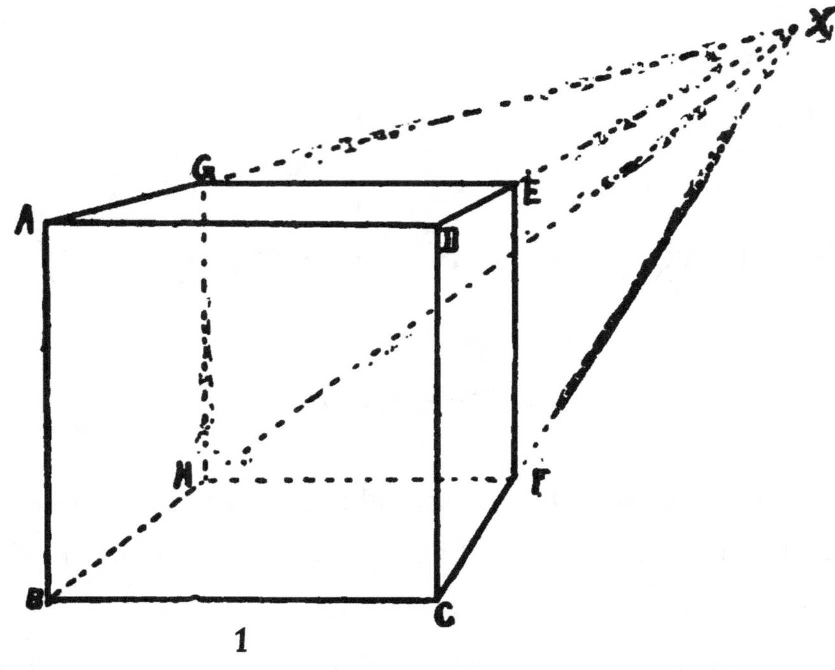

GENERAL DIRECTIONS.

THE CUBE[1] (Fig. 1) is composed of three classes of lines: (1) vertical lines, (2) horizontal lines, and (3) receding lines.

THE VERTICAL LINES A B, E F, G H[2], and D C are drawn parallel with the sides of the paper on which the drawing is made.

THE HORIZONTAL LINES AD, BC, GE, and HF are drawn parallel with the top and bottom of the paper on which the drawing is made.

[1]   A rectangular-shaped box of any kind may be used instead of a cube. It should be held in the hand in the same position as the one represented in the problem. Reference to this box will greatly aid in understanding the problems.

[2]   The dotted lines G H, F H and B H cannot be seen in the real cube unless it is transparent. They are represented here to show their position and to represent all the lines of the cube.

THE RECEDING LINES DE, CF, AG, and BH are drawn from the corners A, B, C, and D to the point X, which is called the Centre of Vision[3] (C. of V.). The receding lines represent *distance away or thickness*. When the drawing of the cube contains both vertical and horizontal lines, the receding lines converge at the C. of V.

These receding lines converging at the C. of V. represent lines in nature that are parallel, and they are spoken of in drawing as parallel lines[4].

Thus the cube has twelve lines, three classes of lines, with four lines in each class, and the lines of each class are parallel.

Each corner of the cube is formed by a vertical, a horizontal, and a receding line, though often only two of these lines can be seen, as at corners B, F, and G where the third line is hidden by the body of the cube.

All proportions and measurements are to be judged by the unaided eye, and each line should be drawn with the unaided hand. For example, after drawing the square ABCD (Fig. 1) and the receding lines to the C. of V., the point E must be chosen by means of the unaided eye[5]. It may be taken for granted that if the drawing looks right, it is right.

3   The C. of V. is the point directly opposite the eye.
4   All receding lines that converge to the same point represent parallel lines.
5   There will be a strong tendency to exaggerate the distance on these receding lines. It may be overcome by going to the other extreme.

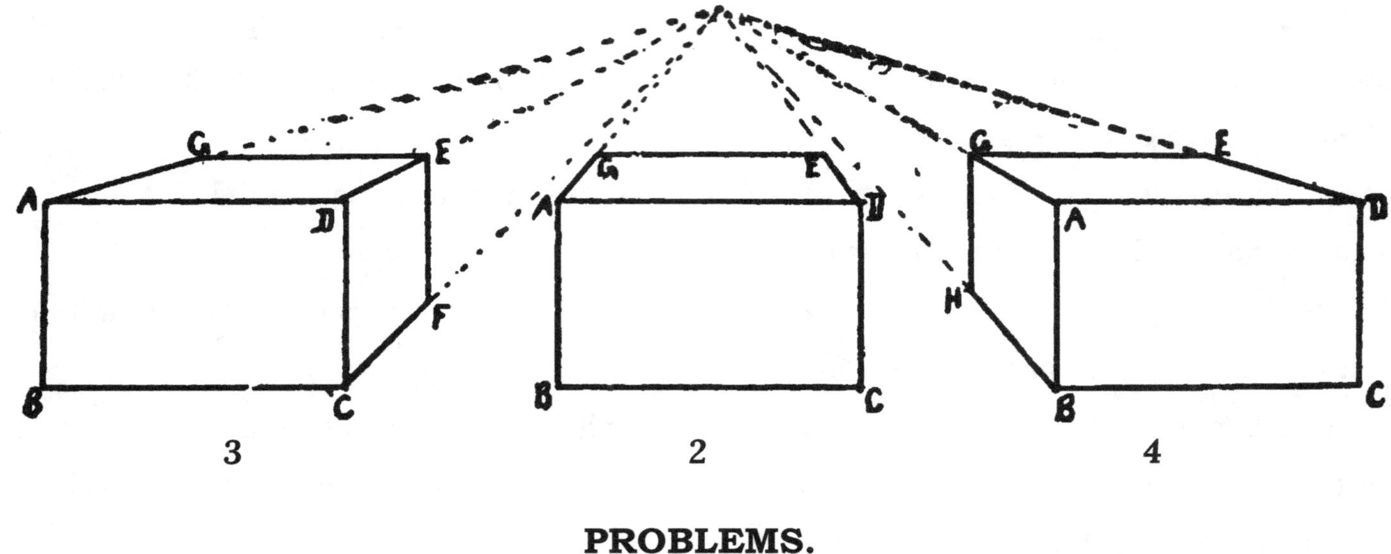

PROBLEMS.

PROBLEM 1. FIG. 2. - *Draw a box[6] below the level of the eye (C. of V.)[7].*

(1) Draw the nearest face of the box ABCD. (2) Place the C. of V. (3) From the corners A and D, draw receding lines to the C. of V. (4) Choose the point E and from it draw the horizontal line GE. (5) Take the real box and hold it before your eye in the same position, and study it, pointing to an edge on the real box and then to the corresponding line in the drawing.

6   A box is preferable to a cube. A common chalk box is an excellent model.

7   The term " eye" " instead of the plural eyes is used because the place of observation is supposed to be a point. The C. of V. and the eye of the observer are opposite points, but being in line with each other are represented by the same point. This point is called the C. of V. when the point beyond the object represented is referred to, and "the eye," or the eye of the observer when the point this side of the object represented is referred to. The object represented is between the eye and the C of V.

PROBLEM 2. FIG. 3. - *Draw a box below and at the left of the eye.*

(1) Draw the nearest face of the box ABCD. (2) Place the C. of V. (3) From the corners A, D, and C draw receding lines to the C. of V. (4) Choose the point E and from it draw a vertical and a horizontal line to F and G. (5) Take the real box and hold it in the same position at the left and below the eye, and study it.

PROBLEM 3. FIG. 4. - *Draw a box below and at the right of the eye.*

(1) Draw the front face of the box ABCD. (2) Place the C. of V. (3) From the corners A, B, and D draw receding lines to the C. of V. (4) Choose the point G and from it draw a vertical line to H and a horizontal line to E. (5) Compare the drawing with the real box held in the same position.

Observe that the receding lines in the above problems slant upward from the corners that they start from.

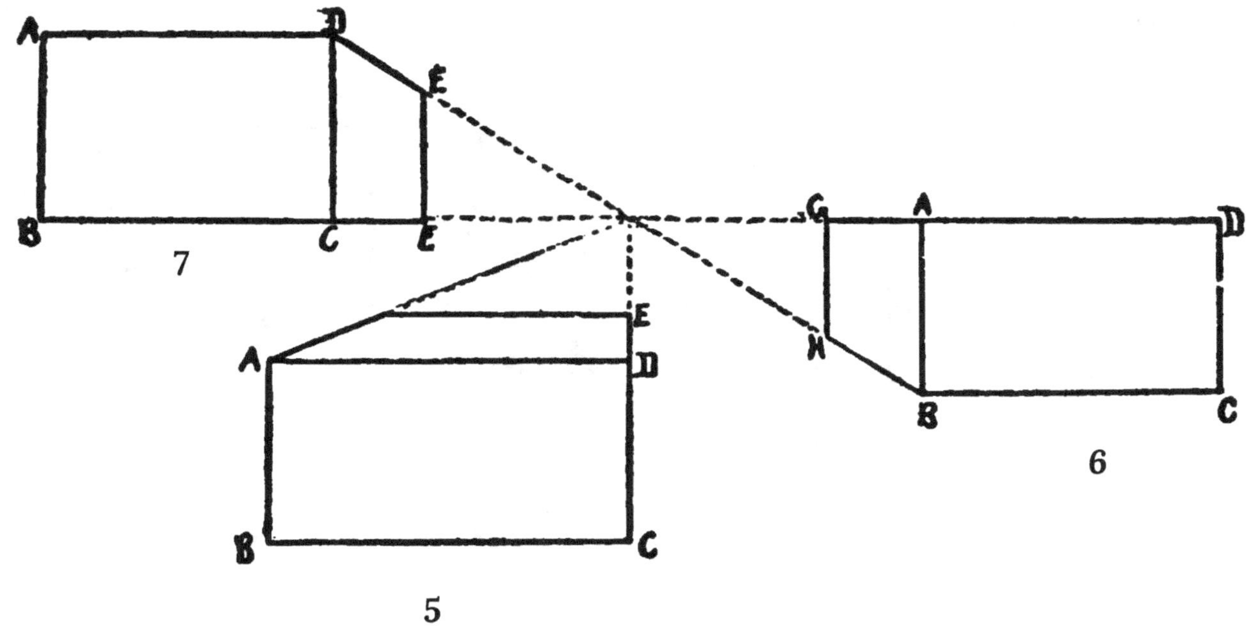

PROBLEM 4. FIG. 5. - *Draw a box with the right side directly below the eye.*

Observe that the receding line DE, being directly in line with the eye, is vertical and in line with the vertical line DC. See this point on the real box by holding it in the same position.

PROBLEM 5. FIG. 6. - *Draw a box at the right of the eye with the top face on a level with the eye.*

(1) Draw the front face of the box ABCD. (2) Place the C. of V. (3) From the corners A and B draw receding lines to the C. of V. (4) Choose the point G and from it draw a vertical line to H. (5) Observe that the receding line AG is horizontal and in line with the horizontal line AD. (6) Observe this on the real box.

PROBLEM 6. FIG. 7. - *Draw a box at the left of the eye with the bottom face on a level with the eye.*

Observe that the receding line CF is horizontal and in line with the horizontal line BC. Observe this on the real box.

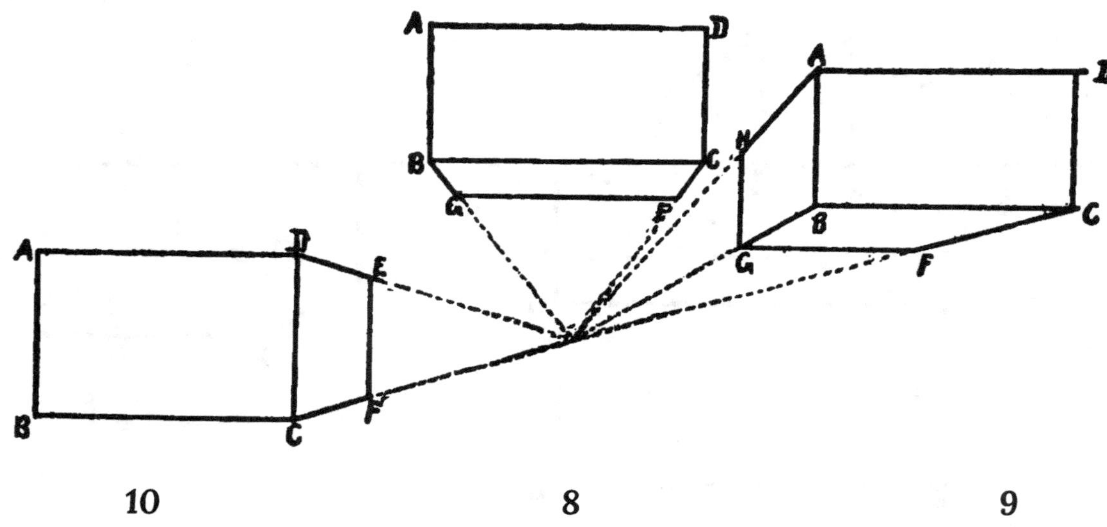

PROBLEM 7. FIG. 8. - *Draw a box above the eye.*

(1) Draw the front face of the box ABCD. (2) Place the C. of V. (3) From the corners B and C draw receding lines to the C. of V. (4) Choose the point G and from it draw a horizontal line. (5) Hold the real box in the same position and study it.

PROBLEM 8. FIG. 9. - *Draw a box[8] at the right and above the eye.*

(1) Draw the front face of the box ABCD. (2) Place the C. of V. (3) From corners A, B, and C draw receding lines to the C. of V. (4) Choose the point G and from it draw a vertical line and a horizontal line. (5) Study the real box in the same position.

PROBLEM 9. FIG. 10. - *Draw a box at the left of the eye[9].*

Observe that all of the receding lines of Figs. 8 and 9 slant downward from the corners that they start from.

Thus we have the following laws governing receding lines:

(1) Receding lines below the level of the eye slant upward.

(2) Receding lines above the level of the eye slant downward.

(3) Receding lines on a level with the eye are horizontal.

(4) Receding lines directly in line with the eye are vertical.

Prove these laws on the real box.

PROBLEM 10. FIG. 11. - *Draw a box directly in front of the eye.*

In this position, only the front face of the box can be seen. Hold the real box directly in front of the eye and see.

8   Care should be taken not to put the C. of V. too far from the box. It will look badly drawn.

9   By changing the C. of V. these problems may be changed indefinitely, thus making it impossible for the pupil to simply copy.

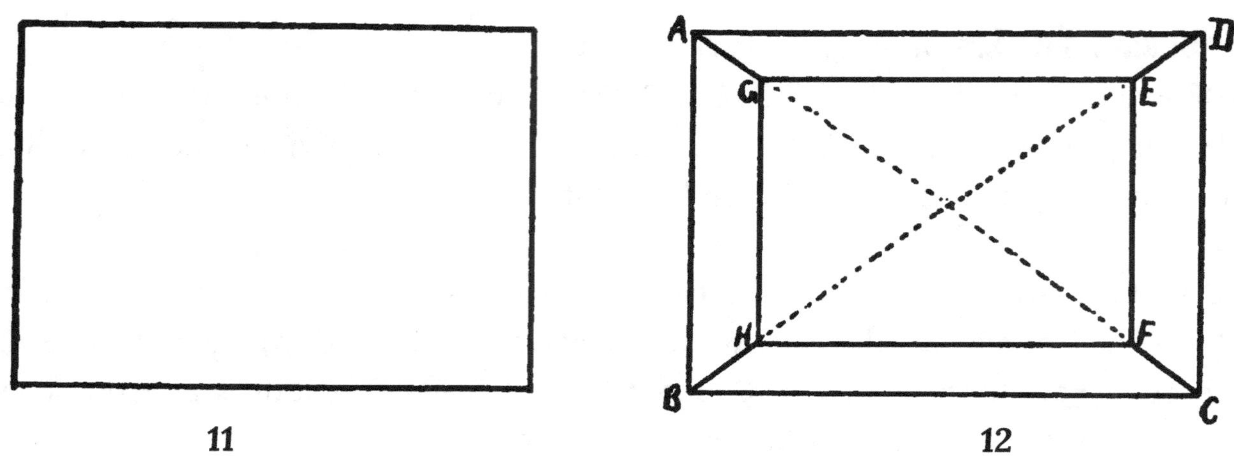

11   12

PROBLEM 11. FIG. 12. - *Draw a box directly in front of the eye with the front face removed so that the inside of the box can be seen.*

(1) Draw the front face ABCD. (2) Place the C. of V. (3) From the corners A, B, C, and D draw receding lines to the C. of V. (4) Choose the point E and from it draw a vertical and a horizontal line. (5) From G draw a vertical line meeting a horizontal line from F at H.

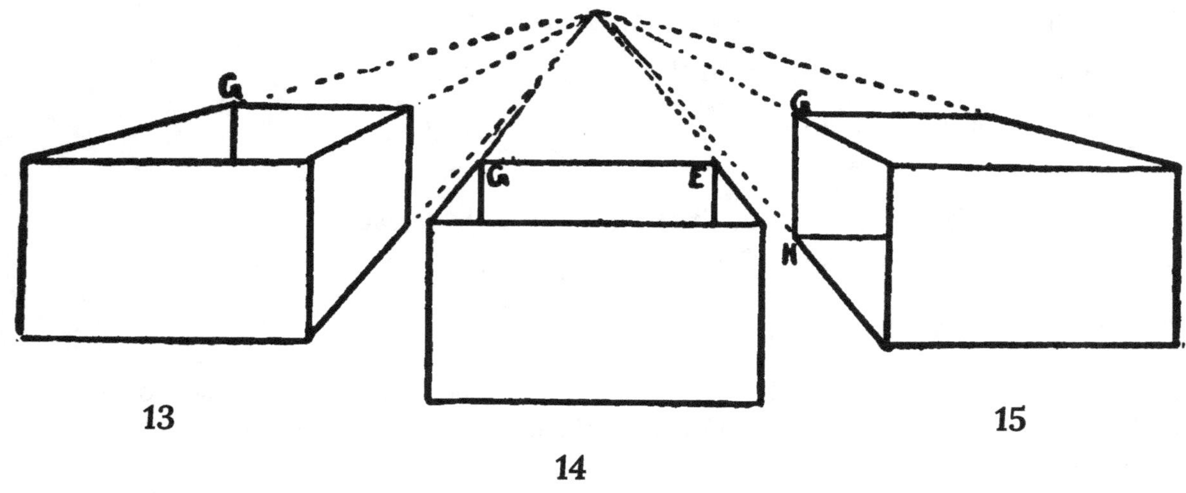

13   15

14

PROBLEM 12. FIG. 13. – *Draw a box below and at the left of the eye and remove the cover from the top face showing the inside.*

(1) Draw the box. (2) From corner G draw a vertical line. (3) See real box in the same position.

Problem 13. – *Draw a box below and at the right of the eye and from the top face remove the cover showing the inside.*

Problem 14. – *Draw a box above and at the left of the eye and from the bottom face remove the cover showing the inside.*

PROBLEM 15. FIG. 14. – *Draw a box below the eye and remove the cover from the top.*

(1) Draw the box. (2) From corners G and E draw vertical lines. (3) See real box held in the same position.

Problem 16. – *Draw a box above the eye and from the bottom remove the cover.*

PROBLEM 17. FIG. 15. – *Draw a box below and at the right of the eye and remove the left side.* (1) Draw the box. (2) From corner H draw a horizontal line. (3) See real box.

Problem 18. – *Draw a box below and at the left of the eye and remove the right side.*

Problem 19. – *Draw a box above and at the right of the eye and remove the left side.*

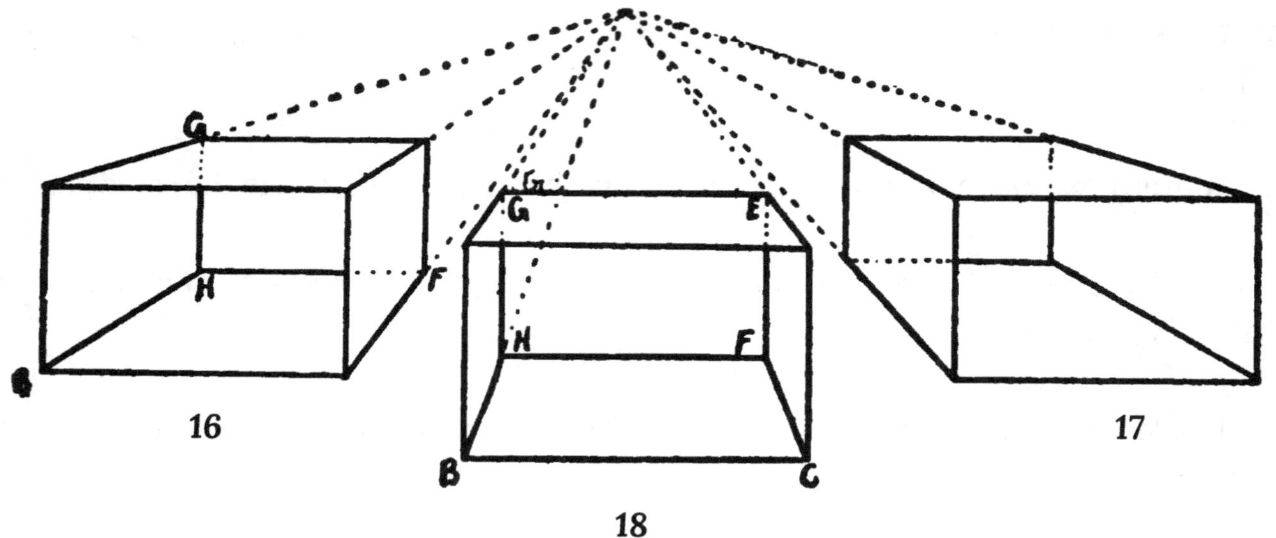

PROBLEM 20. FIG. 16. - *Draw a box below and at the left of the eye and remove the front face showing the inside.*[10]

(1) Draw the box. (2) From corner G, draw a vertical line meeting a horizontal line from corner F, and a receding line from corner B at H. (3) Compare with the real box.

Problem 21. - *At the left and above the eye, draw a box and remove the front face, showing the inside.*

See the real box and Problem 20.

PROBLEM 22. FIG. 17. - *Below and at the right of the eye, draw a box and remove the front face, showing the inside.*

See the real box.

10   Observe that the lines that mark the inside of the box in Figs. 13–17 are drawn from those corners that show only two lines in the solid box or cube.

Problem 23. - *Above and at the right of the eye, draw a box and remove the front face, show-ing the inside.*

PROBLEM 24. FIG. 18. - *Draw a box below the level of the eye and remove the front face, showing the inside.*

(1) Draw the box. (2) From corners E and G, draw vertical lines, meeting receding lines from corners B and C at H and F. (3) Draw the horizontal line H F. (4) Compare with the real box.

Problem 25. - *Draw a box above the eye and remove the nearer end, showing the inside.*

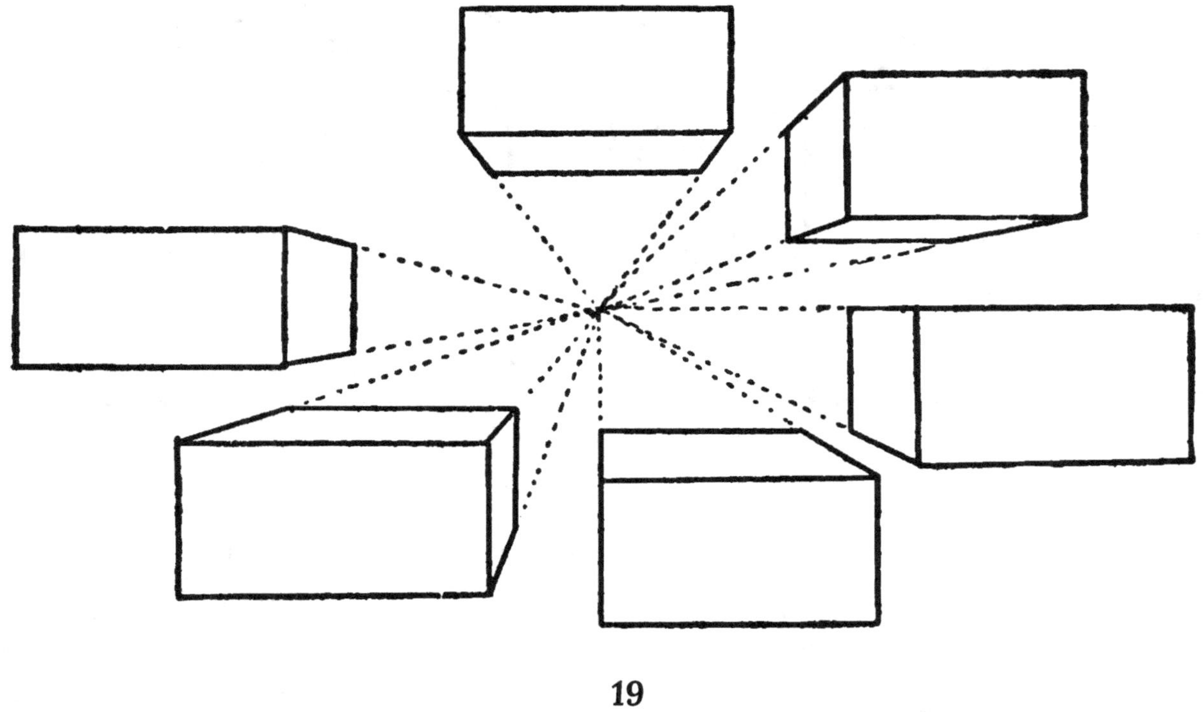

19

PROBLEM 26. FIG. 19. – *Around a center of vision, draw six boxes:*

(1) One below, with the left side directly below the eye.

(2) One at the right, with the top level with the eye.

(3) One at the right and above the eye.

(4) One above the eye.

(5) One at the left of the eye.

(6) One below and at the left of the eye.

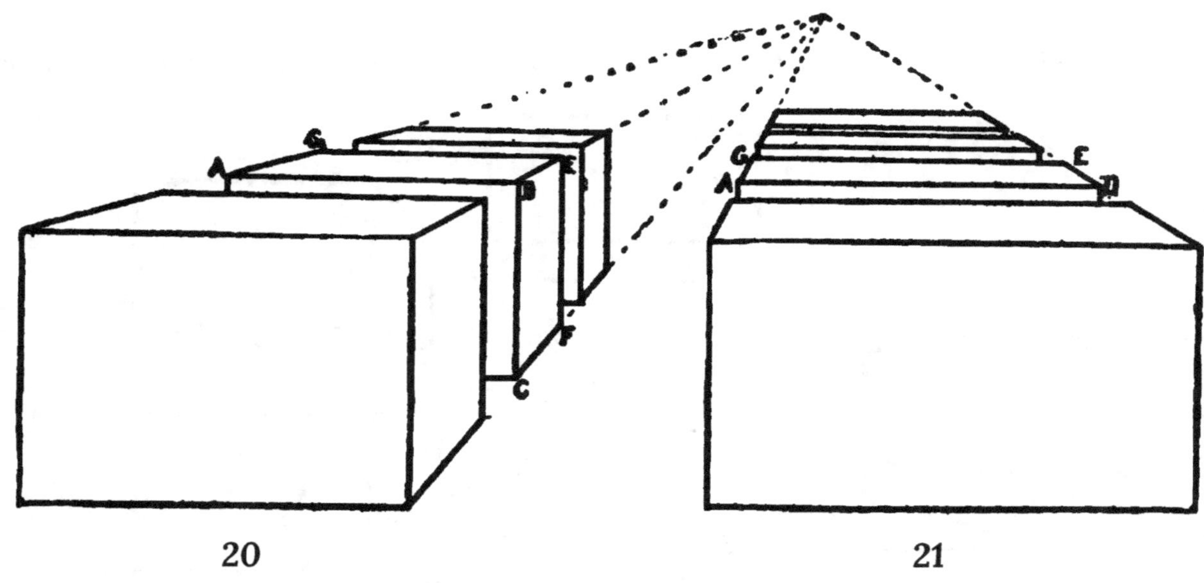

20

21

PROBLEM 27. FIG. 20. - *Below and at the left of the eye, draw a row of three boxes extending toward the C. of V.*

(1) Draw the first box. (2) Choose points D and E, and from each, draw a vertical and a horizontal line. (3) From A, draw a vertical line. (4) From C, draw a horizontal line. (5) Draw the third box in the same manner.

Observe that each box is smaller and each line shorter the farther the box is away.

Problem 28. – *Below and at the right of the eye, draw a row of four boxes extending toward the C. of V. (See Problem 27.)*

PROBLEM 29. FIG. 21 – *Below the level of the eye, draw a row of four boxes extending toward the C. of V.*

(1) Draw the nearest box. (2) Choose points A and G, and from each, draw a horizontal line. (3) From A and D, draw vertical lines. (4) Draw the third and fourth boxes in the same manner.

Problem 30. – *Above the level of the eye, draw a row of three boxes extending toward the C. of V.*

Problem 31. – *Above and at the left of the eye, draw a row of three boxes extending toward the C. of V.*

PROBLEM 32. FIG. 22. – *At the left and above the eye, draw a cube[11].*

(1) Draw the square A B C D. (2) Place the C. of V. and draw the receding lines. (3) Choose corner E at a point that will make it seem as long as the other edges of the cube. (4) Finish as in drawing the box. (5) By drawing diagonal lines across each face, the center of that face may be ascertained, as at E, F, and G.

PROBLEM 33. FIG. 23. – *Draw a cube and divide it into two parts.*

(1) Draw the cube. (2) Choose points A and B, and from each, draw a vertical and a receding line. (3) Erase the horizontal lines E F, A B, and C D. (4) From D, draw a vertical line. (5) From F, draw a horizontal line.

[11]   These problems are suitable for drill work at the blackboard. When drawing the box, you are confined to no particular length, height, or width, but when drawing the cube, all of these dimensions must look equal.

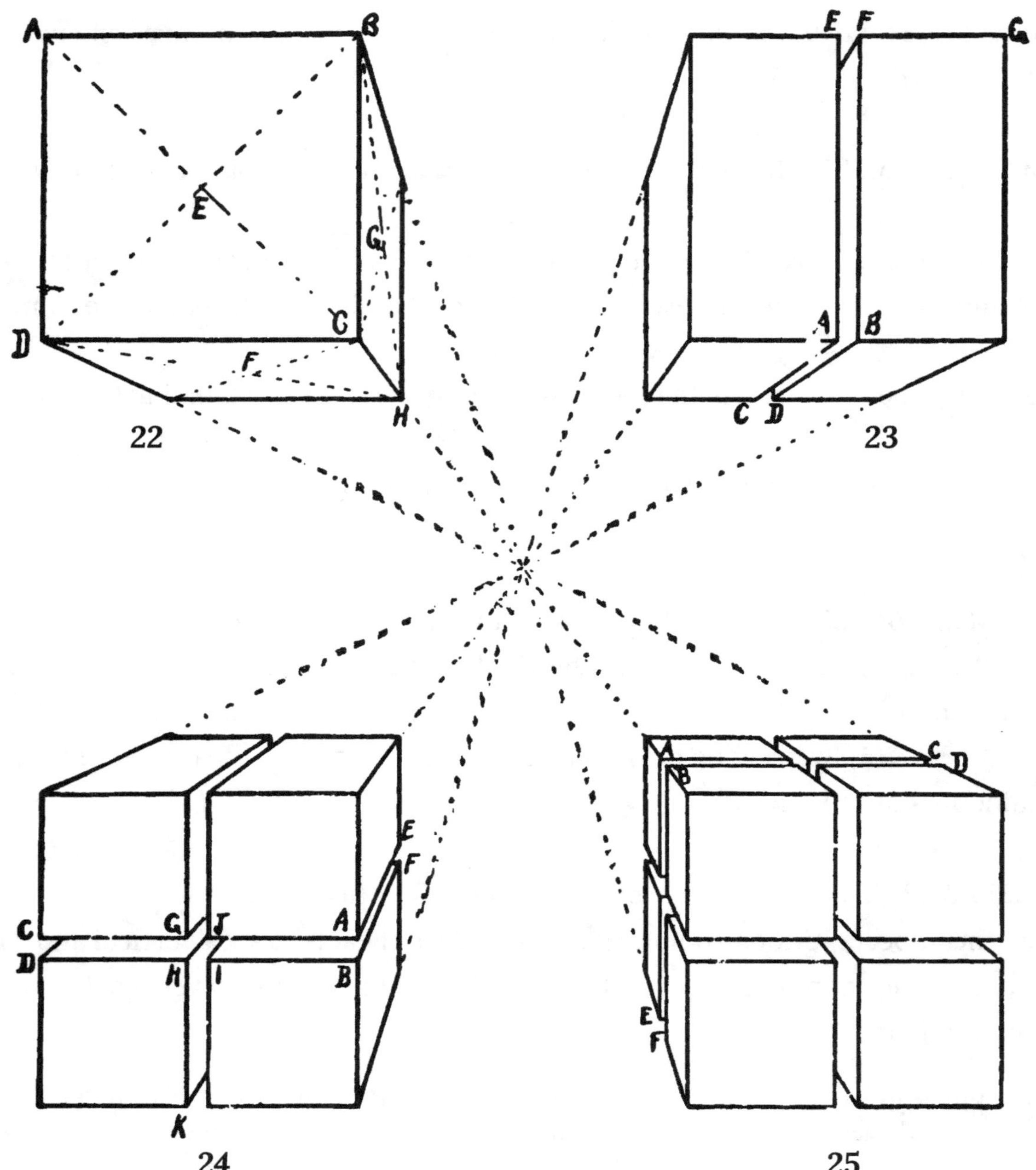

A
B
E
C
D
F
G
H
22
E F
G
A B
C D
23
C
D
G J
H I
A
B
E
F
K
24
B
C D
A
E
F
25

PROBLEM 34. FIG. 24. - *Draw a cube and divide it into four parts.*

(1) Draw the cube. (2) Divide it into two parts. (See Problem 33.)

(3) Choose points A and B, and from each, draw a horizontal and a receding line. (4) Erase the vertical connecting lines C D, G H, I A, B and E F. (5) From F, draw a horizontal line. (6) From D, G, H, I, and K, draw receding lines.

PROBLEM 35. FIG. 25. - *Draw a cube and divide it into eight parts.*

(1) Draw the cube. (2) Divide it into two parts. (See Problem 33.)

(3) Divide it into four parts. (See Problem 34.)

(4) Choose points A and B, and from each, draw a vertical and a horizontal line. (5) Erase the lines that connect the two parts. (6) From the side face, draw horizontal lines and from the top face, vertical lines.

(7) Observe that the lines from the top face are vertical lines, from the side face, horizontal lines, and from the front face, receding lines.

PROBLEM 36. FIG. 26. - *From each corner of a large cube, cut a small cube[12].*

(1) Draw the cube. (2) Choose points A, B, and C. (3) From A, draw a vertical and a receding line. (4) From B, draw a horizontal and a receding line. (5) From C, draw a vertical and a horizontal line. (6) Erase corner G, the corner of the large cube. (7) From E, draw a vertical line, from F a horizontal line, and from D, a receding line. (8) In the same manner, cut small cubes from the remaining corners in the order of their lettering I, J, K, L, M, and N.

The diagonal line G M marks a square on the receding face where it meets the receding lines at E and O.

12   Procure a large potato or apple, cut it to a square corner, like the corner of a cube, and out of this corner cut a small cube to use for reference. Hold the potato or apple with the cut-out part in the position of the cube you are cutting out in your drawing. Cut a potato likewise for Problems 27 and 28.

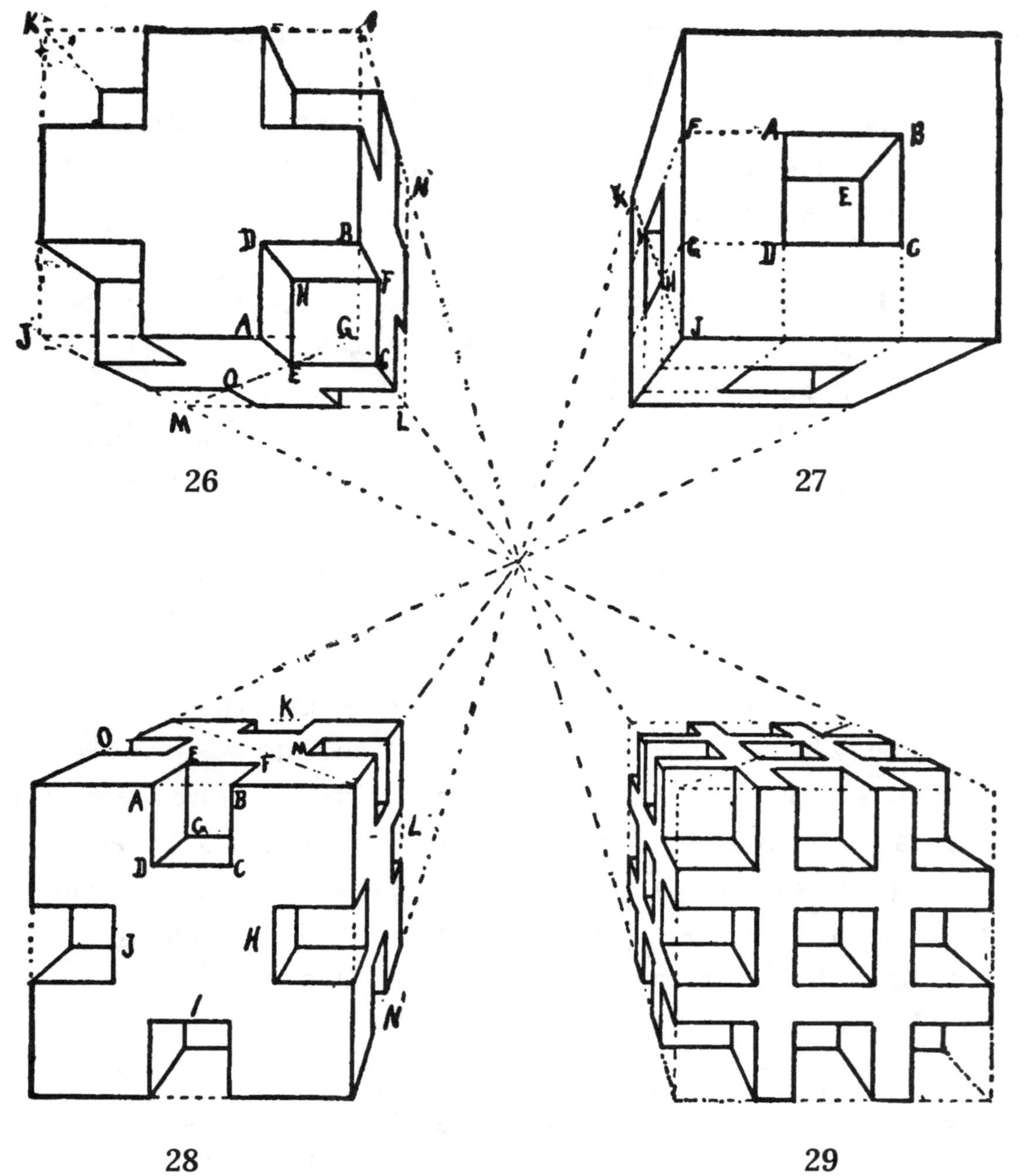

26

27

28

29

PROBLEM 37. FIG. 27. - *From each face of a large cube, cut a small cube*[13].

(1) Draw the cube. (2) Draw the square A B C D. (3) From point B, draw a receding line to the C. of V. (4) Choose point E, and from it, draw a vertical and a horizontal line. (5) From F and G, draw receding lines. (6) Draw the diagonal J K. (7) Where the diagonal line crosses the receding lines at H and I, draw vertical lines. (8) From I, draw a horizontal line. (9) Cut the cube from the bottom in the same manner as from the side.

PROBLEM 38. FIG. 28. - *From each edge of a large cube, cut a small cube.*

(1) Draw the cube. (2) Choose points A and B, and from them, draw the square A C D. (3) From points A, B, and D, draw receding lines. (4) Choose point E, and from it, draw a vertical and horizontal line. (5) From G, draw a horizontal line. (6) In like manner, cut cubes from the remaining edges in the order of their lettering J, K, and O.

PROBLEM 39. FIG. 29. - *Combine Figs. 26, 27, and 28 into one problem.*

PROBLEM 40. FIG. 30. - *From each vertical edge of a cube, cut a rectangular solid the length of that edge.*

PROBLEM 41. FIG. 31. - *From each receding edge of a cube, cut a rectangular solid the length of that edge.*

PROBLEM 42. FIG. 32. - *From each horizontal edge of a cube, cut a rectangular solid the length of that edge.*

13   Many can see and understand these problems better when drawn below and at the left of the eye. There is no objection to drawing them in this position provided they are drawn in other positions afterward.

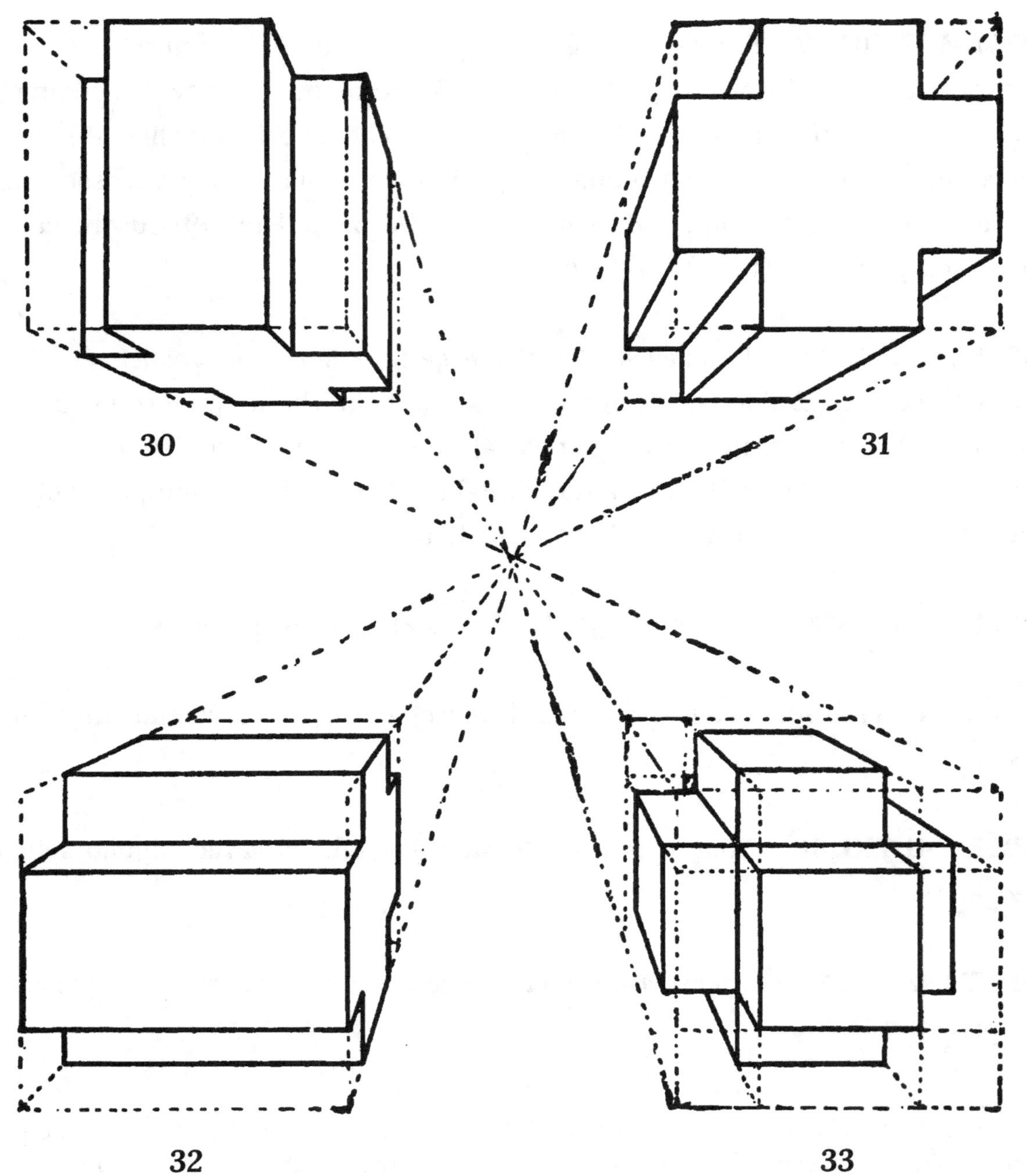

30
31
32
33

PROBLEM 43. FIG. 33. - *Combine Figs. 30, 31, and 32 into one figure.*

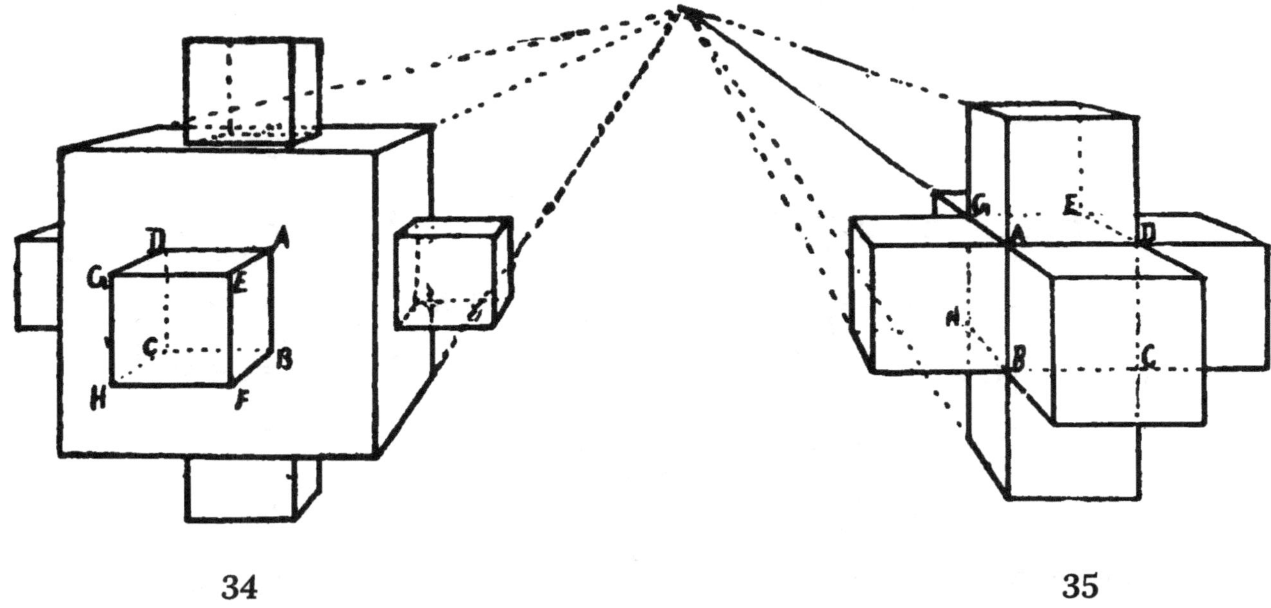

34

35

PROBLEM 44. FIG. 34. - *To each face of a large cube, add a small cube.*

(1) Draw the large cube. (2) Draw the square A B C D. (3) From the C. of V., through points A, B, and D, draw receding lines. (4) Choose point E, and from it, draw a horizontal and vertical line. (5) From G, draw a vertical line, and from F, a horizontal line meeting at H. (6) In like manner, draw the remaining cubes.

Problem 45. Fig. 35. - To each face of a small cube, add another cube of the same size.

(1) Draw the small cube A B C D E G and H. (2) To each face of this cube, add another of the same size.

Problem 46. - *Draw Fig. 35 below and at the left of the eye.*

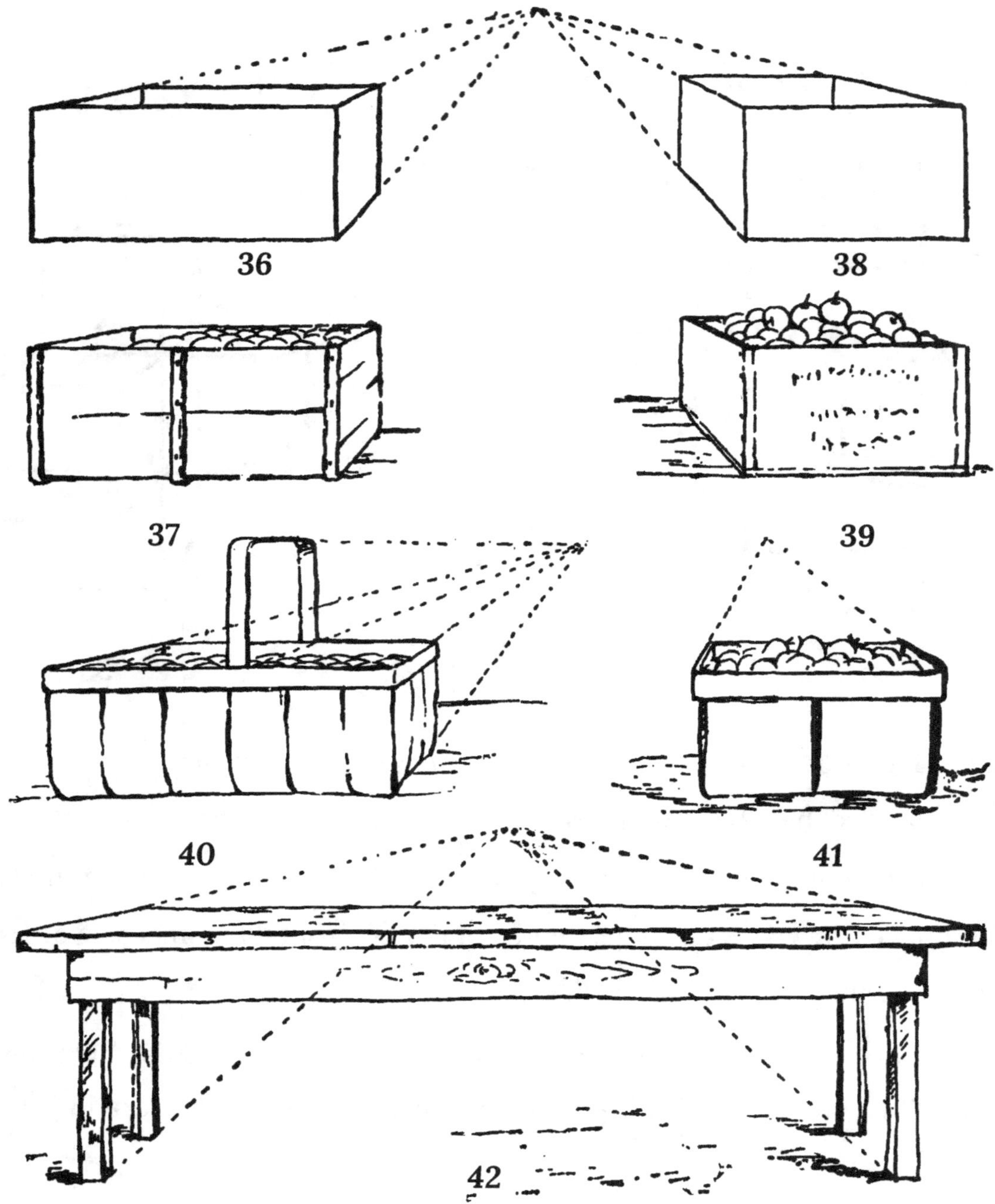

36
38
37
39
40
41
42

Problem 48. - *Draw Fig. 35 above and at the right of the eye.*

Problem 49. - *Draw Fig. 35 directly in front of the eye.*

WITH FIG. 37, another element enters into drawing – the element of *expression.*
Expression may be best learned:

1. *By observation* – by studying the drawings of others and observing how they express ideas by means of lines and forms.

2. *By imitation* – by imitating the manner of drawing, not by copying line by line, but by studying and copying the method, the underlying principle on which the drawing is made.

3. *By application* – a principle is of little practical use if it is not applied.

When a valuable point is gained, it should be applied until it is thoroughly understood. Repetition is a key to knowledge.

Observe in Figs. 37, 39, and 40 that the lines are not all alike as in Figs. 34 and 35, but that some are heavier than others. Notice also that the lines are heavier in some places than in others. This is done to give emphasis to certain parts and to bring out the meaning more clearly. One kind of line throughout would make the work look monotonous and uninteresting.

In general, the farther a line is away, the lighter and less distinct it becomes. For this reason, the further line of the tabletop in Fig. 42 is not so heavy as the line that marks the nearer edge.

It is well to have special drills on the strength of lines. The following is an excellent drill:

Draw (1) A light line. (2) A heavy line. (3) Four lines from light to heavy. (4) Four lines from heavy to light. (5) A line light at each end and heavy in the center. (6) A line heavy at each end and light in the center. (7) A line varying from light to heavy several times, etc., etc.

Commence drawing Figs. 37 and 39 by making an outline similar to Figs. 36 and 38, and then the whole attention may be given to the expression of the outline. The outline should be made with a very light line like Fig. 38, so that it may be easily erased if necessary.

Notice in Figs. 37 and 39 that the construction lines are erased.

These lines should always be erased in the completed drawing.

Figs. 40, 41, and 42 are simple applications of the box problems. Draw each one the same as if it were a simple box, and then turn it into the object it represents.

Problem 50. – (1) Draw the basket (Fig. 40) below and at the right of the eye. (2) Below the eye. (3) Below and at the left of the eye and with the end toward you.

Problem 51. – (1) Draw Fig. 37 at the right and below the eye. (2) Below the eye.

Problem 52. – (1) Draw Fig. 41 below and at the right of the eye. (2) Below and at the left of the eye.

Problem 53. – Draw the table (Fig. 42) with the top on a level with the eye. (2) With the end toward you.

HORIZON LINE.

THE HORIZON LINE (H. L.) is a horizontal line that marks the level of the eye. It is the most important line in the picture and determines the drawing of all receding lines. This line is marked M N in the illustrations.

THE CENTER OF VISION (C. of V.) is the point in the horizon line directly opposite the eye. The C. of V. is the most important point in the picture.

The H. L. should be represented in all drawings whether it can be seen or not. In Fig. 47, this line cannot be seen, but it is represented by a dotted line. When the drawing is completed, this dotted line, along with all the construction lines, should be erased.

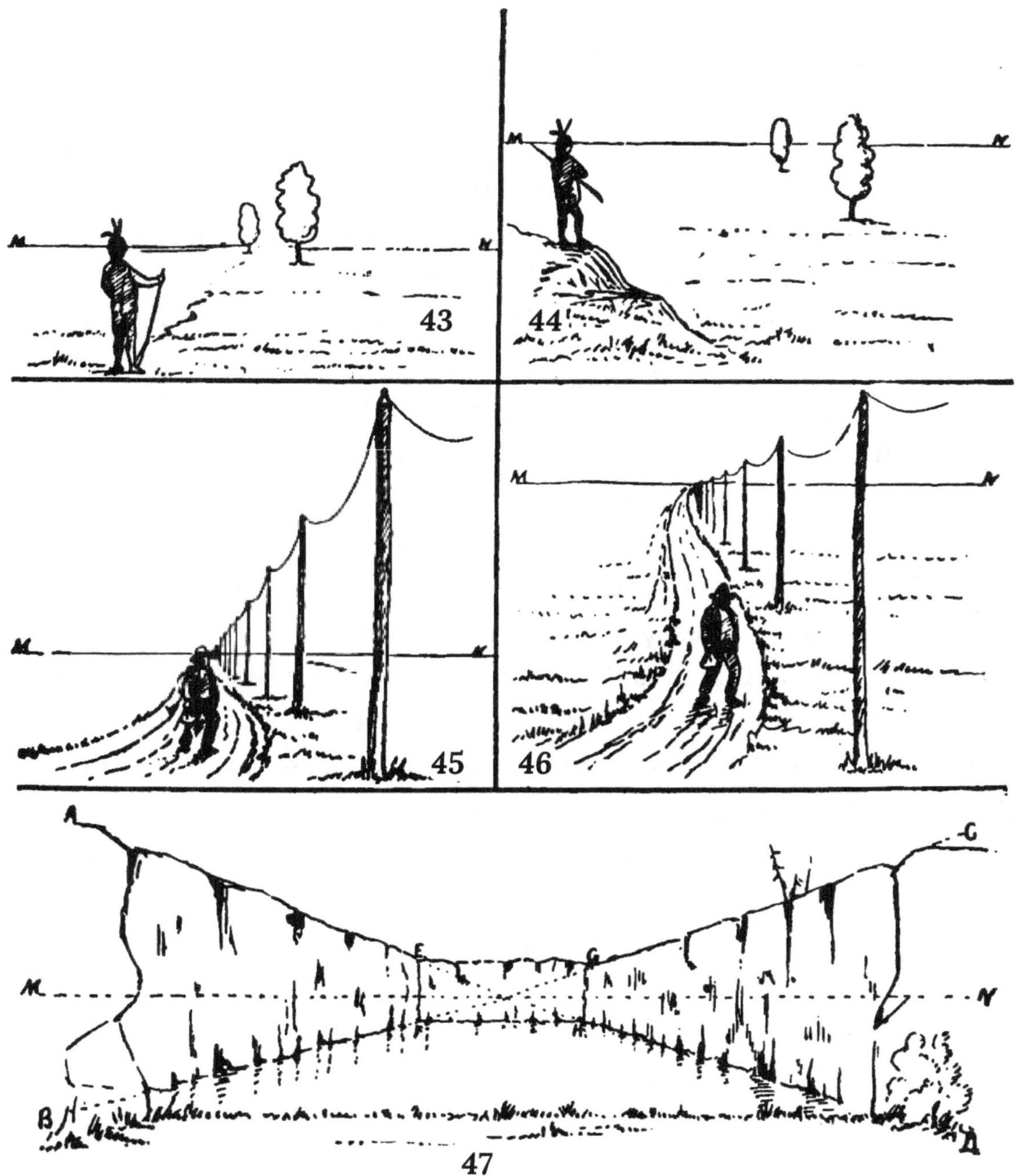

M
N
43
44
45
46
A
C
M
N
B
Д
47

The H. L. may be placed anywhere on the paper, but in general, the most satisfactory place is slightly below the middle of the picture.

The most satisfactory place for the C. of V. is at, or near, the middle of the H. L.

In nature, the H. L. is an imaginary line that exists only in the eye of the observer. On a level plain, this line may be seen where the sky and earth seem to meet, but even here, no two persons will see the same H. L. unless their eyes are level with each other. A person standing on a level plain would not see the same H. L. that he would see from an eminence.

For example, supposing the Indian in Figure 43 is the observer. Then the H. L. will be on a level with his eye, and he sees this line cross the trees below their branches. The Indian ascends a small hill (Fig. 44). As he ascends, the H. L. ascends with him, or rather, he sees a higher H. L. every step he takes upward. At the top of the hill, the H. L. is much higher up and crosses the trees up among their branches. The trees have not changed, but the Indian has, and he sees a new H. L. higher up.

In Figs. 43 and 44, the Indian is the observer, but in Figs. 45 and 46, suppose you are the observer. You see the man coming along the road, and his head is about level with yours, as is shown by the H. L. Now supposing you ascend until your eyes are near the top of the telegraph poles. Now you see a new H. L. far above the man's head, and you can also see much further, showing that the higher the eye, the higher the H. L. will be[14].

PROBLEMS.

FIGURE 47 is drawn the same as a box directly in front of the eye with the top and front face removed. It is drawn very much as Fig. 12.

14   This may be proven very easily on a level plain by means of a spirit-level

(1) Draw the H. L. (2) Place the C. of V. (3) Choose the points A, B, C, and D and from them draw receding lines to the C. of V. (4) Choose the point E and draw EF and EG. (5) Draw GH and FH. (6) Give expression to the different lines.

Problem 54. - Draw Fig. 47 with the H. L. on a level with the top of the bluffs.

Problem 55.- Draw Fig. 47 with the C. of V. directly in line with the face of the bluff on the right.

All of these drawings should be drawn carefully: (1) On paper with a lead pencil. (2) Draw from memory on paper. (3) Reproduce on the blackboard from memory.

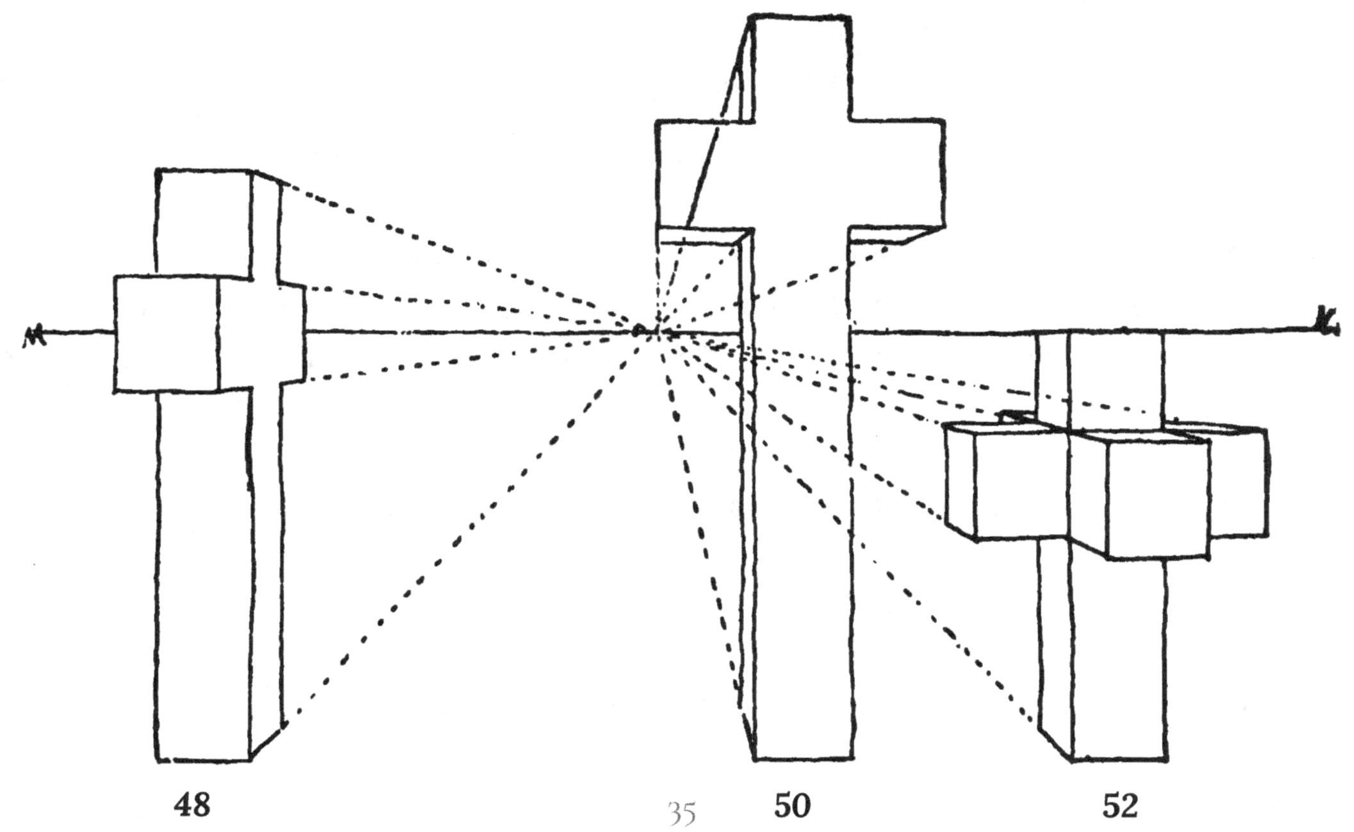

49　　　　　**51**　　　　　**53**

FIGURES 48, 50, AND 52 are outline drawings with their construction lines. These forms are based on Fig. 35. Below, Figs. 49, 51, and 53 are the outlines finished, the construction lines removed, and expression given to the lines. Copy each one and reproduce on the blackboard from memory.

Problem 56. – *Draw Fig. 51 with the arms below the level of the eye.*

Problem 57. – *Draw Fig. 51 directly in front of the eye.*

Problem 58. – *Draw Fig. 49 with the arms entirely below the eye.*

Problem 59. – *Draw Fig. 49 with the arms entirely above the level of the eye.*

FIGURE 54 is based on the box below and at the left of the eye with the top face removed. Copy and draw from memory on the blackboard.

Problem 60. – *Draw Fig. 54 at the right and below the eye.*

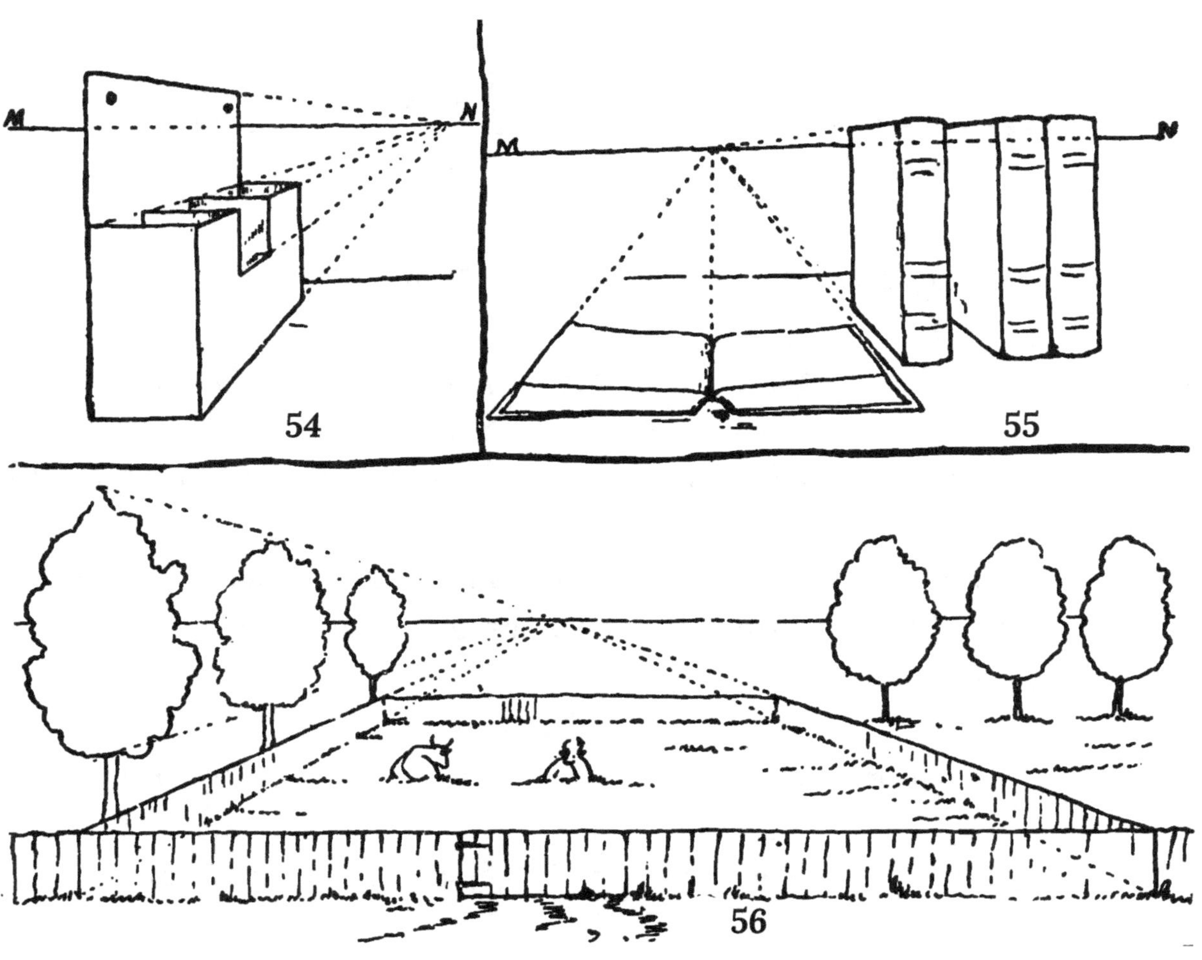

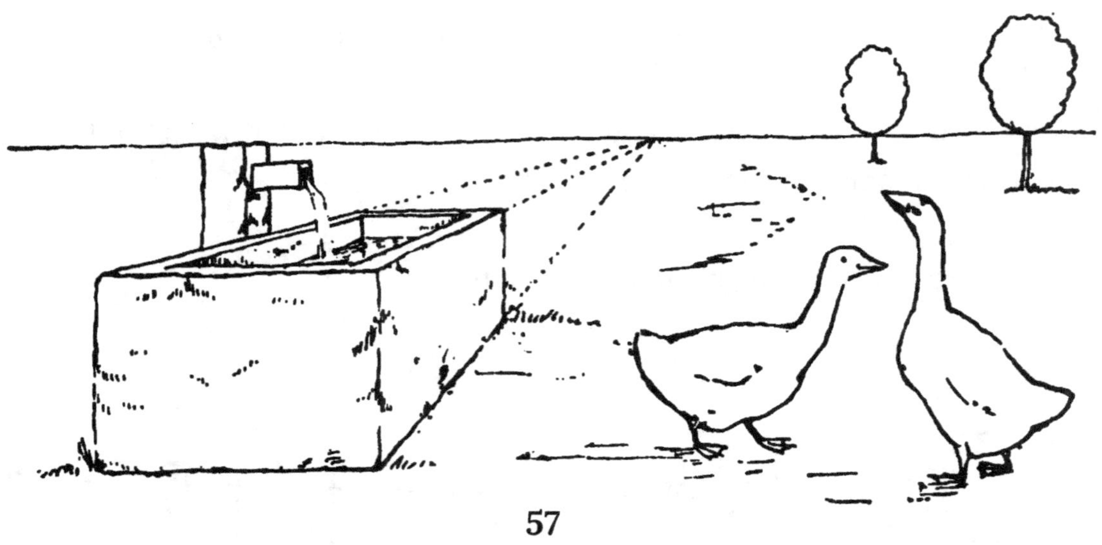

57

Problem 61. - *Place the books standing upright in Fig. 55 at the left of the open book.*

Problem 62. - *Lay the three upright books (Fig. 55) on their side, one above the other.*

FIGURE 56 is the same as a box below the level of the eye with the top face removed, show-ing the inside (See Fig. 14).

The three trees on the right in Fig. 56 are of the same height because they are the same distance in the picture. The three trees on the left are of the same height because they are between the same parallel lines.

Problem 63. - *Draw Fig. 56 with the C. of V. in line with the left side of the enclosure.*

Problem 64. - *Represent another enclosure in Fig. 56, beyond and similar to the one represented.*

FIGURE 57 is the same as a box below and at the left of the eye with the top removed, show-ing the inside (See Fig. 13).

Problem 65. - *Draw Fig. 57 below and at the right of the eye.*

FIGURES 58, 59, AND 60 represent the same object, but with the H. L. in different positions.

In Fig. 58, the H. L. is halfway up the abutments. In Fig. 59, it is at the top of the abutments,

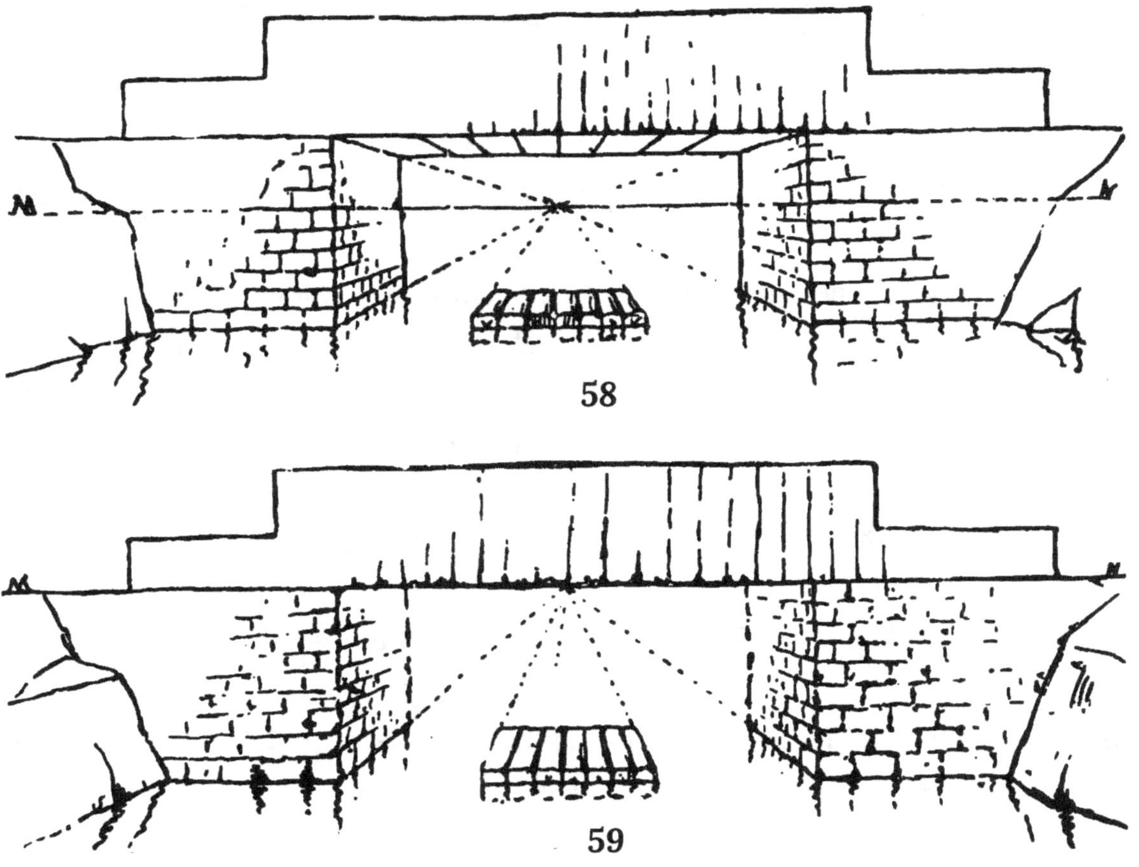

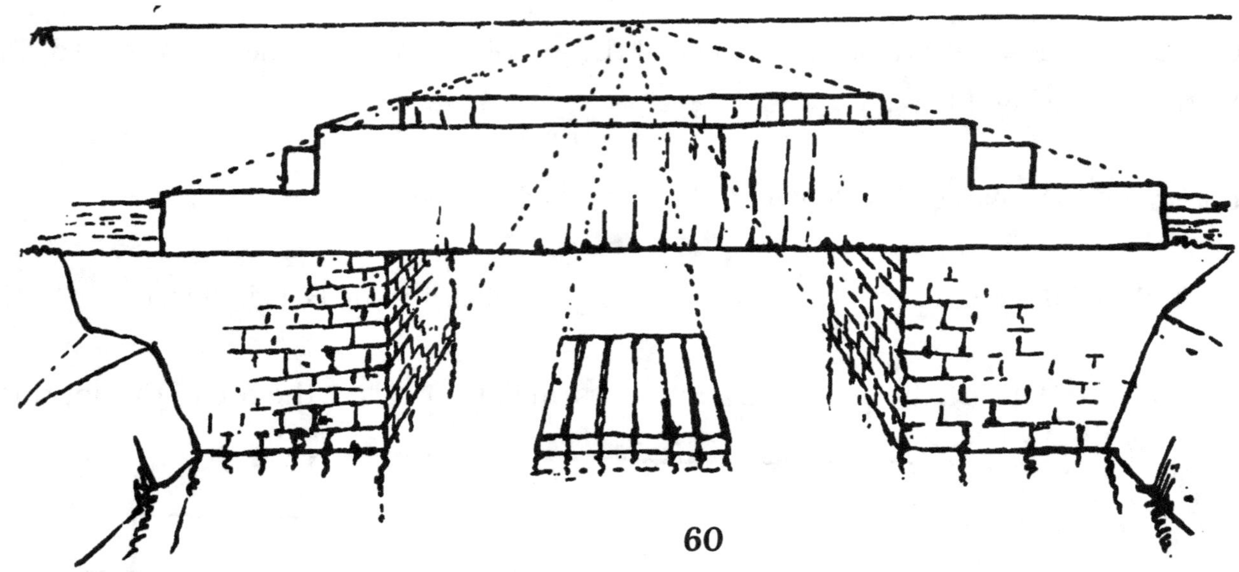

60

and in Fig. 60, it is above the bridge. The opening under the bridge is based on Figs. 12 or 18.

Observe (1) the irregular lines of the mason work and how they gradually diminish in strength from the corners. (2) How the water is suggested by the reflections. (3) The change in the slant of the lines.

Problem 66. – Draw Fig. 58 with the C. of V. in line with the side of the left abutment.

Problem 67. – Draw Fig. 58 with the H. L. where the abutment and water meet.

Problem 68. – Draw Fig. 60 with the C. of V. at the right of the bridge.

IN FIGURE 61, the ruined hut on the right is the same as a box at the right with the bottom on a level with the eye, and the supports represent the vertical lines of a box with the top on a

40

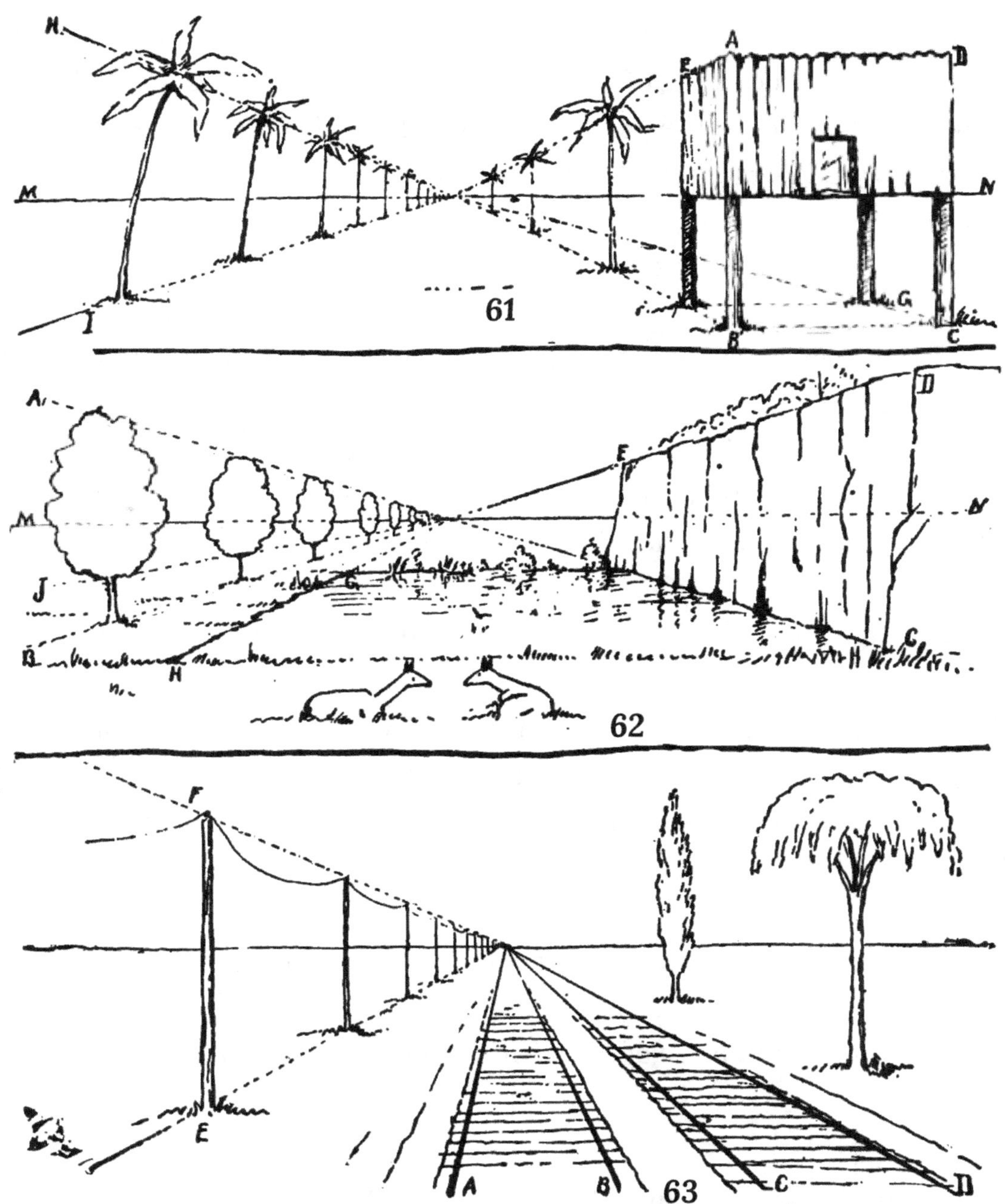

H
A
D
E
M
N
61
I
G
B
C
A
D
E
M
N
J
C
B
H
62
F
E
A
B
63
C
D

level with the eye. The long avenue between the trees is like the top of a box of infinite length.

(1) Draw the H. L. (2) Place the C. of V. (3) Draw the rectangle A, B, C, D. (4) From A, B, and C, draw receding lines. (5) Choose the point E and draw EF and FG. (6) Choose the points A and I and from them draw receding lines. (7) Draw the trees.

Problem 69. – Place the hut in Fig. 69 at the left of the C. of V.

IN FIGURE 62, the surface of the pond is similar to the top of a box, and the bluff is similar to the side face of a box.

(1) Draw the H. L. (2) Place the C. of V. (3) Draw the horizontal line B C. (4) Choose the points A, B, C, D, H, and J and from them draw receding lines to the C. of V. (5) Choose the point G and draw GF and FE. (6) Draw the details. (7) Erase the construction lines.

Problem 70. – Draw Fig. 62 with the H. L. as high up as point D.

FIGURE 63. – (1) Draw the H. L. (2) Place the C. of V. (3) Choose the points A, B, and C D, making A B equal to C D. Also, choose the points E and F and from each draw a receding line to the C. of V. (4) Draw the cross ties, being careful to draw them horizontal. (5) Draw the trees. (6) Erase the construction lines.

Problem 71. – Draw a railroad track with a bluff on each side of it similar to the one in Fig. 62.

Problem 72. – Substitute in place of the telegraph line in Fig. 65 a row of trees similar to the row in Fig. 62.

Problem 73. – Prove that the further tree in Fig. 63 is the taller by means of receding lines.

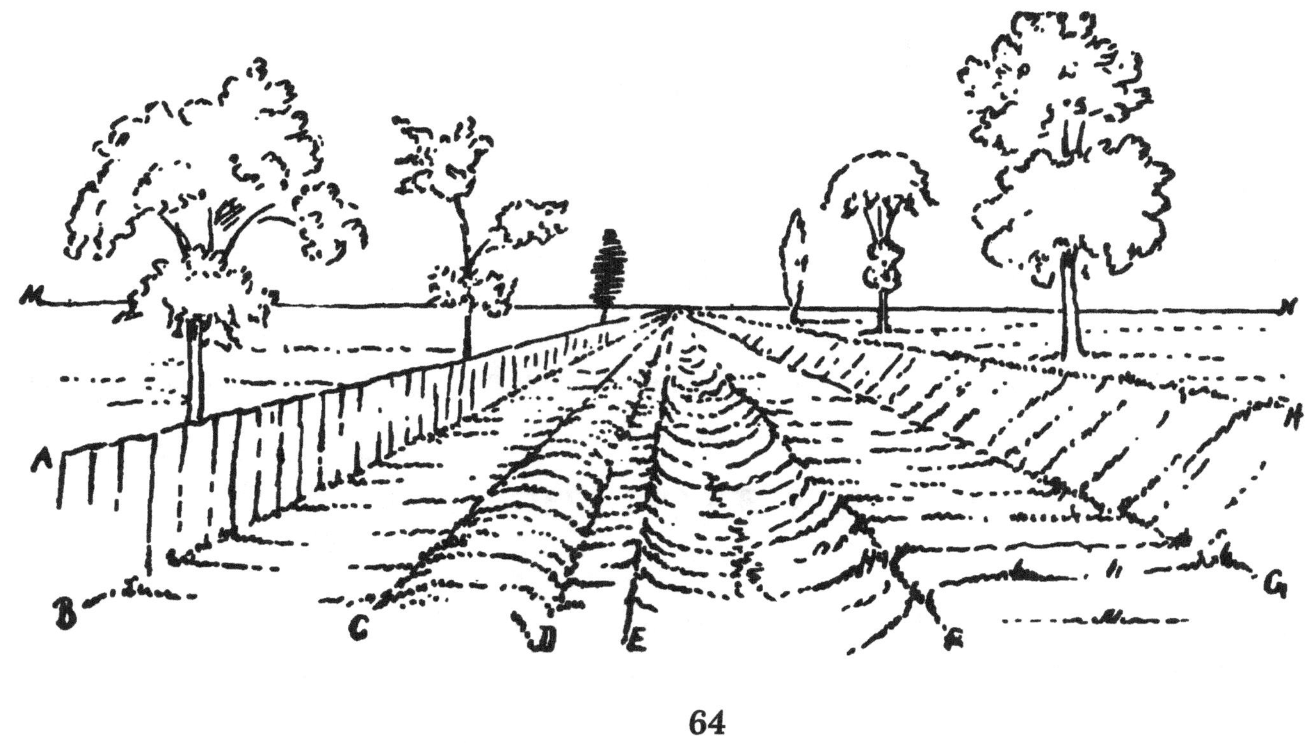

64

FIGURE 64. - The direction of a line suggests the direction of the surface. (1) A vertical line suggests a vertical surface. (2) A horizontal line, a horizontal surface. (3) A receding line, a receding surface. (4) An oblique line, an oblique surface. (5) A curved line, a curved surface.

In the illustration, the vertical lines of the fence AB suggest the vertical surface of the fence, and the receding lines from A and B suggest the surface receding to the C. of V. In like manner, the horizontal, oblique, and curved lines suggest surfaces that correspond to these lines.

Problem 74. - *Change the oblique lines between the receding lines G and H to vertical lines and the vertical lines between A and B to oblique.*

43

Problem 75. - Substitute for the trench in Fig. 64 a railroad track similar to the one in Fig. 63.

Problem 76. - Make the fence in Fig. 64 slant as if it was falling over.

Problem 77. - Substitute in place of the Indian in Fig. 43, Fig. 51.

Problem 78. – Introduce in front of the Indian (Fig. 43) a square or rectangular similar to the one in Fig. 41.

REVIEW QUESTIONS.

1. What class of forms is the cube the basis of?

2. What class of surfaces is the side face of the cube the basis of? The top face of the cube? The inside of the cube?

3. What is the most prominent figure in the cube?

4. What object held in the hand will greatly assist the understanding of the cube?

5. What is the first difficulty the beginning student of drawing meets with?

6. How many classes of lines does a cube or box contain? How many lines in each class? Which are parallel?

7. How are the vertical lines drawn? The horizontal lines? The receding lines?

8. When do the receding lines of a cube or box converge to the C. of V.?

9. What do receding lines represent?

10. What is the C. of V.? Where may it be placed? What lines converge at this point?

11. What is said of lines converging at the same point?

12. How many lines come together at each corner of a cube? Name them. Point out a corner in Fig. 3 that has only two lines. Where is the third one?

13. What is a fairly good rule to guide one in drawing?

14. How are the proportions and measurements to be judged when drawing?

15. What difference is there between the C. of V. and the eye?

16. Where is the object to be drawn placed in regard to the eye and the C. of V.?

17. Where is Fig. 2 in regard to the eye? Fig. 4?

18. When is a receding line horizontal? Vertical?

19. When do receding lines slant downward? Upward?

20. When is a receding line a point? *Ans.* When directly in front of the eye.

21. What effect has distance on an object? *Ans.* Makes it look smaller and less distinct.

22. How can the center of any rectangular face be found? *Ans.* By drawing diagonal lines from the corners or angles.

23. What new element enters drawing with Fig. 37?

24. What are construction lines? Should they appear in the finished drawing?

25. How may expression be learned?

26. Should we copy a drawing line for line? What should we copy?

27. Before we try to give expression to lines, what should we first do?

28. Where is Fig. 37 in regard to the eye? Fig. 39?

29. What is the H. L.? Where may it be placed?

30. Which is the most important line in a picture? Point?

31. What class of lines does the H. L. determine the drawing of?

32. Should the H. L. be represented in all pictures?

33. Where is a satisfactory place on your paper to place the H. L.? The C. of V.?

34. Is the H. L. a real line in nature? Do you always see the same H. L.? Would you see the same H. L. standing on a plain that you would see on a hill?

35. What is the first line drawn when making a picture? *Ans.* H. L.

36. Could the H. L. be seen in Fig. 47? Should it be represented? Why?

37. How should the outline Figs. 48, 50, and 52 be drawn?

38. Can expression be given to lines made with a straight edge or ruler? *Ans.* Very little.

39. Is the open book in Fig. 55 above or below the level of the eye? Why?

40. Which of the three trees on the left in Fig. 56 is the tallest? Why?

41. How is the water suggested in Fig. 58?

42. What is the difference between the three bridges Figs. 58, 59, and 60?

43. How does the avenue in Fig. 61 resemble the top of a box?

44. What part of a box does the pond in Fig. 6 resemble? The bluff?

45. What receding lines are parallel?

46. Are the receding lines A and B (Fig. 62) parallel?

47. What does the direction of a line suggest?

48. What class of lines are necessary to represent a vertical surface? A horizontal surface? An oblique surface? A receding surface?

49. What is a receding surface?

50. Point to a vertical surface in Fig. 62, Fig. 63. Point to a horizontal surface in Fig. 61, Fig. 62.

51. Point to a vertical surface, a horizontal surface, an oblique surface, and a curved surface in Fig. 64.

52. How may all learn how to draw? *Ans.* By drawing.

REVIEW PROBLEMS.

1. Draw a box below the eye.

2. Draw a box above the eye.

3. Draw a box at the right of the eye.

4. Draw a box at the left of the eye.

5. Draw a box below and at the left of the eye.

6. Draw a box below and at the right of the eye.

7. Draw a box above and at the right of the eye.

8. Draw a box above and at the left of the eye.

9. Draw a box with the right side directly below the eye.

10. Draw a box at the left of the eye with the top on a level with the eye.

11. Draw a box directly in front of the eye.

12. Draw a box below and at the left of the eye and remove the top.

13. Draw a box below the eye and remove the top.

14. Draw a box below and at the left of the eye, and remove the right side.

15. Draw a box below and at the left of the eye and remove the front face.

16. Draw a box above the eye and remove the front face.

17. Draw a box above the eye and remove the bottom.

18. Draw Fig. 25 below and at the left of the eye.

19. Draw Fig. 25 above and at the left of the eye.

20. Draw Fig. 25 above and at the right of the eye.

21. Draw Fig. 26 below and at the left of the eye.

22. Below and at the right of the eye.

23. Above and at the right of the eye.

24. Above the eye.

25. Below the eye.

26. At the right of the eye.

27. At the left of the eye.

28. Directly in front of the eye.

29. Draw Fig. 28 below and at the right of the eye.

30. Above and at the left of the eye.

31. Above and at the right of the eye.

32. Below the eye.

33. Above the eye.

34. At the right of the eye.

35. At the left of the eye.

36. Directly in front of the eye.

37. Draw Fig. 29 below and at the left of the eye.

38. Above and at the left of the eye.

39. Below the eye.

40. At the left of the eye.

41. Directly in front of the eye.

42. Draw Fig. 30 below and at the left of the eye.

43. Below the eye.

44. At the left of the eye.

45. Draw Fig. 31 below and at the right of the eye.

46. Below and at the left of the eye.

47. Above the eye.

48. Directly in front of the eye.

49. Draw Fig. 32 above and at the left of the eye.

50. Above and at the right of the eye.

51. Draw Fig. 33 below and at the left of the eye.

52. Below the eye.

53. Draw Fig. 34 below and at the right of the eye.

54. Above and at the right of the eye.

55. With the right side of the large cube directly below the eye.

56. Draw Fig. 35 below and at the left of the eye.

57. Above and at the right of the eye.

58. At the right of the eye.

59. Directly below the eye.

DRAWING THE CUBE.

These general directions are to show how to draw cubical or rectangular forms having the general shape of a box, that is, forms with straight lines and square corners.

Procure a plain, cubical or rectangular box, and with it follow the directions step by step and in the order given.

For convenience, the lines of the real box will be called *edges*, and corresponding lines in the drawing *lines*; *edge or edges* refer to the real box, and *line or lines* in the drawing.

In like manner, *small letters* will refer to points on the *real box*, and large or *capital letters* to points on the *drawing*.

Count the edges of the box. There are twelve. Notice that these edges have three directions, and that there are four edges running in each of the three directions, and that the edges running in the same direction are parallel. The box, then, has twelve edges, three sets of edges, four edges in each set, and the edges in each set are parallel.

CLASSES OF EDGES.

Place the box in front of you and below the level of the eye as in Fig. 65. Place the box at a distance of at least three times its height away[15]. The box may be placed further away than this but not nearer.

15   When drawing any object this rule should be followed. Nearer than this distance objects will look distorted.

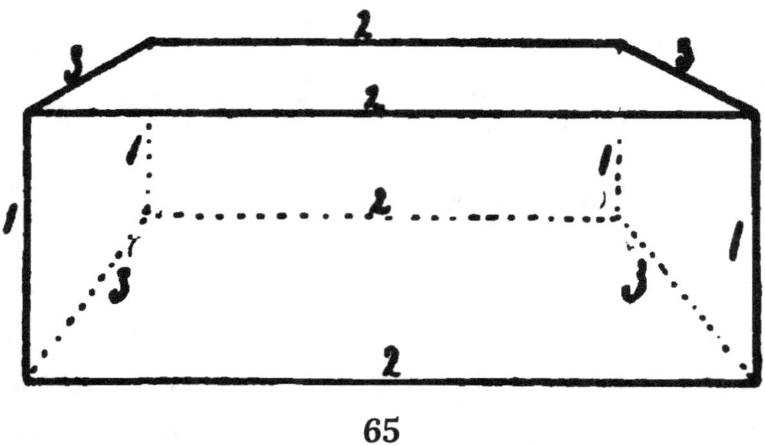

65

Observe that there are three classes of edges to be seen in this position of the box. (1) Two vertical edges. (2) Three horizontal edges. (3) Two receding edges.

There would be four edges of each class if all of them could be seen, but the body of the box hides the edges represented by the dotted lines so that they cannot be seen.

SLANT OF LINES.

Place the box below the level of the eye in such a manner as to show one side slightly as in Fig. 66.

Take a lead pencil of good length, hold it by the end as in Fig. 71 at easy arm's length away, close one eye, and with the other make the upper edge of the pencil correspond, that is, become identical or parallel with edge 1. If the edge is horizontal, the pencil will be horizontal; if the edge slants, the pencil will slant. In this case, the pencil will be horizontal or nearly so.

In the same manner, compare the pencil with edge 2 and edge 3. It will be found that all of them are horizontal and parallel.

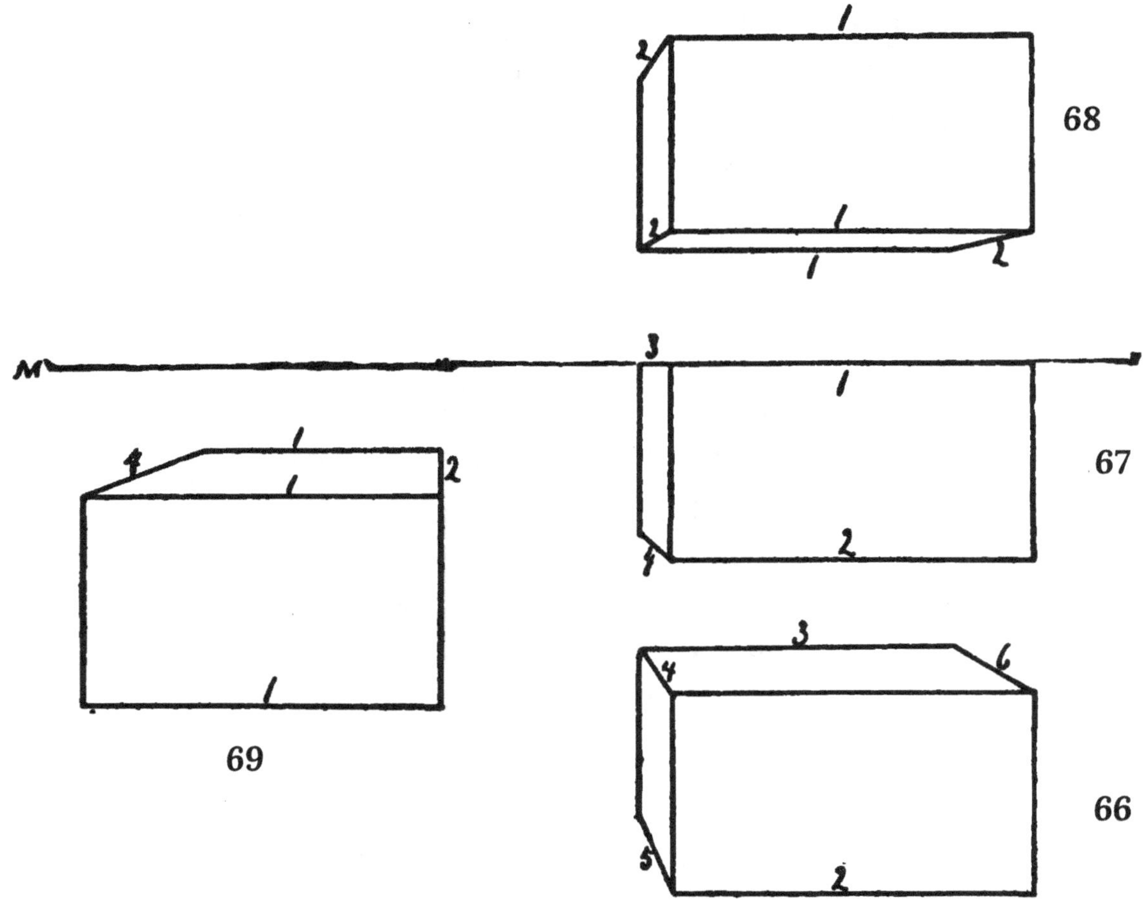

Hold the pencil so it will correspond with edge 4, *being very careful that you do not let your pencil slant in the direction that the receding line recedes.* The pencil must remain at right angles with the arm and hand that holds it. The pencil may slant up or down in a vertical plane, at right angles with the arm, so as to make it correspond with the slant of the receding line, but it must not slant toward or away from you as that will defeat the object to be accomplished.

When taking the slant of edge 4, the pencil ought to incline upward from the nearest corner. Compare the slant of edge 4 with the slant of edge 5 and observe that the lower edge slants more. Compare the slant of edge 4 with that of edge 5.

Place the box in the same position but above the level of the eye as in Fig. 68.

You will observe if you use your pencil as before that the edges marked 1 are still horizontal and those marked 2 slant downward.

Place the box in the same position but with the top on a level with the eye as in Fig. 67.

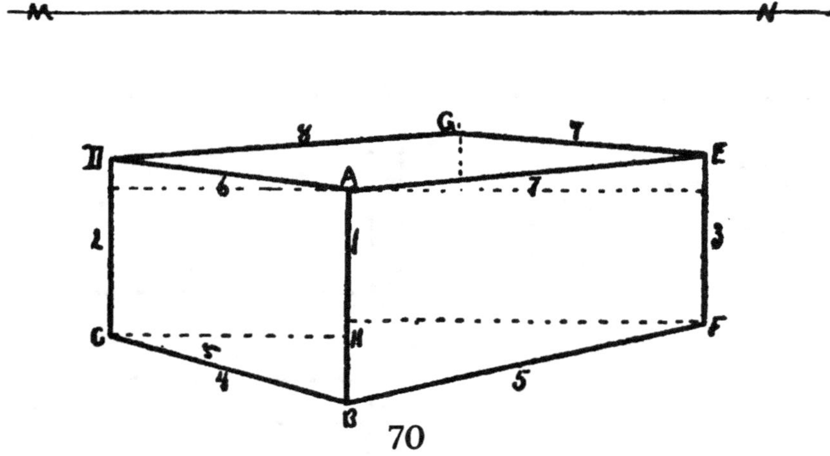

Edges 1 and 2 are still horizontal, and so is the receding edge 3. It is in the same horizontal line with edge 1. Edge 4 will slant upward slightly.

Place the box below the level of the eye so that the right side is directly in line with the eye as in Fig. 69.

Edges marked 1 will be horizontal. The receding edge 2 will be vertical and in line with vertical edge 3. Edge 4 will slant slightly.

In all of these positions, the horizontal and vertical lines have not changed. They do not change. The receding lines alone have changed. They change according to the following seven laws:

1. Receding lines below the level of the eye slant upward.

2. Receding lines above the level of the eye slant downward.

3. Receding lines on a level with the eye are horizontal.

4. Receding lines directly in line with the eye are vertical.

5. The further a receding line is above or below the level of the eye, the more it approaches the vertical.

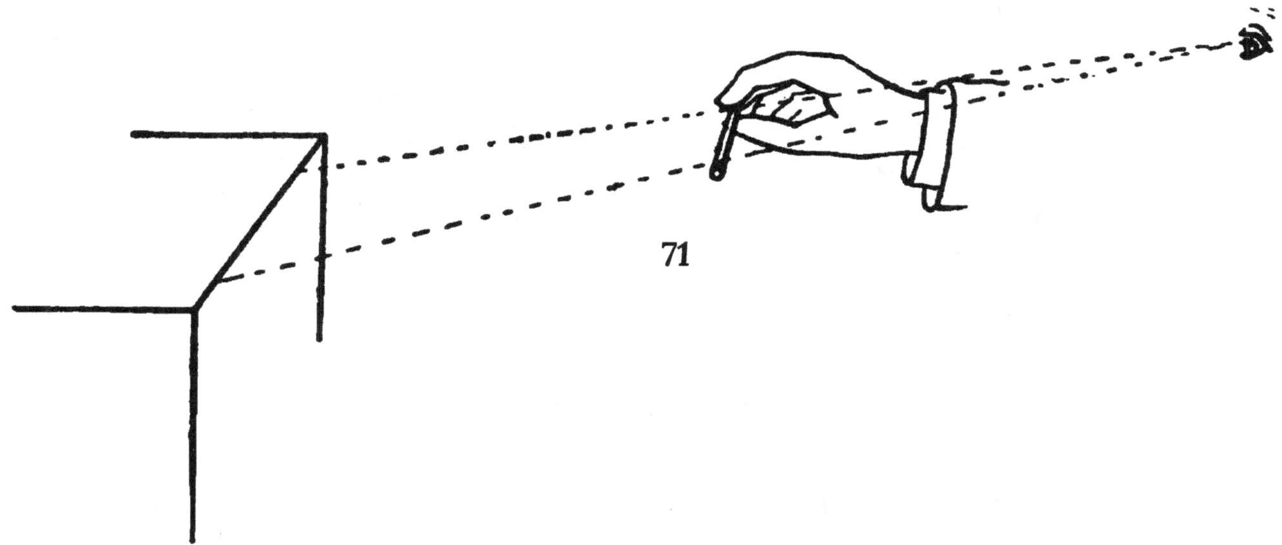

6. The further a receding line is to the right or left of the eye, the more it approaches the horizontal.

7. The nearer a receding line is to the eye, the more it slants.

Take each of these laws separately and prove them. Apply them until they become involuntary, and you follow them without effort. Apply them to common objects about you, to the receding edges of articles of furniture, of rooms, the receding edges of the pavement, streets, sides of buildings, etc.

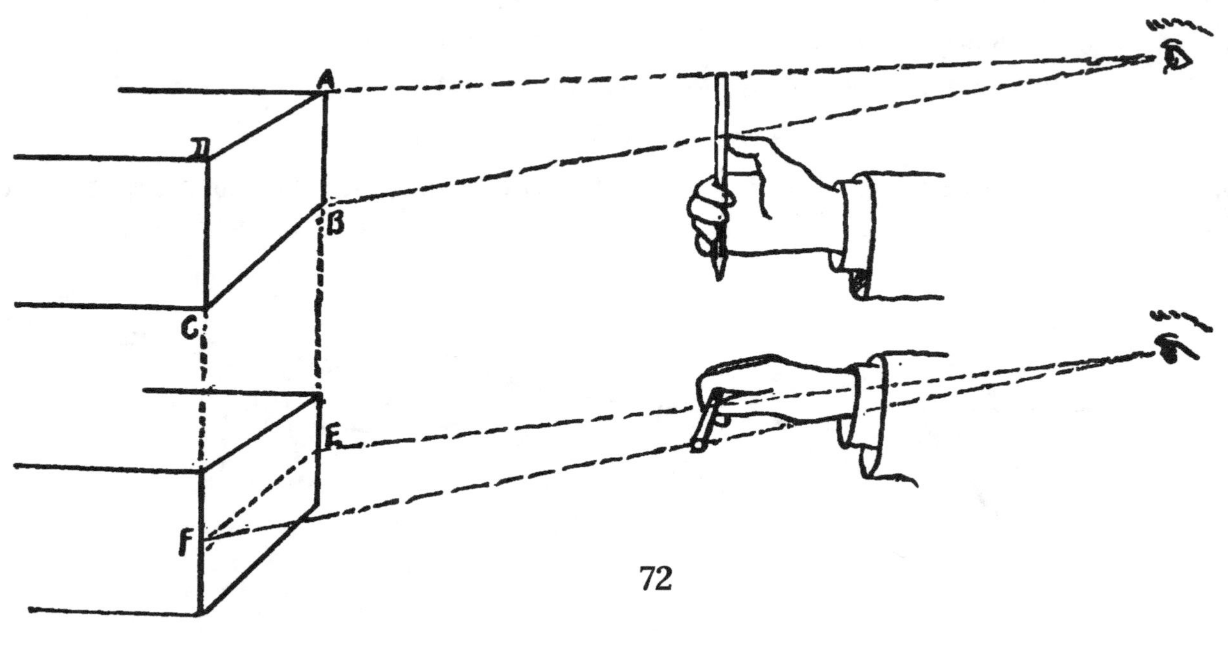

MEASURING.

Place a box before the eye as in Fig. 72. Hold the pencil at easy arm's length away, close one eye, and with the other make the upper end of the pencil correspond with corner a, and with the thumb mark corner b, as shown in the drawing. In order to compare the length of edge ab with the length of edge dc, the hand may be moved slightly to the left and the end of the thumb be made to correspond with corner c, noting how much longer or shorter edge dc is than the pencil above the thumb. By this means, the relative length of the two edges may be judged. Care must be taken not to change the distance between the eye and the hand.

To compare the length of edge ab with the horizontal distance ef, merely turn the hand on the wrist, and the relative measure is readily made.

Place the box below the eye as in Fig. 70. With the pencil, compare the length of edge 1 with the length of edge 2. Edge 1 should be the longer because it is nearer.

Compare the length of edge 2 with the length of edge 3.

Compare the length of edge 1 with the horizontal distance between edges 1 and 2. With the distance between edges 1 and 3.

Measure and compare the relative length of various objects about the room until familiar with the method.

If the directions so far have been followed and clearly understood, we are ready to *draw* the box.

DRAWING THE BOX.[16]

Place the box below the eye as in Fig. 70. (See next page.)

1. Commence by drawing the nearest vertical edge. The line AB that represents this edge may be taken of any length, but when once drawn, it becomes the unit of measure for all the remaining lines and determines the size of the box.

2. Find the position of the remaining vertical lines. This may be done by comparing the length of edge 1 with the horizontal distance between edges 1 and 2 and making the same comparison in the drawing with line 1. For example, supposing that the distance between edges 1 and 2 is the same as the length of edge 1; then in the drawing, take the length of line 1, and lay it off to the left of line 1, and it will give the position of line 2. Not knowing the length of line 2, simply draw an indefinite vertical line. In the same manner, find the position of line 3, and draw an indefinite vertical line.

16   These directions are general and are intended to show how to draw most square or rectangular forms.

3. Locate the corners. The extremities of line 1 represent corners A and B.

To find corner C, pass the lower edge of the pencil *horizontally* through corner C and note where the pencil crosses edge 1, between corner a and b. Mark this point on line 1 as at H, and from it draw a light horizontal line. Where this line crosses line 2, it will mark corner C. Draw line 4.

In like manner, find corner F and draw line 5.

To find corner D, draw a light horizontal line through corner A to line 2. Pass the upper edge of the pencil horizontally through corner a, and note the distance corner c is above it.

Mark this distance above the light horizontal line for corner C. Draw line 6.

In like manner, find corner E and draw line 7.

To find corner G, pass the edge of the pencil vertically through corner g, and note where the pencil crosses edge 6.

Mark this point on line 6, and from it draw a light indefinite vertical line. Corner G will be in this line. From corner D, draw a line slightly converging, but nearly parallel to line 7. Where it crosses the indefinite vertical line, it will mark corner G. Draw line 9, and the outline of the box is complete.

FIGURE 73. – *How to draw the inside of a box.*

1. Place the box as in Fig. 73 so that the eye is near the center of the box.

2. Draw line one for the unit of measure. [17]

3. Find the position of line 2 by comparing the length of edge 1 with the horizontal distance between edges 1 and 2 and making the same comparison with line 1 in the drawing.

4. Not knowing the length of line 2, draw an indefinite vertical line.

5. From corners D and C, draw horizontal lines which will give corners A and B.

6. Find the positions of lines 5 and 6 the same as line 2 was found.

17   Any edge that is not in perspective (that is. a receding line) may be used as a unit of measure.

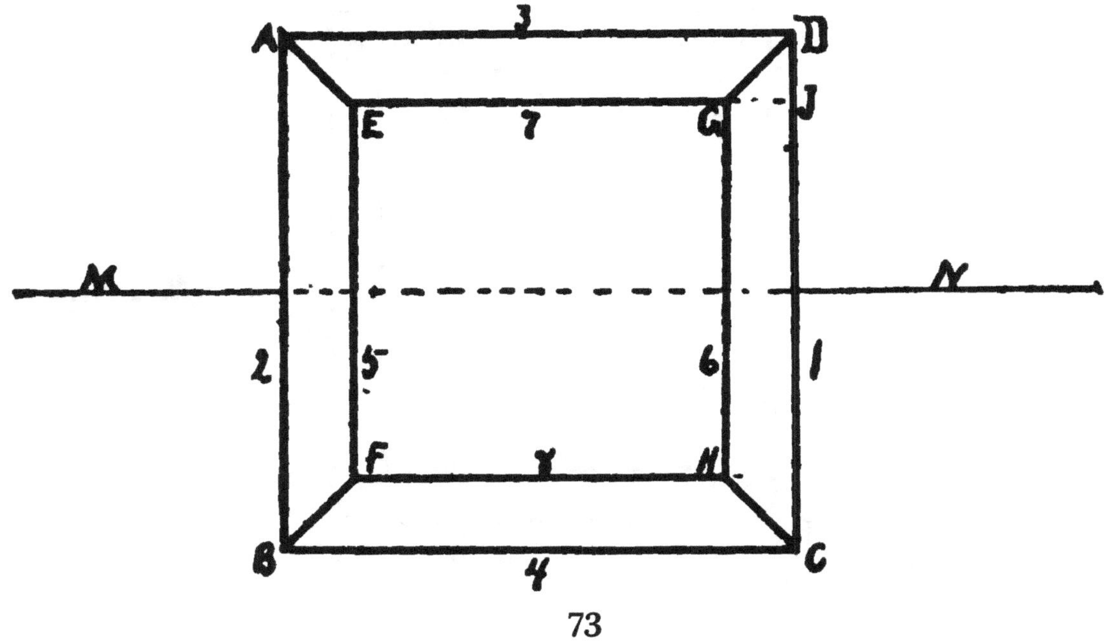

73

7. To find corner G, pass the pencil horizontally through corner g and note where it crosses edge 1.

8. Mark this point on line 1 as at J and from it draw a light horizontal line. Where this line crosses line 6, it will mark corner G.

9. Find corner H in the same manner.

10. From G and H, draw horizontal lines and where they cross line 5, they will mark corners E and F.

11. Draw the receding lines.

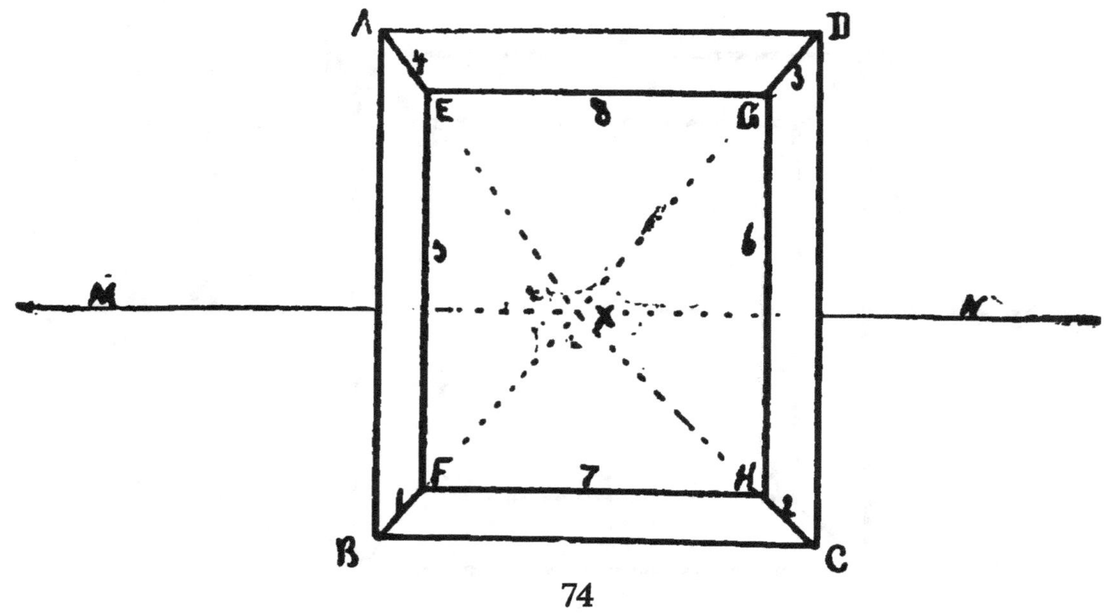

74

SECOND METHOD. FIGURE 74.

1. Place the box as in Fig. 74.

2. Draw the face A B C D as in Fig. 73.

3. Find the C. of V.[18] by taking the slant of two or more receding edges with the pencil and observing where they intersect each other. For example, after drawing ABCD, take the slant of edges 1 and 2 and note the point where they intersect each other as at X.

4. Mark this point in the drawing. It is the C. of V., and to it all the receding lines will converge.

5. Draw the receding lines 3 and 4.

6. Find the point G the same as in Fig. 73 and from it draw a vertical and a horizontal line.

7. Where these lines cross the receding lines, they will mark corners E and H.

8. From E draw a vertical line, from H a horizontal line meeting at F.

18   This can only be done when the box contains both vertical and horizontal lines.

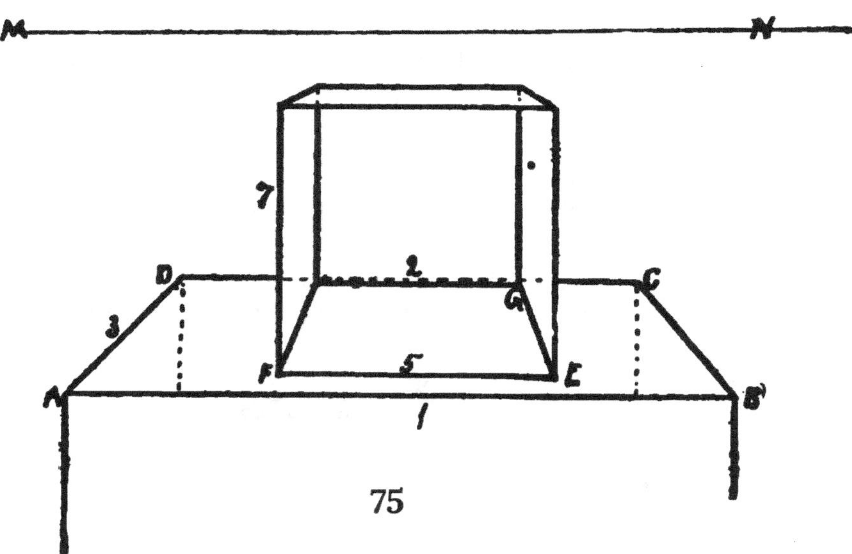

FIGURE 75. – *To draw a box resting on another box with the edges parallel and with both boxes containing vertical and horizontal lines.*

1. Place a small box on a larger one below the level of the eye as in Fig. 75.

2. Draw the upper box the same as Fig. 73.

3. The smaller box, when drawn, may be used as the unit of measure to draw the larger box.

4. Find out how far line 1 is below line 5. This distance is usually so slight that it can hardly be compared with another edge; besides, receding distances are very deceptive. The best way is to measure with the pencil to form a judgment, then mark the distance with the unaided eye.

5. Draw an indefinite horizontal line for line 1.

6. To find corner A, compare edge 5 with the distance from corner F to corner A and make the same comparison with line 5 in the drawing.

7. Find corner B in the same manner.

8. To find line 2, pass the pencil horizontally through corner D and note where the pencil crosses edge 7. Mark this point on line 7 and draw an indefinite horizontal line for line 2.

9. To find corner D, pass the pencil vertically through corner D and note where the pencil crosses edge 1.

10. Mark this point on line 1 and from it draw a vertical line. Where this line crosses line 2, it will mark corner D.

11. Draw line 3.

12. Find corner C in the same manner and draw line 4.

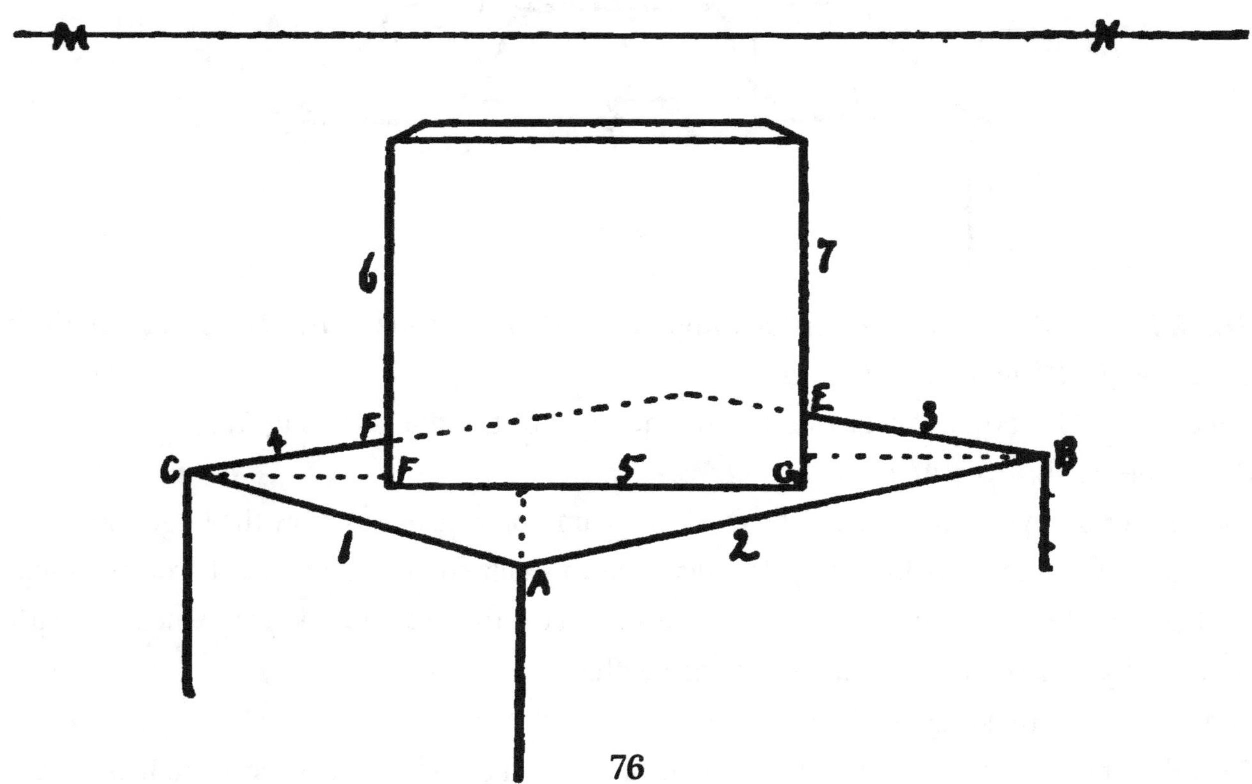

76

SECOND METHOD. – Find the C. of V. as in Fig. 74 and to it draw all of the receding lines.

FIGURE 76[19]. – *To draw a box resting another box with the edges of each box at angles with each other.*

1. Place the boxes as in Fig. 76.

2. Draw the smaller box, and use it as the unit of measure to draw the larger box.

3. Find corner A by passing the pencil vertically through corner A, and noting where the pencil crosses edge 5.

4. Mark this point on line 5, and from it draw a vertical line. Corner A is somewhere in this vertical line.

5. Find the position of corner A by comparing the length of edge 6 with the distance between edge 5 and corner A, and make the same comparison in the drawing.

6. To find corner C, pass the pencil horizontally through corner C and note where the pencil crosses edge 6.

7. Mark this point on line 6, and from it draw an indefinite horizontal line. Corner C will be in this horizontal line.

8. Compare the length of edge 5 with the distance between edge 6 and corner C, and make the same comparison in the drawing with line 5. Draw line 1.

9. Find corner B in the same manner and draw line 2.

10. To find point F, note where edge 4 crosses edge 6 and mark this point on line 6 and draw line 4.

11. Find point E and draw line 3 in the same manner.

19   The small box in Fig. 76 may be drawn by using the C. of V., but the large box cannot because it does not contain horizontal lines.

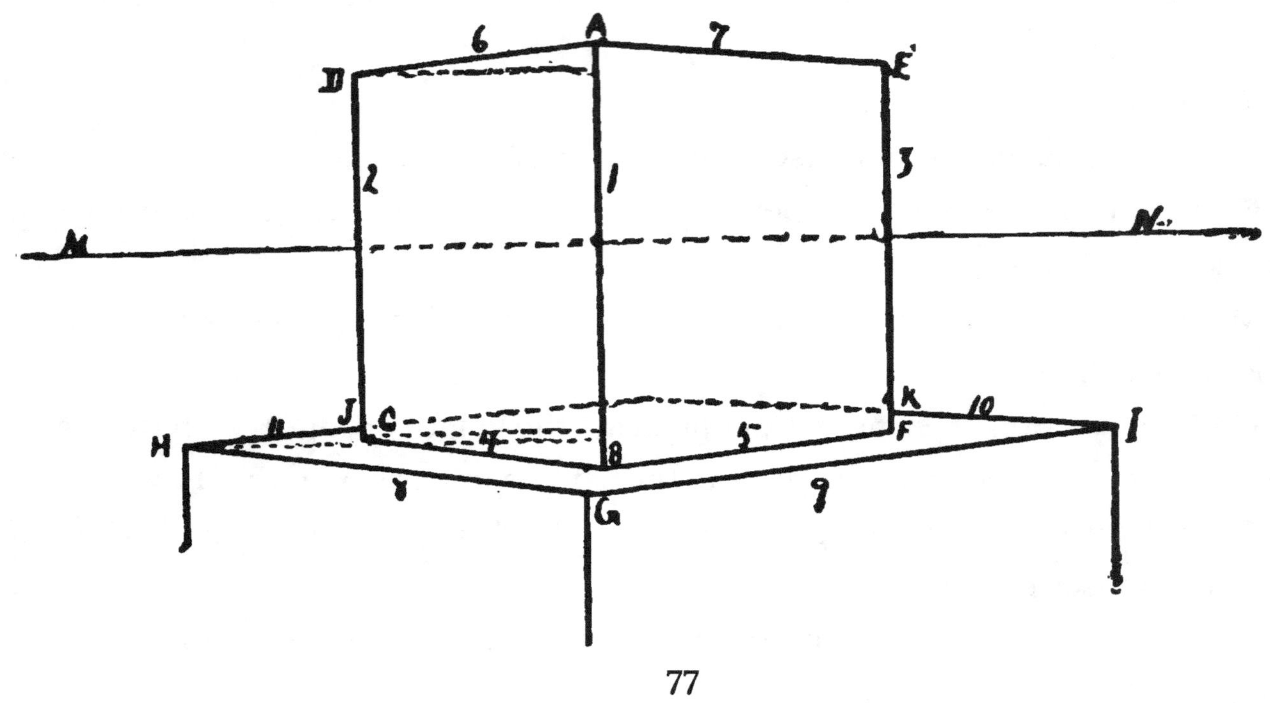

FIGURE 77. – To draw one box resting on another with edges parallel with each other, the boxes composed of vertical and receding lines.

(1) Draw line 1. (2) Find the position of lines 2 and 3. (3) Find corner C and draw line 4. (4) Find corner F and draw line. (5) Find corner D and draw lines 2 and 6. (6) Find corner E and draw lines 3 and 7. (7) Find corner G. (8) Find corner H and draw line 8. (9) Find corner I and draw line 9. (10) Find points J and K and draw lines 10 and 11.

78

79

80

81

After the mechanical process of drawing is understood, apply the principles to surrounding objects such as those represented in Figs. 78 - 81, proceeding exactly in the same manner. For example, when drawing an object similar to Fig. 80:

(1) Draw the nearest vertical line AB. (2) Find the position of the vertical lines CD and EF. (3) Find corner D and draw DB. (4) Find corner C and draw AC. (5) Find corner E and draw AE. (6) Find corner F and draw BF. (7) Draw all of these lines lightly, then go over the work giving expression to the lines as much as possible.

FIGURE 81. – (1) Draw AB for the unit of measure. (2) Find corner C. (3) Find corner D and draw A D and DC. (4) Find corner E and draw E A and E C. (5) Find the point F and draw B F. (6) Find the point G and draw B G. (7) Draw and give expression to the details.

Objects that are drawn similar to the box are found on every hand and include barns, sheds, level fields, fences, bridges, tunnels, tables, chairs, stools, desks, beds, trunks, chests, rooms, halls, stairs, books, shelves, platforms — in fact, any object bounded by straight lines and square corners.

It is not necessary to draw the objects that surround another object. The object sought after may be drawn, and the objects that surround it entirely omitted, or suggested by a slight sketch. Do not form the habit of measuring with the pencil any more than can be helped, but depend on the eye as much as possible. With use, the eye becomes far more rapid and accurate than measuring with the pencil.

REVIEW QUESTIONS.

1. How many edges does the box contain? How many sets of edges? How many edges in each set?

2. How many classes of edges may a box contain?

3. What edges of the box are parallel?

4. What classes of lines do not change?

5. Repeat the seven laws governing receding lines.

6. When taking the slant of a line with the lead pencil, what precaution is necessary?

7. When drawing an object similar to a box, which line should be drawn first? How long should it be drawn?

8. Name the three steps in drawing a box.

9. What is a receding distance?

10. When may the C. of V. be used in drawing objects?

11. Can a horizontal edge be used as a unit of measure?

12. Is it well to form the habit of measuring with the pencil? Why?

13. How many classes of lines can be seen in Fig. 65? In Fig. 70? Fig. 73? Fig. 77? Fig. 78?

14. Are there any horizontal lines in Fig. 70? Then can it be drawn by using the C. of V.?

15. How can we tell when the box is below the level of the eye?

REVIEW OF PART I.

THE CUBE AND ITS APPLICATIONS.

REVIEW QUESTIONS.

(1) What class of forms is the cube the basis of? *Ans.* Forms having straight lines and square corners.

(2) What class of surfaces is the side face of the cube the basis of? *Ans.* All square or rectangular vertical surfaces. Give examples.

(3) What class of surfaces is the top of the cube the basis of? *Ans.* All square or rectangular horizontal surfaces. Give examples.

(4) What is the inside of a hollow cube the basis of? *Ans.* All enclosed cubical or rectangular spaces. Give examples.

(5) What is the most prominent figure in the cube? *Ans.* The square. In the box? *Ans.* The rectangle.

(6) How many classes of lines does a cube or box contain? How many lines in each class?

(7) In the cube, what lines are parallel? *Ans.* The lines of each class are parallel.

(8) How are vertical lines in a picture drawn? *Ans.* Parallel with the sides of the paper on which the drawing is made.

(9) How are the horizontal lines in a picture drawn? *Ans.* Parallel with the top and bottom of the paper on which the drawing is made.

(10) When the drawing contains vertical and horizontal lines, how are the receding lines drawn? *Ans.* To the center of vision.

(11) What do receding lines represent? *Ans.* Thickness or distance away.

(12) What is the center of vision? *Ans.* It represents the point directly opposite the eye. In nature, it is the point directly opposite the eye.

(13) What lines converge at the center of vision? *Ans.* Lines at right angles to horizontal and vertical lines in the picture.

(14) What is said of lines converging at the same point? *Ans.* They are parallel. That is, they represent parallel lines.

(15) How many lines come together at each corner of a cube?

(16) What is a fairly good rule to guide one in drawing? *Ans.* When the drawing looks right, it may be taken for granted that it is right.

(17) How are the proportions and measurements to be judged when drawing? *Ans.* By the appearance.

(18) What difference is there between the center of vision and the eye? *Ans.* They are opposite points.

(19) When is a receding line horizontal? *Ans.* When it is on a level with the eye. Prove it with the model.

(20) When is a receding line vertical?

(21) When do receding lines slant downward? Upward?

(22) When is a receding line a point? *Ans.* When directly in front of the eye. Prove it.

(23) What effect has distance on an object? *Ans.* Makes the object look smaller and less distinct. Prove it.

(24) How can the center of a rectangular face be found? *Ans.* By means of diagonal lines from opposite corners.

(25) What are construction lines? *Ans.* Light or dotted lines drawn to mark points. They should be erased in the finished drawing.

(26) How may expression be learned? *Ans.* By observing, studying, and practicing the methods of others.

(27) Should we copy a drawing line for line? *Ans.* No. We may copy the principle, method, or idea.

(28) Before we try to give expression to lines, what should we do? *Ans.* Draw the proportion with light lines.

(29) What is the horizon line? *Ans.* A horizontal line that marks the level of the eye. It is the most important line in the picture and determines the drawing of receding lines. The center of vision is always in the horizon line directly opposite the eye.

(30) Should the horizon line be represented in all drawings? *Ans.* Yes. Either represented, or its position understood.

(31) Is the horizon line a real line, and the center of vision a real point in nature? *Ans.* No. They are no more real than the equator and North Pole, but are as essential in the study of drawing as the equator and pole are in the study of geography.

(32) Can expression be given to lines made with a straight edge or ruler? *Ans.* Very little.

(33) What receding lines are parallel? *Ans.* Those that converge to the same point.

(34) What does the direction of a line suggest? *Ans.* The direction of the surface.

(35) What class of lines are necessary to suggest a vertical surface? A horizontal surface? A receding surface?

(36) How do you know when an object is below the level of the eye? *Ans.* When an object is in that position, the top can be seen.

(37) How do you know when an object is above the eye?

(38) How do you know an object is at the right or left of your eye? *Ans.* When it is at the right or left of the point you have chosen for your center of vision.

(39) When is an object directly in front of the eye? *Ans.* When it is between your eye and the center of vision.

(40) Are all square-cornered objects composed of vertical, horizontal, and receding lines? *Ans.* No. They may be placed so as to contain only vertical and receding lines, or only receding

lines alone. Prove it.

(41) When can the center of vision be used in drawing square-cornered objects? *Ans.* When the object is placed so that it contains the three classes of lines, viz: vertical, horizontal, and receding, and at no other time.

(42) When square-cornered objects contain only vertical and receding lines, how should they be drawn? *Ans.* See Part I, under "DRAWING THE BOX."

(43) What class of lines change as the object is changed? *Ans.* Receding lines.

(44) Repeat the seven laws governing receding lines.

(45) When taking the slant of a receding line with the lead pencil, what precaution is necessary? *Ans.* To keep the pencil at right angles with the hand and not let it recede in the direction that the receding line recedes, as there will be a strong tendency to do.

(46) How near may we be to an object when drawing it? *Ans.* Not nearer than three times the height of the object.

(47) When drawing an object similar to a box, what line should be drawn first and how long may it be drawn? *Ans.* The nearest vertical line. It may be drawn as long as you wish. It determines the size of the drawing.

(48) Name the three general steps in drawing the box. *Ans.* (1) Draw the nearest vertical line. (2) Find the remaining vertical lines. (3) Find the corners.

(49) What is a receding surface? Point to one.

(50) Can a horizontal edge be used as a unit of measure? *Ans.* Yes.

(51) What is a unit of measure in drawing? *Ans.* An edge or line with which we compare other edges or lines.

(52) Should the unit of measure of the object and the unit of measure of the drawing be kept separate? *Ans.* Yes, distances on the object should be compared with the unit of measure of the object, and distances in the drawing with the unit of measure of the drawing.

(53) Is it well to form the habit of measuring with the pencil? *Ans.* No, it is necessary at first

in order to assist the judgment and learn certain truths, but as soon as these are learned, it is best to discontinue its use.

(54) What is the dividing line between the lines that slant upward and those that slant downward?

(55) When will the receding lines of a box or similar object converge at the center of vision?

(56) What is a marked tendency in the beginning student of drawing? *Ans.* Exaggeration. The tendency to place the center of vision too far away, to make receding lines slant too much, and to make receding distances too wide. This may be overcome by going to the other extreme.

(57) In a group of objects, which should be drawn first? *Ans.* The nearest object usually.

REVIEW PROBLEMS FOR THE BLACK-BOARD.

The pupil should work these problems outside of the class and be prepared to put them on the blackboard in the class without the aid of a drawing or from the teacher.

In the following nine problems, require the pupil, after the problem is finished, to stand directly before the problem and hold a box in the same position as the drawing, to point to corresponding lines in each, and to answer such questions as will show that he clearly understands the problem.

(1) Draw a box below and at the left of the eye.

(2) Draw a box below and at the right of the eye.

(3) Draw a box above and at the left of the eye.

(4) Draw a box above and at the right of the eye.

(5) Draw a box below the eye.

(6) Draw a box above the eye.

(7) Draw a box at the right of the eye.

(8) Draw a box at the left of the eye.

(9) Draw a box directly in front of the eye.

(10) Draw a box below and at the left of the eye and remove the top face showing the inside. Remove the side face. Remove the front face. Remove the back face. Remove the remaining side face.

(11) Draw a box below and at the right of the eye and remove the top face. Remove the side face. Remove the front face. Remove the back face. Remove the remaining side face. Restore the box face by face as it was.

(12) Draw a box above and at the left of the eye and remove the front face.

(13) Draw a box above and at the right of the eye and remove the bottom face. Front face. Side face. Back face. Top face. Restore the box face by face as at first.

(14) Draw a box below the eye and remove the top face. Remove the front face. Remove both the top and front faces. Replace the faces.

(15) Draw a box at the right of the eye and remove the front face. Remove the front and side faces. Restore it as at first.

(16) Draw a box at the left of the eye and remove the front, side, and top faces.

(17) Draw a box above the eye and remove the bottom face. Remove the front face. Remove the front, bottom, and side faces.

(18) Draw a box at the left and above the eye and remove the front, side, and bottom faces.

(19) Draw the box in its nine positions.

(20) Draw a box below and at the right of the eye and place a similar box on top of it.

(21) Draw a box below and at the left of the eye and place two similar boxes on top of it.

(22) Draw three boxes, one below and at the left, one directly below, and one below and at the right of the eye.

(23) Draw three boxes, one above and at the left, one at the left, and one below and at the

left of the eye.

(24) Below and at the left of the eye, draw three boxes, one behind the other and extending toward the center of vision.

(25) Directly below the eye, draw three boxes in a row, extending toward the center of vision.

(26) Draw a box directly in front of the eye and remove the front face. Remove the front and top faces. Remove the front, top, and one side face.

(27) Draw a cube below and at the left of the eye and from each corner cut a small cube.

(28) Draw a cube below and at the right of the eye and from each corner cut a small cube.

(29) Draw a cube above and at the left of the eye and from each corner cut a small cube.

(30) Draw a cube above and at the right of the eye and from each corner cut a small cube.

(31) Draw a cube directly in front of the eye and from each corner cut a small cube.

(32) Draw a cube at the left of the eye and from each corner cut a small cube.

(33) Draw a cube below and at the left of the eye and from each edge cut a small cube.

(34) Draw a cube below and at the right of the eye and from each edge cut a small cube.

(35) Draw a cube above and at the left of the eye and from each edge cut a small cube.

(36) Draw a cube above and at the right of the eye and from each edge cut a small cube.

(37) Draw a cube directly in front of the eye and from each edge cut a small cube.

(38) Draw a cube below the eye and from each edge cut a small cube.

(39) Draw a cube at the right of the eye and from each edge cut a small cube.

(40) Draw a cube below and at the left of the eye and to each face add a small cube.

(41) Draw Problem 40 below and at the right of the eye.

(42) Draw Problem 40 below the eye.

(43) Draw Problem 40 above and at the left of the eye.

(44) Draw Problem 40 at the right of the eye.

(45) Below and at the left of the eye, draw a small cube and to each face add another cube of the same size.

(46) Draw Problem 45 at the right of the eye.

(47) Draw Problem 45 below and at the right of the eye.

(48) Draw Problem 45 above and at the left of the eye.

(49) Draw Problem 45 above and at the right of the eye.

(50) Draw Problem 45 at the left of the eye.

(51) Draw a box placed below the eye containing only vertical and receding lines.

(52) Draw a box placed with the top face on a level with the eye, containing only vertical and receding lines.

(53) Draw a box below the eye containing vertical, horizontal, and receding lines, using a center of vision.

PART II.

THE CYLINDER.

SUGGESTIONS TO TEACHERS.

PRINCIPLES. — The same principles are used through the four parts of Drawing Simplified, but always in a progressive manner. It is almost impossible for the pupil to begin with this part and do successful work without a knowledge of Part I.

MATERIALS. — The materials necessary for work are: (1) A model for each pupil and one for the teacher. (2) A medium soft lead pencil. (3) A rubber eraser. (4) Paper.

MODELS. — Fruit, salmon or spice cans, baking powder boxes, round pasteboard or tin boxes, cartridge shells, etc., are all excellent models and are so common that each pupil can procure one for himself. A turned handle of any sort, such as a broom handle, may be cut into pieces one or two inches long and a whole class supplied.

MODELS NEGLECTED. — There will be a strong tendency to ignore and neglect the use of the model. Do not do this. If the model is neglected, the progress will be slow and the work unsatisfactory.

A GOOD PLAN. — (1) Point out and explain to the class the principle from the model. (2) Explain the same principle by means of drawings placed on the blackboard. This may be reversed and the principle explained through drawings made on the blackboard, and then verified by the model. (3) The pupil will then explain the same principle from the model and illustrate it by means of drawings on the blackboard. (4) Apply the principle to objects similar to the model in form.

PROBLEMS. — A clear understanding of the problems is the basis of thorough work in drawing. Do not hasten to picture making. Use the greater part of the time with drill work in the problems. Draw each problem in at least four positions and often in nine.

COPYING. — Do not tolerate copying without understanding. Teach your pupils to work independently from the principle—to be guided by the idea. Then drawing will mean something and be a pleasure to them; otherwise, it will be drudgery and a waste of time.

USE OF RULERS or Straight Edges should not be allowed. Let each pupil depend on his unaided hand and eye. After control over the hand has been gained so that the execution is rapid and accurate, then there will be time to teach the use of the ruler or straight edge.

THE BLACK-BOARD. — Much of the class work should be at the blackboard. No work will show to the teacher the pupil's knowledge as plainly and accurately or give the pupil greater confidence and independence than this work. The pupil should be able to work the problem when given verbally by the teacher.

DRAWING FROM THE OBJECT. — It is of little use for the pupil to draw from nature or the real object until he has some knowledge to draw with — some principle that will aid him to draw intelligently. Nature's laws are so subtle that a pupil cannot understand them by copying from the real object. They must be explained through the model and drawing first. Blindly copying from nature is but a step higher than blindly copying from a picture. Neither will alone teach the pupil to draw intelligently. By such methods, the pupil, through repeated failure, soon dislikes drawing. The method also requires too much time.

A better plan is to commence with the idea or principle and always keep this idea back of the drawing as a propelling force. To teach the principle first and then use it to draw the real form — to learn how to represent the principle and then the form afterward. This may be done by using the type form and the blackboard drawing together, using one to explain the other, and then applying the knowledge to similar forms.

THE FOUNDATION. — Four studies are the foundation of all branches. They are number, language, drawing, and music. These studies take more time to master because they are the basis of whole departments and are not based on other studies. They are not like geography, geometry, physiology, etc., but are the basis of these studies. *For this reason, the drawing class should meet every day.*

In proportion as a thorough knowledge of these fundamental branches is acquired, the time for the mastery of all other branches is shortened.

TEXT BOOK. — Each pupil in drawing should have a textbook of his own, the same as in other studies. Some teachers take the place of the textbook and impart to the pupil all they know of the subject. This is right in the primary grades but not in the higher. It may work fairly well with teachers of marked ability, but at the best, the knowledge will be fragmentary and the work unsatisfactory.

THREE BRANCHES OF DRAWING. — It is best not to teach the three branches of drawing, viz.: Representative, constructive, and decorative drawing, together in the same class. Representative drawing is the basis of constructive and decorative drawing very much as arithmetic is the basis of geometry and algebra, and if all are taught together, confusion is almost sure to follow unless in the hands of a very experienced teacher. If representative drawing is taught first, constructive and decorative drawing is acquired in a very short time and the whole course of drawing is shortened.

Representative drawing is largely expressed through the unaided hand; constructive and decorative drawing require the use of instruments. If all are taught together, the pupil will depend on the instruments for all that he can possibly use them for, and the hand, eye, and judgment remain comparatively uncultivated.

SIZE OF DRAWING. — In general, the size of the drawing is adapted to the size of the paper on which the drawing is made. This is not an arbitrary rule, however. In general, a drawing with the pencil may be made 2x3 inches for single objects and 8x10 inches on the blackboard. The habit of making small drawings should be discouraged.

THE OBJECTIVE POINT. — A pupil should not only be taught how to reproduce objects placed before him, but his own thoughts as well. He should (1) be able to draw the object as placed before him, (2) draw from memory, and (3) draw from the imagination.

THE CYLINDER.

THE CYLINDER[20] is made the basis of forms having curved lines and surfaces.

The cylinder should be studied in three positions: (1) The vertical cylinder (Figs. 2-7), (2) The horizontal cylinder (Figs. 29-35), and (3) The receding cylinder (Figs. 50-54). Two

20　　A cylinder should be in the hand or where it can be easily referred to when studying these principles. Constant reference to this cylinder cannot be emphasized too much. A common fruit can is a very good model.

classes of lines are used in drawing the cylinder in each of these three positions: (1) The vertical and curved lines to draw the vertical cylinder, (2) The horizontal and curved lines to draw the horizontal cylinder, and (3) The receding and curved lines[21] to draw the receding cylinder.

The most prominent figure in the cylinder is the circle.

The word *edge or edges* will refer to the real cylinder, and "line" or "lines" to corresponding points in the drawing. In the same manner, small letters will refer to the real cylinder and *large or capital* letters to corresponding points in the drawing.

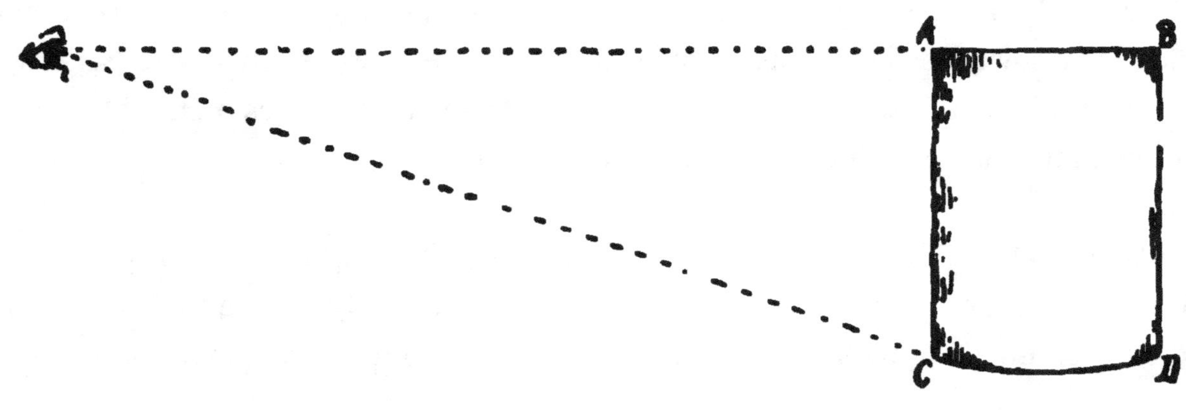

FIG. 1.

THE VERTICAL CYLINDER.

The position of the Horizon Line[22] determines the drawing of the cylinder in the vertical

---

21   Observe that in addition to the vertical, horizontal, and receding lines of the cube, the curved line is added.

22   The drawing of the vertical cylinder is, to some extent, dependent on the C. of V. ; but for practical

position.

Procure a cylinder and follow the directions below step by step. Hold the cylinder in the hand vertically before the eye, as in Fig. 1. Hold the cylinder so that the upper edge ab is on a level with the eye. Observe that the curved edge ab is horizontal[23], the same as AB in the drawing.

Observe also that cd curves downward, the same as C D in the drawing.

Hold the cylinder so that the bottom is on a level with the eye, as in Fig. 6. Now cd is horizontal, the same as C D in the drawing, and ab curves upward slightly, the same as A B in the drawing.

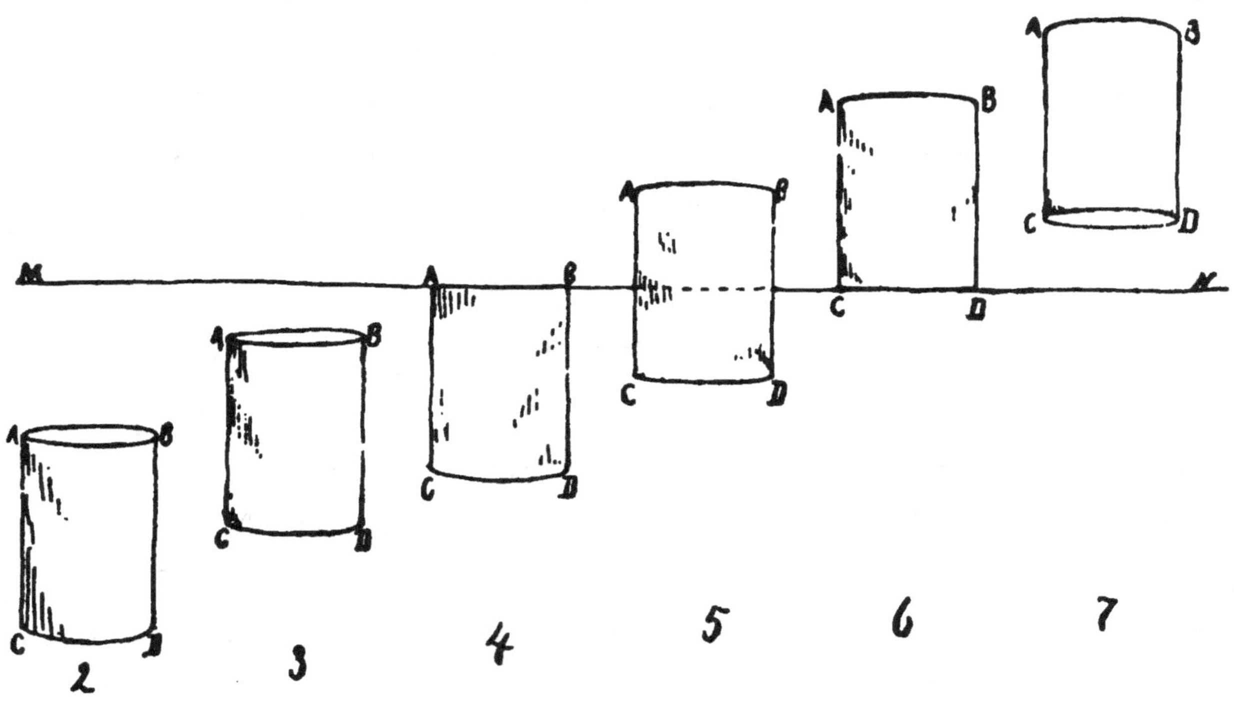

____

purposes it is best to ignore this relation and draw it in its relation to the H. L. alone.

23   'This can be readily seen if a peucil is held level with the top, after the manner of taking the slant of a line.

Hold the cylinder as in Fig. 5, so that the eye is about at the middle of the cylinder. Edge ab curves upward lightly, and cd downward, the same as A B and C D in the drawing.

Hold the cylinder below the level of the eye, as in Fig. 3. Edge ab has become an ellipse, the same as AB in the drawing, and cd curves downward more than in Figs. 4 and 5.

Hold the cylinder still further below the eye, as in Fig. 2. The edge ab has become more circular than in Fig. 3, and cd curves downward still more, the same as AB and CD in the drawing.

Hold the cylinder above the level of the eye, as in Fig. 7. The edge cd has become elliptical, and ab curves upward, the same as CD and AB in the drawing.

In all of these positions, the degree of curvature of the ends of the cylinder depends on the distance above or below the HL. The edge of the cylinder at the level of the eye is horizontal, and the further the edge is above or below this line, the more it curves.

PROBLEMS.

Problem 1. — *Draw a vertical cylinder below the level of the eye (Fig. 2).*

Problem 2. — *Draw a vertical cylinder above the level of the eye (Fig. 7).*

Problem 3. — *Draw a vertical cylinder with the top on a level with the eye (Fig. 4).*

Problem 4. — *Draw a vertical cylinder with the top above the level of the eye and the bottom below the level of the eye (Fig. 5).*

Problem 5. — *Draw a vertical cylinder with the bottom on a level with the eye (Fig. 6).*

Problem 6. — *Draw two vertical cylinders of unequal distances below the level of the eye.*

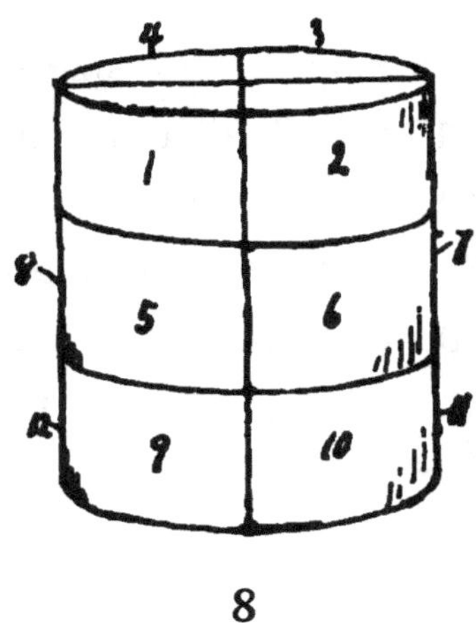

8

FIGURE 8 is a vertical cylinder below the level of the eye, divided horizontally into thirds, and each third is divided vertically into quarters, thus dividing the cylinder into twelve equal parts. Each part is numbered for convenience of reference. These parts in the following problems are to be removed as suggested in each problem.

It is a good plan, when drawing the cylinder, to draw the proportions in straight lines, as in Fig. 9, and then place points to mark the curvature of the lines, as in Fig. 10. The general directions are as follows:

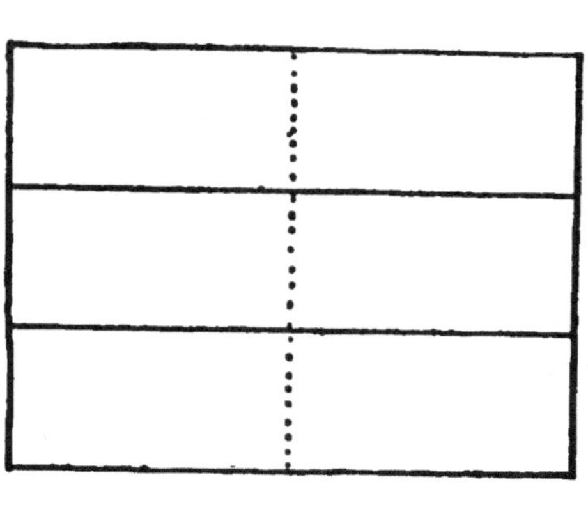

9

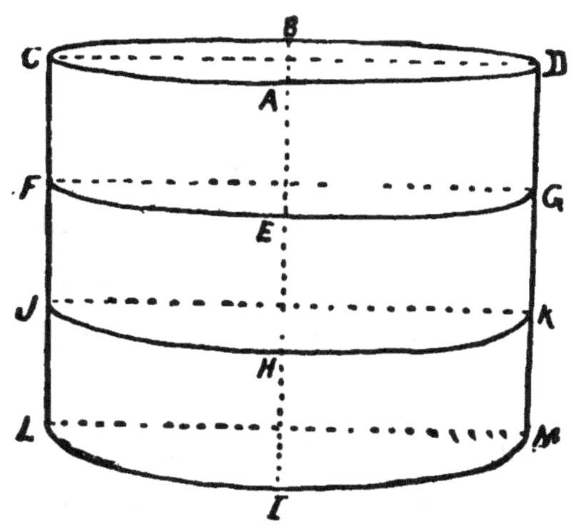

FIGURES 9 AND 10 — (1) Draw a diagram the size you wish the cylinder, as in Fig. 9. (2) Choose the points A and B in Fig. 10 equally distant from the horizontal line C D. (3) Choose the point E a little further below the horizontal line FG than the point A is below C D. Choose H still further than E and I than H. (4) Through these points, draw the curved lines F E G, J H K, and L I M. (5) Observe that the parts of the circles that curve most are at the points C F J L and D G K M, and that at the points A E H and I, the circle curves very little.

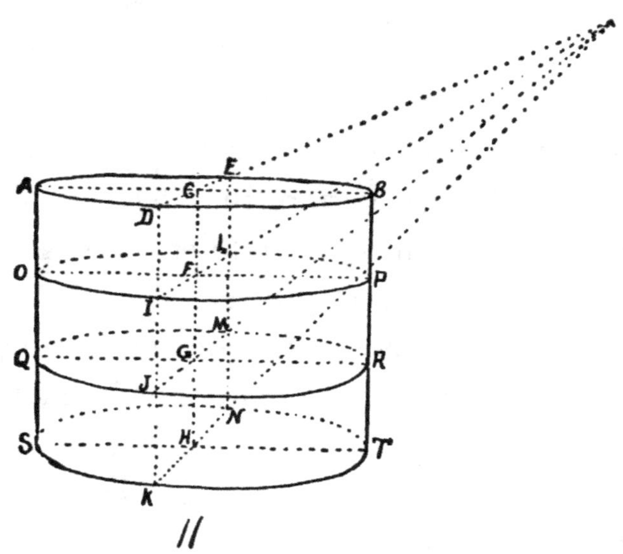

FIGURE 11 — To *divide the cylinder into parts*: (1) Draw the diagram as in Fig. 9. (2) Draw the circle ADBE. (3) Choose the CV some distance away. (4) From the CV, draw a receding line through the point C, the center of AB. This will give the points D and E. (5) From the point C, draw a vertical line, which will give the points F, G, and H. (6) Through the points F, G, and H, draw receding lines which, meeting vertical lines from the points D and E, will give the points I, J, K, and L, M, N. (7) The points O, I, P, L will mark a circle, and the point F will be its center. Q, J, R, M will mark the next one, and the point G will be its center, and S, K, T, N will mark the last, and H is its center. These are all the points necessary to work the problems given below.

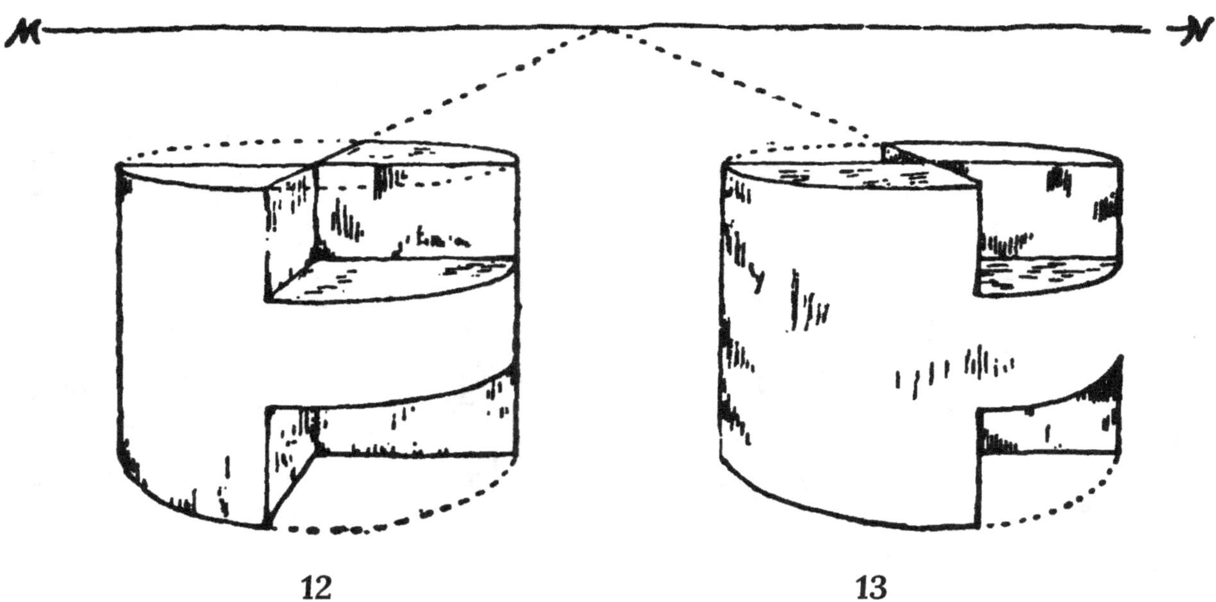

12   **13**

PROBLEM 7[24] **(FIG. 12)**[25] — *Draw a vertical cylinder below and at the left of the eye and remove parts 2, 4, and 10 (See Fig. 8).*

PROBLEM 8[26] **(FIG. 13)** — *Draw a vertical cylinder below and at the right of the eye and remove parts 2, 4, and 10.*

Problem 9. — *Draw a vertical cylinder below and at the left of the eye and remove parts 1, 3, and 9.*

Problem 10. — *Draw a vertical cylinder below and at the right of the eye and remove parts 1, 3, and 9.*

24   Do not attempt to draw the cylinder and the cut-out parts at the same time, but first draw the entire cylinder and then cut out the parts.

25   Observe that the vertical, horizontal, and receding lines are used in very much the same manner as in the cubes.

26   It is suggested that each problem be drawn as accurately as possible. The drill is as essential as the understanding of the problem.

83

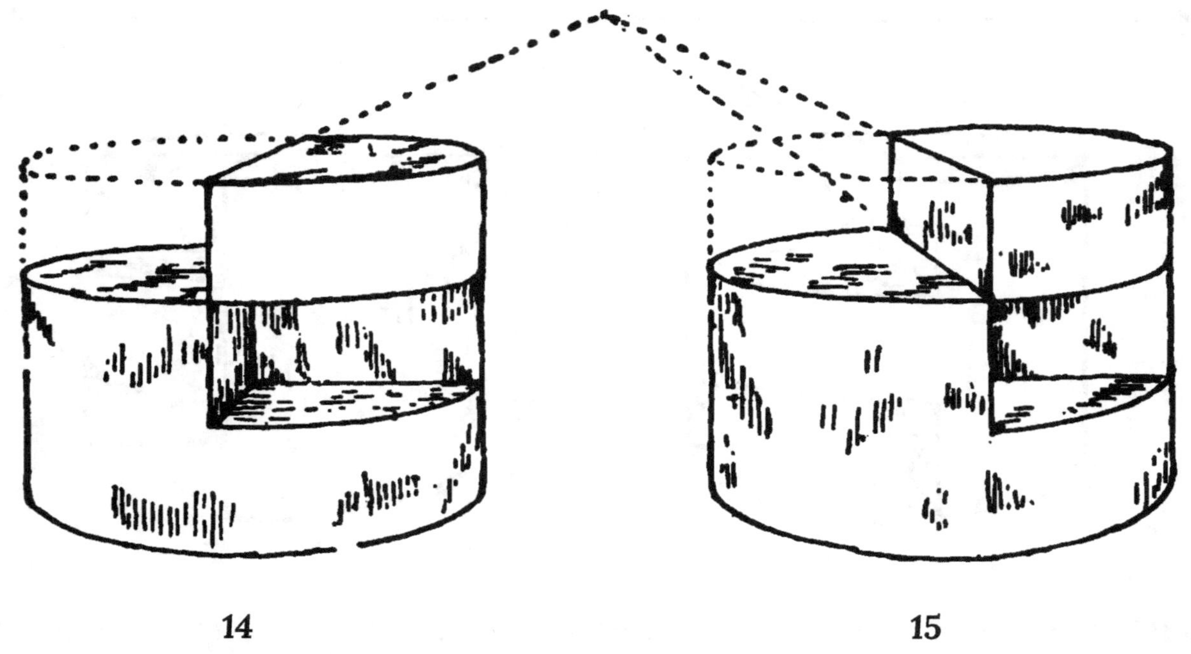

14   **15**

PROBLEM 11 (FIG. 14) — *Draw a vertical cylinder below and at the left of the eye and remove parts 1, 4, and 6.*

PROBLEM 12 (FIG. 15) — *Draw a vertical cylinder below and at the right of the eye and remove parts 1, 4, and 6.*

Problem 13. — Draw a vertical cylinder directly below the level of the eye and remove parts 1, 2, 9, and 10.

Problem 14. — Draw a vertical cylinder directly below the eye and remove parts 5 and 6; also 3 and 4.

Problem 15. — Draw a vertical cylinder below and at the left of the eye and remove parts 2, 3, 10, and 11.

Problem 16. — Draw a vertical cylinder below and at the right of the eye and remove parts 2, 3, 10, and 11.

84

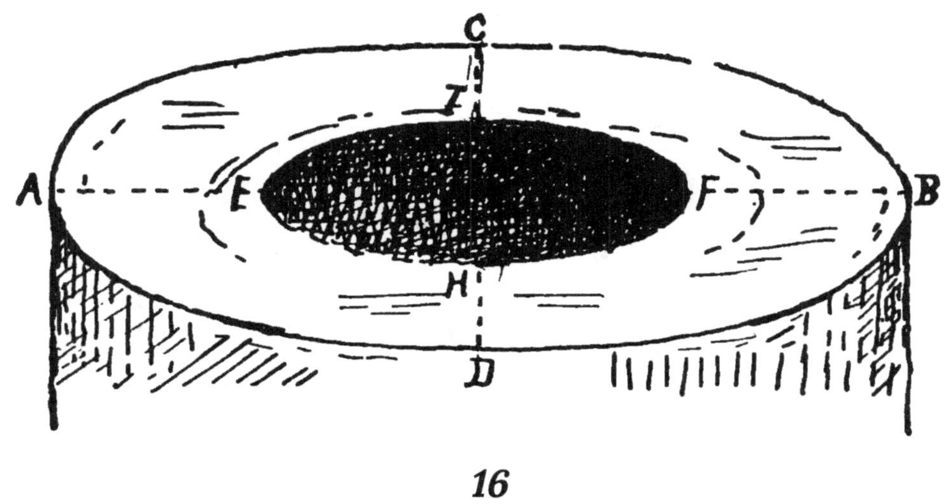

16

FIGURE 16 — *To make the inside circle proportional to the outside circle:* (1) Draw the horizontal line A B and bisect it. (2) Place the points C and D equally distant above and below the horizontal line A B at its center. (3) Through the points A D B C, draw the circle. This will be a circle in perspective. (4) Bisect the radii at E H F and I and through these points draw the other circle. The two circles will be proportional.

The radii may be divided into any proportion.

The distance I C being farther away than D H, will be drawn shorter. The amount must be determined by the judgment.

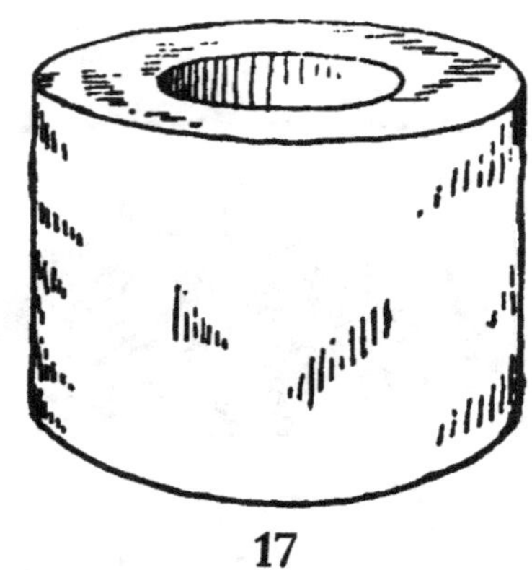

17

PROBLEM 17 (FIG. 17) — *Draw a vertical cylinder below the level of the eye and bore a round hole through it vertically (See Fig. 16).*

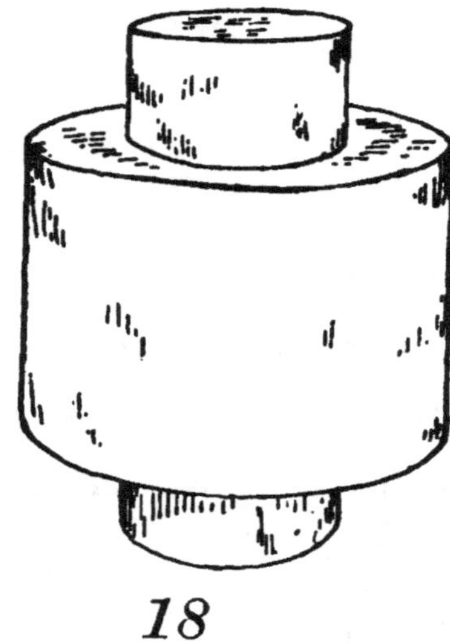

18

PROBLEM 18 (FIG. 18) — *Draw a vertical cylinder below the level of the eye and to each end add a small vertical cylinder.*

Problem 19. — *Draw a vertical cylinder above the level of the eye, and to each end add a smaller cylinder.*

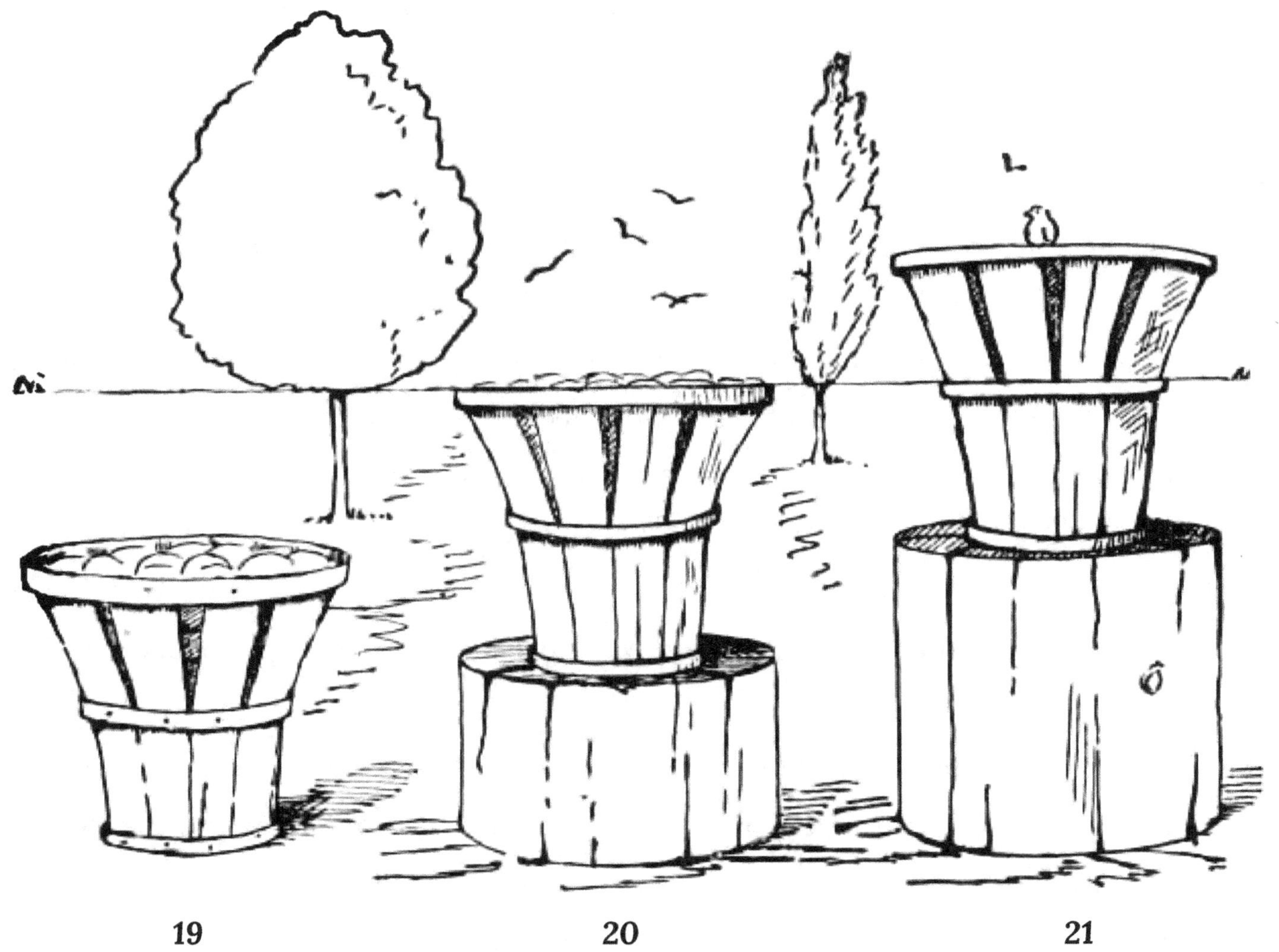

19   20   21

FIGURES 19, 20, AND 21 are practical applications of the vertical cylinder at various levels of the eye.

Observe: —

(1) That the top of Fig. 19 can be seen, that of Fig. 20 is horizontal, and that of Fig. 21 curves upward. State the cause of this.

(2) That the top of the block in Fig. 20 is wider and shows more than the top of the block in Fig. 21. State the reason for this.

(3) That the middle hoop of the basket in Fig. 20 is not drawn correctly. How may it be corrected?

Problem 20. — *Draw Fig. 19 and fill it with apples, with potatoes, with watermelons, with pumpkins.*

Problem 21. — *Place a board across the top of the basket in Fig. 20 and on it place a pumpkin.*

Problem 22. — *Draw Fig. 21 with the top of the block on a level with the eye.*

FIGURES 22, 23, 24, AND 25 are forms based upon the vertical cylinder.

Draw each one of these figures carefully on paper and then reproduce from memory on the blackboard.

Observe in Fig. 24 how the courses of stone in the lighthouse curve upward above the H.L. and downward below that line.

Observe in Fig. 25 the end of the stumps. The ends below the level of the eye (H.L.) are elliptical, the one on a level with the eye is horizontal, and the one above the eye curves upward.

Problem 23. — *Draw Fig. 22 with the eye on a level with the rim of the standard.*

Problem 24. — *Draw Fig. 23 with the eye level with the rim of the saucer.*

Problem 25. — *Draw Fig. 24 with the H.L. where the bird is flying.*

Problem 26. — *Draw Fig. 24 with the H.L. level with the base of the lighthouse.*

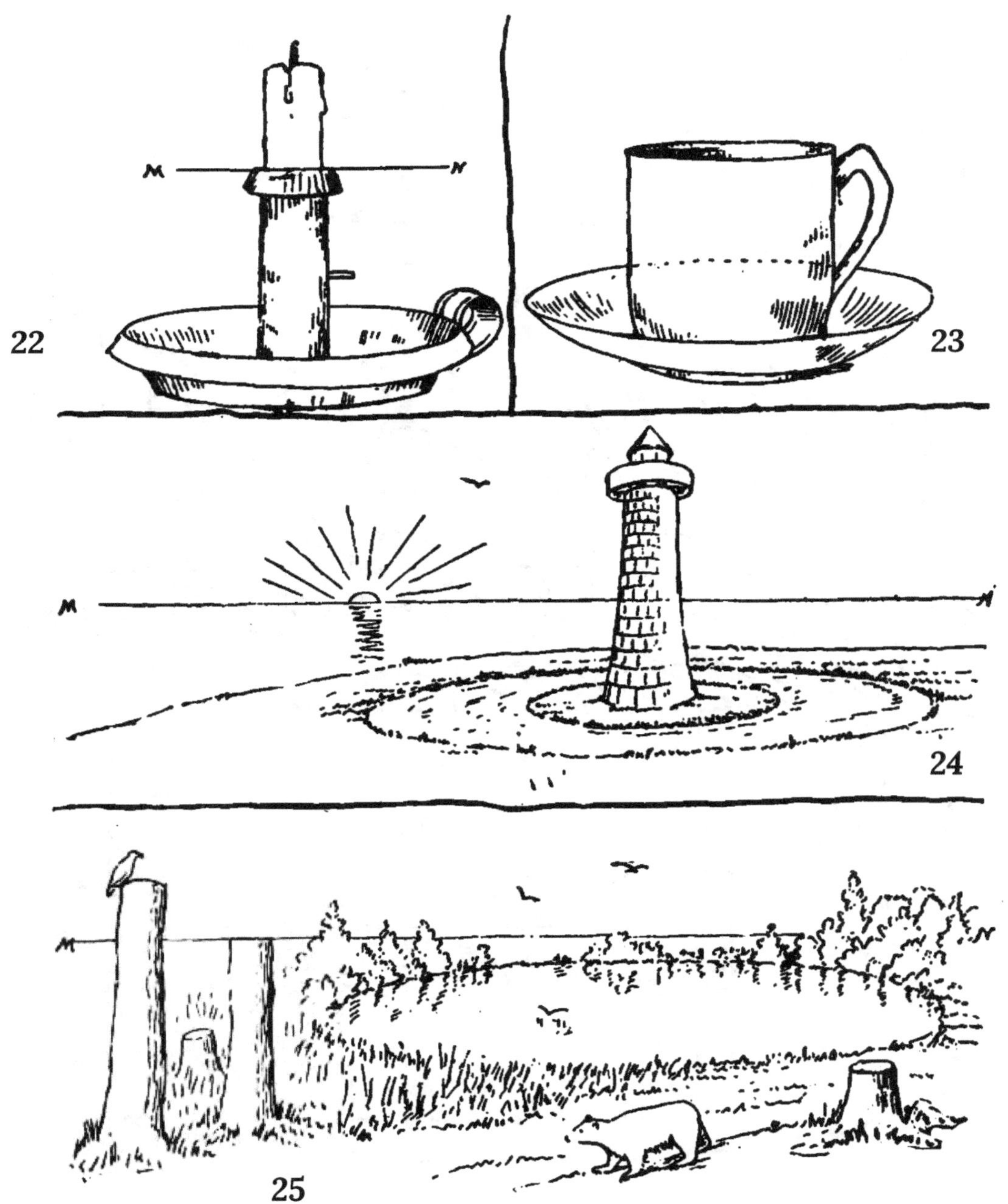

M
N
22
23
M
N
24
M
N
25

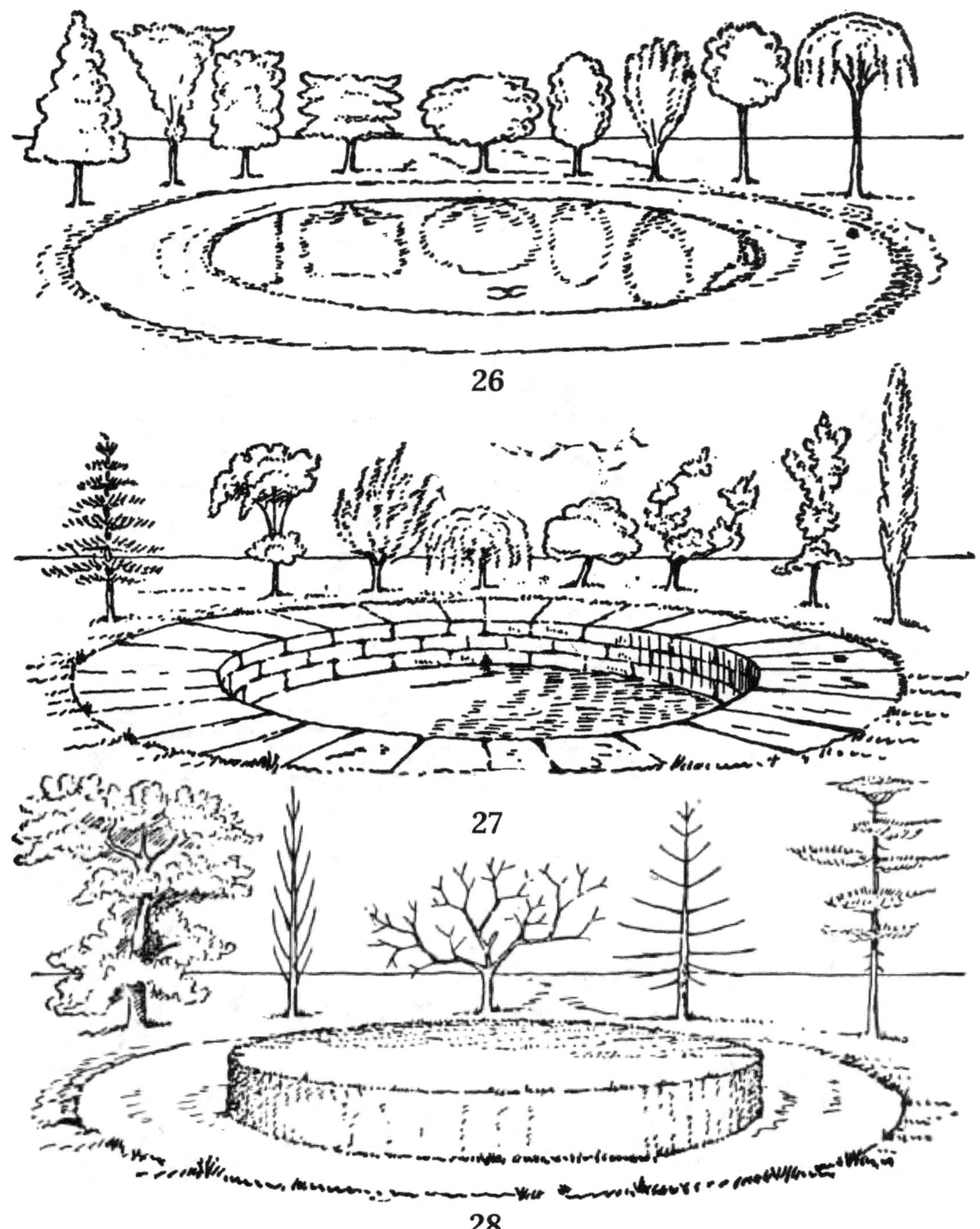

26

27

28

FIGURES 26, 27, AND 28 are applications of the top of the cylinder and are based on Fig. 16. Observe that the surface of 26 is level. That Fig. 27 is the same as Fig. 26 with the surface sunk below the level. That Fig. 28 is the same as Fig. 26 with the surface raised above a level.

Observe the shape of the trees in Fig. 26. Beginning at the left, the first two are triangular in shape, the next two rectangular, the next two elliptical, the next one balloon-shaped, the next round, and the last umbrella-shaped.

In Fig. 27, the trees are, with the exception of the one on the extreme right and left, irregular in shape. Beginning at the left and in the order given, there is an evergreen, elm, willow, weeping willow, apple, an old chestnut, elm, and Lombardy poplar.

The three trees in Fig. 28 without foliage represent the three kinds of branching: (1) Regular branching, of which the evergreens are types. (2) Irregular branching, of which the maple is a good type and deciduous trees generally. (3) Vertical branching, of which the Lombardy poplar is a type.

The first tree on the left in Fig. 26 is a pear tree, and the one on the right is an elm; the remainder are of no particular kind. The tree on the left in Fig. 28 is an oak, and the one on the right is a pine.

Cultivate habits of observation. When walking along, observe the different forms of trees. Most trees have irregular tops, but many of them are of definite form. Try and recognize these forms.

Find a tree with a round top. Find trees with triangular, rectangular, elliptical, balloon-shaped, and umbrella-shaped tops.

Observe the shape of the pear, apple, and peach trees. Of maple, oak, chestnut, and willow trees. Notice (1) whether the stem is straight or divides into branches. (2) Whether the limbs are regular, irregular, or vertical. (3) The shape of the top. (4) The character of the foliage.

Find what kind of trees are conical and what kind are rounding on top.

Notice the difference in shape between young and old trees of the same species. Notice the difference between trees that grow in a wood and those of the same species that grow in an open field.

Observe and point out the three kinds of branching.

PROBLEMS.

Problem 27. — *Draw Fig. 26 and omit the trees.*

Problem 28. — *Draw Fig. 27 and omit the trees.*

Problem 29. — *Draw Fig. 28 and omit the trees.*

Problem 30. — *Draw Fig. 26 and sink the pond below the surface of the ground.*

Problem 31. — *Draw Fig. 26 with a round fence around it in place of the larger circle.*

Problem 32. — *Draw Fig. 27 with the center level with the surrounding surface.*

Problem 33. — *Draw Fig. 28 with the center raised until level with the eye.*

Problem 34. — *Draw Fig. 28 with the path around the mound sunk below the surrounding surface.*

Problem 35. — *Draw Fig. 28 with the center sunk below the surrounding surface.*

Problem 36. — *Draw on the blackboard a round-topped tree, a broad rectangular tree, a tall rectangular tree, a tall elliptical tree, a broad elliptical tree, an umbrella-shaped tree, a balloon-shaped tree, a triangular-shaped tree, and a conical-shaped tree.*

Problem 37. — *Draw a pear tree on the blackboard, an apple tree, a Lombardy poplar, a willow, a weeping willow, a pine, an oak, and an evergreen.*

Problem 38. — *Draw a tree with regular branches, with irregular branches, and with vertical branches.*

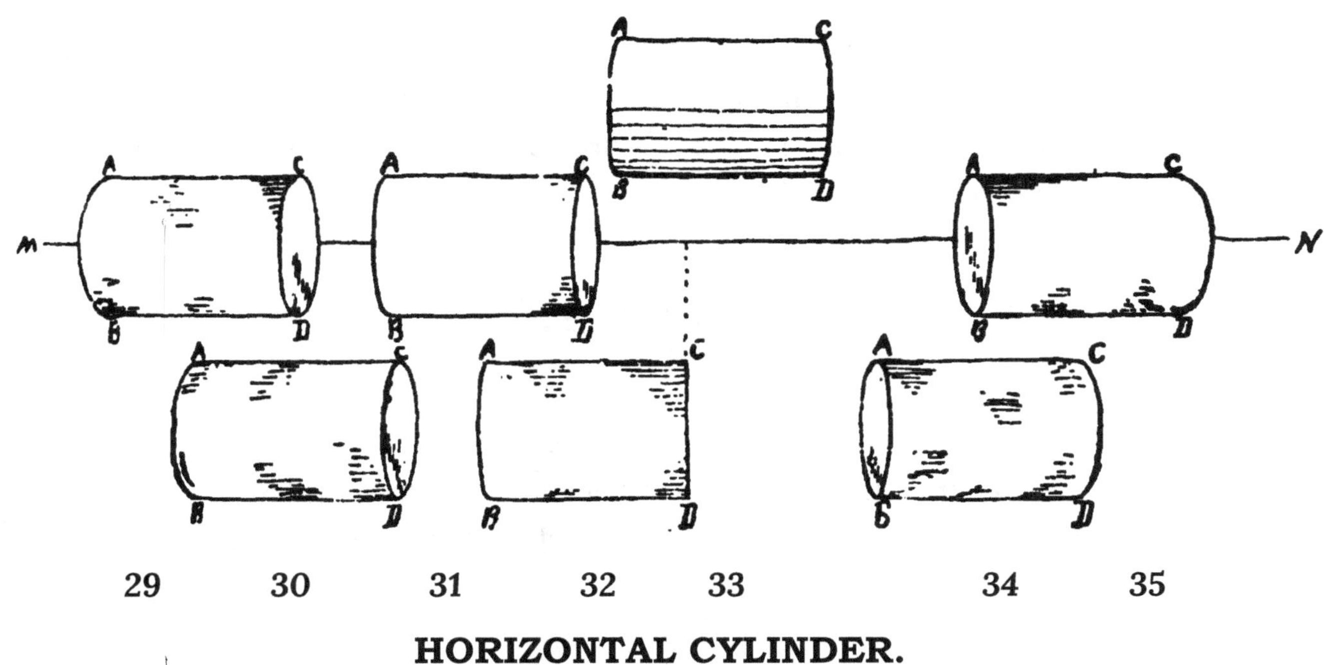

HORIZONTAL CYLINDER.

The drawing of the horizontal cylinder depends on its position in relation to the C. of V[27].

Hold the cylinder horizontally before the eye so that the right end is in line with the eye, as in Fig. 32. The curved edge C D will be vertical, the same as C D in the drawing, and edge A B will curve to the left as A B in the drawing.

Hold the cylinder to the left of the eye as in Fig. 30, and the edge C D becomes an ellipse like C D in the drawing and the edge AB curves still more to the left like A B in the drawing.

Hold the cylinder so that the eye is in line with the middle of the cylinder, as in Fig. 33. Now the edge A B curves to the left and the edge C D to the right, like A B and C D in the drawing.

27   The position of the horizontal cylinder above or below the H.L. does affect its drawing to some extent, but for all practical purposes, this may be ignored and the cylinder drawn in relation to the C. of V. alone.

Observe that the further to the right or left the horizontal cylinder is from the C. of V. (eye), the more circular one end becomes and the more curving the other. Thus CD in Fig. 29 is more circular than CD in Fig. 31, and AB in Fig. 29 is more curving than AB in Fig. 31, and the same may be noticed in Figs. 34 and 35.

PROBLEMS.

Problem 1. — Draw a horizontal cylinder at the left of the eye.

Problem 2. — Draw a horizontal cylinder at the right of the eye.

Problem 3. — Draw a horizontal cylinder with the left end directly in front of the eye.

Problem 4. — Draw a horizontal cylinder with one end at the left and the other at the right of the eye.

Problem 5. — Draw two cylinders at the left of the eye but of unequal distance.

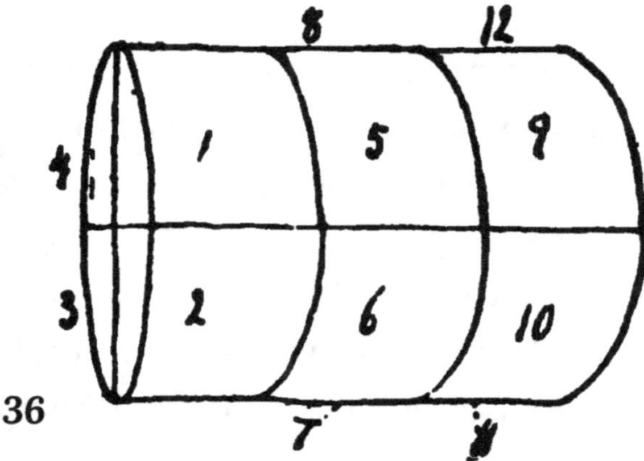

FIGURE 36 is a horizontal cylinder divided into thirds and each third is divided into quarters and numbered for convenience of reference in the following problems.

Commence drawing the problems as follows:

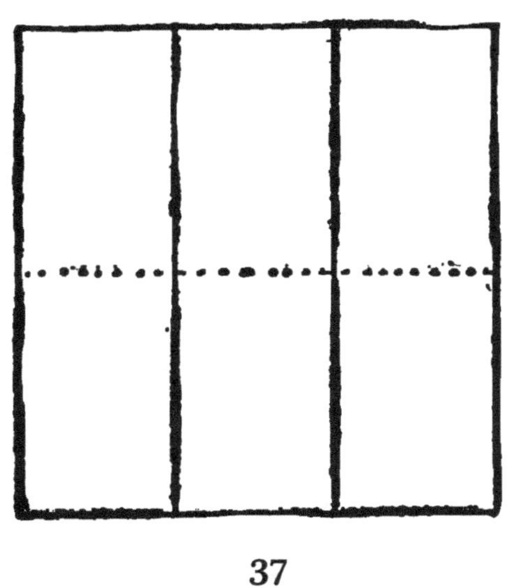
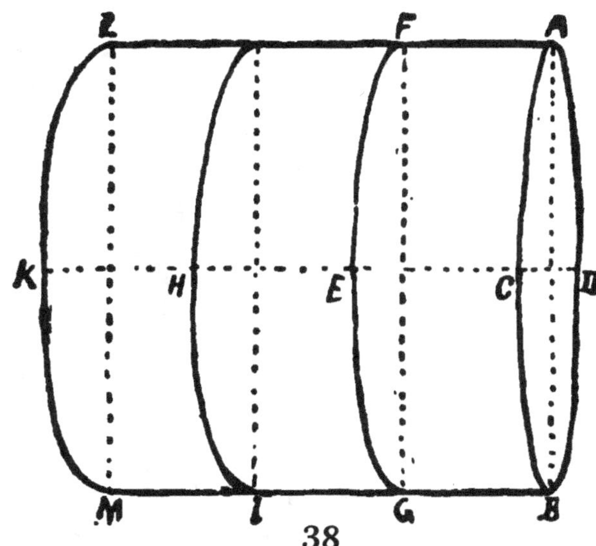

37   38

FIGURES 37 AND 38. - (1) Draw a diagram with light lines the size you wish the cylinder, like Fig. 37. (2) Choose the points C and D in Fig. 38, equally distant from the vertical line A B. (3) Choose the point E, a little further from the vertical line F G, than C is from A B. Choose H still further than E and K, than H. (4) These points will mark the amount of curvature of the lines F E G, I H J and L K M. Observe that the curvature is mostly at the points A F J L B G I and M, and that the circle curves very little at the points D C E H and K.

FIGURE 39. - To find the points used in drawing the problems. (1) Draw the diagram as in Fig. 37. (2) Draw the circle A D B E as in Fig 39. (3) Choose the C. of V., and through the point C, the cente of the circle, draw a receding line. This line will mark the points D and E. (4) From the point C, draw a horizontal line which will mark the points F G and H. (5) Through the points F G and H, draw receding lines, which meeting horizontal lines from the points D and E will mark the points I J K and L M N. (6) The points O I D L will mark the second circle, Q J R M the third, and S K T N the fourth. (7) The points C F G H are the centers of their respective circles.

95

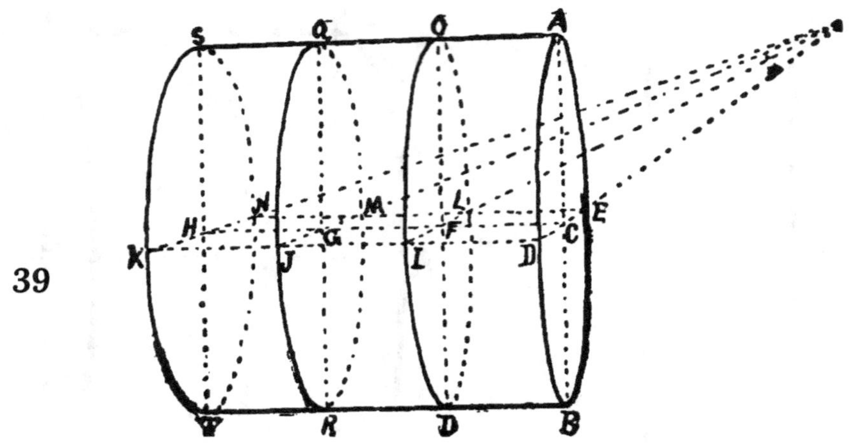

Problem 6. — Draw Fig. 39 below and at the right of the eye.

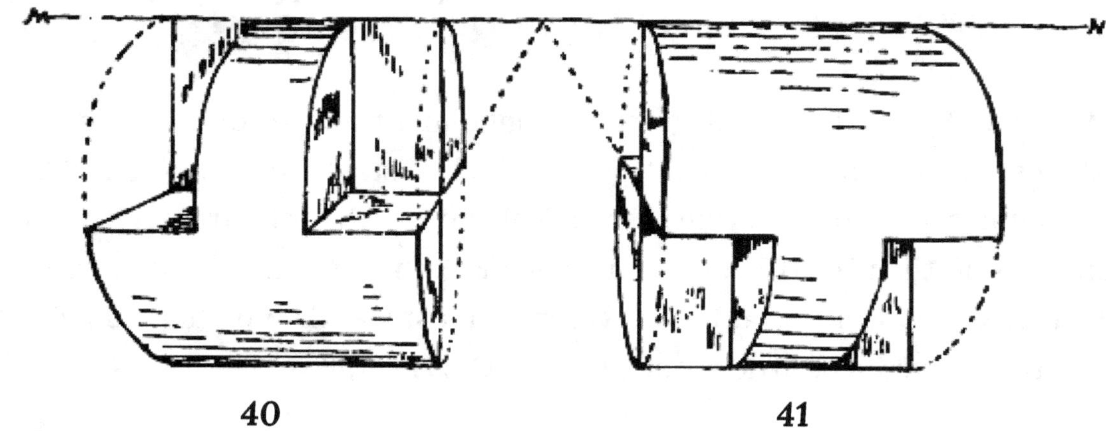

PROBLEM 7. FIG. 40. — *Draw a horizontal cylinder slightly below and at the left of the eye, and remove parts 9, 11, and 1. (See Fig. 36.)*

PROBLEM 8. FIG. 41. — *Draw a horizontal cylinder slightly below and at the right of the eye and remove parts 2, 4, and 10. (See Fig. 36.)*

Problem 9. — *Draw a horizontal cylinder slightly below and at the right of the eye and remove quarters 1, 6, and 9.*

Problem 10. — *Draw a horizontal cylinder below and at the right of the eye and remove parts 4, 5, and 9.*

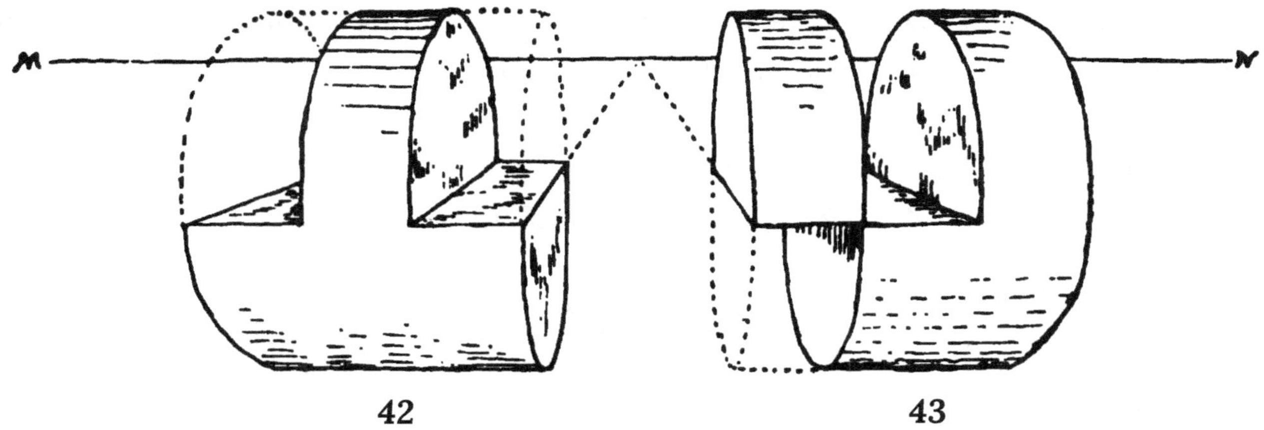

PROBLEM 11. FIG. 42. — *Draw a horizontal cylinder slightly below and at the left of the eye and remove parts 4, 1, 9, and 12. (See Fig. 36.)*

PROBLEM 12. FIG. 43. — *Draw a horizontal cylinder below and at the right of the eye and remove parts 2, 3, 5, and 8. (See Fig. 36.)*

Problem 13. — *Draw a horizontal cylinder below and at the left of the eye and remove parts 6 and 7.*

Problem 14. — *Draw a horizontal cylinder at the left of the eye and remove parts 1, 2, 9, and 10.*

Problem 15. — *Draw a horizontal cylinder directly below the eye and remove part 5.*

Problem 16. — *Draw a horizontal cylinder below and at the left of the eye and bore a round hole through it horizontally.*

Problem 17. — *Draw a horizontal cylinder at the right of the eye and to each end add a small horizontal cylinder.*

Problem 18. — *Draw a horizontal cylinder below the eye and remove parts of the upper half. Remove parts 1, 5, 9, 4, 8, and 12.*

Problem 19. — *Draw a horizontal cylinder at the right and slightly below the eye and remove the parts of the lower half. Remove parts 2, 6, 10, 3, 7, and 11.*

FIGURES 44, 45, 46, AND 47 are applications of the horizontal cylinder. Copy each figure carefully and then draw it on the blackboard from memory.

Problem 20. — *Draw Fig. 44 at the right of the eye.*

Problem 21. — *Draw Fig. 44 as a vertical cylinder below the level of the eye.*

Problem 22. — *Draw Fig. 45 at the left of the eye.*

Problem 23. — *Draw the pyramid of logs in Fig. 46 at the left of the eye, and the row of logs at the right.*

Problem 24. — *Draw the bridge in Fig. 47 at the right of the eye.*

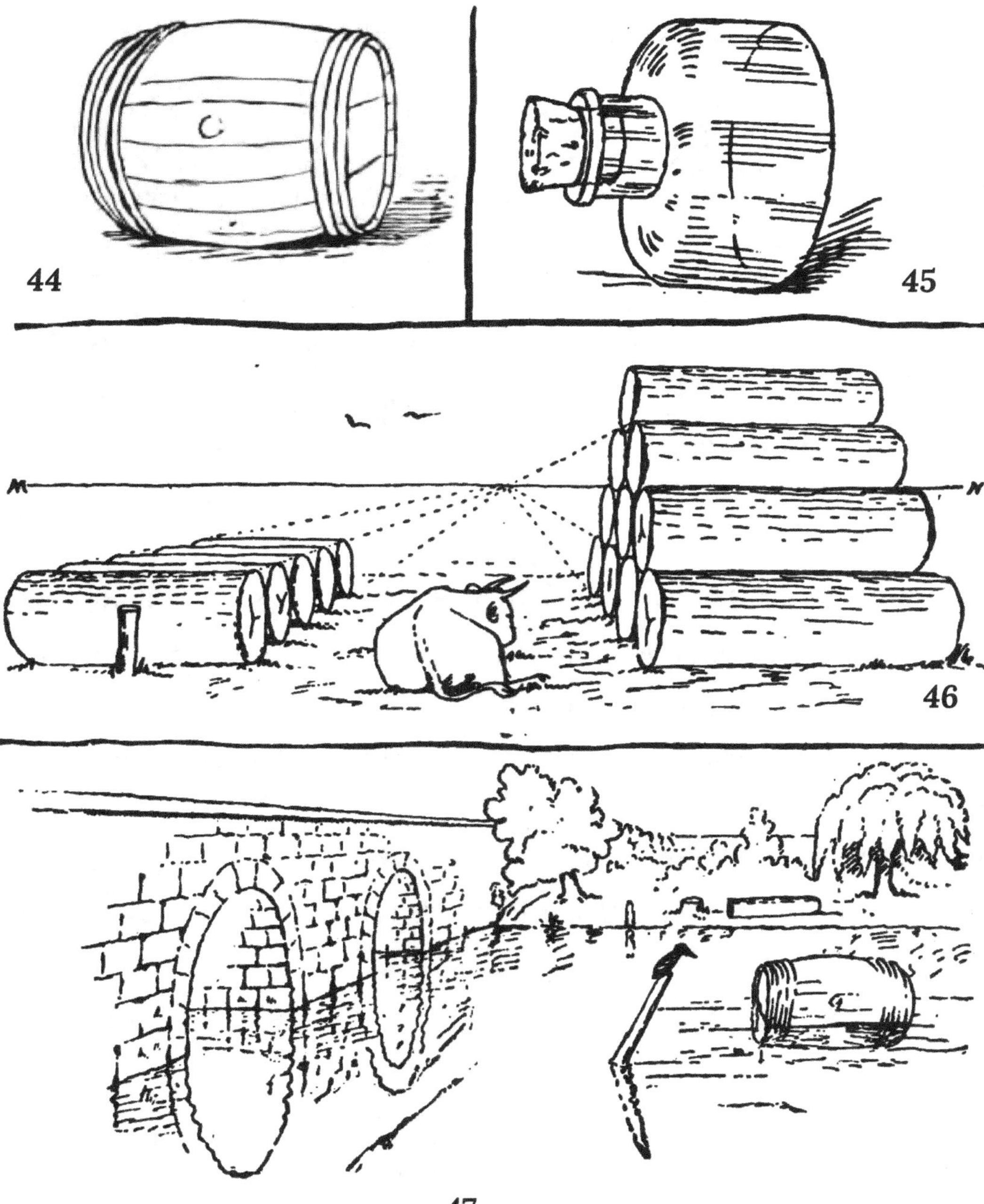

44

45

46

47

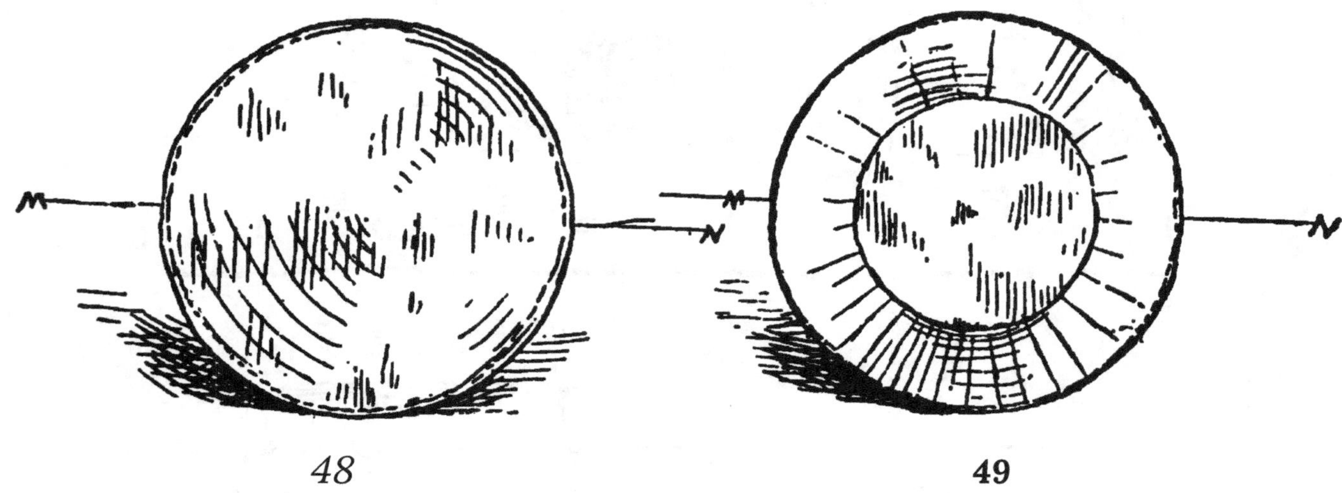

48

49

The position of the C. of V. determines the drawing of the receding cylinder[28].

Hold the receding cylinder directly in front of the eye so that only the nearer end can be seen. The end will be simply a circle like Fig. 48.

Remove one end from the cylinder. Hold it in front of the eye so that the inside can be seen. It will appear similar to Fig. 49.

PROBLEM 1. FIG. 48. — *Draw a receding cylinder directly in front of the eye.*

PROBLEM 2. FIG. 49. — *Draw a receding cylinder directly in front of the eye with the nearer end removed.*

28   When the end of a cylinder is a circle, the receding lines of the sides converge to the C. of V., and conversely, when the sides converge to the C. of V., the end must be a circle.

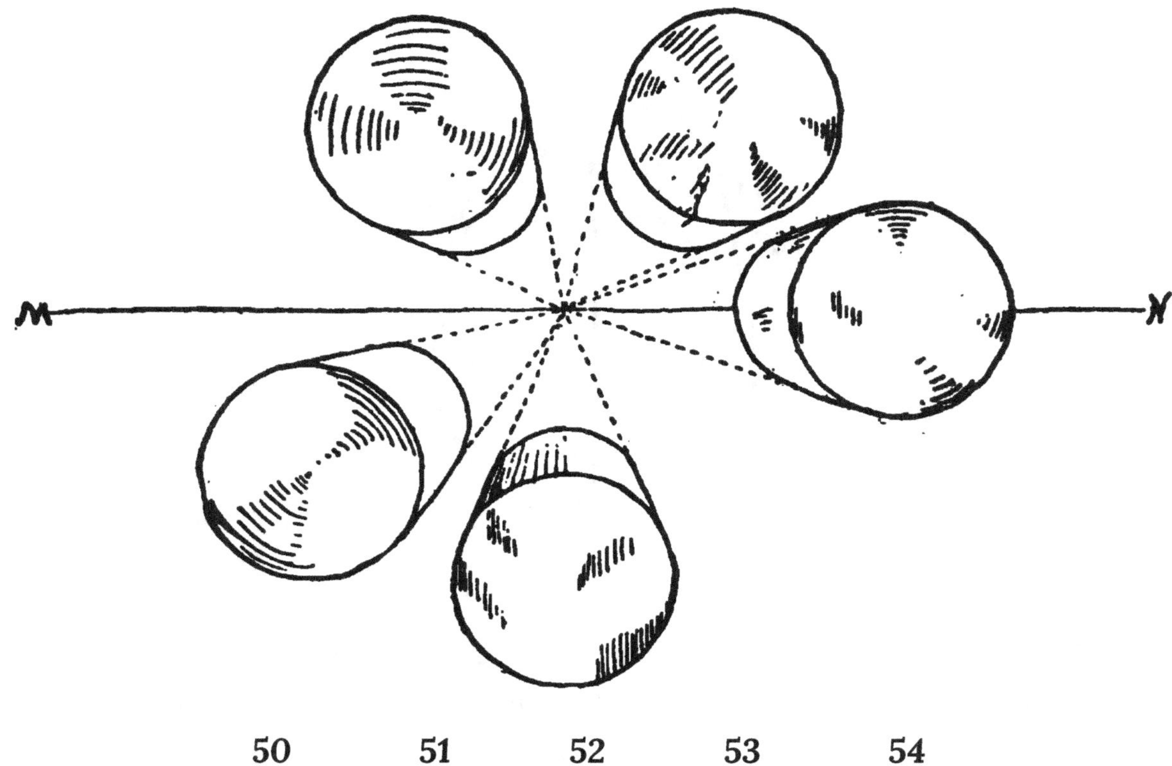

50   51   52   53   54

Hold the cylinder below the level of the eye. The nearer end and part of the side will be seen as in Fig. 52.

Hold the cylinder at the right of the eye. The nearer end and part of the side can be seen as in Fig. 54.

Hold the cylinder above and below, at the right or left of the eye, and the circular end and a part of the side will show as represented by Figs. 50 - 54.

PROBLEM 3. FIG. 52. — *Draw a receding cylinder below the level of the eye.*[29]

PROBLEM 4. FIG. 50. — *Draw a receding cylinder below and at the left of the eye.*

PROBLEM 5. FIG. 51. — *Draw a receding cylinder above and at the left of the eye.*

PROBLEM 6. FIG. 53. — *Draw a receding cylinder above and at the right of the eye.*

29 Care must be taken to draw the further end of the cylinder as curving as the corresponding part of the nearer end.

101

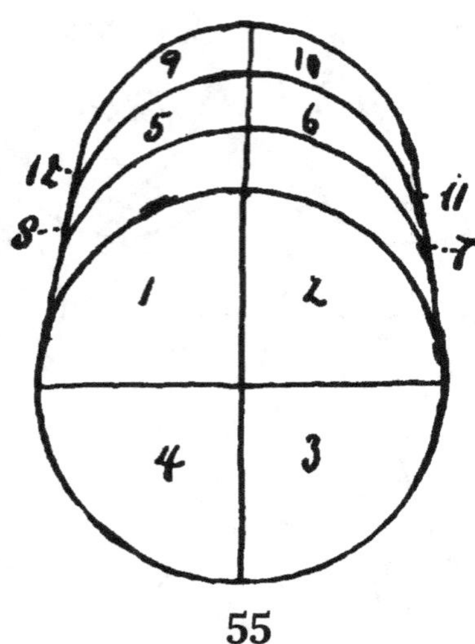

55

FIGURE 55 is a cylinder below the eye divided lengthwise into thirds and each third divided into quarters, and numbered for convenience of reference in the following problems.

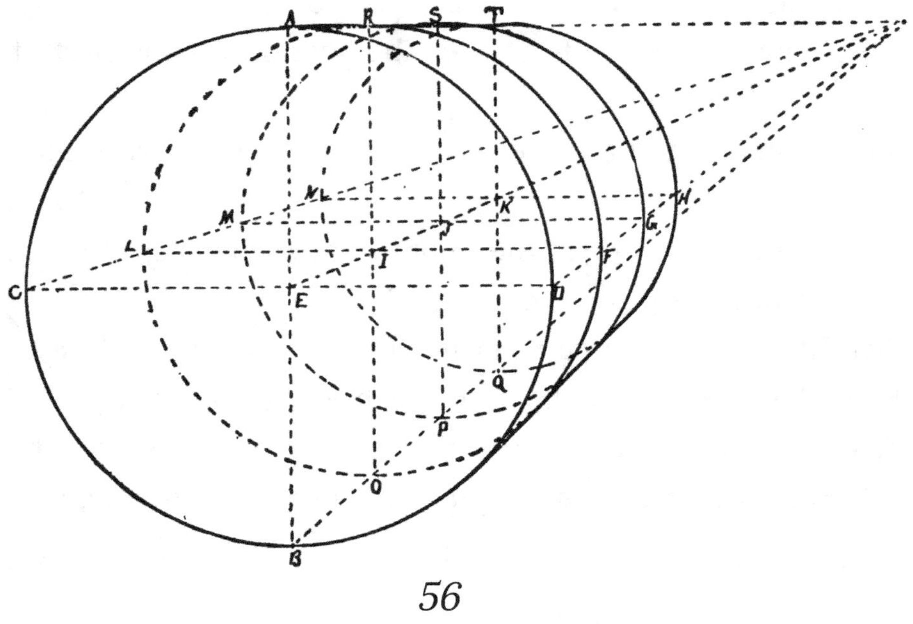

56

FIGURE 56. — To find the different points in the receding cylinder problems: (1) Draw the circle A C B I D and through its center E the vertical line A B and the horizontal line C D. (2) Choose the C. of V. and from the points A, B, C, D, and E draw receding lines. (3) Choose the points F, G, H, and I, and from them draw horizontal lines. Where these horizontal lines cross the receding lines, they will mark the points I, J, K, and L, M, N. (4) Vertical lines through I, J, K mark the points O, P, Q, and R, S, T. (5) E is the center of the first circle, I of the second, J of the third, and K of the fourth.

These are all the points necessary to draw the following problems in the receding cylinder.

Problem 7. — *Draw Fig. 56 below and at the right of the eye.*
Problem 8. — *Draw Fig. 56 directly below the eye.*
Problem 9. — *Draw Fig. 56 at the right of the eye.*

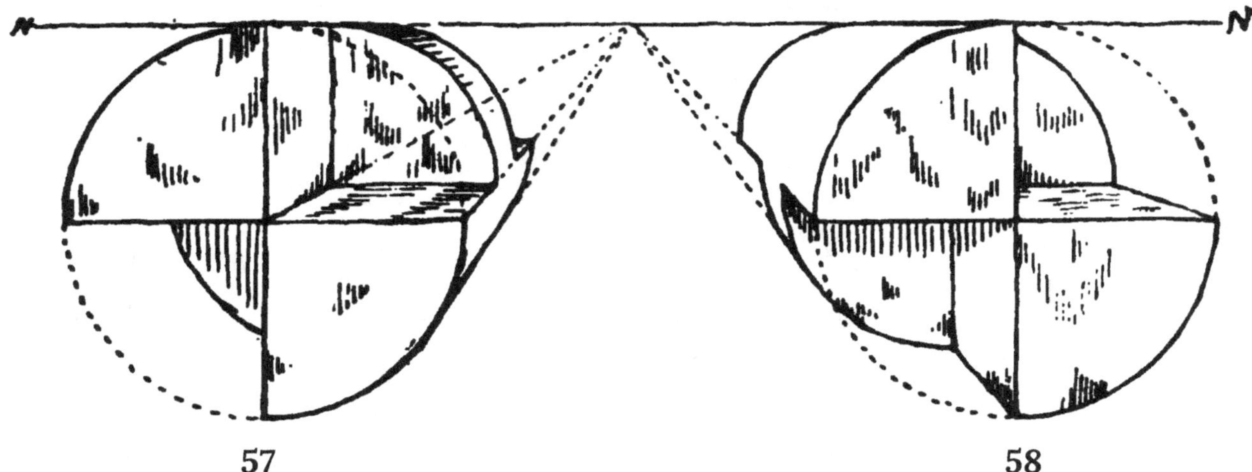

57   58

PROBLEM 10. FIG. 57. — *Draw a receding cylinder below and at the left of the eye and remove parts 2, 4, and 10. (See Fig. 55.)*

PROBLEM 11. FIG. 58. — *Draw a receding cylinder below and at the right of the eye and re-*

move parts 2, 4, and 12.

Problem 12. — Draw a receding cylinder below the eye and remove parts 1, 2, 9, and 10.

Problem 13. — Draw a cylinder below and at the right of the eye and remove parts 5, 4, and 12.

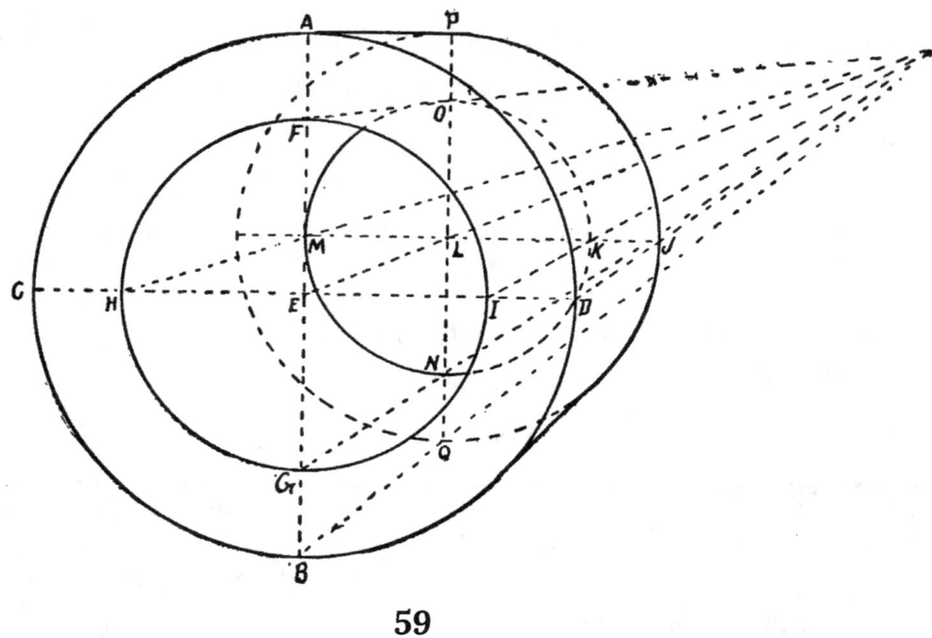

59

FIGURE 59. — To bore a round hole through a receding cylinder: (1) Draw with a common center the two circles A C B I D and F H G J. (2) Through the center E draw the vertical line A B, and the horizontal line CD. (3) Choose the C. of V. and from the points D, I, E, H, F, and G draw receding lines. (4) Choose the point J and from it draw a horizontal line. Where this line crosses the receding lines, it will mark the points K, L, and M. (5) A vertical line through L will mark the points O and N, P and Q. (6) Through the points O K N M and P J Q draw circles.

Problem 14. — Draw Fig. 59 below and at the right of the eye.

Problem 15. — Draw Fig. 59 below the eye and at the right of the eye.

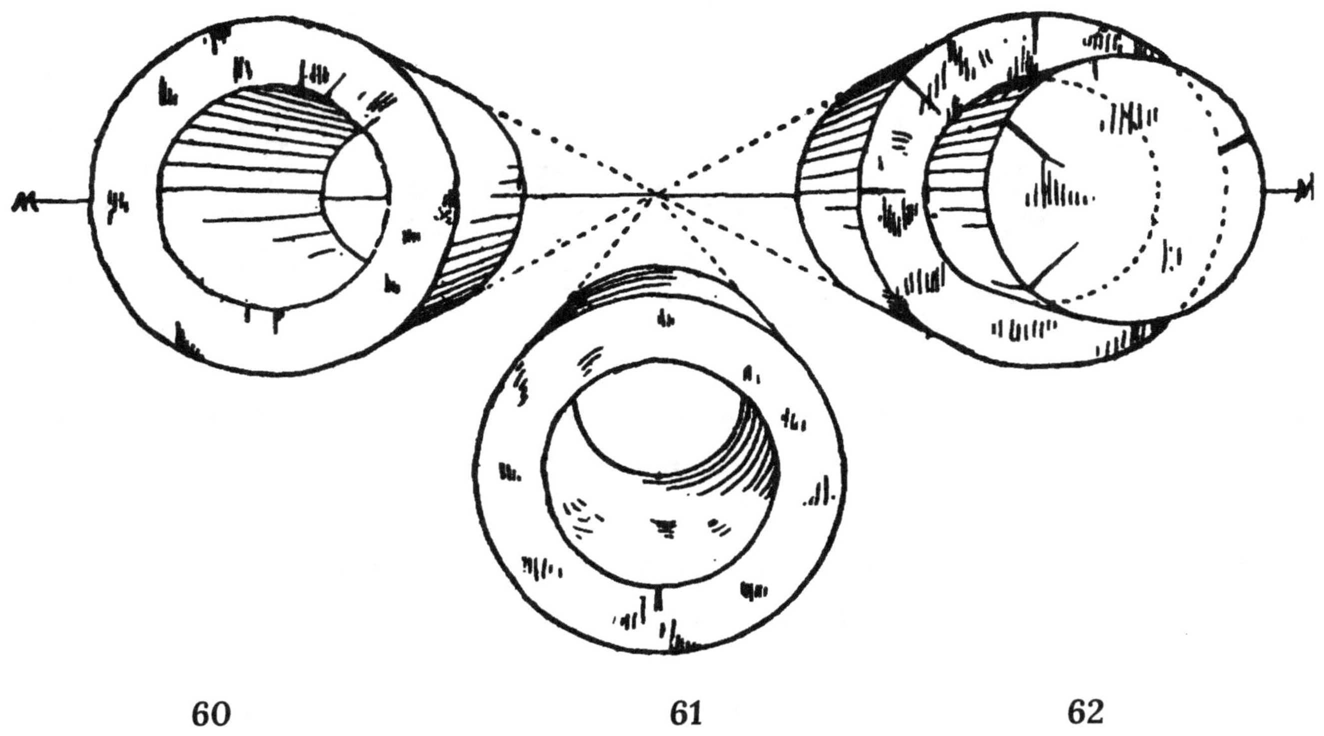

60 **61** **62**

PROBLEM 16. FIG. 60. — *Draw a receding cylinder at the left of the eye and bore a round opening through it. (See Fig. 59.)*

PROBLEM 17. FIG. 61.— *Draw a receding cylinder below the eye and bore a round hole through it. (See Fig. 59.)*

PROBLEM 18. FIG. 62. — *Draw a receding cylinder at the right of the eye and to the end add a smaller receding cylinder.*

PROBLEM 19. — *Draw Fig. 60 at the right of the eye. Below and at the right of the eye. Above the eye.*

PROBLEM 20. — *Draw Fig. 62 below the eye. Above the eye. Below and at the left of the eye.*

105

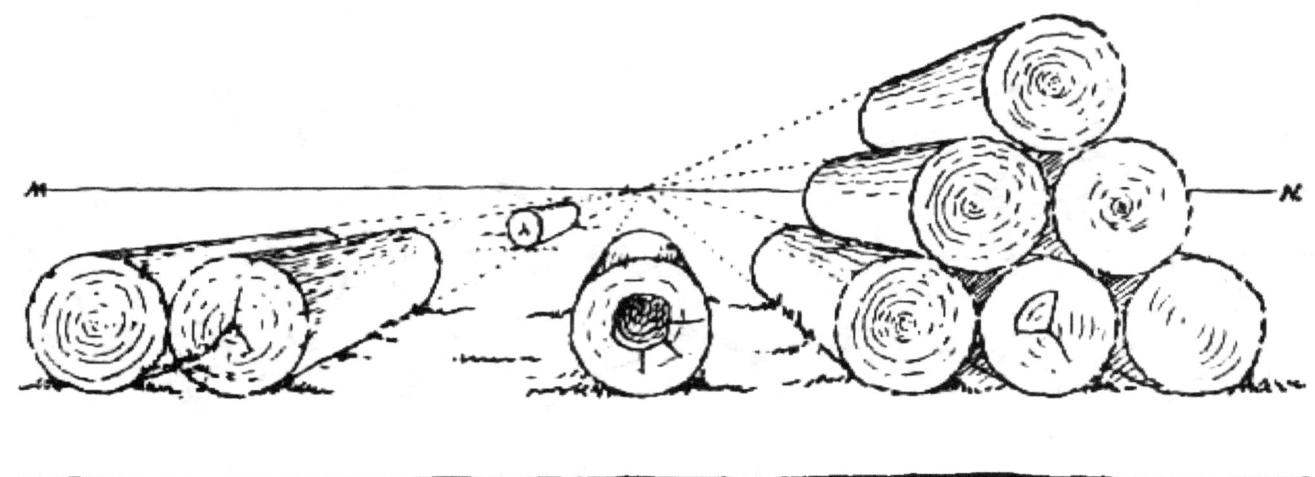

63

FIGURES 63, 64, AND 65 are simple applications of the receding cylinder. Copy each carefully and reproduce from memory on the blackboard.

Problem 21. — *Draw a pyramid of logs at the left of the eye similar to those in Fig. 63.*

Problem 22. — *Draw the pyramid of logs in Fig. 63 as horizontal logs at the right of the eye.*

Problem 23. — *Draw the roller in Fig. 64 at the right of the eye.*

Problem 24. — *Draw Fig. 65 with the C. of V. in the center of the pier at A.*

Problem 25. — *Draw Fig. 65 with the C. of V. above the arches.*

64

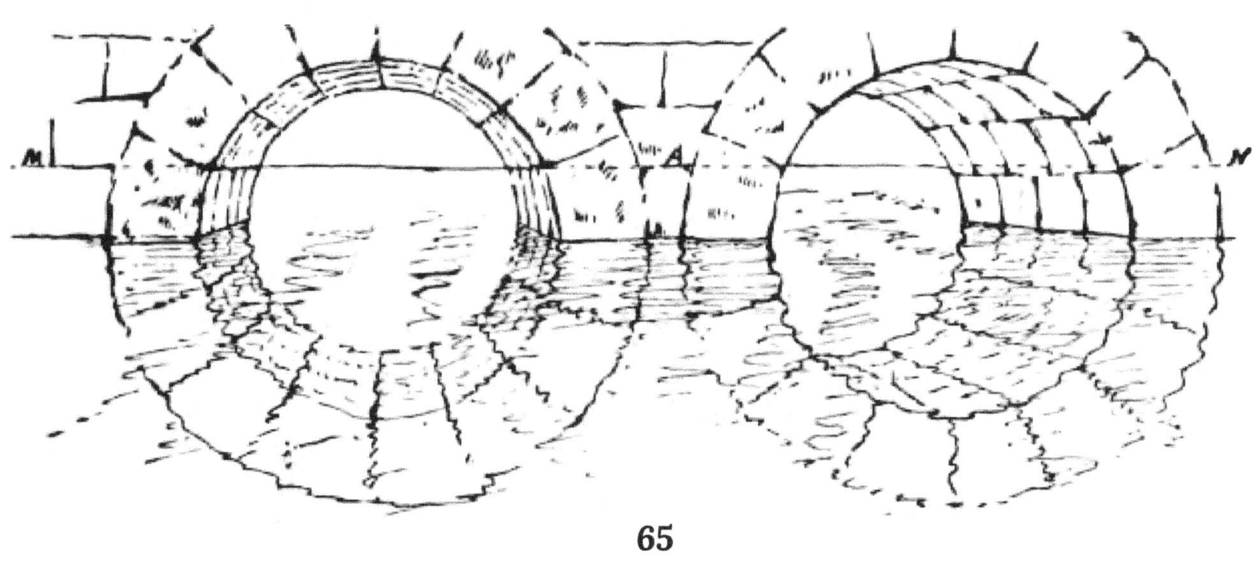

65

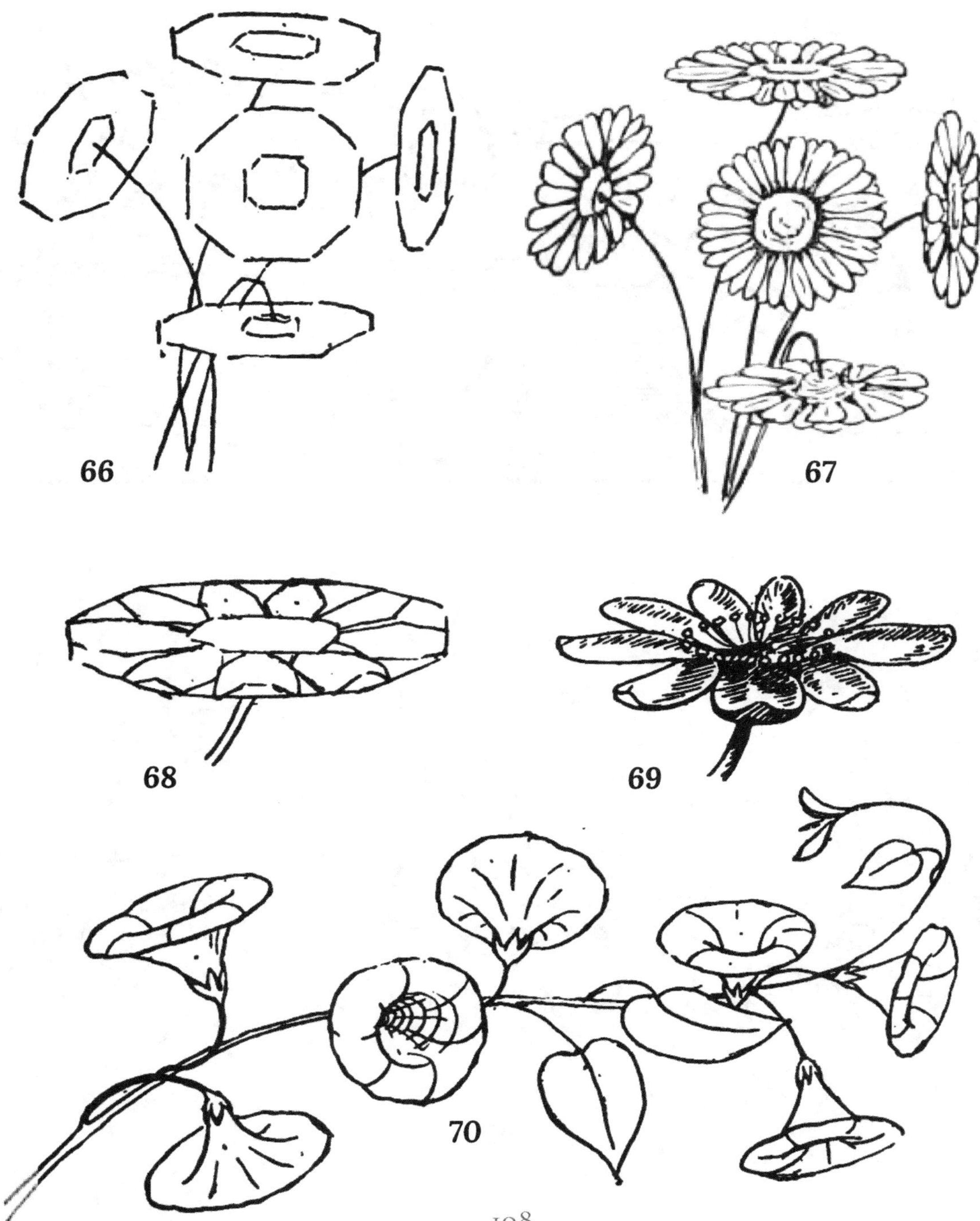

66
67
68
69
70

FIGURE 67 representing a bunch of daisies, shows a combination of the vertical, horizontal, and receding cylinder. The upper and lower daisy represent a figure similar to the end of the vertical cylinder; the daisies at the right and left represent the end of a horizontal cylinder; and the daisy in the center represents the end of the cylinder held directly in front of the eye.

FIGURE 66 represents a proportion sketch or drawing of Fig. 67. This proportion drawing is called "Blocking in." All drawings should be first *blocked* in with light lines, which may be easily erased before adding the details or giving expression to the lines.

FIGURE 68 represents the blocking in Fig. 69. It is best to use *straight lines* when blocking in, ignoring the small details and aiming at the general proportion alone.

FIGURE 70 represents various positions of the ends of vertical, horizontal, and receding cylinders.

Problem 26. — *Draw a single daisy below the eye based on the end of the vertical cylinder. Above the eye. At the right of the eye. At the left of the eye.*
Problem 27. — *Draw a single daisy based on the end of the receding cylinder directly in front of the eye.*
Problem 28. — *Block in Fig. 70.*
Problem 29. — *Copy Fig. 70, Fig. 69, Fig. 67.*
Problem 30. — *Represent a flower of Fig. 70 as based on the end of the vertical cylinder, the horizontal cylinder, and the receding cylinder.*

THE HALF CYLINDER.

The study of the half cylinder may be divided like the cylinder into three parts: (1) The vertical half cylinder, (2) The horizontal half cylinder, (3) The receding half cylinder.

Models may be: (1) Moulded from clay or plaster of Paris, (2) Whittled from soap, paraffin, clay, or plaster, (3) By splitting a cylinder into halves, (4) Made from card or pasteboard.

There are no principles in the half cylinder that have not been passed over in the cylinder, so no explanation is deemed necessary.

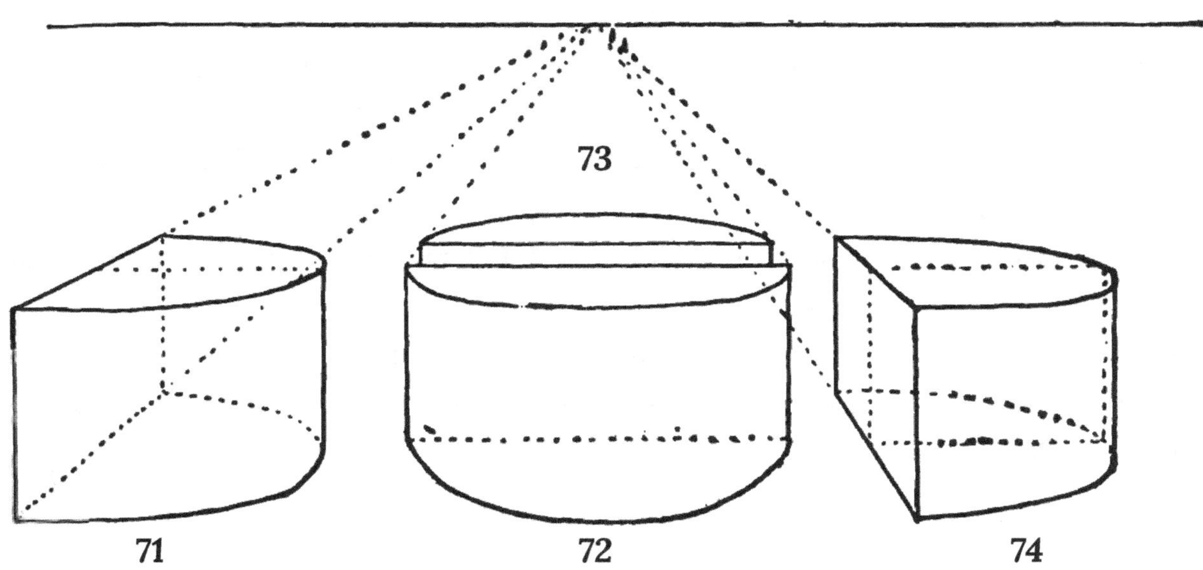

THE VERTICAL HALF CYLINDER.

FIGURES 71, 72, 73, 74 are vertical half cylinders below, below and at the left, and below and at the right of the eye.

PROBLEMS.

PROBLEM 1. FIG. 71. — *Below and at the left of the eye draw a vertical half cylinder with the plane face to the left. With the plane face to the right.*

PROBLEM 2. FIG. 72 AND 73. — *Below the eye draw a vertical half cylinder with the plane face away from you. With the plane face toward you.*

PROBLEM 3. FIG. 74. — *Below and at the right of the eye, draw a vertical half cylinder with the plane face to the left. With the plane face to the right.*

Problem 4. — Draw Fig. 71 above the eye. At the left of the eye. Below the eye. Remove the top face showing the inside.

Problem 5. — Draw Fig. 74 and remove the top face showing the inside. Remove the plane face. Remove both top and plane faces.

Problem 6. — Draw Fig. 74 above and at the right of the eye. At the right of the eye. Below the eye. Below and at the left of the eye.

Problem 7. — Draw Fig. 73 below the eye. Above. Below and at the left of the eye.

Problem 8. — Draw Fig. 72 above the eye. With the bottom on a level with the eye. Below and at the left of the eye.

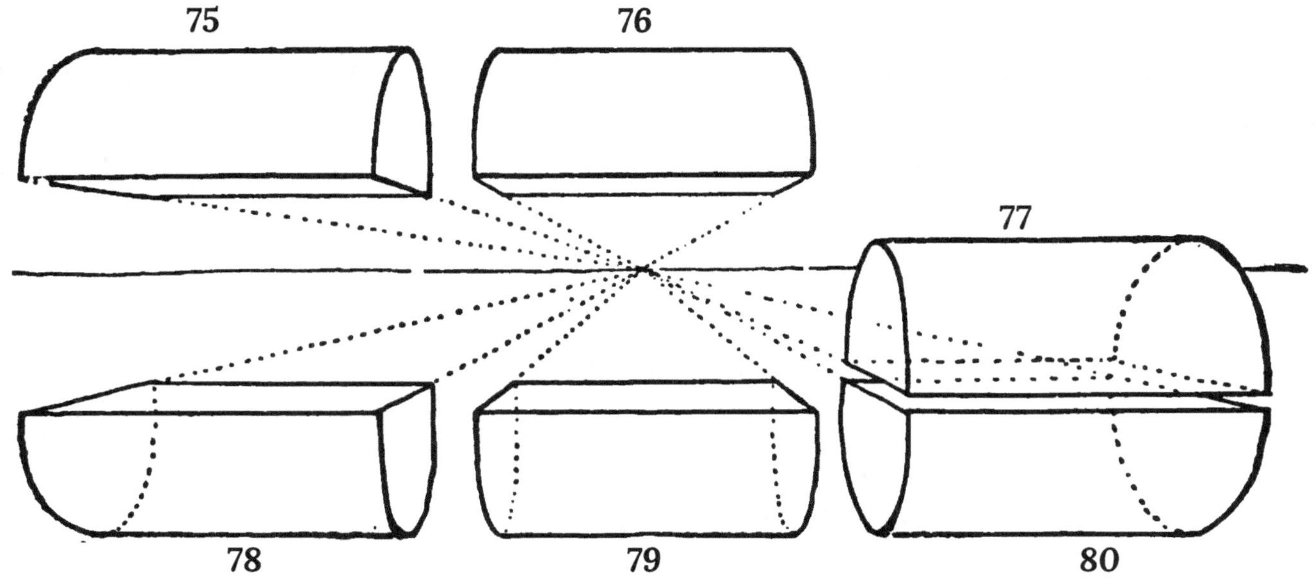

THE HORIZONTAL HALF CYLINDER.

FIGURES 75 – 80 are horizontal half cylinders above and at the left, below and at the left, above and below, and below and at the right of the eye.

PROBLEMS.

PROBLEM 9. FIG. 79. — *Below the eye draw a horizontal half cylinder with the plane face up. With the plane face down. Remove the top face.*

PROBLEM 10. FIG. 78. — *Below and at the left of the eye draw a horizontal half cylinder with the plane face up. With the plane face down. Remove the top face. Remove the end.*

PROBLEM 11. FIG. 75. — *Above and at the left of the eye draw a horizontal half cylinder with the plane face down. With the plane face up.*

PROBLEM 12. FIG. 76. — *Above the eye draw a horizontal half cylinder. Remove the plane face showing the inside. Draw with the plane face on a level with the eye.*

PROBLEM 13. FIG. 77. — *At the right of the eye draw a horizontal half cylinder with the plane face down. Remove the end face. Remove the curved face. Draw with the plane face on a level with the eye.*

PROBLEM 14. FIG. 80. — *Below and at the right of the eye draw a horizontal half cylinder with the plane face up. With the plane face down. Remove the top face.*

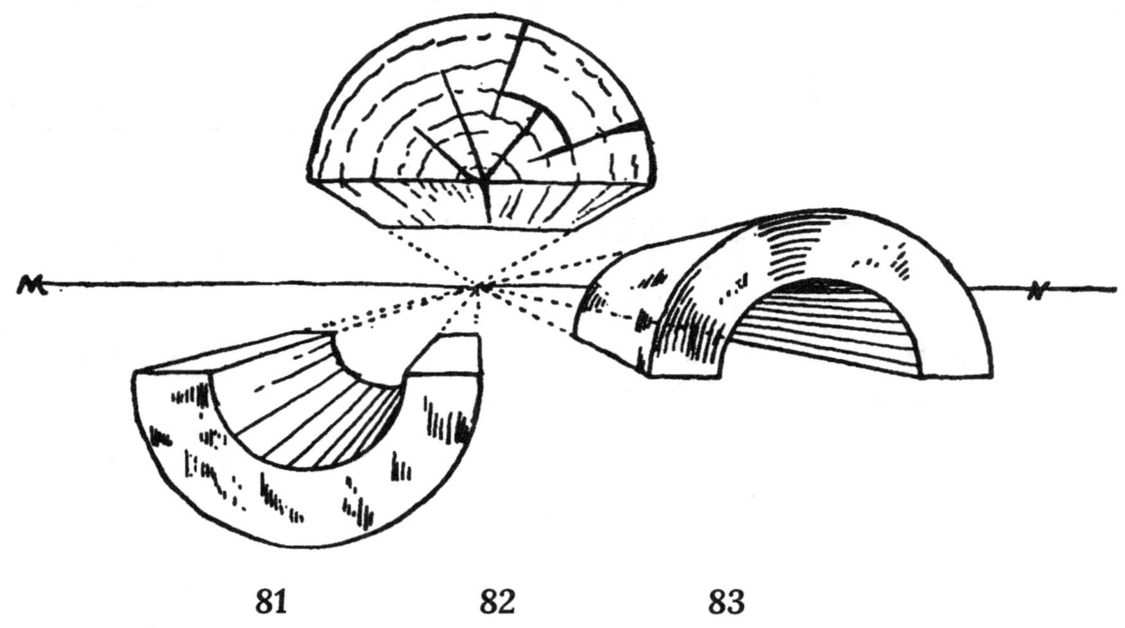

81   82   83

THE RECEDING HALF CYLINDER.

FIGURES 81, 82, AND 83 are receding half cylinders above, below, and at the right of the eye.

114

PROBLEMS.

PROBLEM 15. FIG. 81. — *Below and at the left of the eye draw a receding half cylinder with the plane face up. Hollow it out. Draw it plane face down.*

PROBLEM 16. FIG. 82. — *Directly above the eye draw a receding half cylinder with the plane face down. With the plane face up. Remove the nearer face. Remove the bottom face. Remove both.*

PROBLEM 17. FIG. 83. — *At the right of the eye draw a receding half cylinder with the plane face down and hollowed out. With the plane face up. Draw it at the left of the eye. Above the eye.*

Problem 18. — *Draw Fig. 82 below the eye. At the right of the eye. At the left of the eye. Directly in front of the eye. Below and at the right of the eye.*

Problem 19. — *Draw a receding half cylinder directly in front of the eye and remove the front face showing the inside.*

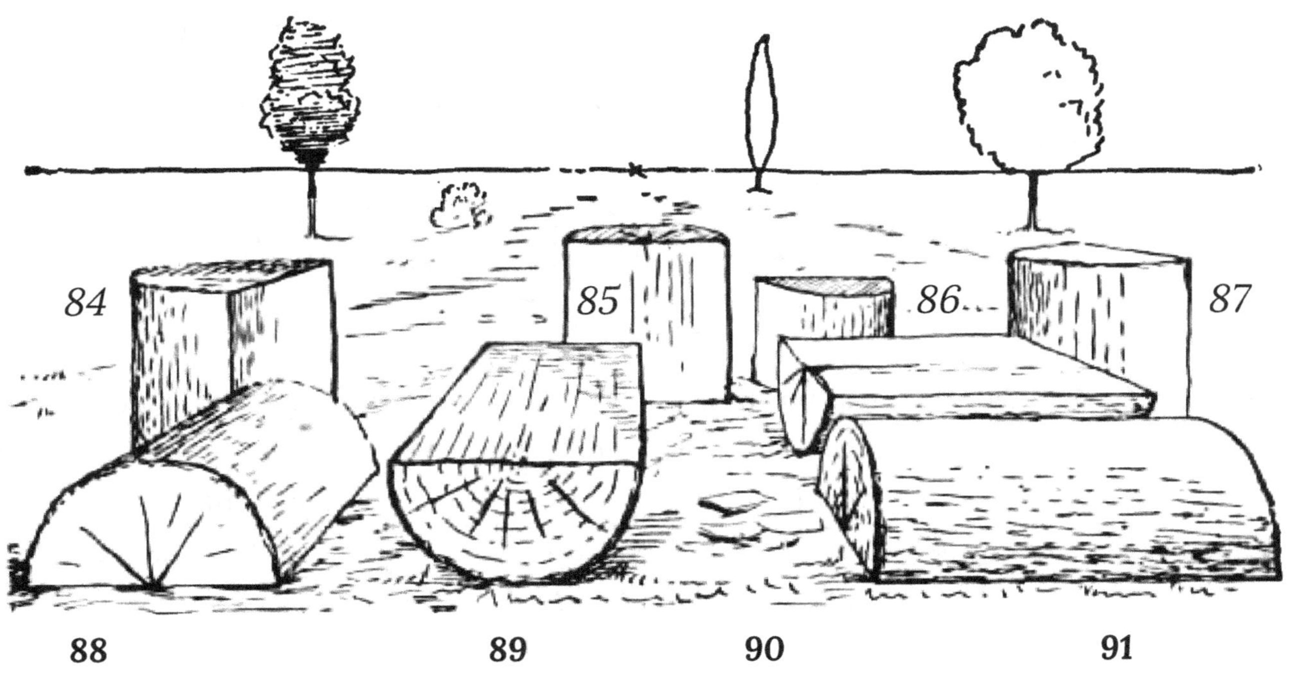

FIGURES 84 - 91 is a group of vertical, horizontal, and receding half cylinders in the form of logs split in halves.

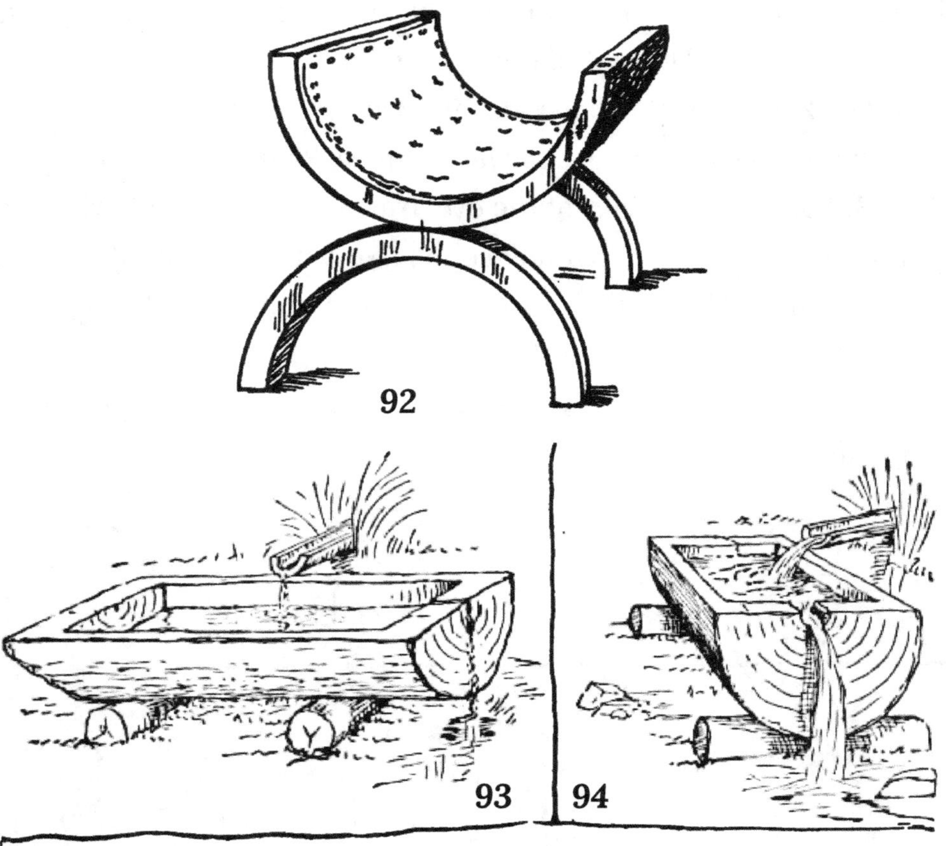

FIGURES 92, 93, AND 94 are applications of the half cylinder arranged in a picture.

Problem 20. — *Directly below the eye, draw a half log with the plane face up, in a receding position. The same below and at the left of the eye. Below and at the right of the eye.*

Problem 21. — *Directly below the eye, draw a receding half log with the plane face down. Draw the same below and at the left of the eye. Below and at the right of the eye.*

Problem 22. — *Draw Fig. 92 below and at the right of the eye. Below the eye.*

Problem 23. — *Directly below the eye, draw a horizontal half log with the plane face up. Draw the same below and at the left of the eye. Below and at the right of the eye.*

Problem 24. — *Below and at the left of the eye, draw a vertical half log with the plane face to the right. To the left. Towards you. Away from you.*

Problem 25. — *Draw Fig. 93 below and at the right of the eye. Directly below the eye.*

Problem 26. — *Draw Fig. 94 below and at the left of the eye, without any water in it. Directly below the eye.*

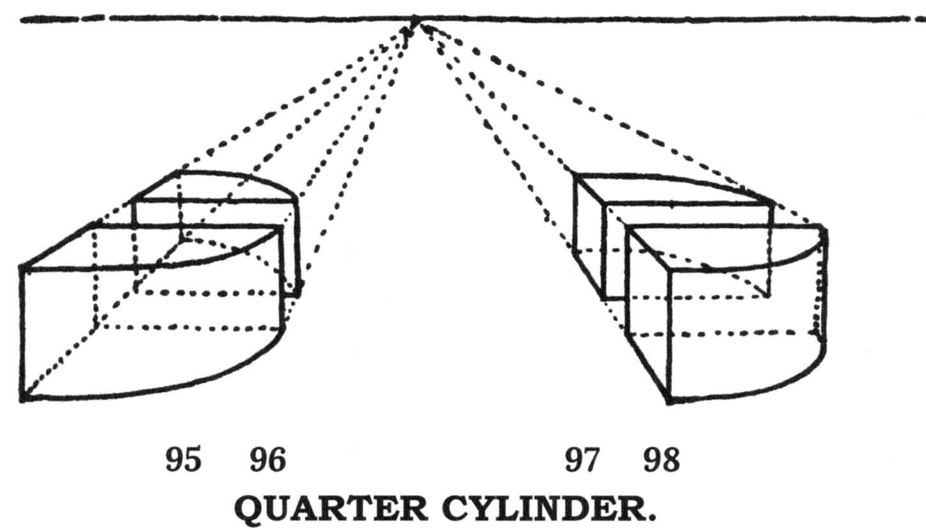

95   96   97   98

QUARTER CYLINDER.

In order to show the quarter cylinder in its most common positions, the oblique line is necessary. For this reason, the quarter cylinder will be taken up in Part III. Only the vertical, horizontal, receding, and curved lines are used in this part.

The study of the quarter cylinder is divided the same as the cylinder and half cylinder, into three parts: the vertical, horizontal, and receding quarter cylinder.

FIGURES 95 – 98 represent the vertical quarter cylinder.

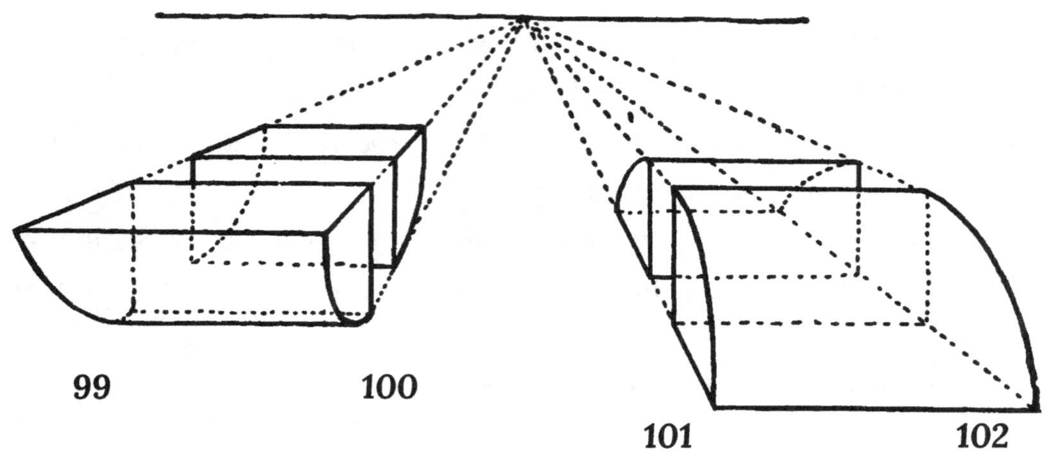

99   100   101   102

FIGURES 99 – 102 represent the horizontal quarter cylinder.

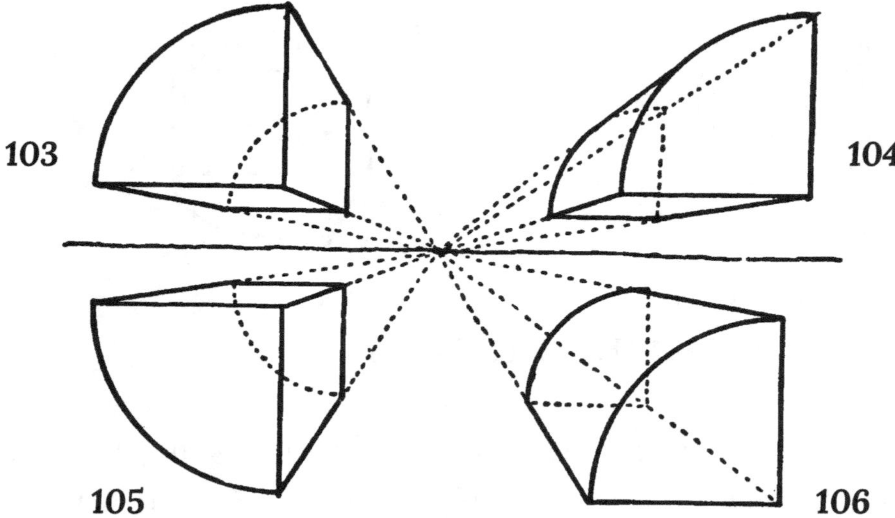

103   104   105   106

FIGURES 103 – 106 represent the receding quarter cylinder. Each is represented in four different positions, so simple as to need no explanation.

The models may be made the same as those of the half cylinder.

PROBLEMS.

Problem 1. — *Draw Fig. 95 below and at the left of the eye, and remove the top face showing the inside. Remove the curved face. Remove both. Draw it below the eye. Above and at the left of the eye.*

Problem 2. — *Draw Fig. 98 below and at the right of the eye. Below and at the left of the eye. Below the eye. Above and at the left of the eye. Remove the top face. Remove the curved face.*

Problem 3. — *Draw Fig. 96 below and at the left of the eye. Above and at the right of the eye. Remove the front face. Remove the top face.*

Problem 4. — *Draw Fig. 99 below and at the left of the eye. Remove the top face. Remove the end face. Remove the curved face. Draw below and at the right of the eye. Above and at the right of the eye.*

Problem 5. — *Draw Fig. 102 below and at the right of the eye. Above and at the left of the eye. Below the eye. Remove the curved face. Remove the end face. Remove both.*

Problem 6. — *Draw Fig. 100 below and at the left of the eye. Below the eye. Above and at the right of the eye. Remove the front face. Remove the top face.*

Problem 7. — *Draw Fig. 105 below and at the left of the eye. Remove the nearer face. Remove the right face. Draw below and at the right of the eye. At the left of the eye. Above the eye.*

Problem 8. — *Draw Fig. 106 below and at the right of the eye. Remove the curved face. The nearer end. Draw above and at the right of the eye. Below the eye. At the right of the eye. At the left of the eye.*

Problem 9. — *Draw Fig. 101 below and at the right of the eye. Remove the front face. The end. Both the end and front face.*

Problem 10. — *Draw Fig. 104 above and at the right of the eye. Remove the nearer end. Remove the curved face. Draw it below and at the right of the eye.*

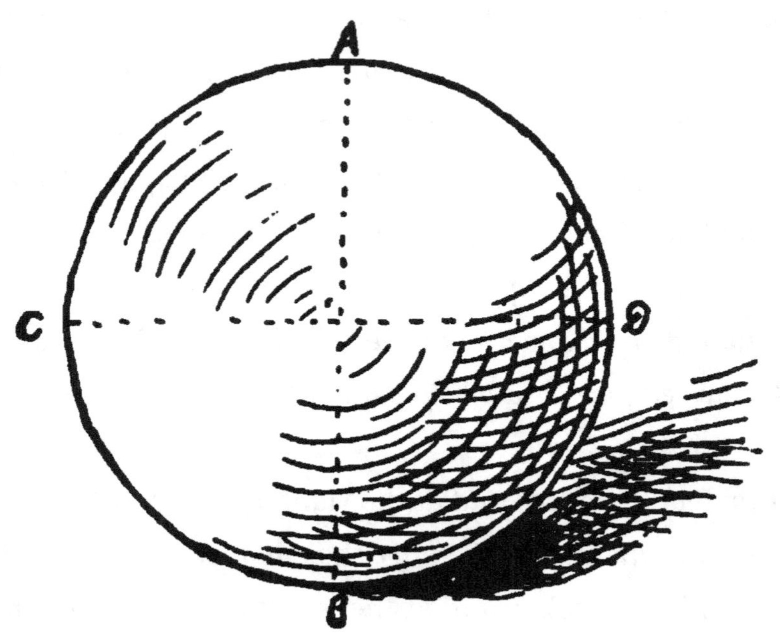

THE SPHERE.

In Elementary Drawing Simplified, the sphere is recognized as a type form, but in Drawing Simplified, it is placed under the cylinder because it has so much in common with this type form as to make it unnecessary to place it by itself. (See Elementary Drawing Simplified.)

The outline of the sphere is a circle in whatever position it may be held.

It is the same as the outline of the receding cylinder held directly in front of the eye.

The sphere may be made the basis of all round objects, such as apples, pears, pumpkins, etc.

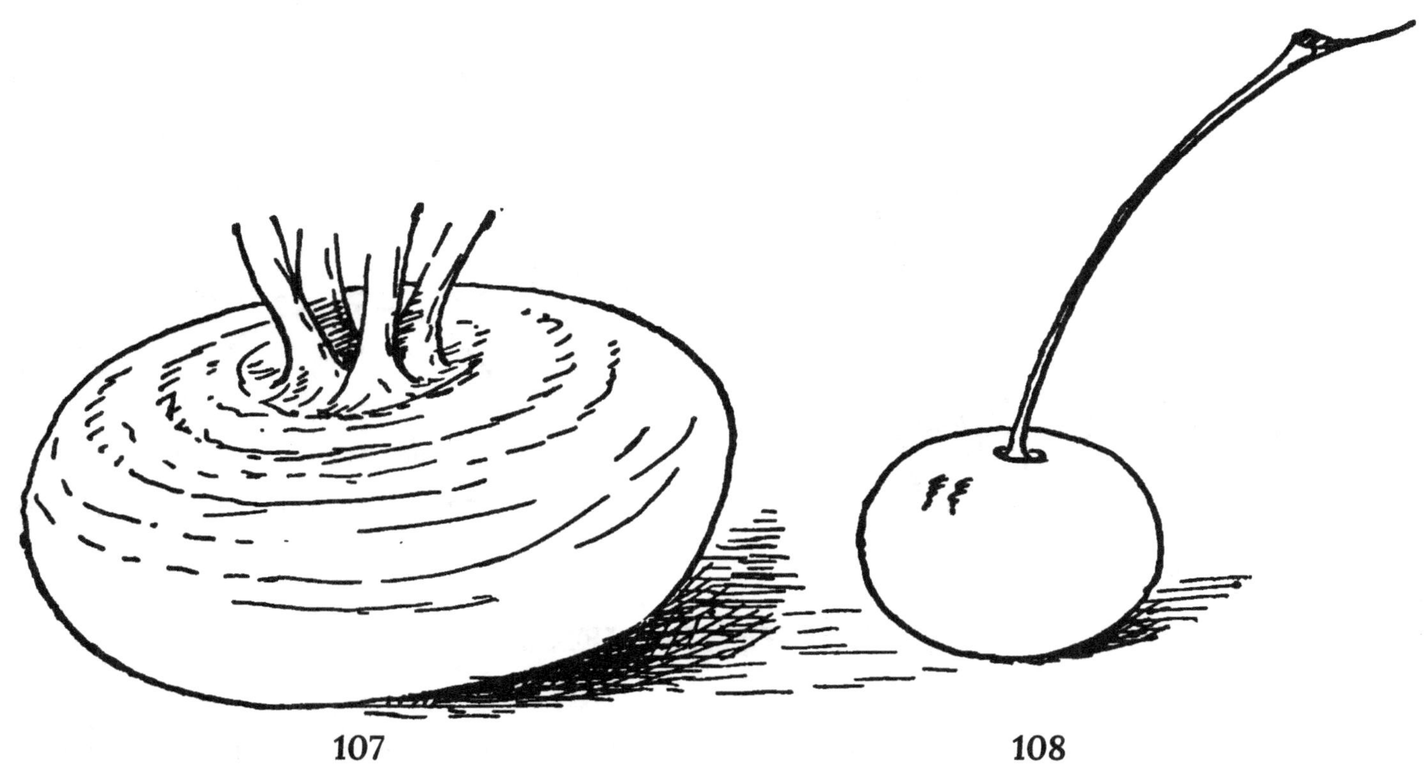

107

108

A knowledge of the cylinder is necessary to draw most round objects intelligently, as nearly all have some part based on the principles found in the cylinder. For example, in Fig. 107, notice that the markings of the turnip are similar in principle to those that mark the top of the vertical cylinder. In Fig. 108, where the stem joins the cherry, the small circle is that of the top of the cylinder.

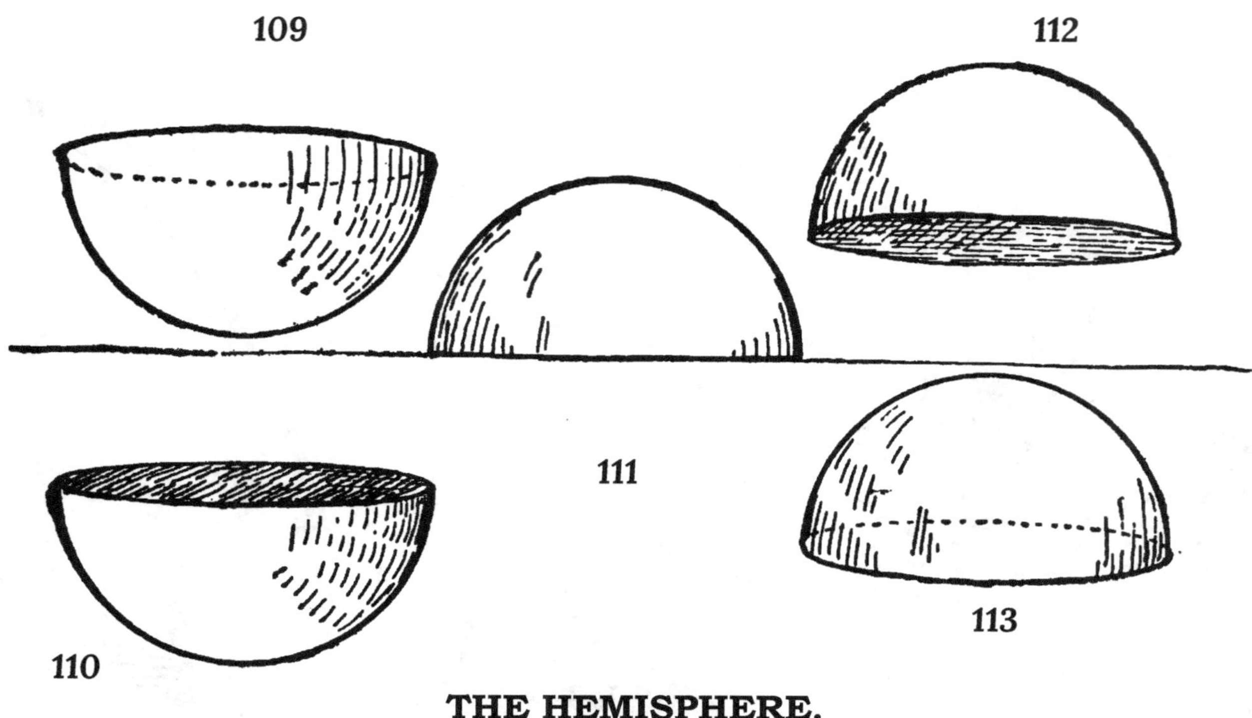

THE HEMISPHERE.

The hemisphere may be studied in two positions: (1) When the plane face is up, as in Figs. 109 and 110. In this position, it is like the top of the vertical cylinder. (2) When the plane face is down, as in Figs. 111, 112, and 113. In this position, it is like the bottom of the vertical cylinder.

FIGURES 109 AND 112 are above the eye.

FIGURES 110 AND 113 are below the eye.

FIGURE 111 is with the plane face on a level with the eye.

The hemisphere is seldom seen as horizontal or receding, and for that reason, is not represented so here.

114
115
116
117

PROBLEMS.

Problem 1. — Draw a hemisphere below the level of the eye, with the plane face up. With the plane face down.

Problem 2. — Above the eye, draw a hemisphere with the plane face down. With the plane face up.

Problem 3. — Directly in front of the eye, draw a hemisphere with the plane face down and on a level with the eye. With the plane face up and on a level with the eye.

Problem 4. — Represent Fig. 110 as hollow.

FIGURES 114 – 117 are simple applications of the hemisphere.

FIGURES 114 is a hemisphere above the level of the eye with the plane face down.

FIGURES 115 AND 116 are hemispheres below the level of the eye, with the plane face up.

FIGURES 117 is a hemisphere below the level of the eye, with the plane face down.

Problem 5. — Draw Fig. 114 below the level of the eye.

Problem 6. — Draw Fig. 115 bottom up.

Problem 7. — Draw Fig. 115 with the rim on a level with the eye.

Problem 8. — Draw Fig. 114 bottom side up.

Problem 9. — Draw a toadstool on the blackboard from memory. A bird's nest. An Eskimo hut. A kettle.

Would one naturally see a toadstool above or below the level of the eye? A kettle?

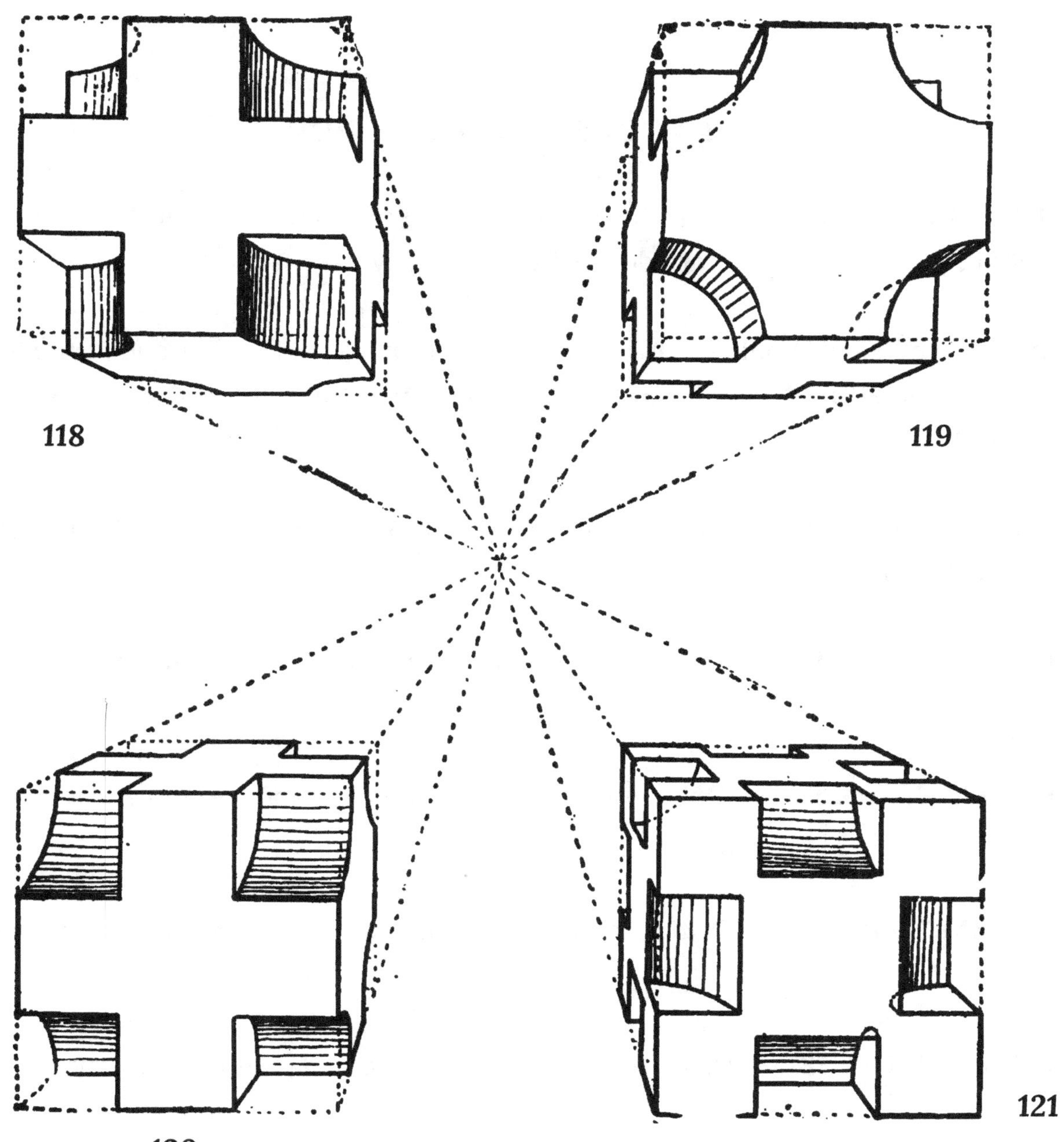

118
119
120
121

THE CUBE AND CYLINDER.

FIGURES 118 – 122 are problems involving both the cube and cylinder. No new principles are introduced, so explanations are deemed unnecessary.

Each problem below should be drawn in four positions, viz: (1) Below and at the left of the eye. (2) Below and at the right of the eye. (3) Above and at the right of the eye. (4) Above and at the left of the eye.

In combinations of the cube and cylinder, four classes of lines are used: (1) Vertical; (2) Horizontal; (3) Receding; (4) Curved.

PROBLEM 1. FIG. 118. — *Draw a cube, and from each corner cut a vertical quarter cylinder.*

PROBLEM 2. FIG. 119. — *Draw a cube and from each corner cut a receding quarter cylinder.*

PROBLEM 3. FIG. 120. — *Draw a cube and from each corner cut a horizontal quarter cylinder.*

PROBLEM 4. FIG. 121. — *Draw a cube and from each edge cut a quarter cylinder.*

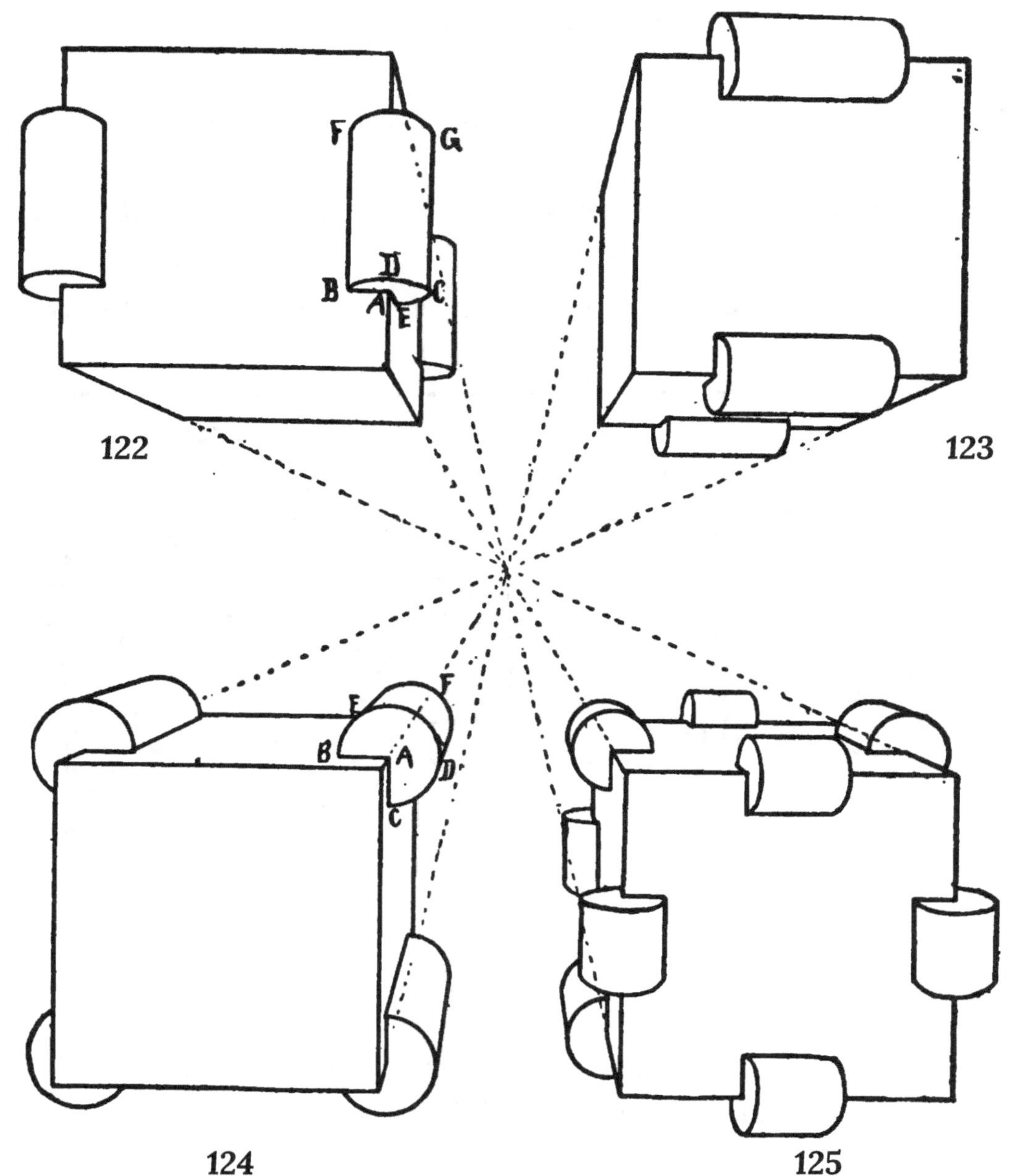

F
G
D
B
C
A
E
122
123
E
F
B
A
D
C
124
125

PROBLEM 5. FIG. 122. — *Draw a cube and to each vertical edge add a three-quarters vertical cylinder.*

PROBLEM 6. FIG. 123. — *Draw a cube and to each horizontal edge add a three-quarters horizontal cylinder.*

PROBLEM 7. FIG. 124. — *Draw a cube and to each receding edge add a receding three-quarters cylinder.*

PROBLEM 8. FIG. 125. — *Draw a cube and to each edge add a three-quarters cylinder.*

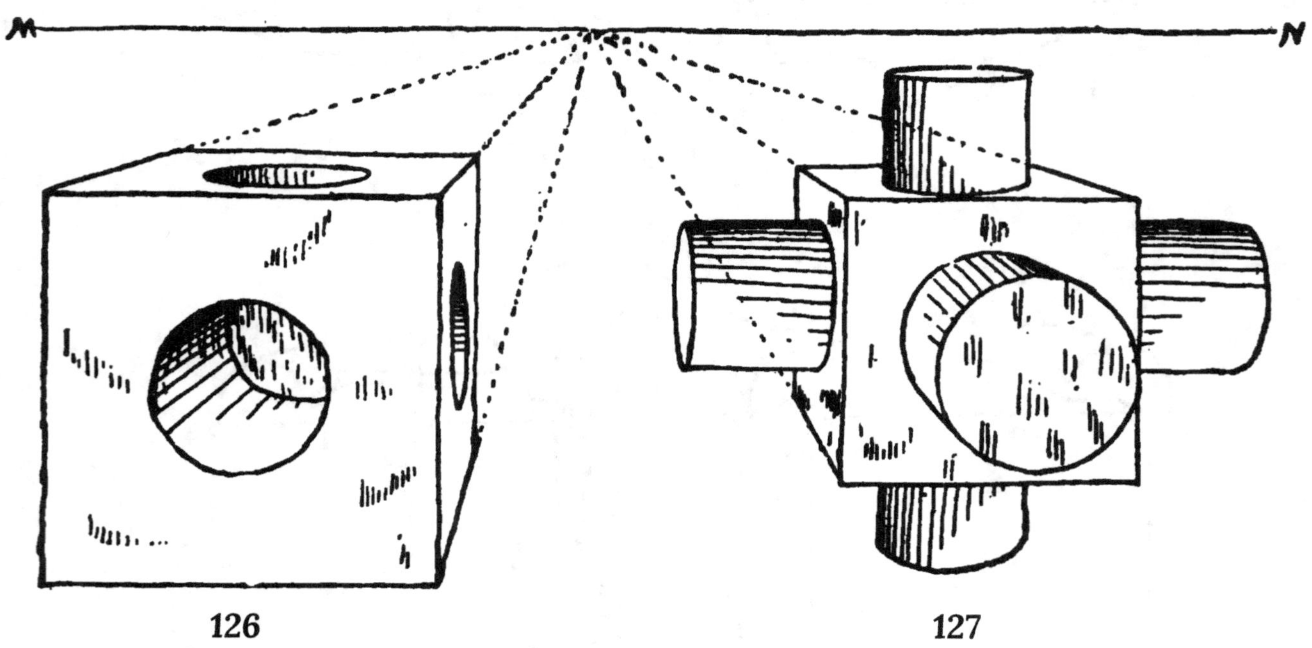

PROBLEM 9. FIG. 126. — *Draw a cube and into each face bore a round hole.*

PROBLEM 10. FIG. 127. — *Draw a cube and to each face add a cylinder perpendicular to the face.*

The quarter cylinder is an application of the cube and cylinder combined.

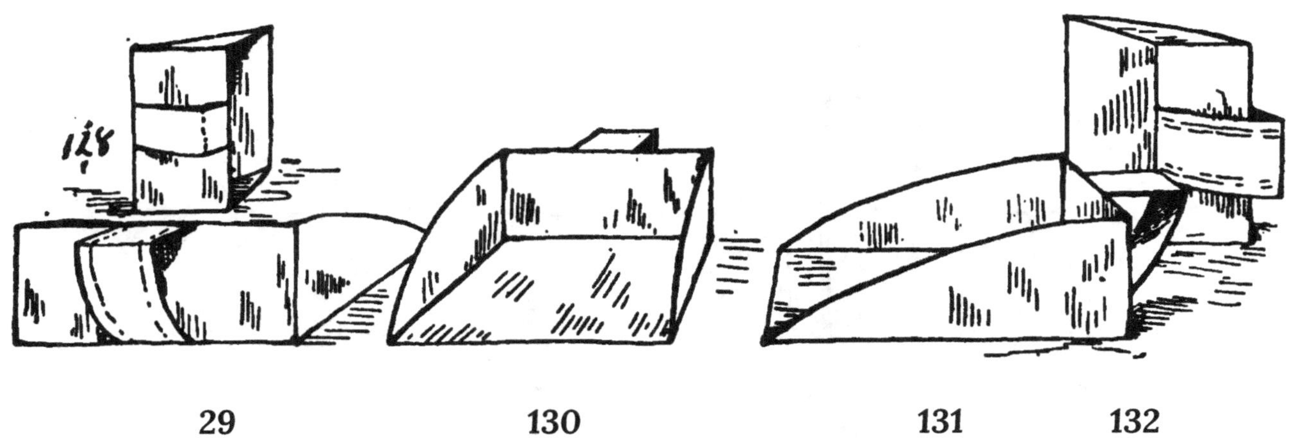

29   130   131   132

FIGURES 129 – 132 are applications of the quarter cylinder or cube and cylinder.

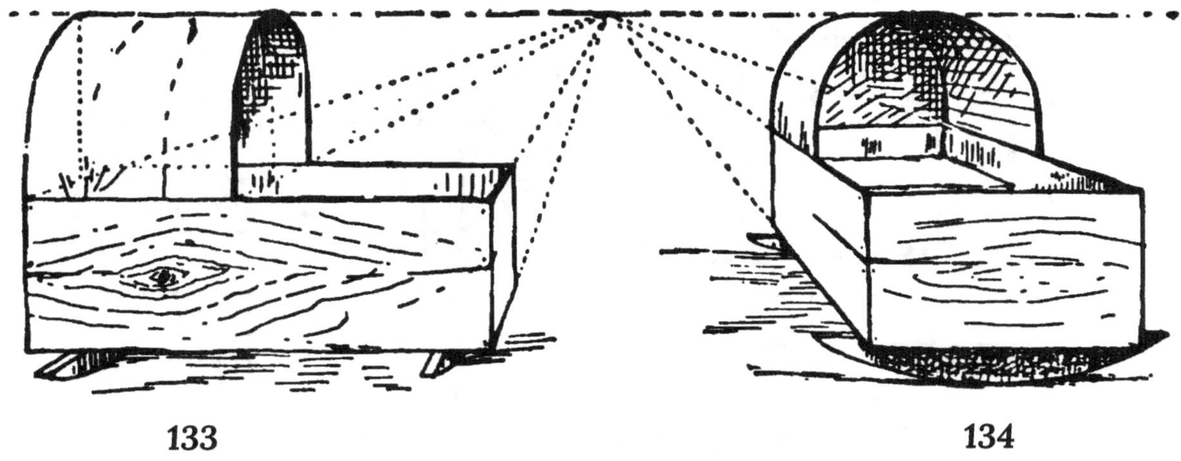

133   134

FIGURES 133 AND 134 are applications of the cube and half cylinder.

FIGURES 135 is an application of the cube, cylinder, and half cylinder.

FIGURES 136 AND 137 are applications of the cube and half cylinder.

135   136   137

PROBLEMS.

Problem 11. — Draw Fig. 129 turned end for end.

Problem 12. — Draw Fig. 130 turned end for end.

Problem 13. — Draw Fig. 132 turned end for end.

Problem 14. — Draw Fig. 131 resting on its side and open toward you.

Problem 15. — Draw Fig. 131 below and at the left of the eye.

Problem 16. — Draw Fig. 133 below and at the right of the eye.

Problem 17. — Draw Fig. 133 on the blackboard from memory.

Problem 18. — Draw Fig. 134 end for end.

Problem 19. — Draw Fig. 134 below and at the left of the eye.

Problem 20. — Draw Fig. 133 with the left end toward you.

FIGURES 136. — (1) Draw the rectangle ABCD. (2) Bisect AB at F, and from this point erect an indefinite vertical line. (3) Choose the point E and draw the curved line AEB. (4) Draw GKHIJ in the same manner. (5) Choose the center of vision and draw the horizontal line. (6) From KHIB and C draw receding lines to the center of vision. (7) Choose the point L and draw LO and LP. (8) Draw PQ and QR. (9) Add the details.

FIGURES 137. — (1) Draw the rectangle ABCD. (2) Draw the abutments of OPIJ and QRKL. (3) Draw the semi-circular arches A0, PQ, and RB. (4) Draw the horizontal line and choose the center of vision. (5) From the points ADPQKB and C draw receding lines to the center of vision. (6) Choose the point E and draw EH. (7) From E draw a horizontal line which will mark the points ST and F. (8) Draw the vertical lines SU, TV, and FG. (9) Add the details.

Problem 21. — Draw a squirrel cage similar to Fig. 135 on the blackboard from memory.

Problem 22. — Draw the squirrel cage at the right of the eye.

Problem 23. — Draw the squirrel cage turned so the wheel will be horizontal.

Problem 24. — Draw Fig. 136 on the blackboard from memory.

Problem 25. — Draw the building Fig. 136 so that the nearer end will be receding and the side horizontal.

Problem 26. — Draw Fig. 137 on the blackboard from memory.

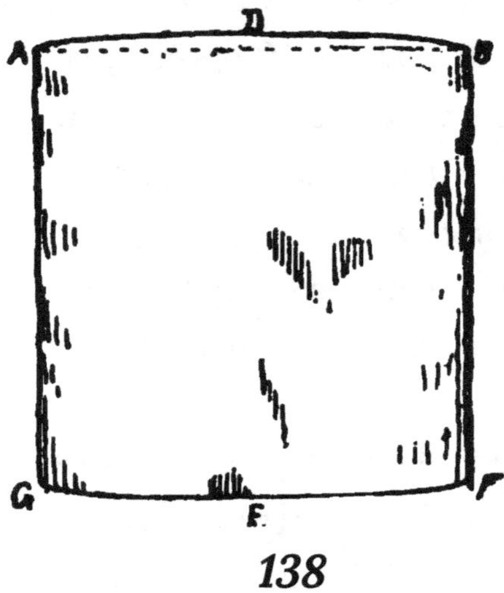

138

DRAWING THE CYLINDER.

The unit of measure when drawing the real cylinder is its longer diameter, as indicated by AB in the illustrations. Thus, in Fig. 139, AB, the longer diameter, is the unit of measure. CD is the shorter diameter.

Small letters refer to points on the real cylinder and large letters to the corresponding points in the drawing.

PROBLEM 1. FIG. 138. — *Draw a vertical cylinder with the eye level with the middle part.*

(1) Place the cylinder as in Fig. 138. (2) Draw the unit of measure A B[30] as long as the cylin-

30   A B is the longer diameter. The shorter diameter cannot be seen.

der is to be in width. (3) Find the height D E by comparing the length of ab with the distance between d and e, and make the same comparison in the drawing with the line A B. (4) From A and B draw vertical lines for the sides. (5) Draw the curved lines of the ends. A D B and G E F[31].

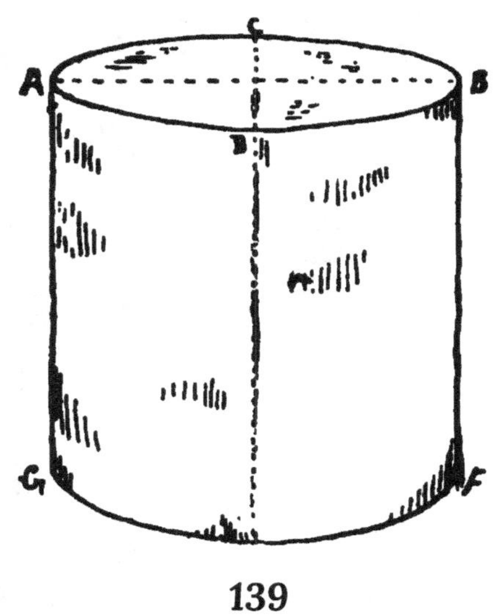

139

PROBLEM 2. FIG. 139. — *Draw a vertical cylinder below the level of the eye.*

(1) Place the cylinder below the level of the eye as in Fig. 139. (2) Draw the unit of measure AB the width the cylinder is to be. (3) Find the points C and D by comparing the length of ab with the distance from c to d, and make the same comparison in the drawing with line AB. Place the distance CD half above and half below the line AB. (4) Draw the ellipse ABCD. (5) From the points A and B draw indefinite vertical lines. (6) To find the point E, compare ab with the distance from d to e, and make the same comparison in the drawing with the line AB. (7) Draw the curved line through GEF.

31   Care must be taken not to exaggerate the curvature of these lines. Hold the pencil so as to judge how much they curve.

Problem 3. — *Draw a vertical cylinder above the eye.*

Problem 4. — *Draw a vertical cylinder with the top on a level with the eye.*

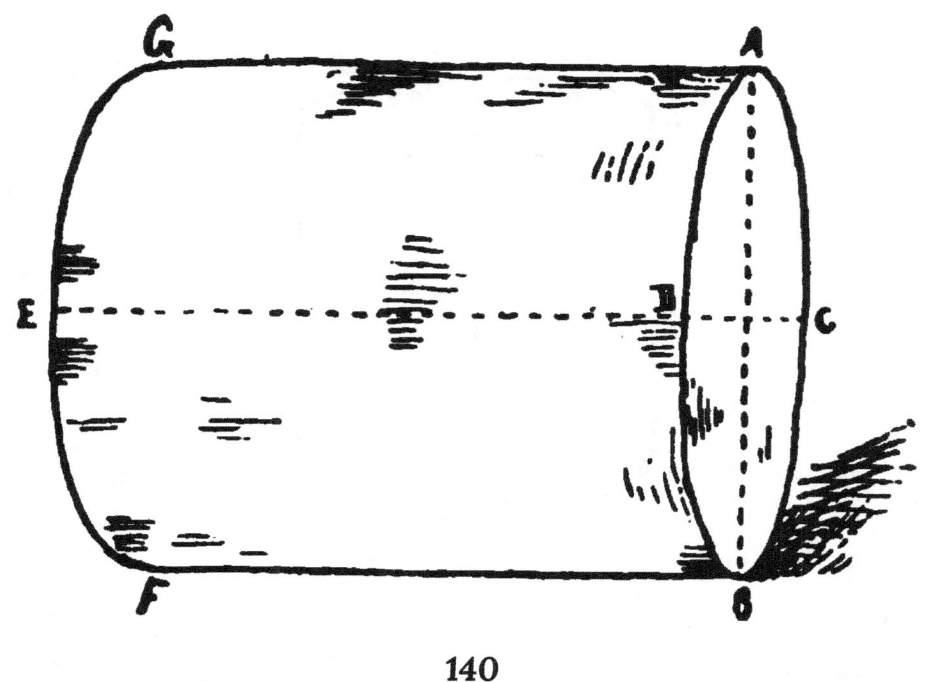

140

PROBLEM 5. FIG. 140. — *Draw a horizontal cylinder at the left of the eye.*

(1) Place the cylinder as in Fig. 140. (2) Draw the unit of measure AB. (3) Find the shorter diameter CD by comparing ab with Cd, and make the same comparison in the drawing with AB. (4) Draw the ellipse ABCD. (5) From A and B draw indefinite horizontal lines. (6) To find the point E, compare ab with the distance between d and e, and make the same comparison in the drawing with AB. (7) Draw the curved line through E.

Problem 6. — *Draw a horizontal cylinder at the right of the eye.*

Problem 7. — *Draw a horizontal cylinder directly in front of the eye. (See Prob. 1.)*

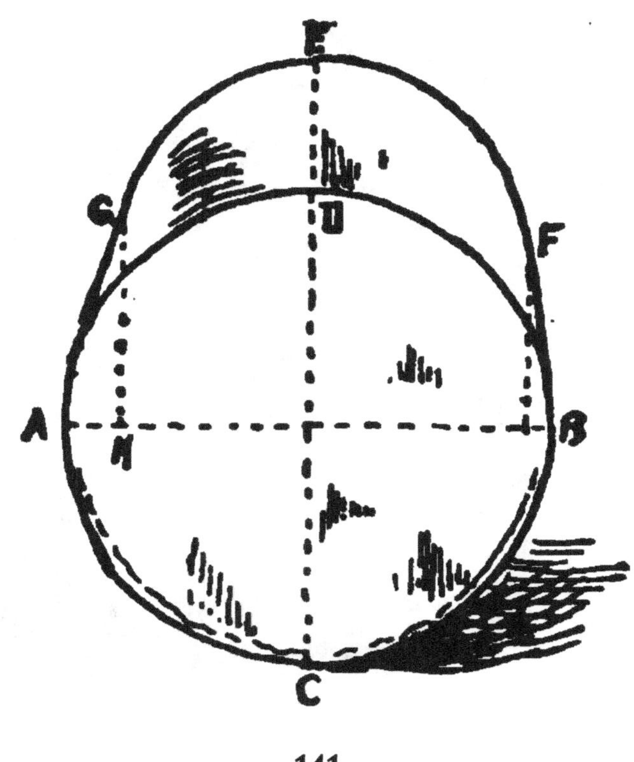

141

PROBLEM 8. FIG. 141. — *Draw a receding cylinder below the eye.*

(1) Place the cylinder as in Fig. 141. (2) Draw the unit of measure A B. (3) Find the shorter diameter C D by comparing ab with Cd and making the same comparison in the drawing with A B. (4) Draw the ellipse A B C D. (5) Find point E by comparing ab with the distance from d to e and make the same comparison in the drawing with A B. (6) To find the point G, pass the pencil vertically through g and note how far the pencil passes to the right of the point a. Mark this distance at the right of the point A as at H, and from it draw a vertical line which will pass through G. (7) Find a similar line for F. (8) Draw the curved line G E F by the eye with the aid of the lines and point found.

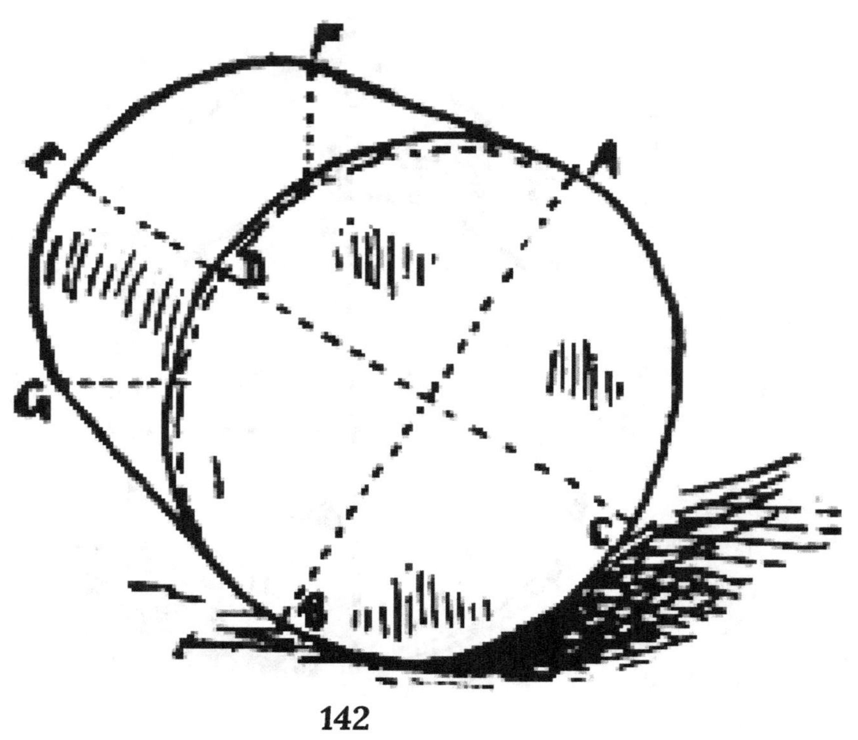

142

PROBLEM 9. FIG. 142. — *Draw a receding cylinder below and at the right of the eye.*

(1) Draw the longer diameter A B for the unit of measure. (2) Find the points D and C and draw the ellipse A B C D. (3) Find the point E. (4) Find the point G by passing the pencil horizontally through g and noting where it crosses edge db. Mark this point on line D B, and from it draw an indefinite horizontal line. The point G will be in this line. (5) To find the point F, pass the pencil vertically through f and note where the pencil crosses edge da. Mark this point on D A and from it draw an indefinite vertical line. The point F will be in this line. (6) With the aid of these lines and point E, draw the curved line G E F.

Problem 10. — *Draw a receding cylinder below and at the left of the eye.*

Problem 11. — *Draw a receding cylinder above and at the right of the eye.*

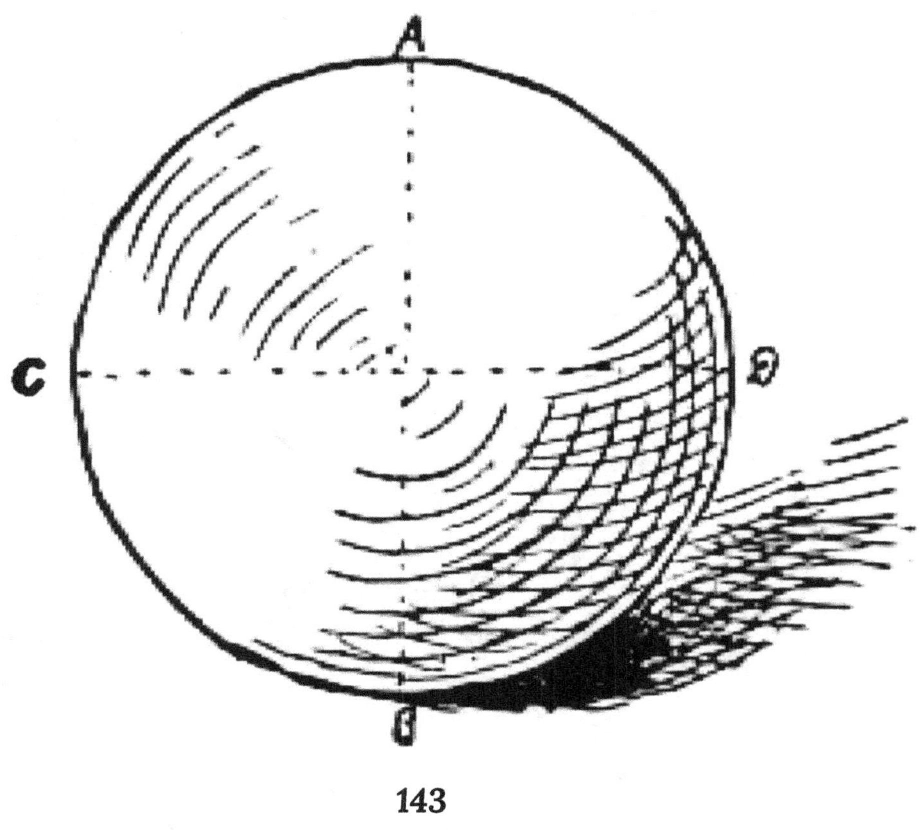

143

THE SPHERE.

The outline of the sphere is a circle similar to Fig. 143, in whatever position it may be placed. It is the same as the outline of the receding cylinder directly in front of the eye.

The unit of measure when drawing the sphere is its diameter. The vertical diameter is the most convenient.

The directions are: (1) Place the sphere in position. (2) Draw the vertical diameter A B for the unit of measure. (3) Bisect A B and draw C D equal to A B, making the distance of C and D from line A B equal. (4) Through the points A, C, B, and D draw the circle.

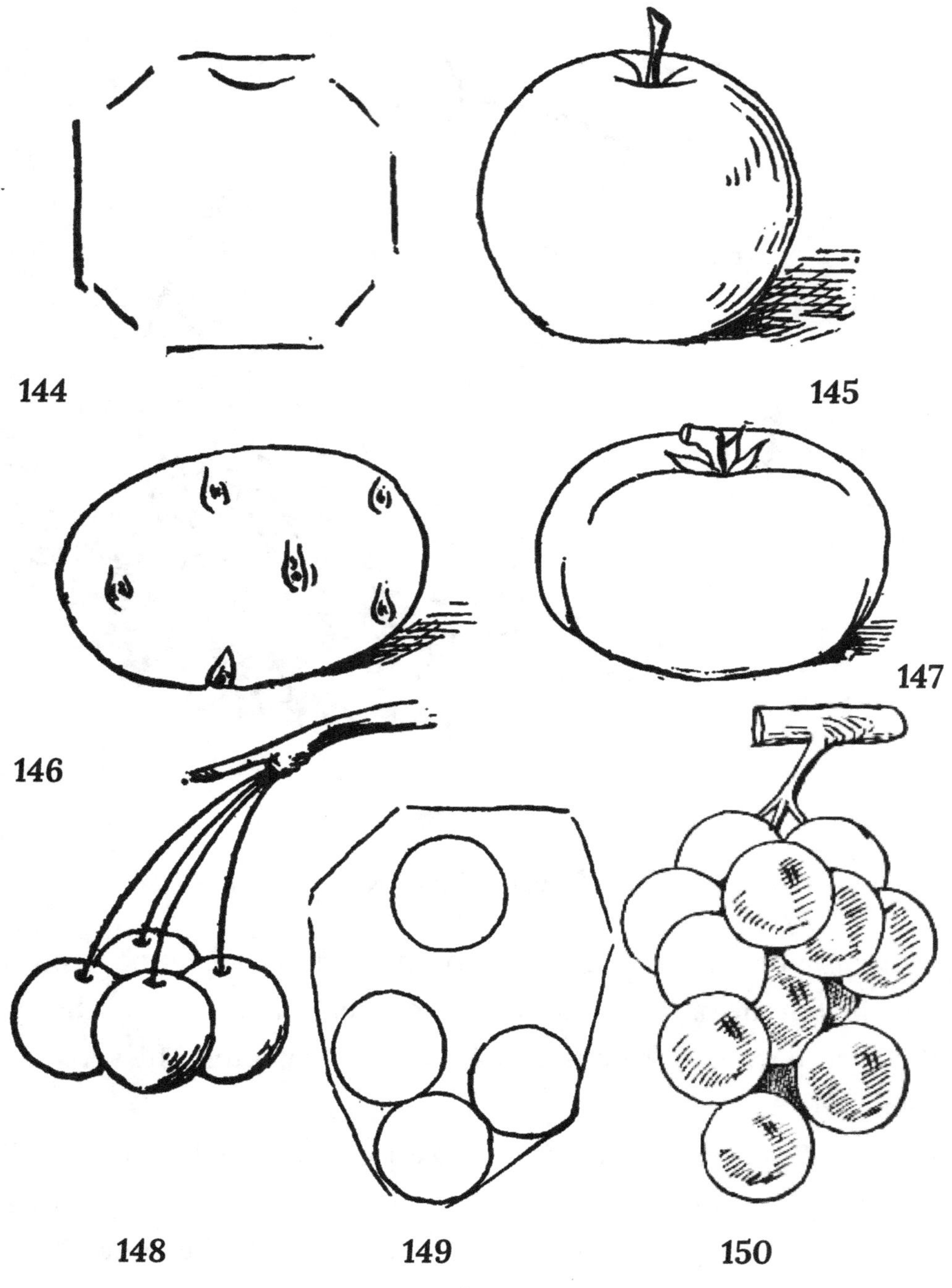

144

145

146

147

148

149

150

FIGURES 144 – 150 are applications of the sphere to drawing natural objects. When drawing objects similar to the apple (Fig. 145), find and then mark the height and width as shown by Fig. 144 before beginning to draw the outline. This may be done by measuring with the pencil, comparing the height with the width, the same as when drawing the sphere.

FIGURES 146 AND 147 are elliptical in form, but the principle is the same as in drawing the sphere.

When drawing a group of objects, such as the cherries in Fig. 148, draw the nearest one first. The outline of this one is usually entire. Draw the remainder in their order from the nearest to those furthest away, thus: (1) Draw the nearest cherry. (2) Draw the one on the left. (3) Draw the one on the right. (4) Draw the furthest one away. (5) Draw the eye where the stem joins the cherry. (6) Draw the branch. (7) Draw the stems.

When drawing a bunch of objects, such as grapes (Fig. 150), (1) Sketch an outline of the whole branch as shown by Fig. 149. (2) Draw those that have their outline entire as in Fig. 149. (3) Draw the remainder in the order of their distance away.

Procure and draw the following objects: an apple, a pear, a lemon, a potato, a tomato, a turnip, an onion, a squash, and a pumpkin.

Procure and draw a bunch of cherries, crab-apples, grapes, plums, strawberries, gooseberries, and currants.

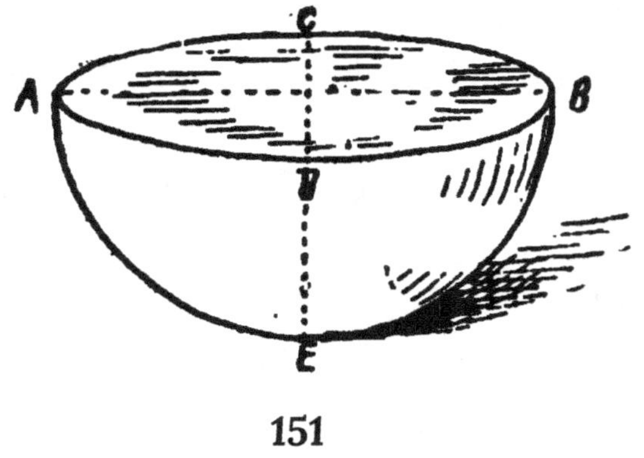

151

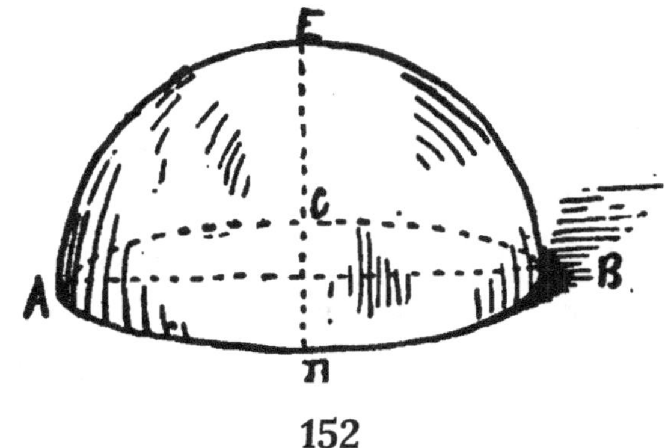

152

THE HEMISPHERE.

FIGURES 151 AND 152 are drawn in the same manner and by the same laws as the cylinder.

The unit of measure is the longer diameter AB, the same as in the cylinder. It is drawn as follows: (1) Place the hemisphere in position as in Fig. 151 or 152. (2) Draw the longer diameter AB for the unit of measure. (3) Find CD, the shorter diameter, by comparing ab with the distance from c to d and make the same comparison in the drawing with AB. (4) Through the points A, C, B, and D draw the ellipse. (5) Find the point E by comparing ab with the distance from d to e and making the same comparison in the drawing with AB. (6) Draw the semi-circle AEB.

Problem 1. — *Draw Fig. 151 above the level of the eye.*

Problem 2. — *Draw Fig. 152 above the level of the eye.*

REVIEW QUESTIONS.

1. What line is used in drawing the cylinder that is not used in drawing the cube?

2. In what three positions is the cylinder studied?

3. What is the most prominent figure in the cylinder? The cube? The box?

4. What line determines the drawing of the vertical cylinder?

5. For practical purposes, is it well to notice the center of vision when drawing the vertical cylinder?

6. When will the nearer edge of a vertical cylinder curve upward? Downward? Be horizontal?

7. In Fig. 10, why does the curved line LIM curve more than FEG?

8. How do you know that Fig. 16 is below the level of the eye?

9. Which should appear wider in Fig. 16, the distance IC or HD? Which should be drawn wider?

10. Why can the top of the basket in Fig. 19 be seen, and not that in Fig. 20?

11. What is the difference between the horizon line in nature and in a drawing? Ans. The first is the level of the eye; the second *represents*.

12. Where is the H L in Fig. 23? How do you know?

13. In Fig. 24, why do some of the lines that mark the courses of stone curve upward, and some downward?

14. What is the shape of the pond in Fig. 25?

15. In Fig. 26, the pond appears circular. Why does it measure so much more from right to left than directly across it? Why is the path around the pond wider at the right and left than at any other place?

16. In Fig. 26, how can the size of the reflections be determined? *Ans.* The reflections are the same size as the object reflected. The top of the tree is as far above the roots as the reflection of the top is below.

17. How does the central part of Fig. 27 differ from Fig. 26? Fig. 28 from Fig. 26?

18. Do real trees have definite shapes like those in Fig. 26? *Ans.* Yes.

19. Name the three classes of branching.

20. What kind of trees have regular branching? Name four varieties.

21. What kind of trees have irregular branching? Name four varieties.

22. What is the difference in shape between a young and old pine?

23. How may habits of observation be cultivated?

24. What is the shape of a pear tree? A young pine tree? A spruce?

25. What is the difference in the amount of foliage between trees that grow in the wood and those that grow in the open field?

26. What point determines the drawing of the horizontal cylinder?

27. What determines the curvature of the edges of the horizontal cylinder?

28. When does the nearer edge of a horizontal cylinder curve to the right? To the left? When is it vertical?

29. How do you know that the barrel in Fig. 44 is at the left of the eye?

30. How can you find the center of vision in Fig. 47?

31. What determines the drawing of the receding cylinder?

32. When is the nearer end of a receding cylinder a circle?

33. What is the H. L.? C. of V.? The eye?

34. Find the C. of V. in Fig. 64. In Fig. 65.

35. What is "blocking in?"

36. Show how Fig. 67 is based on the cylinder.

37. How is the study of the half cylinder divided?

38. What lines are used in drawing the half cylinder?

39. What part of the half cylinder is similar to the cube?

40. How may models for the cylinder be prepared? For the half cylinder?

41. Name twelve objects similar in form to the half cylinder.

42. What lines are necessary to draw the quarter cylinder?

43. How is the study of the quarter cylinder divided?

44. Can you point to parts in the quarter cylinder that resemble the cube?

45. Why is the sphere not treated in this book as a separate type form?

46. What figure is the outline of the sphere in all positions?

47. What may the sphere be the type form for?

48. What in Fig. 107 is very much like the cylinder? In Fig. 108?

49. What form is the hemisphere a part of?

50. In what two positions is the hemisphere studied? Why is it not studied in the horizontal and receding positions?

51. How does the hemisphere resemble the vertical cylinder?

52. Name 12 objects that are similar to the hemisphere in form.

53. About where is the H. L. in Fig. 114? Fig. 115? Fig. 116?

54. What type forms are represented in Fig. 135? Fig. 136? Fig. 137? Fig. 133?

55. About where is the H. L. in Fig. 138? In Fig. 139?

56. What is the unit of measure when drawing the cylinder? The sphere?

57. Tell how to draw a cylinder from nature.

58. Tell how to draw objects similar to Fig. 145.

59. When drawing a group, what part should be drawn first?

60. Tell how to draw Fig. 148. Fig. 150.

61. How may one become a good draughtsman? By intelligent practice.

REVIEW OF PARTS I AND II.

THE CUBE AND CYLINDER AND THEIR APPLICATIONS.

REVIEW QUESTIONS.

(1) What class of forms is the cube the basis of?

(2) What class of surfaces is the top of the cube the basis of? The sides of the cube.

(3) What is the inside of a hollow cube the basis of?

(4) What class of forms is the cylinder the basis of? Forms having curved lines.

(5) What is the top of the vertical cylinder the basis of? Horizontally circular surfaces. Give examples.

(6) What is the most prominent figure in the cube? In the cylinder?

(7) How many classes of lines are used in drawing the cube? In drawing the cylinder?

(8) How are vertical lines in a picture drawn? Horizontal lines?

(9) What do receding lines in a picture represent?

(10) What is the center of vision? The horizon line?

(11) What lines converge at the center of vision?

(12) What is said of lines converging at the same point?

(13) What difference is there between the center of vision and the "eye"?

(14) When is a receding line horizontal?

(15) When is a curved line horizontal? *Ans.* When it is on a level with the eye.

(16) When is a receding line vertical? A curved line?

(17) When do receding lines slant downward? Upward?

(18) When is a receding line a point?

(19) What effect has distance on an object?

(20) What are construction lines?

(21) Should a drawing be copied line for line?

(22) In what line is the center of vision found?

(23) Is the horizon line a real line and the center of vision a real point? *Ans.* No. They are no more real than the equator and north pole, but are as essential in the study of drawing as the equator and pole are in the study of geography.

(24) What receding lines are parallel? *Ans.* Those that converge at the same point.

(25) What class of lines suggest a vertical surface? A horizontal surface? A receding surface? A vertical receding surface? A curved surface? A horizontal receding surface?

(26) How do you know when an object is below the level of your eye? Above?

(27) When is an object directly in front of the eye?

(28) When can the center of vision be used to draw square-cornered objects?

(29) What class of lines change as their position changes? *Ans.* Receding lines.

(30) Repeat the seven laws governing receding lines.

(31) How near may we be to an object when drawing it?

(32) What is the dividing line between the lines that slant upward and those that slant downward?

(33) In a group of objects, which should be drawn first?

(34) What line is used in drawing the cylinder that is not used in drawing the cube? *Ans.* The curved line.

(35) In what three positions is the cylinder studied?

(36) What line determines the drawing of the vertical cylinder? What point the horizontal and receding cylinders?

(37) When will the nearer edge of a vertical cylinder curve upward? Downward? Be horizontal?

(38) What is the difference between the horizon line in nature and in a drawing? *Ans.* In

nature the horizon line is the level of the eye; in the drawing it represents the level of the eye.

(39) What determines the curvature of the edges in a horizontal cylinder? *Ans.* The distance right or left from the center of vision.

(40) When does the nearer edge of a horizontal cylinder curve to the right? To the left? When is it vertical?

(41) What is meant by "blocking in"? *Ans.* Marking in the general proportions with light lines.

(42) How is the study of the half cylinder divided? The quarter cylinder?

(43) What part of the quarter cylinder is like the cube?

(44) What lines are used in drawing the half cylinder? The quarter cylinder?

(45) How may models for the half cylinder be prepared? For the quarter cylinder?

(46) Name five suitable cylinder models.

(47) Name ten objects similar in form to the cylinder. Half cylinder. Quarter cylinder. Sphere. Hemisphere.

(48) What form is the hemisphere a part of?

(49) In what two positions is the hemisphere studied?

(50) What is the unit of measure when drawing the cylinder? The half cylinder? The sphere? The hemisphere?

(51) When drawing a group, what part should be drawn first?

REVIEW PROBLEMS FOR THE BLACK-BOARD.

The pupil should work these problems outside of the class and be prepared to put them on the black-board in the class without aid from the teacher or from a drawing.

(1) Draw a box below and at the left of the eye. Below and at the right. Above and at the

right. Above and at the left. Above. Below. At the right. At the left. Directly in front of the eye.

(2) Draw a box below and at the left of the eye and remove the top face. The side face. The front face. The top, side, and front faces.

(3) Draw a box below the eye and remove the top face. The front face. Both the top and front faces.

(4) Draw the box in its nine positions.

(5) Draw three boxes: one below, one below and at the right, and one below and at the left of the eye.

(6) Draw a box directly in front of the eye. Remove the front face. Remove the front and top faces. Remove the front, top, and side faces.

(7) Draw a cube below and at the left of the eye, and from each corner cut a small cube.

(8) Draw a cube below and at the left of the eye, and from each edge cut a small cube.

(9) Draw a cube below and at the left of the eye, and from each face cut a small cube.

(10) Draw a cube below and at the right of the eye, and to each face add a small cube.

(11) Draw a small cube below and at the left of the eye, and to each face add another cube of the same size.

(12) Draw a vertical cylinder below the level of the eye. Above. With the top on a level. With the bottom on a level.

(13) Draw a vertical cylinder below the eye, and remove the top face, showing the inside.

(14) Draw a vertical cylinder below and at the left of the eye, and divide it into two parts.

(15) Draw a vertical cylinder below the eye, and bore a round hole through it.

(16) Draw a vertical cylinder below the eye, and to each end add another and smaller vertical cylinder.

(17) Draw a horizontal cylinder at the left of the eye.

(18) Draw a horizontal cylinder at the right of the eye.

(19) Draw a horizontal cylinder with the left end directly below the eye. With the middle

directly below the eye.

(20) Draw a horizontal cylinder below and at the left, and below and at the right of the eye.

(21) Draw a horizontal cylinder below and at the left of the eye, and bore a round hole through it horizontally.

(22) Draw a horizontal cylinder below and at the right of the eye, and to each end add a small horizontal cylinder.

(23) Draw a horizontal cylinder at the left of the eye, and remove the end, showing the inside.

(24) Draw a receding cylinder directly in front of the eye.

(25) Draw a receding cylinder directly in front of the eye, and remove the nearer end, showing the inside.

(26) Around a center of vision, draw six receding cylinders.

(27) Draw a receding cylinder below the eye, and bore a round hole through it. The same at the left of the eye. Above the eye. Directly in front of the eye.

(28) Draw a receding cylinder below the eye, and to the end add a small receding cylinder. The same at the right of the eye. Below and at the left of the eye.

(29) Draw a vertical half cylinder below and at the right of the eye, with the plane face to the left. To the right.

(30) Draw a vertical half cylinder below the eye, with the plane face toward you. Away from you. With the plane face to the right. To the left.

(31) Draw a horizontal half cylinder below and at the left of the eye, with the plane face up. With the plane face down.

(32) Draw a horizontal half cylinder below the eye, with the plane face up. With the plane face down.

(33) Draw a receding half cylinder above the eye, with the plane face down. With the plane face up.

(34) Draw a receding half cylinder below and at the left of the eye, with the plane face up.

With the plane face down.

(35) Draw a vertical quarter cylinder below the eye with the curved face toward you. Below and at the left. Below and at the right of the eye.

(36) Draw a horizontal quarter cylinder below and at the left of the eye with the curved face toward you. Below and at the right of the eye. Below the eye.

(37) Draw a receding quarter cylinder above and at the left, above and at the right, below and at the left, and below and at the right of the eye, with the curved face to the right.

(38) Draw a sphere.

(39) Draw a hemisphere below the eye with the plane face up. Down. With the plane face on a level with the eye.

(40) Draw a hemisphere above the eye with the plane face up. Down.

(41) Draw a cube below and at the left of the eye, and from each corner cut a vertical quarter cylinder. A horizontal quarter cylinder. A receding quarter cylinder.

(42) Draw a cube below and at the left of the eye, and from each edge cut a quarter cylinder.

(43) Draw a cube below and at the right of the eye, and to each edge add a three-quarters cylinder.

(44) Draw a cube below and at the left of the eye, and to each face add a cylinder perpendicular to the face.

(45) Draw a cube below and at the right of the eye, and in each face bore a round hole.

PART III.

TRIANGULAR PRISM.

THE TRIANGULAR PRISM is made the basis of objects having oblique lines. Its most prominent figure is the triangle.

In addition to the vertical, horizontal, and receding lines, the oblique line is used.

Models of the triangular prism may be: (1) Made from cardboard or similar substance. (2) Whittled from wood, plaster of Paris, paraffin, soap, or clay. (3) Molded from plaster of Paris or clay.

The prism is studied the same as the cylinder, in three positions: (1) the vertical prism, (2) the horizontal prism, (3) the receding prism.

For convenience of study, one of the three lines that mark the end of each prism is made in the drawings either vertical, horizontal, or receding, and is marked AB and the apex E. There is no oblique line that is vertical, horizontal, or that recedes to the C. of V. The base is marked AB.

Take a prism in your hand and count the edges. There are nine. Observe: (1) that the three edges that mark the length of the prism are parallel, (2) that the three edges that mark the end of the prism are not parallel, (3) that the two corresponding edges of each end are parallel.

VERTICAL PRISM.

THE VERTICAL PRISM may be studied in two parts: (1) When the apex is toward or away from you (Figs. 1–6), (2) When the apex points to the right or left (Figs. 7, 8, and 9).

When the apex is toward or away from you, the prism contains vertical, horizontal, and oblique lines.

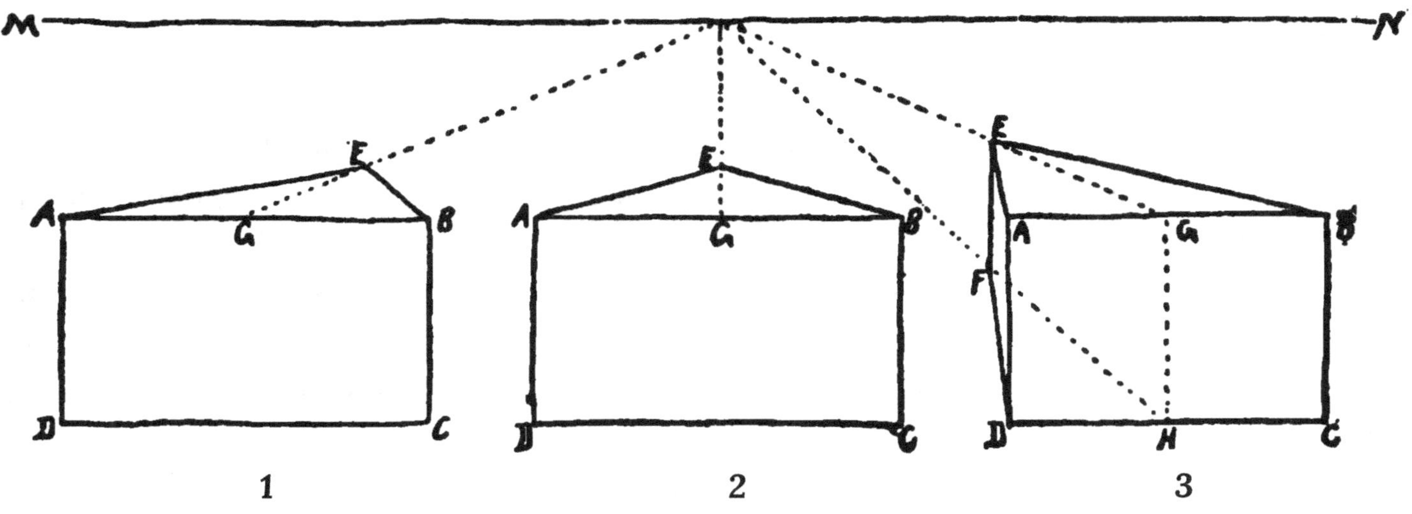

FIGURES 1, 2, AND 3. - How to draw vertical prisms when the apex is away from you:

1. Draw the base A B C D.

2. Draw the H. L. and place the C. of V.

3. Bisect AB as at G and draw a receding line to the C. of V.

4. Choose the point E and draw EA and EB.

5. If one of the oblique sides of the prism shows as in Fig. 3, then from H, the middle of DC, draw a receding line to the C. of V.

6. From E, draw a vertical line.

7. Draw FD.

PROBLEMS.

Use the model constantly when working these problems and refer to it whenever in doubt.

PROBLEM 1. FIG. 1. — *Draw a vertical prism below and at the left of the eye with the apex away from you.*

PROBLEM 2. FIG. 2. — *Draw a vertical prism below the eye with the apex away from you.*

PROBLEM 3. FIG. 3. — *Draw a vertical prism below and at the right of the eye with the apex away from you.*

Problem 4. — *Above and at the left of the eye, draw a vertical prism with the apex away from you.*

Problem 5. — *Above the eye, draw a vertical prism with the apex away from you.*

Problem 6. — *Above and at the right of the eye, draw a vertical prism with the apex away from you.*

Problem 7. — *At the right of the eye, draw a prism with the apex away from you.*

Problem 8. — *Draw a prism similar to Fig. 3 at the left of the eye.*

Problem 9. — *Draw a prism similar to Fig. 3 below and at the left of the eye.*

Problem 10. — *Draw Fig. 1 and remove the top face. The nearest face. Both the top and nearest face.*

Problem 11. — *Draw Fig. 2 and remove the top face. The nearest face. Both.*

FIGURES 4, 5, AND 6 – How to draw a vertical prism with the apex toward you:

1. Draw the base ABCD.

2. Draw the H. L. and place the C. of V.

3. Bisect AB as at G and from the C. of V. through this point, draw a receding line.

4. Choose the point E in this line and draw EA and EB.

5. Through H, draw a receding line meeting a vertical line from E at F.

6. Draw FD and FC.

7. When the point E, as in Fig. 5, is directly in front of the eye, the point F may be found by drawing a receding line through A, meeting a horizontal line from E at J.

8. From J, draw a vertical line meeting a receding line through D at K.

9. From K, draw a horizontal line meeting a vertical line from E, forming F.

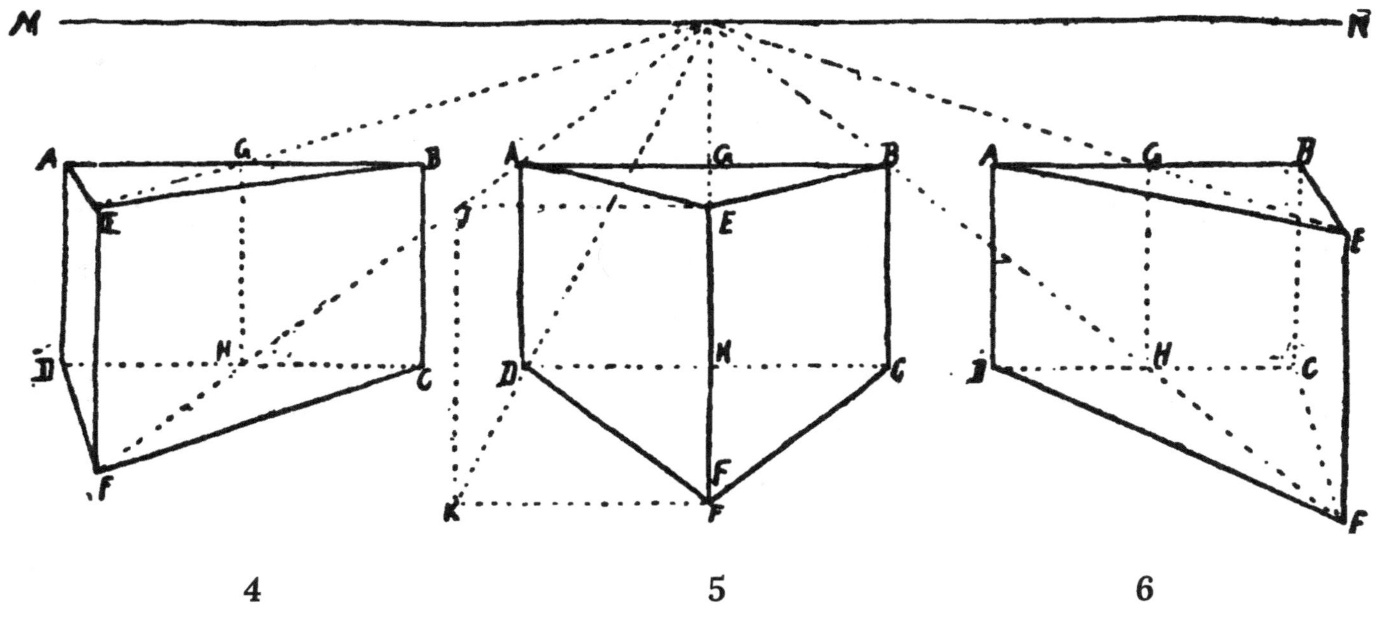

PROBLEM 1. FIG. 4. — *Draw a vertical prism below and at the left of the eye with the apex toward you.*

PROBLEM 2. FIG. 5. — *Draw a vertical prism below the eye with the apex toward you.*

PROBLEM 3. FIG. 6. — *Draw a vertical prism below and at the right of the eye with the apex toward you.*

Problem 4. — *Above and at the left of the eye, draw a vertical prism with the apex toward you.*

Problem 5. — *Above the eye, draw a vertical prism with the apex toward you.*

Problem 6. — *Above and at the right of the eye, draw a vertical prism with the apex toward you.*

Problem 7. — *At the left of the eye, draw a vertical prism with the apex toward you. Draw the same at the right of the eye.*

Problem 8. — *Below and at the right of the eye, draw a vertical prism with the apex toward you, and remove the top face. Remove both the top and left faces.*

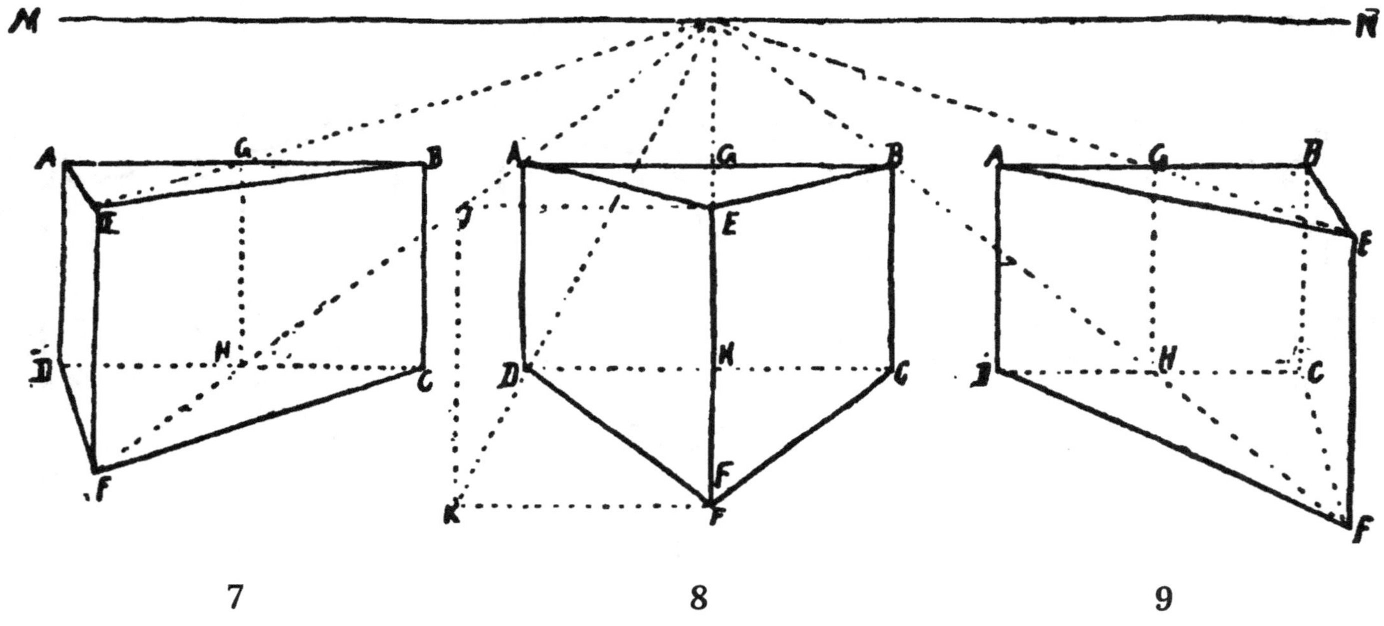

FIGURES 7, 8, AND 9 – When the apex of the vertical prism points to the right or left, it contains vertical, receding, and oblique lines and is drawn as follows:

1. Draw the vertical line A D.

2. Draw the H. L. and place the C. of V.

3. From the points A and D, draw receding lines.

4. Choose the point B and draw B C.

5. Choose the point G[32], half-way between A and B, and from it draw a horizontal and a vertical line.

6. From H, draw a horizontal line.

7. Choose the point E and draw E F.

32   The point G may be found by drawing diagonals across the base.

8. Draw E B, E A, and F D.

9. When A B, as in Fig. 8, is directly in line with the eye, the point F may be found by:

10. Drawing a receding line through E, meeting a horizontal line from A at J.

11. From J, draw a vertical line meeting a horizontal line from D at K.

12. From K, draw a receding line meeting a vertical line from E at F.

13. Draw E B, E A, and F D.

PROBLEM 1. FIG. 7. — *Draw a vertical prism below and at the left of the eye with the apex to the left.*

PROBLEM 2. FIG. 9. — *Draw a vertical prism below and at the right of the eye with the apex to the left.*

PROBLEM 3. FIG. 9. — *Draw a vertical prism with the base directly below the eye and the apex to the left. With the apex to the right.*

Problem 4. — Above and at the left of the eye, draw a vertical prism with the apex to the left. With the apex to the right.

Problem 5. — Above and at the right of the eye, draw a vertical prism with the apex to the left. With the apex to the right.

Problem 6. — At the left of the eye, draw a vertical prism with the apex to the left. To the right.

Problem 7. — At the right of the eye, draw a vertical prism with the top on a level with the eye and the apex to the left. To the right.

Problem 8. — Draw Fig. 7 and remove the top face. Remove the right face. Remove the left face.

Problem 9. — Draw Fig. 9 and remove the top face. Remove the nearest face. Remove both.

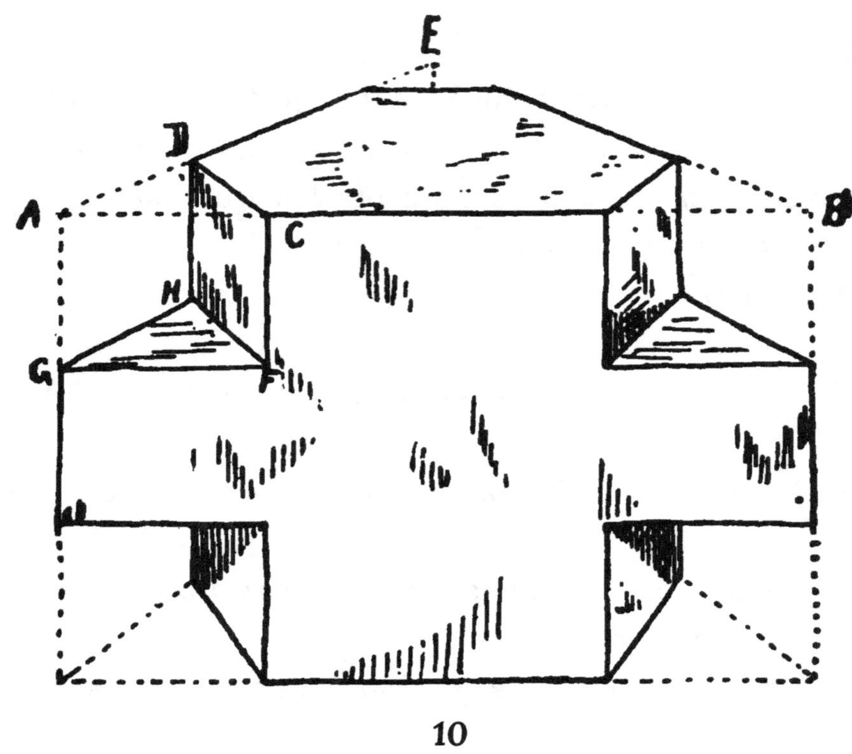

10

PROBLEM 1. FIG. 10.[33] — *Draw a vertical prism below the level of the eye with the apex away from you, and from each corner cut a small vertical prism.*

Observe that the small prisms cut from each corner of the large prism are of the same shape as the large prism, and that the lines of the small prism correspond to and are parallel with the corresponding lines of the large prism. Thus lines DC and HF are parallel with EB, GH with AE, and GF with AB.

Problem 2. — *Draw Fig. 10 below and at the left of the eye.*

Problem 3. — *Draw Fig. 10 above the eye.*

33   Figures 10 - 14 are drill problems to be drawn on the black-board. It is well not to use the vanishing points here, but to have them drawn entirely by the unaided eye.

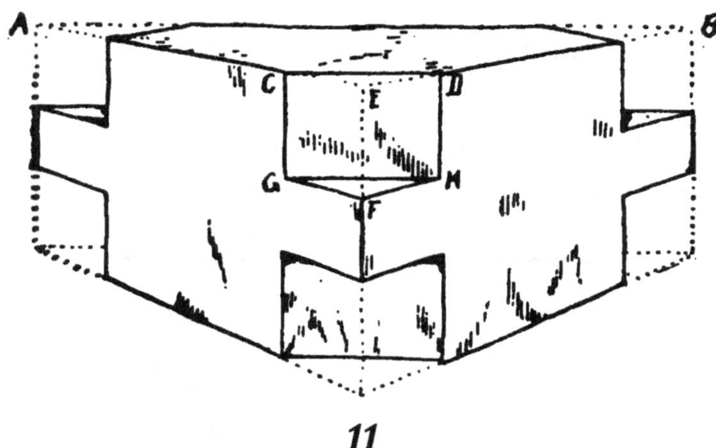

11

PROBLEM 1. FIG. 11. — *Draw a vertical prism below the eye with the apex toward you, and from each corner cut a small vertical prism.*

Observe that lines CD and GH are parallel with AB, FH with EB, and FG with EA. The same is true with all the small prisms.

Problem 2. — *Draw Fig. 11 below and at the right of the eye.*

Problem 3. — *Draw Fig. 11 above the eye.*

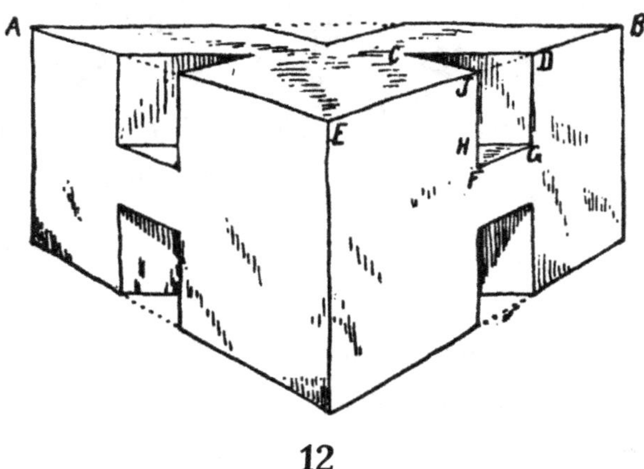

12

PROBLEM 1. FIG. 12. — *Draw a vertical prism below the eye with the apex toward you, and from each line cut a small vertical prism.*

Observe that CD and GH are horizontal, the same as AB, and that FG is parallel with EB and CJ with AE.

Problem 2. — *Draw Fig. 12 above the level of the eye.*

Problem 3. — *Draw Fig. 12 below and at the left of the eye.*

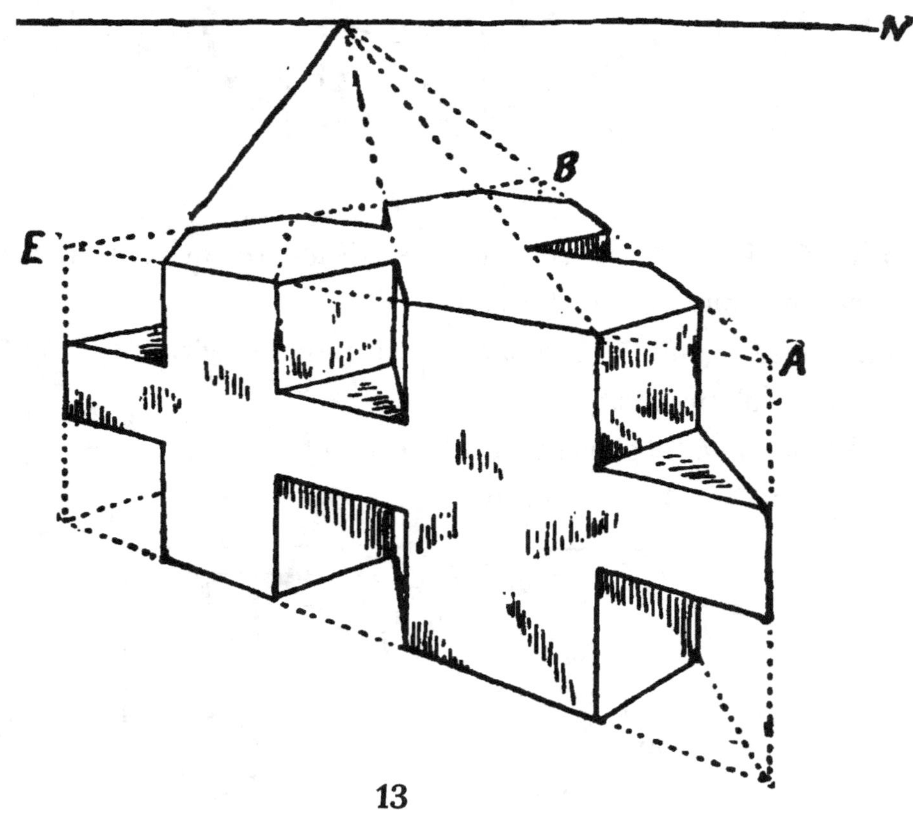

13

PROBLEM 1. FIG. 13. — *Draw a vertical prism below the eye with the apex to the left, and from each corner and each line cut a small vertical prism.*

Problem 2. — *Draw Fig. 13 below and at the left of the eye.*

Problem 3. — *Draw Fig. 13 with the base line directly in line with the eye.*

Problem 4. — *Draw Fig. 13 with the apex to the right.*

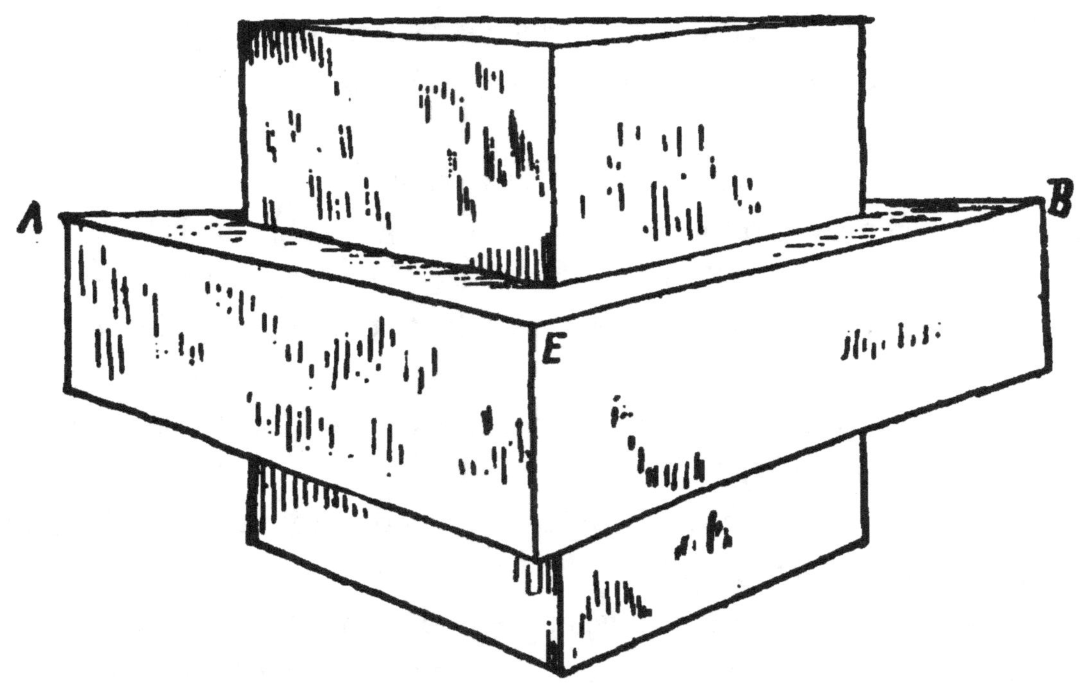

14

PROBLEM 1. FIG. 14. — *Draw a vertical prism below the eye with the apex toward you, and to the upper and lower face add a small vertical prism.*

Problem 2. — *Turn Fig. 14 so the apex will be away from you.*

Problem 3. — *Turn Fig. 14 so the apex will be to the left. To the right.*

Problem 4. — *Draw a vertical prism below the eye with the apex away from you and cut a triangular opening through it vertically.*

VANISHING POINTS.

The **BASE LINE** of a picture is the line on which it rests, as line CD, Fig. 15.

The **PICTURE PLANE** is the real surface on which the picture is drawn, as the paper or blackboard.

The **GROUND PLANE** is that apparent surface at right angles with the picture plane that reaches from the base line out to the H. L. In Fig. 15, the ground plane is that part of the picture reaching from the base line CD out to the horizon line MN. Lines perpendicular to the ground plane are vertical lines, and lines perpendicular to the picture plane are receding lines converging at the C. of V.

The **CENTRAL RAY** is the imaginary line connecting the C. of V. with the eye of the observer. There can be only one central ray.

There are two classes of receding lines: (1) Those that converge at the C. of V., (2) Those that converge at a point outside of the C. of V.

The class of receding lines that converge at the C. of V. are those parallel with the central ray and perpendicular to the picture plane. All other parallel lines have a vanishing point (V. P.) of their own.

IN FIGURE 15, there are three straight roads starting from AB. One directly forward to the C. of V., one to a vanishing point on the right, and one to a vanishing point on the left. Any number of roads might start from AB and run to as many V. P.s.

The receding lines that start from AB and run along the surface of the ground plane to the C. of V. are perpendicular to the picture plane. Those receding lines that run along the surface of the ground plane to the other V.P.s are at an angle with the picture plane.

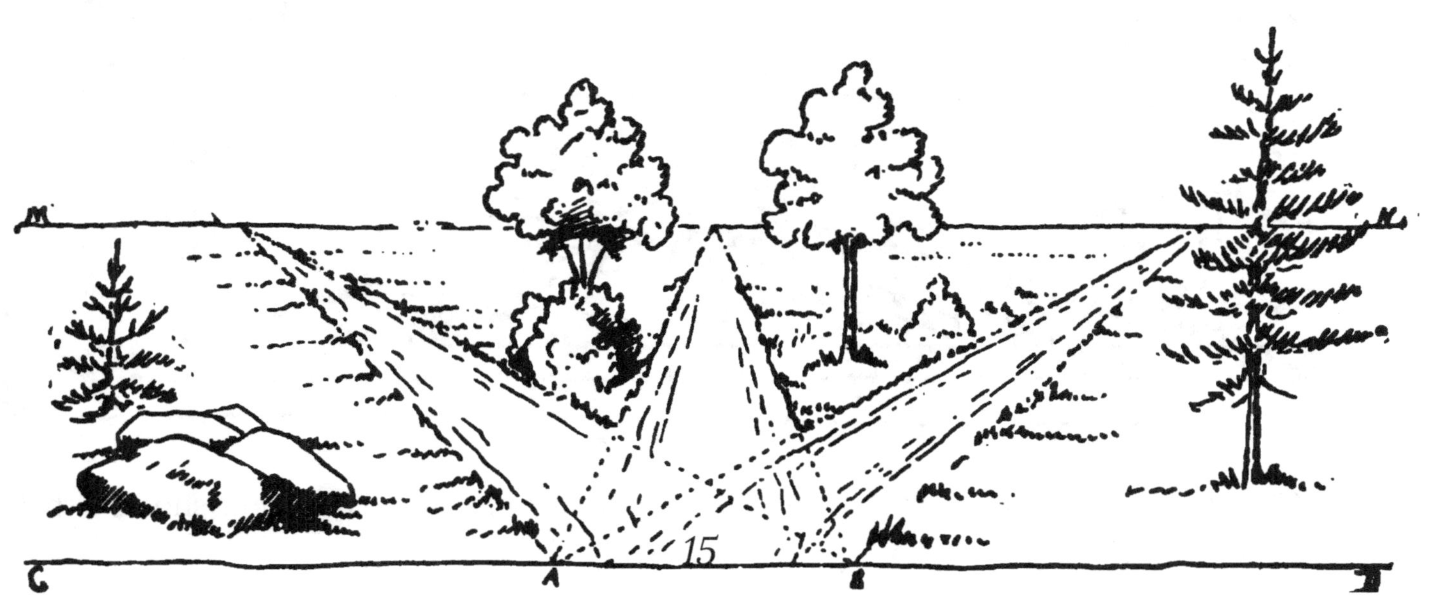

Figure 15 may be drawn as follows:

(1) Draw the H. L. and the base line. (2) Choose the points A and B, and from them draw receding lines to the C. of V. (3) Choose the V. P. on the right and the V. P. on the left, and from A and B draw lines to each.Problem 1. — *Draw Fig. 15 with two roads on the right of the C. of V. and three on the left.*

Problem 2. — *Make a drawing similar to Fig. 15 on the blackboard from memory*[34].

Problem 3. — *Make a drawing of the tree on the right in Fig. 15 on the blackboard.*

34   Before a picture can be drawn from memory, it must be copied carefully. The power of drawing from memory increases very rapidly with practice.

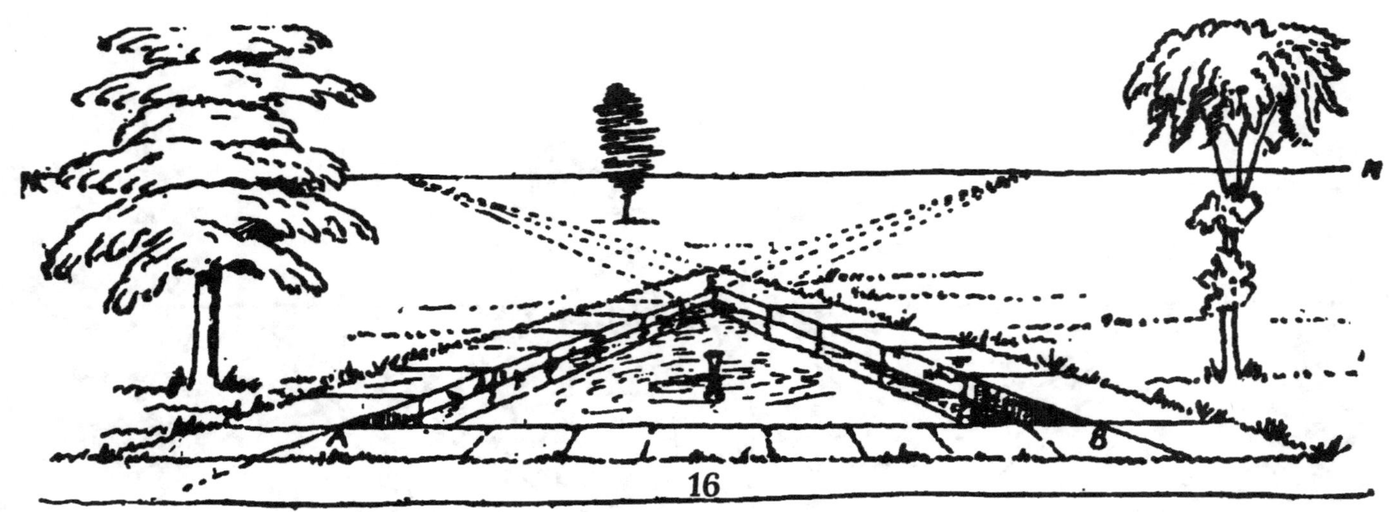

FIGURE 16 is an application of the vertical prism with the apex away from you, showing the use of V.P.s in drawing it.

Figure 16 may be drawn as follows:

(1) Draw the H. L. (2) Draw the triangle A B E. (3) Continue the lines A E and B E until they intersect the H. L., which will give the V. P.'s for all lines parallel with these lines.

Problem 1. — *Draw Fig. 16 with the apex toward you.*

Problem 2. — *Draw Fig. 16 on the blackboard from memory.*

Problem 3. — *Draw the elm tree on the right in Fig. 16 on the blackboard. Draw the hickory tree on the left.*

Problem 4.[35] — *Draw Fig. 10 by using V.P.s the same as in Fig. 16.*

35   The V.P.s in Fig. 10 may be found by continuing two or more parallel lines to their point of interception. Lines CD and BE are parallel.

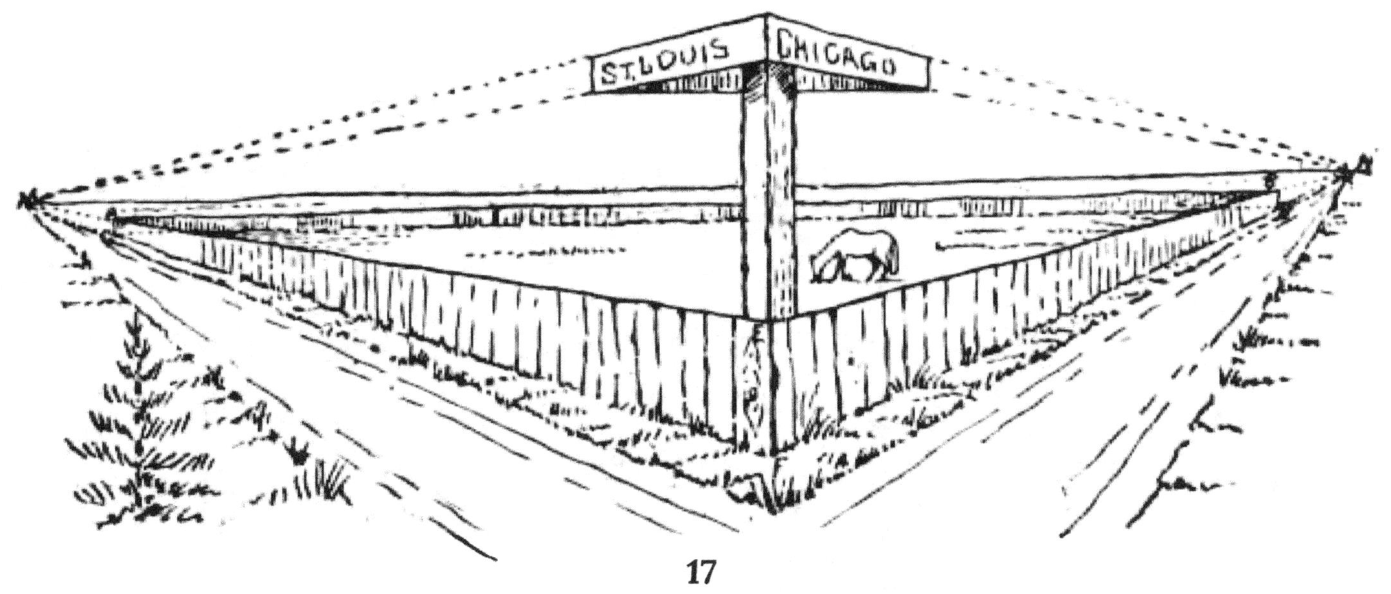

17

FIGURE 17 is an application of the vertical prism with the apex toward you, showing the use of V. P's. in drawing it.

Figure 17 may be drawn as follows:

(1) Draw the H. L. (2) Draw the triangle A B E. (3) Continue E A and E B until they intersect the H. L., which will give the V. P's. (4) Draw the vertical line E F. (5) From the point F draw a receding line to each V. P. (6) From A draw the vertical line A C. (7) From C draw the horizontal line C D. (8) Draw the roads. (9) The sign-board at E is the same problem above the level of the eye.

Problem 1. — *Draw a sign similar to the one in Fig. 17 where two roads meet.*

Problem 2. — *Draw Fig. 11 using V.P.s as in Fig. 17.*

Problem 3. — *Draw Fig. 12 using V.P.s as in Fig. 17.*

Problem 4. — *Draw Fig. 17 on the blackboard from memory.*

Problem 5. — *Make a drawing of the little bush on the left in Fig. 17 on the blackboard.*

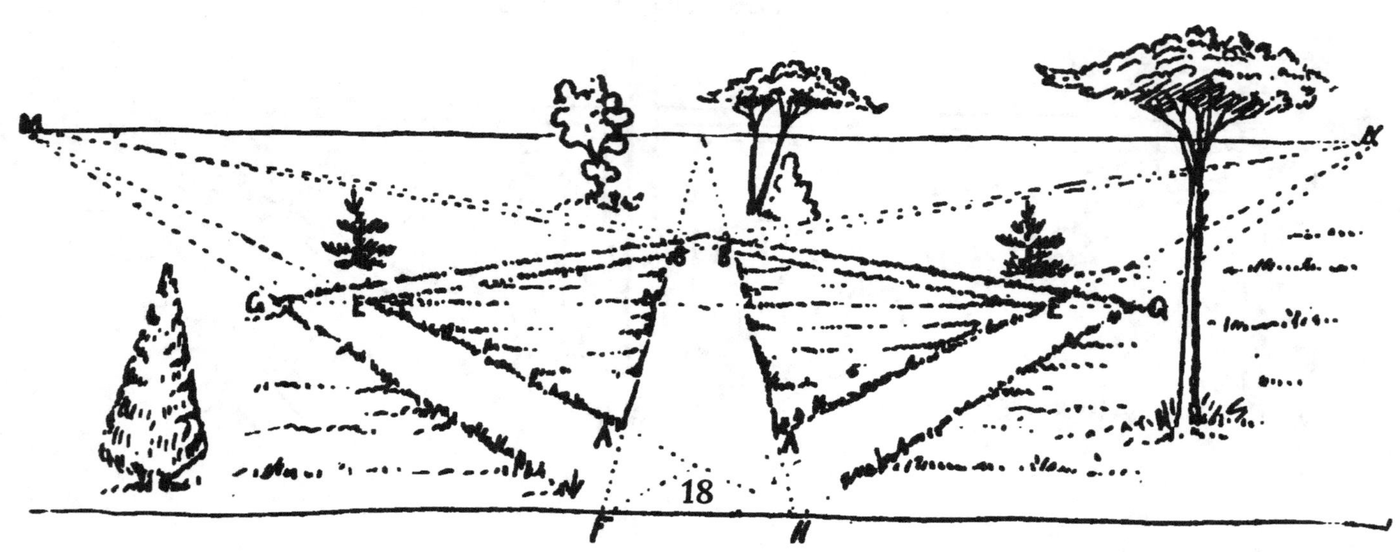

FIGURE 18 is an application of the vertical prism with the apex turned to the right and left from the receding lines of the base.

Figure 18 may be drawn as follows:

(1) Draw the H. L. and place the C. of V. (2) Choose the points F and H and from them draw receding lines to the C. of V. (3) Choose the V. P.'s equally distant from the C. of V. and draw the receding lines from the points F and H. (4) Choose the point E and through it draw a horizontal line marking the points E E and G G. (5) From the points E E and G G draw receding lines to the V. P.'s.

Problem 1. — *Draw Fig. 18 with the triangular grass plats at the left of the C. of V.*
Problem 2. — *Draw Fig. 18 on the blackboard from memory.*
Problem 3. — *Draw Fig. 13 using two V.P.s and the C. of V., the same as in Fig. 18.*
Problem 4. — *Draw the tree on the right in Fig. 18 on the blackboard.*

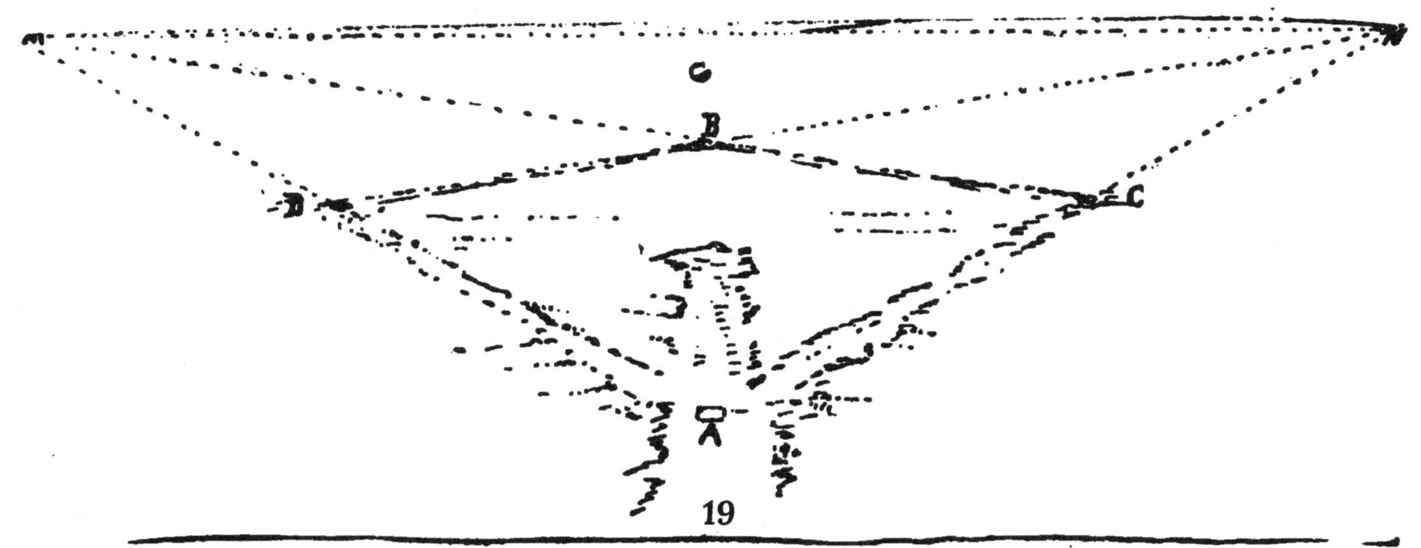

FIGURE 19 is a square made in the figure of a baseball diamond and composed of receding lines alone.

It may be studied as the base of two prisms together.

Figure 19 may be drawn as follows:

(1) Draw the H. L. and place the C. of V. (2) Choose the V. P.'s equally distant from the C. of V. (3) Choose the point A and from it draw a receding line to each V. P. (4) Choose the point D and draw a horizontal line marking point C. (5) From the points C and D, draw a receding line to the V. P.'s.

Problem 1. — *Draw a ball-field similar to Fig. 19 on the blackboard from memory.*

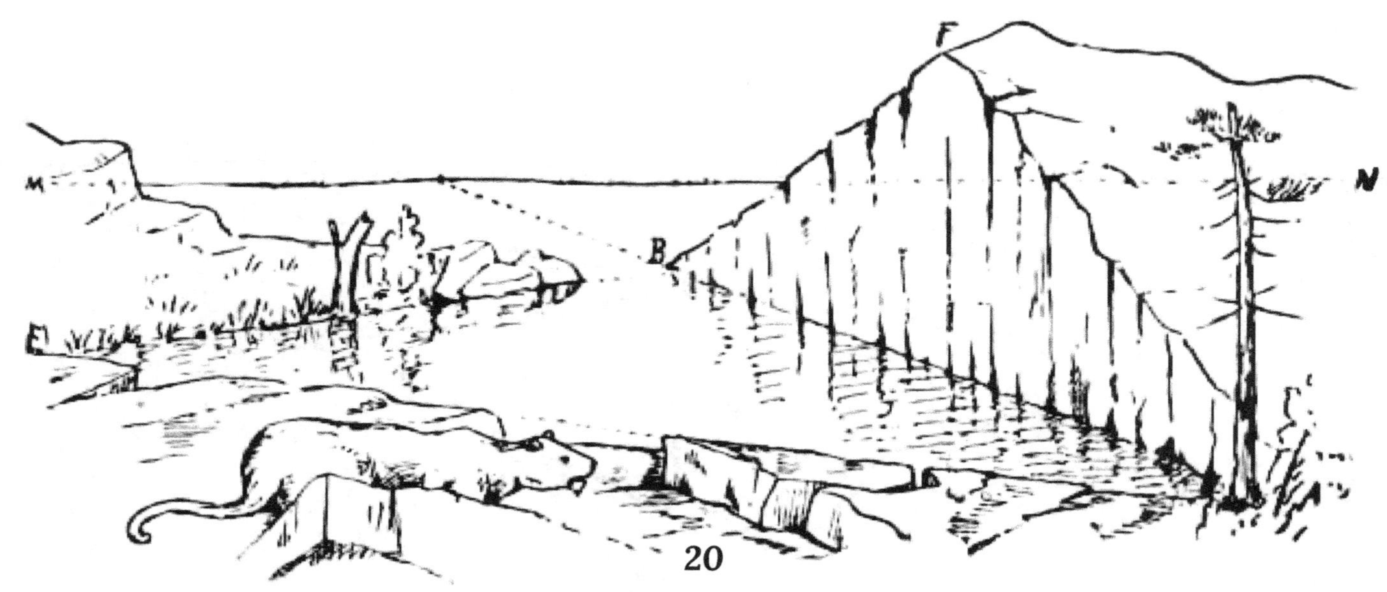

FIGURE 20 is a practical application of the triangular prism to figures sometimes seen in nature.

Figure 20 may be drawn as follows:

(1) Draw the H. L. and place the C. of V. (2) Choose the point A and draw a receding line to the C. of V. (3) Choose the point B and the point E and draw E A and E B. (4) Choose the point F and draw F A and F B. (5) Add the details.

Problem 1.[36] — *Draw Fig. 20 on the blackboard from memory.*

Problem 2. — *Draw a triangular-shaped island in the midst of the ocean.*

Problem 3. — *Draw a triangular-shaped peninsula.*

36   Birds, animals, trees, etc., are often introduced in the drawing to add life and interest to the picture. Of course, it is understood that objects of this sort may be added or omitted at pleasure, as long as it does not detract from the central idea.

THE HORIZONTAL PRISM.

THE HORIZONTAL PRISM may be studied in four positions:

(1) When the apex points upward. (2) When the apex points downward. (3) When the apex is toward you. (4) When the apex is away from you.

When the horizontal prism rests on its base, it contains horizontal, receding, and oblique lines. See Figures 21-24.

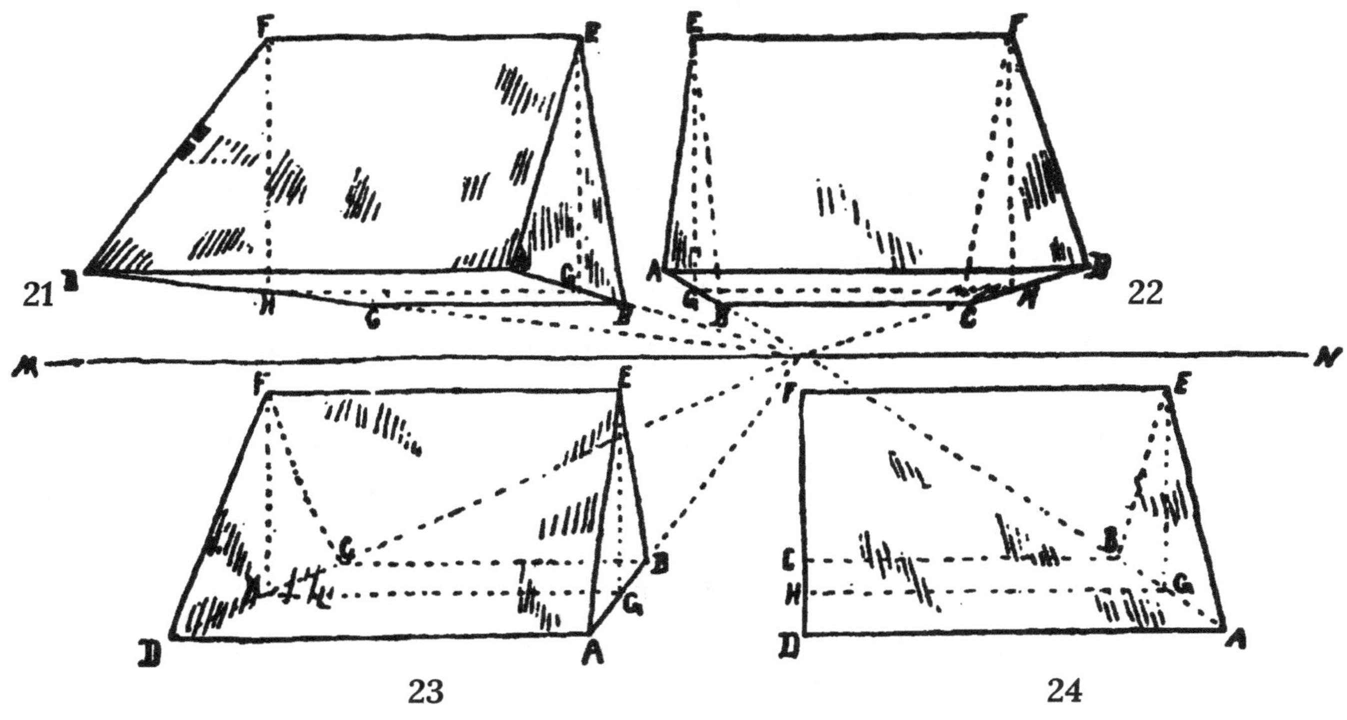

FIGURE 21 is a horizontal prism above and at the left of the eye. Fig. 22 is above the eye. Fig. 23 is below and at the left of the eye, and Fig. 24 is below with one end directly in line with

the eye.

Figures 21, 22, 23, and 24 may be drawn as follows:

(1) Draw the H. L. (2) Draw the horizontal line A D the length of the prism. (3) Choose the C. of V. (4) From the points A and D draw receding lines to the C. of V. (5) Choose the point B and draw B C. (6) Bisect A B as at G and draw the horizontal line G H and an indefinite vertical line. (7) Choose the point E and draw a horizontal line meeting a vertical line from H. (8) Draw E A, E B, and F D, or such of the oblique lines as can be seen.

PROBLEM 1. FIG. 21. — *Draw a horizontal prism above and at the left of the eye. Remove the bottom face. The nearest side.*

PROBLEM 2. FIG. 23. — *Draw a horizontal prism below and at the left of the eye. Remove the nearest side. The end. Both.*

PROBLEM 3. FIG. 22. — *Draw a horizontal prism directly above the eye. Remove the bottom face. The side.*

PROBLEM 4. FIG. 24. — *Draw a horizontal prism below the eye. Remove the side.*

Problem 5. — *Draw a horizontal prism below and at the left of the eye with the apex pointing downward.*

Problem 6. — *Below the eye draw a horizontal prism with the apex pointing downward.*

Problem 7. — *Above and at the right of the eye draw a horizontal prism with the apex pointing downward.*

When the apex of the horizontal prism is toward or away from you, it is composed of vertical, horizontal, and oblique lines as in Figs. 25 and 26. The principle is exactly the same when the apex points downward.

FIGURE 25 is a horizontal prism with the apex toward you, and Fig. 26 is one with the apex away from you.

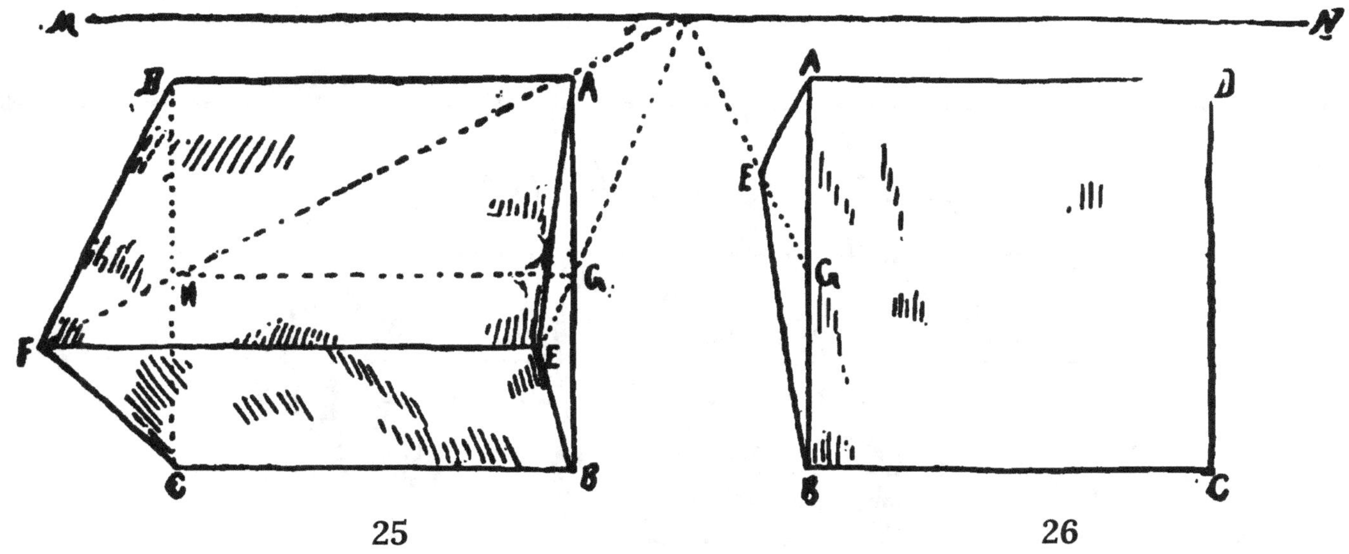

25　　　　　　　　**26**

Figures 25 and 26 may be drawn as follows:

(1) Draw the H. L. (2) Draw the base A B C D. (3) Choose the C. of V. (4) Bisect A B as at G and through this point from the C. of V. draw a receding line. (5) Choose the point E and draw E A and E B. (6) From G draw a horizontal line. (7) From E draw a horizontal line meeting a receding line through H at F. (8) Draw F D and F C.

PROBLEM 1. FIG. 25. — *Draw a horizontal prism below and at the left of the eye with the apex toward you.*

PROBLEM 2. FIG. 26. — *Draw a horizontal prism below and at the right of the eye with the apex away from you.*

Problem 3. — *Above and at the left of the eye draw a horizontal prism with the apex toward you. With the apex away from you.*

Problem 4. — *Draw Fig. 26 and remove one end. Remove the nearest face. Remove both.*

Problem 5. — *Draw Fig. 25 and remove the upper face.*

169

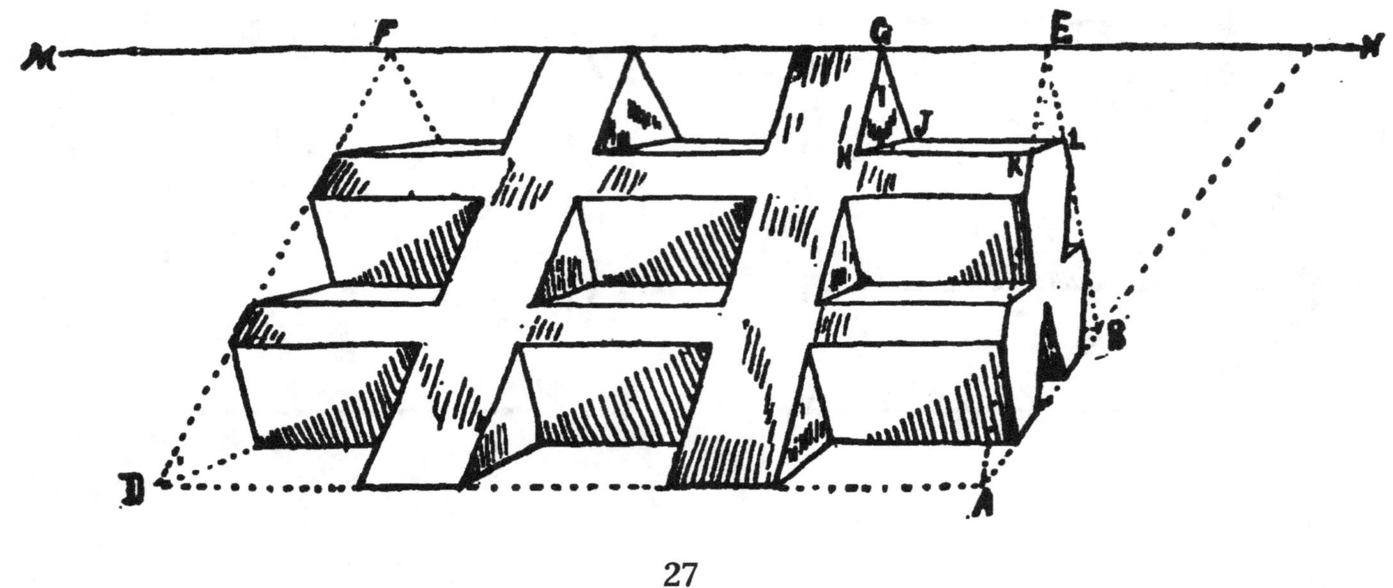

27

PROBLEM 1. FIG. 27. — *Below and at the left of the eye draw a horizontal prism with the apex pointing upward, and from each corner and edge cut a small horizontal prism.*

In **FIGURE 27** observe that the small prisms cut from the corners and edges of the large prism are like the large prism, and that the corresponding lines in each are parallel. Thus, the lines HJ and KL are receding lines the same as AB. GH is parallel with EA and GJ with EB. Draw Fig. 27.

Problem 2. — *Draw a horizontal prism resting on its base below and at the right of the eye, and from each corner cut a small horizontal prism.*

Problem 3. — *Below and at the right of the eye draw a horizontal prism resting on its base and from each edge cut a small horizontal prism.*

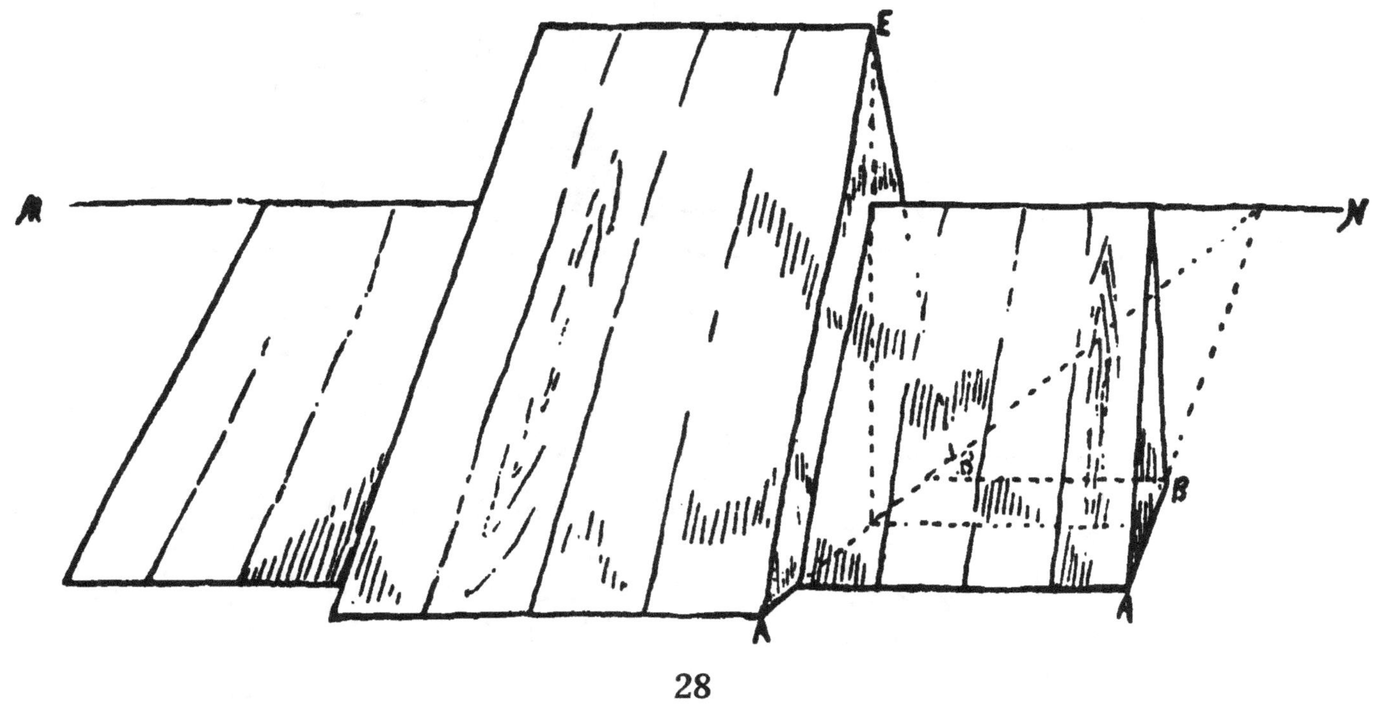

PROBLEM 1. FIG. 28. — *Below and at the left of the eye draw a horizontal prism resting on its base and to each end add another and smaller prism also resting on their bases.*

Problem 2. — *Draw Fig. 28 at the right of the eye.*

Problem 3. — *Below and at the left of the eye draw a horizontal prism resting on its base, and through it cut a triangular-shaped opening.*

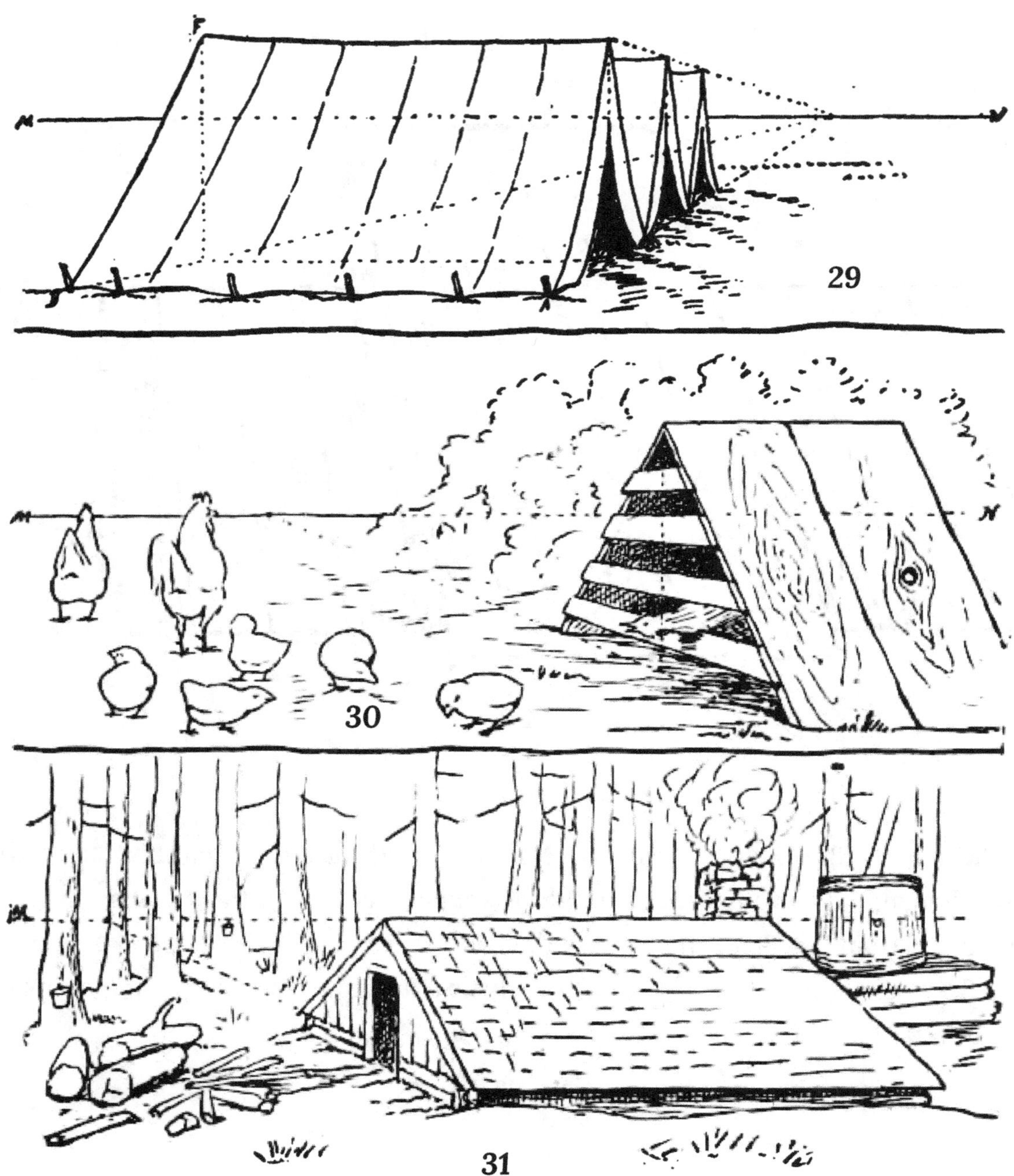

29

30

31

FIGURE 29, 30, AND 31 are applications of the horizontal prism resting on its base to familiar objects.

Problem 4. — *Draw Fig. 29 on the blackboard.*

Problem 5. — *Draw the tents in Fig. 29 at the right of the eye.*

Problem 6. — *Draw Fig. 30 on the blackboard.*

Problem 7. — *Draw the rooster and the hen on the blackboard from memory.*

Problem 8. — *Draw the hen-coop in Fig. 30 at the left of the eye.*

Problem 9. — *Draw the sugar shanty in Fig. 31 on the blackboard.*

Problem 10. — *Draw the sugar shanty in Fig. 31 at the left of the eye.*

THE RECEDING PRISM.

THE RECEDING PRISM may be studied in four positions:

(1) When the apex points upward. (2) When the apex points downward. (3) When the apex points to the right. (4) When the apex points to the left.

When the apex of the receding prism points upward or downward, the prism is composed of horizontal, receding, and oblique lines (Figs. 32-35).

FIGURE 32 is a receding prism above and at the left of the eye; Fig. 34 is below and at the left of the eye; Fig. 33 is above the eye; and Fig. 35 is below the eye.

Figures 32, 33, 34, and 35 may be drawn as follows:

(1) Draw the H. L. (2) Draw the nearest line of the base A B. (3) Bisect A B as at G and from it erect an indefinite vertical line. (4) Choose the point E and draw E A and E B. (5) Choose the C. of V. and to it draw receding lines from A B, G, and E. (6) Choose the point C and from it draw

the horizontal line D C. (7) From H draw H F. (8) Draw F C and F D if they can be seen.

PROBLEM 1. FIG. 34. — *Draw a receding prism below and at the left of the eye. Below and at the right of the eye.*

PROBLEM 2. FIG. 32. — *Draw a receding prism above and at the left of the eye. Above and at the right of the eye.*

PROBLEM 3. FIG. 33. — *Draw a receding prism above the eye.*

PROBLEM 4. FIG. 35. — *Draw a receding prism below the eye.*

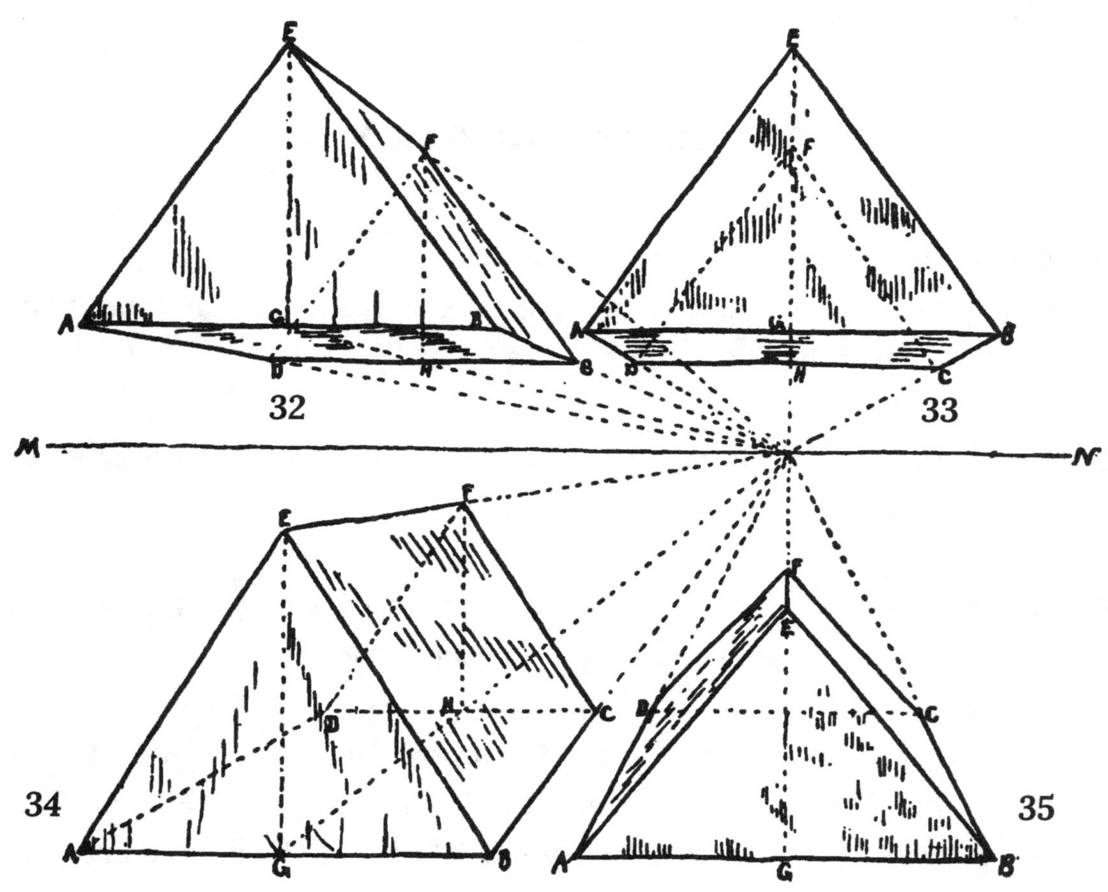

Problem 5. — *Draw Fig. 35 with the apex down.*

Problem 6. — *Draw Fig. 33 with the apex up.*

Problem 7. — *Draw Fig. 34 with the apex down.*

Problem 8. — *Draw Fig. 32 with the apex down.*

When the apex of the prism points to the right or left, it is composed of vertical, receding, and oblique lines (Figs. 36 and 37).

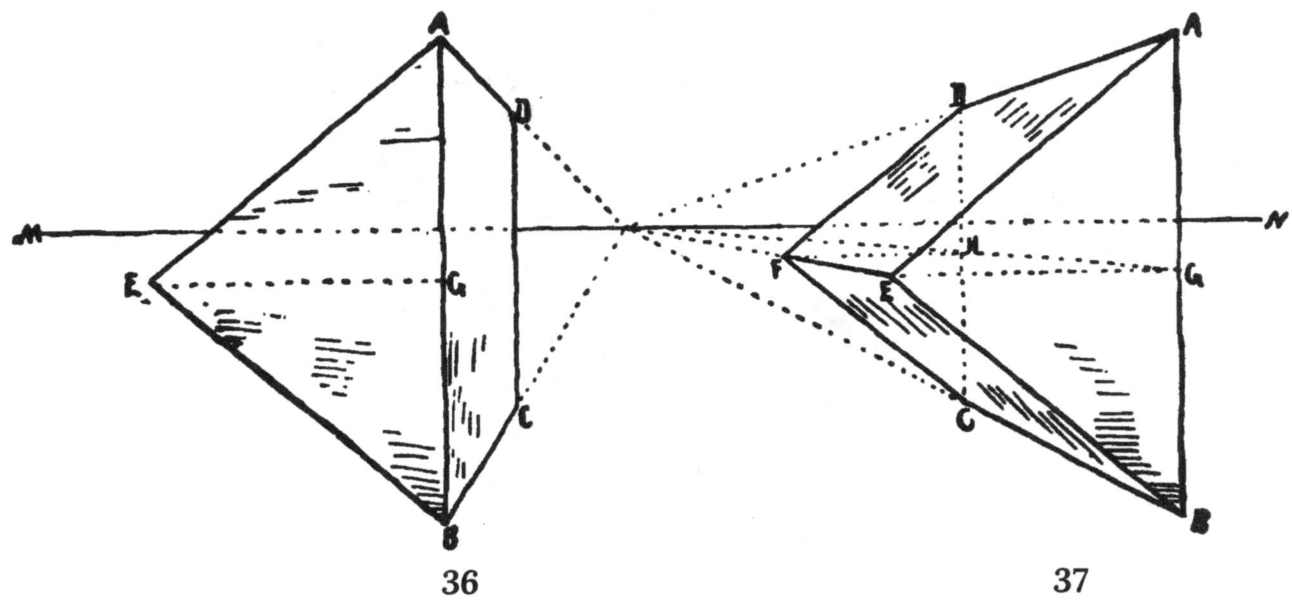

Figures 36 and 37 may be drawn as follows:

(1) Draw the H. L. (2) Draw the nearest line of the base A B. (3) Bisect A B as at G and from it draw an indefinite horizontal line. (4) Choose the point E and draw E A and E B. (5) Choose the C. of V. and to it draw receding lines from the points A and B and, if necessary, from G and E. (6) Choose the point C and draw the vertical line C D. (7) In Fig. 37, draw the horizontal line H F. (8) Draw the lines F C and F D.

PROBLEM 1. FIG. 36. — *Draw a receding prism with the apex to the left, at the left of the eye. Below and at the left.*

PROBLEM 2. FIG. 37. — *Draw a receding prism with the apex to the left, at the right of the eye. Below and at the right of the eye.*

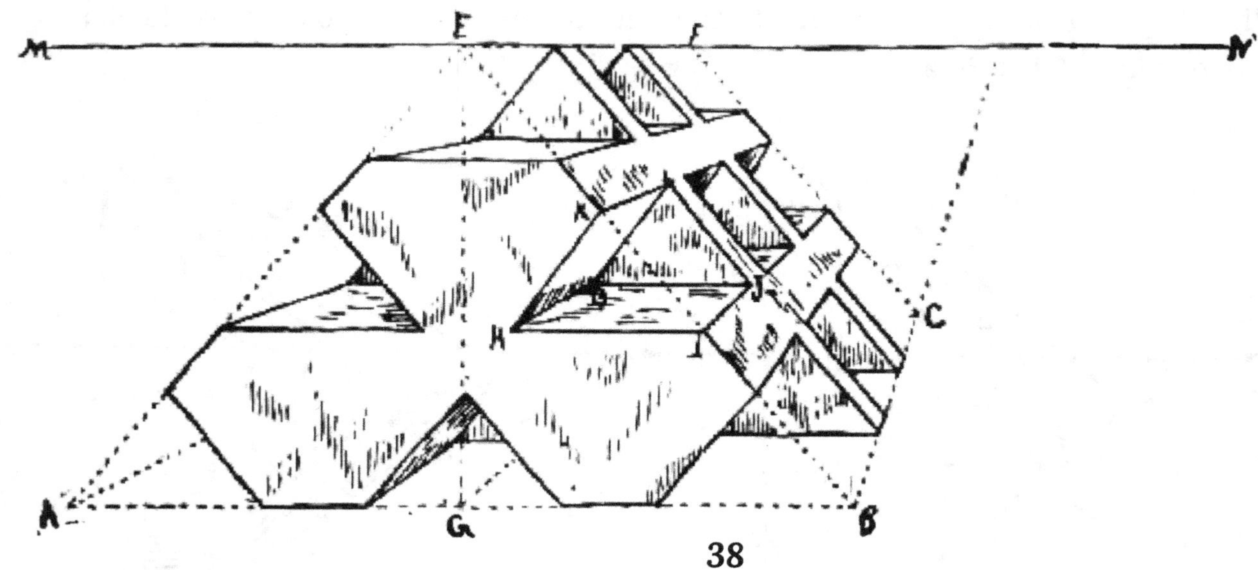

FIGURE 38 is a receding prism drawn slightly below and at the left of the eye, with small, receding prisms cut from each corner and line. Observe that the small prisms are similar in shape and position to the large prism and that the corresponding lines in each are parallel. Thus, the lines KL, HJ, and IJ are parallel with EF and BC, and of course will converge at the C. of V. OJ and HI are parallel with AB; KH and LO with EA; and LJ with EB and FC.

PROBLEM 1. FIG. 38. — *Below and at the left of the eye draw a receding prism resting on its base and from each corner and edge cut a small receding prism.*

PROBLEM 2. FIG. 38. — *Draw a receding prism below and at the left of the eye and from each corner cut a small receding prism.*

PROBLEM 3. FIG. 38. — *Draw a receding prism below and at the left of the eye and from each edge cut a receding prism.*

Problem 4. — Below and at the right of the eye draw a receding prism resting on its base and from each edge cut a small receding prism.

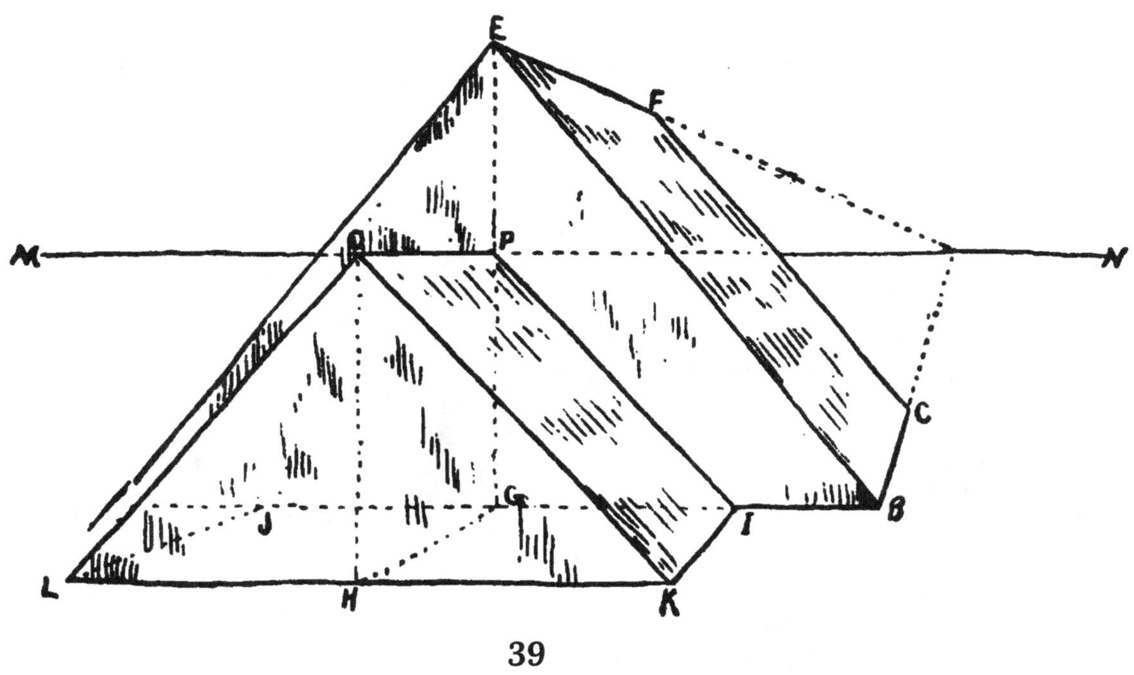

39

FIGURE 39 is a receding prism slightly at the left of the eye and resting on its base, with a small receding prism added to the end, also resting on its base.

Figure 39 may be drawn as follows:

(1) Draw the large prism. (2) Choose the points J and I equally distant from G and in the line G E choose the point P. (3) From the C. of V. through the points P, J, G, and I draw indefinite receding lines. (4) Choose the point H and through it draw the horizontal line L K and from it the vertical line H O. (5) Draw O L, O K, and P I.

PROBLEM 1. FIG. 39. — *At the left of the eye draw a receding prism and to each end add a small prism. All resting on their bases.*

Problem 2. — Draw Fig. 39 at the right of the eye.

Problem 3. — Draw Fig. 39 at the left and above the eye.

Problem 4. — At the left of the eye draw a receding prism resting on its base and through it cut a triangular opening.

Problem 5. — Directly in front of the eye draw a receding prism and through it cut a triangular-shaped opening.

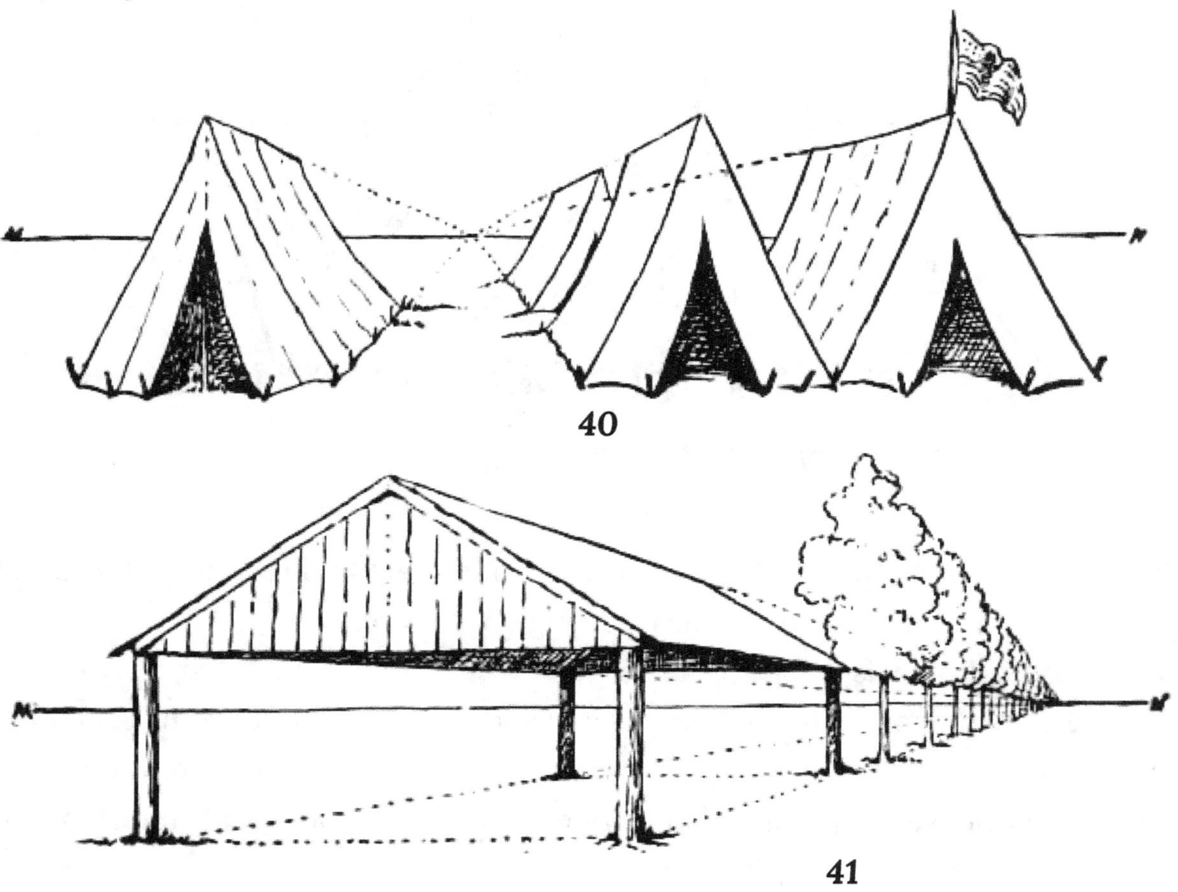

40

41

FIGURE 40, 41, AND 42 are practical applications of the receding prisms.

Problem 1. — *Draw Fig. 40 on the blackboard from memory.*
Problem 2. — *Draw the shed (Fig. 41) on the blackboard from memory.*
Problem 3. — *Draw the shed (Fig. 41) at the right of the eye.*

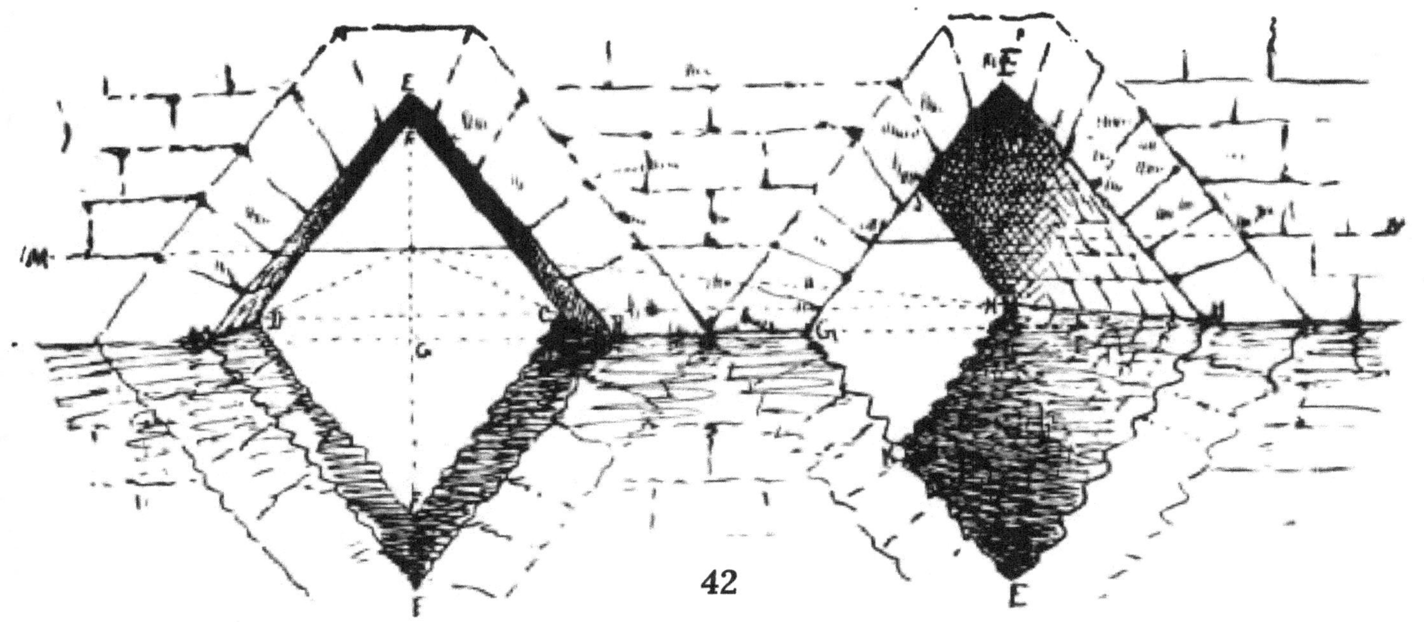

FIGURE 42 represents a waterway through a thick wall and its reflection in the water, making a double receding prism with the bases together.

Figure 42 may be drawn as follows:

(1) Draw the diamond-shaped outlines A E B E and G E H E. (2) Draw the H. L. and place the C. of V. (3) From the points A, B, E, G, and H draw receding lines to the C. of V. (4) Choose the point D and draw the horizontal line D H, marking the points D, C, and H. (5) From D, C, and H draw lines parallel with A E, B E, and H E. (6) Draw the details.

Problem 1. — Draw Fig. 42 on the blackboard from memory.

Problem 2. — Draw Fig. 42 with the C. of V. in the center of the right-hand arch.

Problem 3. — Draw Fig. 42 with the C. of V. halfway between the two arches.

PYRAMID.

Study your model.

The pyramid is placed under the triangular prism because it contains oblique lines.

Hold a pyramid in the hand and observe:

(1) That it has eight edges. (2) That its base is a rectangle or square, the same as the bottom of a cube or box. (3) That the apex of the pyramid is directly over the center of the base. (4) That the edges that mark the sides are oblique and at the same time receding.

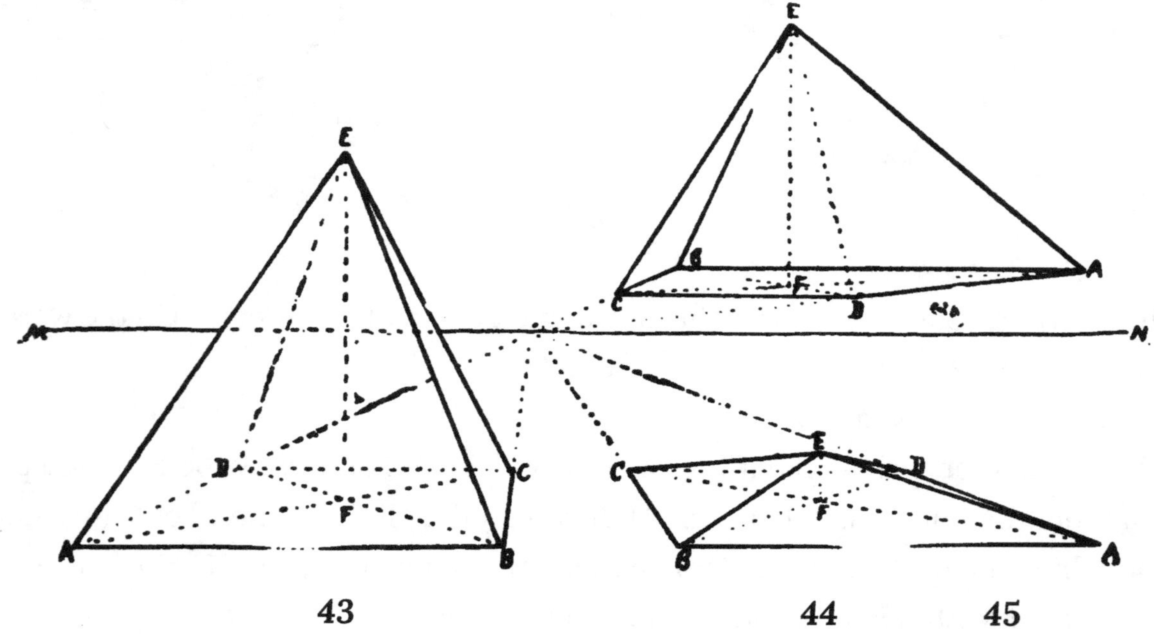

FIGURE 43, 44, AND 45 are pyramids drawn below and at the left, below and at the right, and above and at the right of the eye.

They are drawn as follows:

(1) Draw the H. L. and place the C. of V. (2) Draw the base A B C D. (3) Find the point F, the center of the base, by drawing the diagonals A C and B D. (4) From the point F draw an indefinite vertical line. (5) Choose the apex E and draw E A, E B, and E C, and if it can be seen, E D.

PROBLEMS.

PROBLEM 1. FIG. 43. — *Below and at the left of the eye draw a pyramid.*

PROBLEM 2. FIG. 44. — *Below and at the right of the eye draw a pyramid.*

PROBLEM 3. FIG. 45. — *Above and at the right of the eye draw a pyramid.*

Problem 4. — *Below and at the left of the eye draw a pyramid with the apex down.*

Problem 5. — *Above and at the right of the eye draw a pyramid with the apex down.*

Problem 6. — *Draw Fig. 43 and remove the front face. Remove the right face. Remove both.*

Problem 7. — *Draw a pyramid directly below the eye. Above the eye. Above the eye with the apex down.*

FIGURE 46 – 49 are practical applications of the pyramid to common forms.

Problem 1. — *Draw a glass fruit dish (Fig. 46) using the C. of V.*

Problem 2. — *Draw the fruit dish (Fig. 46) at the left of the eye.*

Problem 3. — *Draw Fig. 47 on the blackboard from memory.*

Problem 4. — *Draw a tent similar to Fig. 48 on the blackboard using the C. of V.*

Problem 5. — *Draw Fig. 48 directly in front of the eye so as to show the inside more clearly.*

Problem 6. — *Draw Fig. 48 at the left of the eye.*

Problem 7. — *Draw Fig. 49 on the blackboard*

Problem 8. — *Draw Fig. 49 with the pyramids at the left of the eye, using the C. of V.*

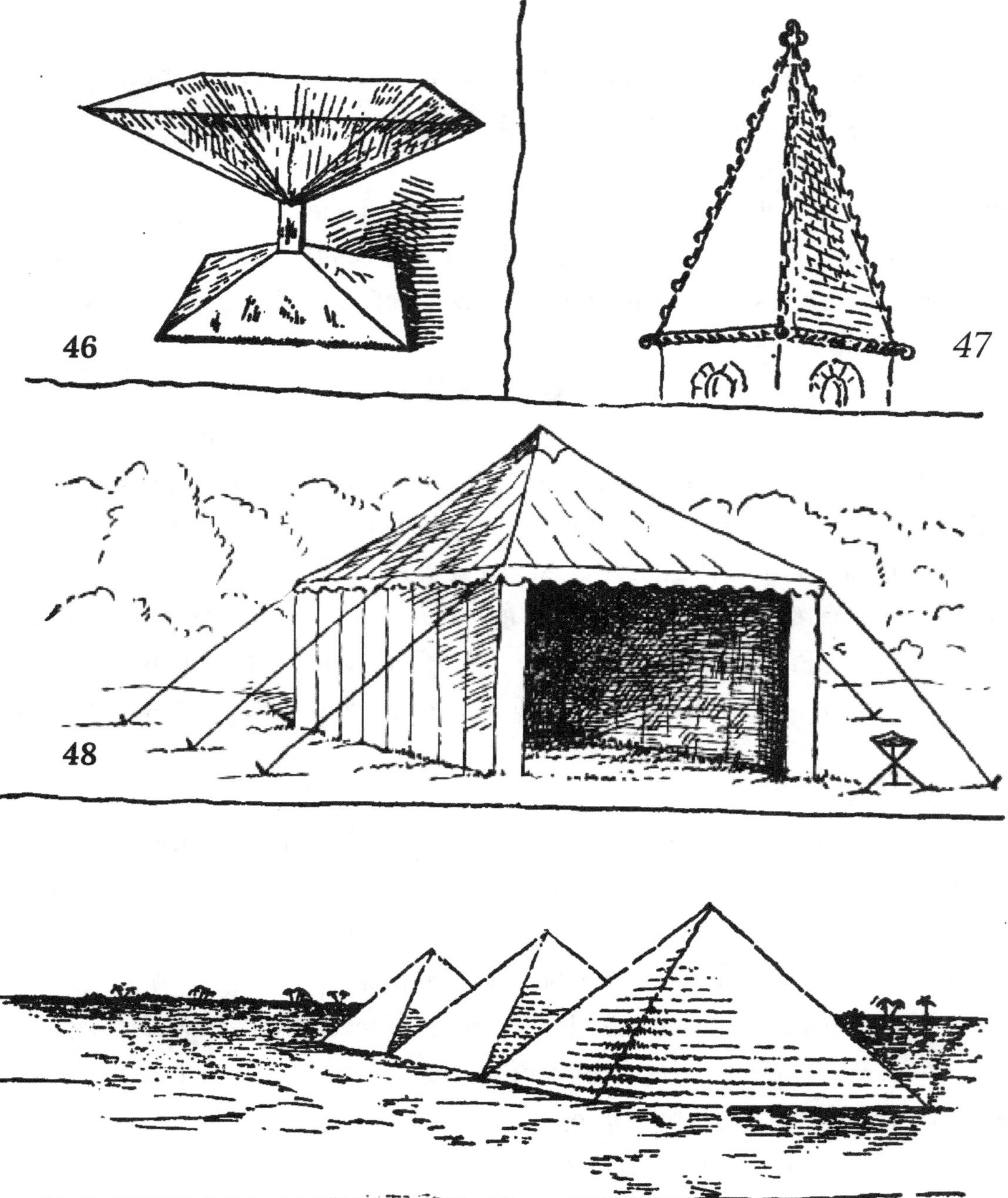

46

47

48

49

CONE.

The base of the cone is like the bottom of the cylinder. It is placed under the triangular prism because it contains oblique lines.

Hold a cone in your hand and observe:

(1) That the base is the same as the base of a cylinder. (2) That the apex is directly over the center of the base. (3) That the cone is composed of curved and oblique lines. (4) That the outline is made up of two oblique and one curved line.

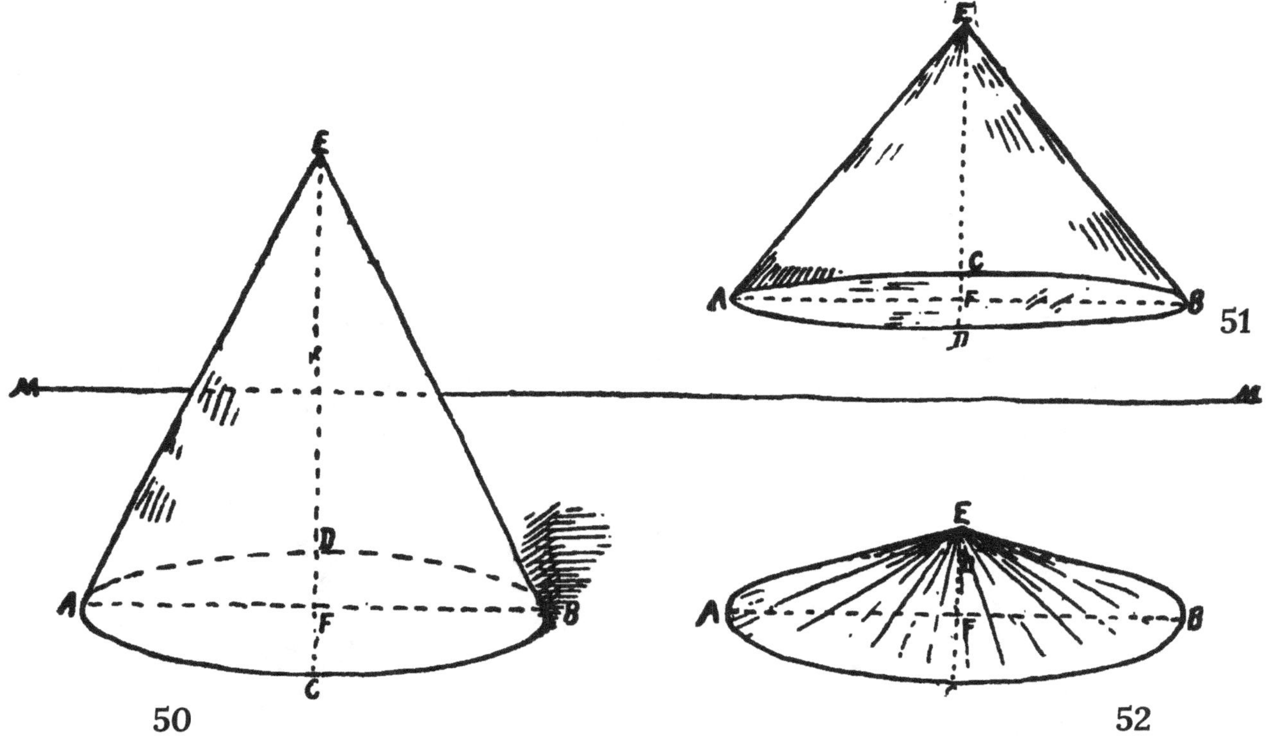

FIGURE 50, 51 AND 52 are cones drawn above and below the level of the eye. They may be drawn as follows:

(1) Draw the H. L. (2) Draw the base A B C D. (3) Bisect the longer diameter of the base as at F and from it erect an indefinite vertical line. (4) Choose the point E and from it draw lines tangent with the longer diameter of the base.

PROBLEM 1. FIG. 50. — Draw a cone with the base below the eye.

PROBLEM 2. FIG. 51. — Draw a cone with the base above the eye.

PROBLEM 3. FIG. 52. — Draw a cone entirely below the eye.

Problem 4. — Draw a cone with the apex pointing downward below the level of the eye. Remove the top face.

Problem 5. — Draw a cone with the base above the eye. With the base on a level with the eye.

Problem 6. — Draw Fig. 51 and remove the bottom face.

53

54

FIGURE 53 – 57 are practical applications of the cone to common forms.

Problem 1. — Draw the wine-glass (Fig. 53) on the blackboard from memory.

Problem 2. — Draw the wine-glass (Fig. 53) with the upper edge of the bowl on a level with the eye.

Problem 3. — Draw the funnel (Fig. 54) on the blackboard from memory.

Problem 4. — Draw the funnel (Fig. 54) lying on the table with the small end pointing upward.

Problem 5. — Draw the wigwams (Fig. 55) on the blackboard.

Problem 6. — Draw two rows of wigwams extending toward a C. of V.

Problem 7. — Draw Fig. 56 on the blackboard from memory.

Problem 8. — Draw the oil-can (Fig. 57) on the blackboard from memory.

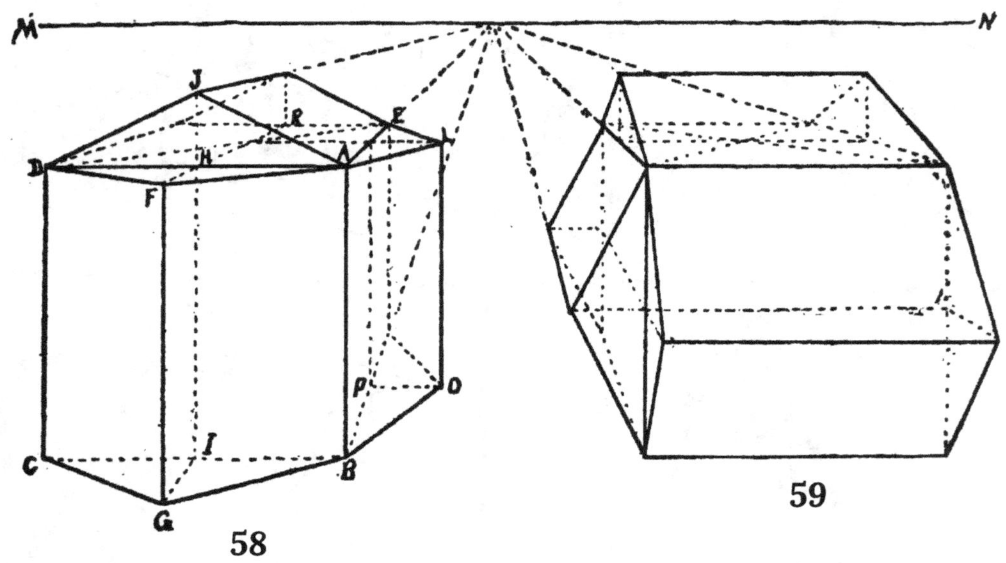

CUBE AND PRISM.

PROBLEM 1. FIG. 58. — To each of the exposed surfaces of a cube add a triangular prism.

(1) Draw the cube. (2) To draw the prism on the front face, bisect A D at H and through it draw a receding line from the C. of V. as far as the apex of the prism is to be, as at F. (3) From F draw a vertical line meeting a receding line from I. (4) Draw F D, F A, G C, and G B. (5) To draw the prism on the top face of the cube, erect a vertical line from H as high as the apex is to be, as at J. (6) Draw J A and J D and from J a receding line to the C. of V., meeting a vertical line from R at K. (7) Draw E K. (8) To draw the prism on the side face of the cube, draw from the middle

of A E a horizontal line as far as the apex L is to be. (9) Draw L E and L A and a vertical line from L meeting a horizontal line from F at O. (10) Draw O B. (11) Erase the construction lines.

FIGURE 59 is the same problem with the prisms placed at right angles to those in Fig. 61.

Problem 2. — *To each of the exposed faces of a cube, add a pyramid.*
Problem 3. — *To each face of a cube, add a cone.*

FIGURE 60, 61, AND 62 are practical applications of the cube and prism to common forms.

Problem 1. — *Find the C. of V. in Fig. 60 and draw the picture.*
Problem 2. — *Draw Fig. 60 on the blackboard from memory, using the C. of V.*
Problem 3. — *Find the C. of V. in Fig. 61 and draw the picture.*
Problem 4. — *Place the barn in Fig. 61 at the right of the C. of V.*
Problem 5. — *Find the C. of V. in Fig. 62 and draw the picture.*
Problem 6. — *Draw Fig. 62 on the blackboard from memory.*
Problem 7. — *Draw the wagon shed in Fig. 62 alone.*
Problem 8. — *Draw Fig. 62 with the wagon shed in the center.*

60
61
62

QUARTER CYLINDER.

Study your model.

Such positions of the quarter cylinder as require the oblique line in drawing them are taken up here.

FIGURE 63 - 66 represent the vertical quarter cylinder. Figs. 67, 68, and 69 the horizontal quarter cylinder, and Figs. 70, 71, and 72 the receding quarter cylinder.

The vertical quarter cylinder, Figs. 63 - 66, may be drawn by using vanishing points if so desired. The vanishing points may be found by following the receding lines until they intercept the H. L.

PROBLEMS.

PROBLEM 1. FIG. 63. — *Draw a vertical quarter cylinder below and at the left of the eye with the curved face to the left. To the right.*

PROBLEM 2. FIG. 66. — *Draw a vertical quarter cylinder below and at the right of the eye with the curved face to the right. To the left.*

PROBLEM 3. FIG. 65. — *Below the eye, draw a vertical quarter cylinder with the curved face toward you. To the right. To the left.*

PROBLEM 4. FIG. 64. — *Below the eye, draw a vertical quarter cylinder with the curved face away from you. With the curved face to the right. To the left.*

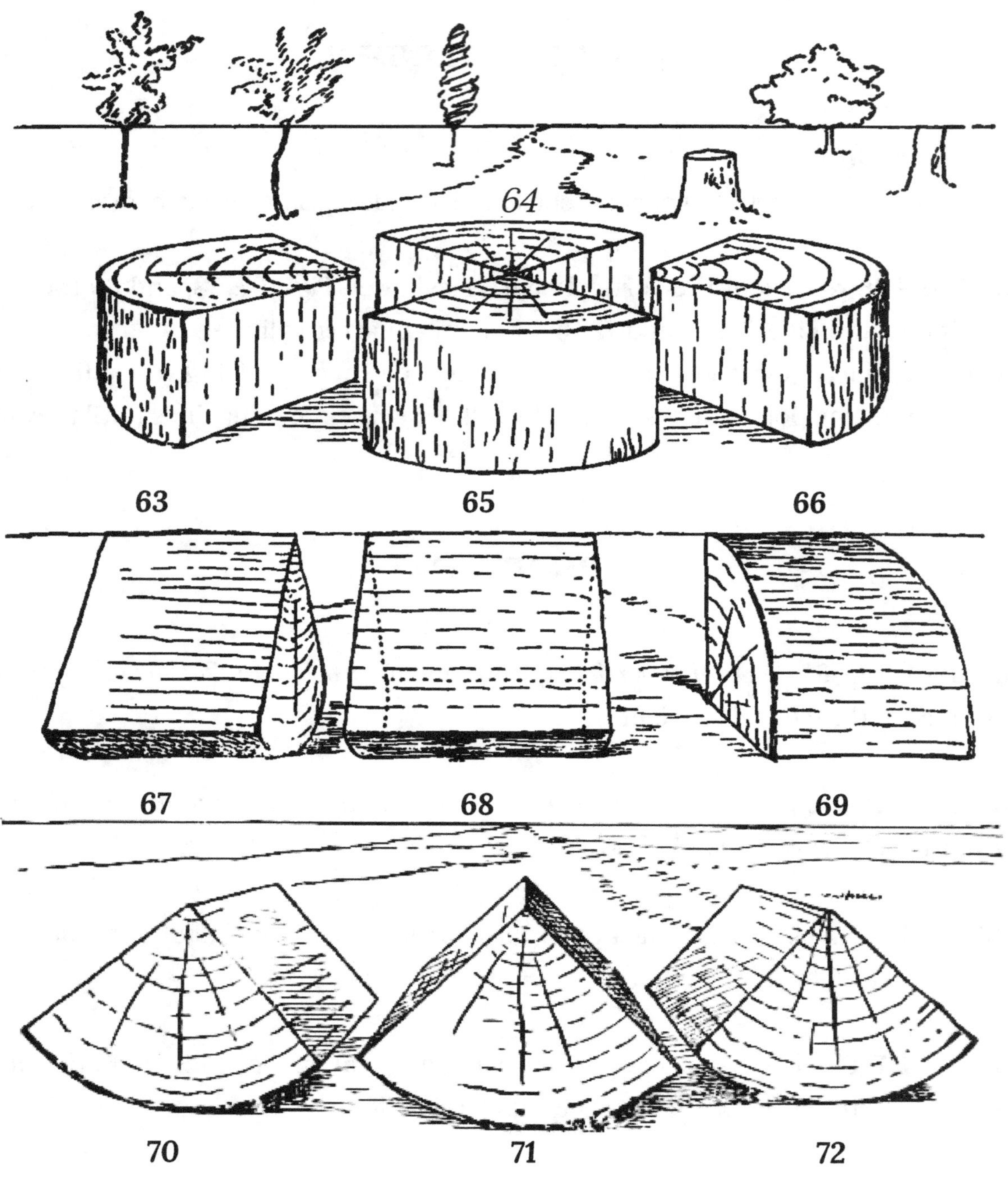

64
63
65
66
67
68
69
70
71
72

PROBLEM 5. FIG. 67. — *Below and at the left of the eye, draw a horizontal quarter cylinder with the curved face down. With the curved face away from you. With the curved face toward you.*

PROBLEM 6. FIG. 68. — *Below the eye, draw a horizontal quarter cylinder with the curved face down. Draw it at the right of the eye. Turn it so the curved face is toward you.*

Problem 7. — *Draw Fig. 69 with the curved face away from you.*

PROBLEM 8. FIG. 70. — *Below and at the left of the eye, draw a receding quarter cylinder with the curved face down. To the left. To the right.*

PROBLEM 9. FIG. 71. — *Below the eye, draw a receding quarter cylinder with the curved face down. Remove the nearer end showing the inside.*

Problem 10. — *Draw Fig. 72 and remove the nearer end. The left side. Both the end and side.*

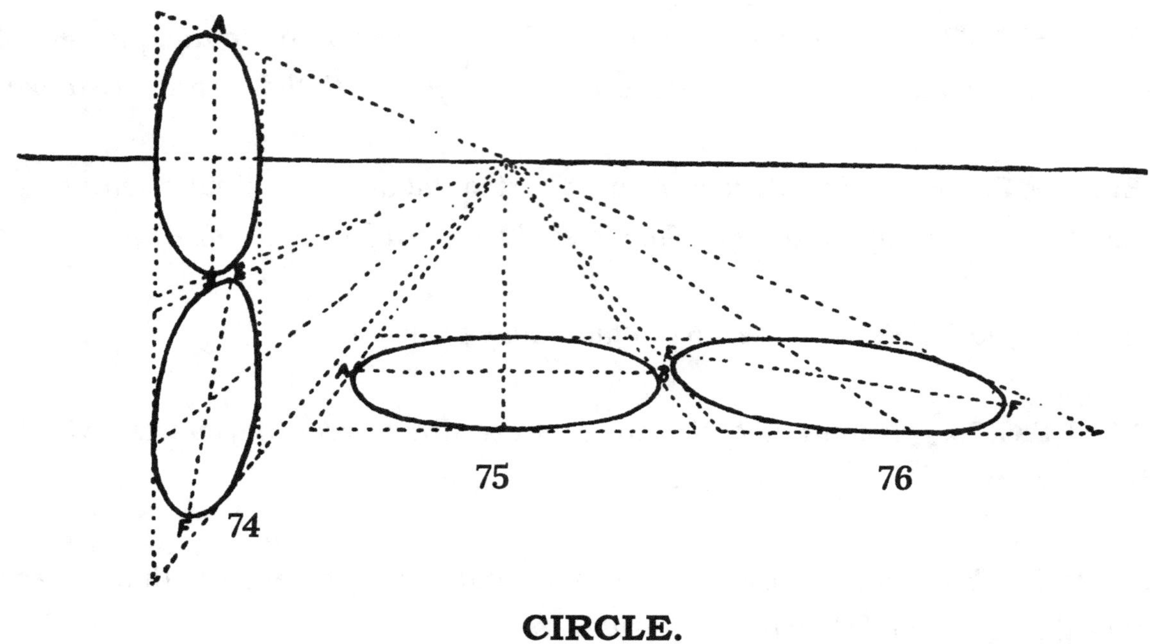

CIRCLE.

FIGURES 73 AND 74. — When a vertical receding circle is at the left of the eye, its longer diameter AB is vertical. When the circle is below and at the right of the eye, as in Fig. 74, the longer diameter is no longer vertical but slightly inclined as EF, and the further below the eye, the more inclined it becomes.

This is the same when the vertical receding circle is above and at the right, above and at the left, and below and at the right of the eye.

This can easily be seen on the model. Hold the end of a horizontal cylinder at the right of the eye and gradually lower it below the eye, and note the change of the longer diameter from a vertical to the oblique. Hold it above and at the right, above and at the left, and below and at the left of the eye, and a like change will be seen.

If the vertical receding circle is drawn in a square, as in Figs. 73 and 74, this will be demonstrated clearly.

FIGURES 75 AND 76. — In the horizontal receding circle, the same change in the longer diameter takes place as the circle is moved to the right or left. AB, the longer diameter in Fig. 75, is changed in Fig. 76 as shown by EF. The same change would take place below and at the left, above and at the right, and above and at the left of the eye.

PROBLEMS.

PROBLEM 1. FIG. 73. — *At the left of the eye, draw a vertical receding square, and in it inscribe a circle.*

PROBLEM 2. FIG. 74. — *Below and at the left of the eye, draw a vertical receding square, and in it inscribe a circle.*

Problem 3. — *Below and at the right of the eye, draw a vertical receding square, and in it inscribe a circle.*

PROBLEM 4. FIG. 75. — *Directly below the eye, draw a horizontal receding square and in it inscribe a circle.*

PROBLEM 5. FIG. 76. — *Below and at the right of the eye, draw a horizontal receding square and in it inscribe a circle.*

Problem 6. — *Below and at the left of the eye, draw a horizontal receding square and in it inscribe a circle.*

QUARTER AND THREE-QUARTER SPHERES.

The quarter and three-quarter spheres are combinations of the vertical, horizontal, receding, and oblique lines, both straight and curved, and require a very close study of the model to get a correct understanding of each position.

Like the cylinder and prism, the study of the quarter and three-quarter sphere is divided into the vertical, horizontal, and receding.

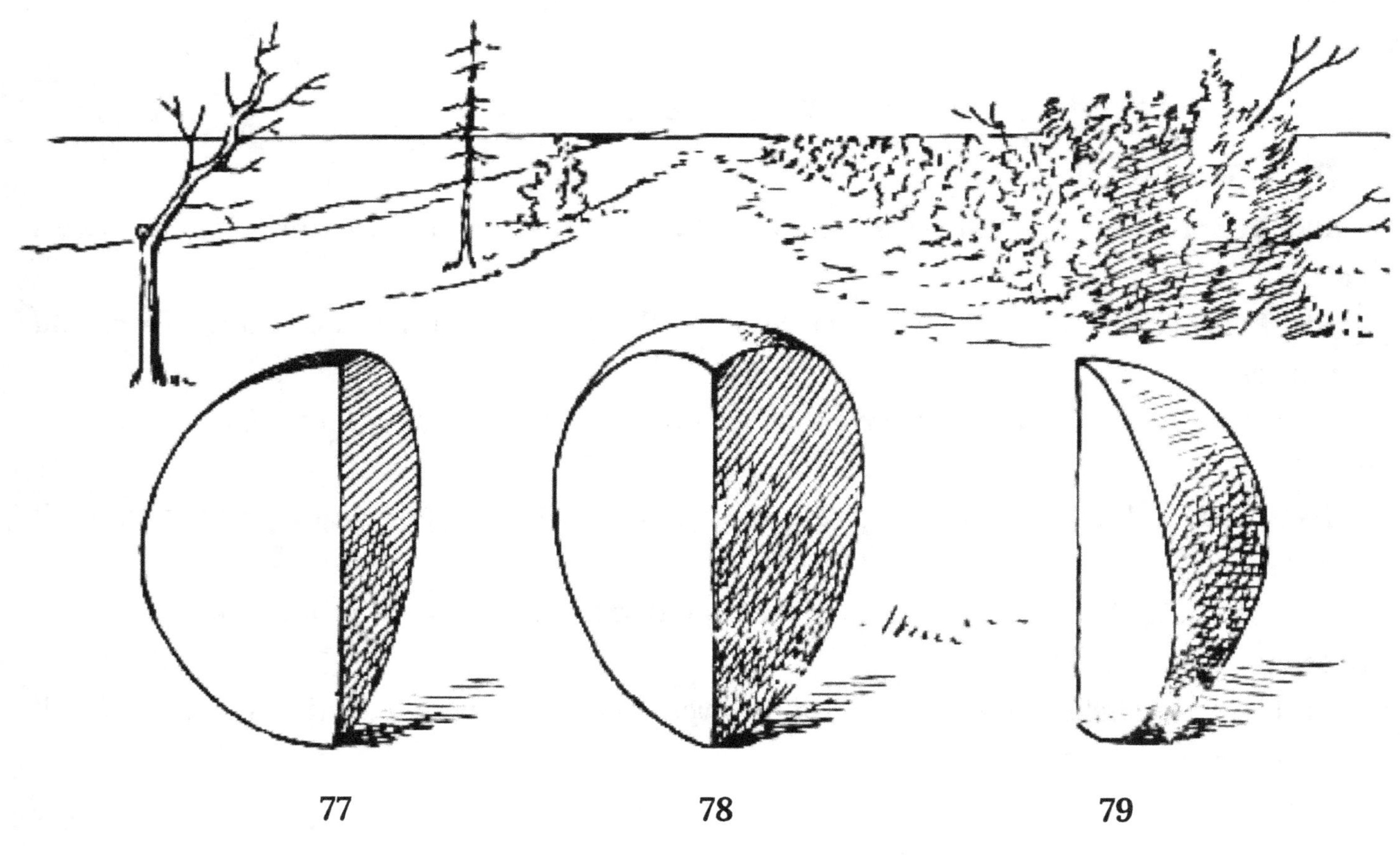

77   78   79

VERTICAL QUARTER SPHERE.

FIGURES 77, 78, AND 79 are vertical quarter spheres below and at the left, below, and below and at the right of the eye.

194

Observe that each vertical quarter sphere may be drawn in eight positions according to the direction of the curved face. (1) When the curved face is toward you. (2) When the curved face is away from you, Fig. 78. (3) When the curved face is to the right. (4) When the curved face is to the left. (5) When the curved face is to the left and away, Fig. 77. (6) When the curved face is to the left and toward you. (7) When the curved face is to the right and away from you. (8) When the curved face is to the right and toward you, Fig. 79.

Hold the model in each of these positions until learned.

PROBLEMS.

PROBLEM 1. FIG. 78. — *Below the eye, draw a vertical quarter sphere with the curved face away from you. Toward you. With the curved face to the right. To the left. With the curved face to the left and away from you. To the right and away. To the right and toward you. To the left and toward you.*

PROBLEM 2. FIG. 77. — *Below and at the left of the eye, draw a vertical quarter sphere with the curved face at the left and away from you. At the left and toward you. At the right and away from you. At the right and toward you. At the left. At the right. Toward you. Away from you.*

PROBLEM 3. FIG. 79. — *Below and at the right of the eye, draw a vertical quarter sphere with the curved face at the right and toward you. With the curved face toward you. Away from you.*

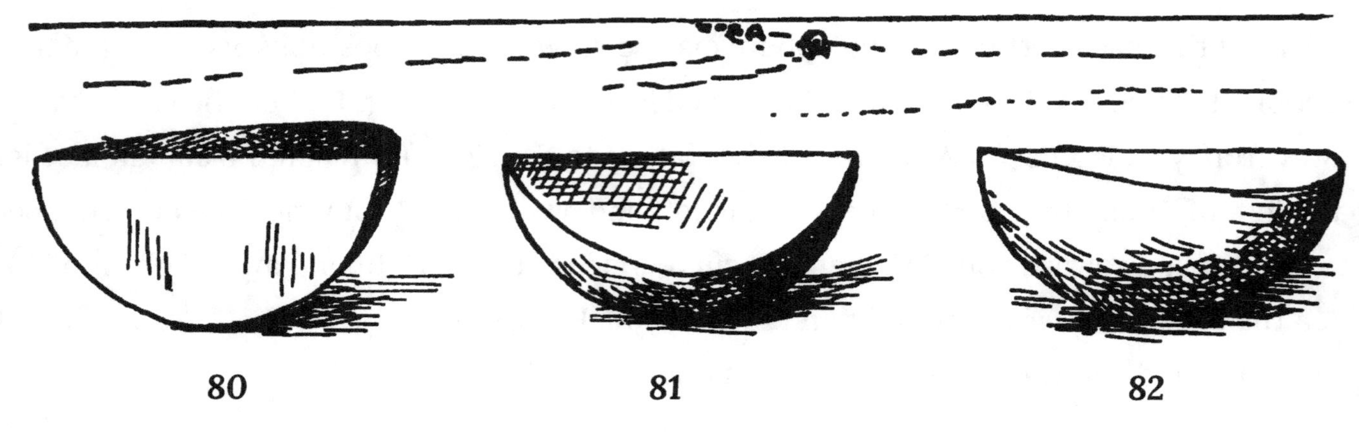

80   **81**   **82**

HORIZONTAL QUARTER CYLINDER.

Study your model.

FIGURES 80, 81, AND 82 are horizontal quarter spheres below and at the left, below, and below and at the right of the eye.

Observe that each horizontal quarter sphere may be drawn in eight positions. (1) When the curved face is down, Fig. 81. (2) Up. (3) Toward you. (4) Away from you. (5) Down and away from you, Fig. 80. (6) Up and away from you. (7) Down and toward you, Fig. 82. (8) Up and toward you.

PROBLEMS.

PROBLEM 1. FIG. 81. — *Below the eye, draw a horizontal quarter sphere with the curved face down. With the curved face up. Toward you. Away from you. Down and toward you. Down and away from you. Up and toward you. Up and away from you.*

PROBLEM 2. FIG. 80. — *Below and at the left of the eye, draw a horizontal quarter sphere with the curved face down and away from you. Up and away from you. Down and toward you. Down. Away from you.*

PROBLEM 3. FIG. 82. — *Below and at the right of the eye, draw a horizontal quarter sphere with the curved face down and toward you. Down and away from you. Down.*

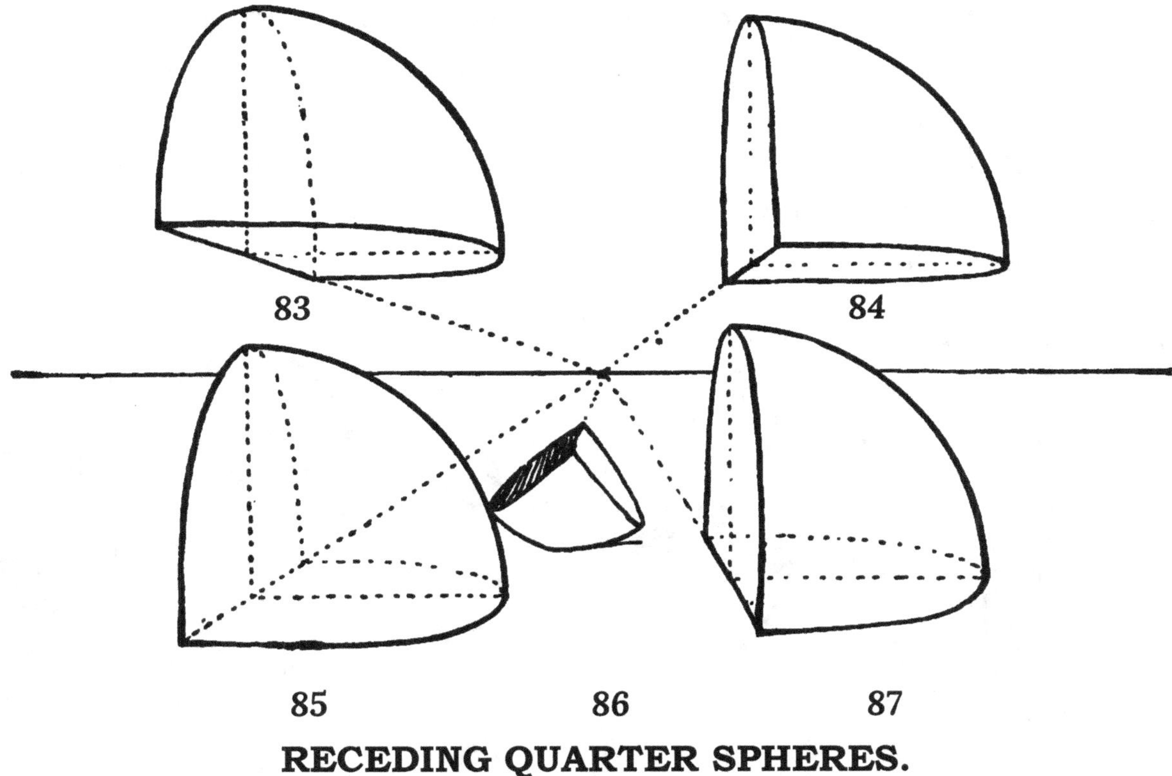

RECEDING QUARTER SPHERES.

FIGURES 83 – 87 are receding quarter spheres below and at the left, below, below and at the right, above and at the right, and above and at the left of the eye.

Observe that each receding quarter sphere may be drawn in each of the following positions. (1) With the curved face down, Fig. 86. (2) Up. (3) To the right. (4) To the left. (5) To the right and up, Figs. 83, 84, 85, and 87. (6) To the left and up. (7) To the right and down. (8) To the left and down.

PROBLEMS.

PROBLEM 1. FIG. 85. — *Below and at the left of the eye, draw a receding quarter sphere with the curved face at the right and up. At the left and up. At the left and down. At the right and down. At the left and down. Down. At the right. At the left.*

PROBLEM 2. FIG. 87. — *Below and at the right of the eye, draw a receding quarter sphere with the curved face at the right and up. At the right and down. At the left and up. At the left and down. With the curved face down.*

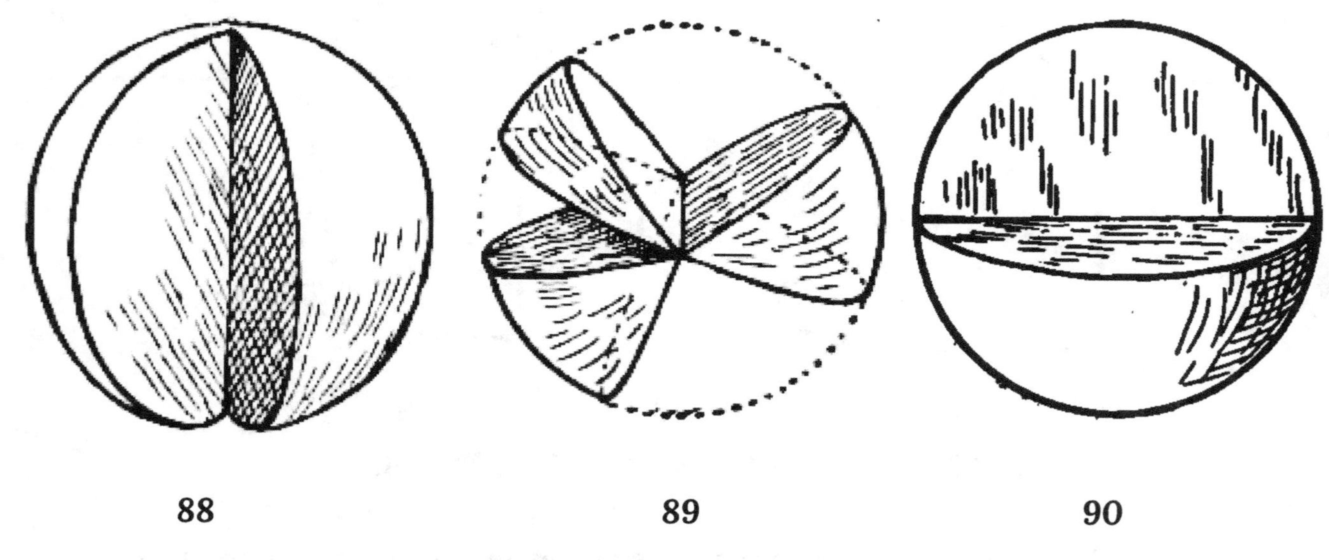

88   89   90

THREE QUARTERS SPHERE.

FIGURES 88 is a sphere below and at the left of the eye with a vertical quarter sphere cut from the face toward you.

FIGURES 89 is a sphere below the eye with two receding quarters and an eighth cut, one from above, one from below and at the right, and one from the left of the sphere.

FIGURES 90 is a sphere below the eye with a horizontal quarter cut above and toward you.

PROBLEMS.

PROBLEM 1. FIG. 88. — *Draw a sphere below and at the left of the eye and cut a vertical quarter from the face toward you.*

Problem 2. — Draw a sphere directly below the eye and from in front cut a vertical quarter. A horizontal quarter. From the right and toward you, cut a vertical quarter. From the left and toward you.

PROBLEM 3. FIG. 89. — *Directly below the eye, draw a sphere and from the upper face cut a receding quarter. From the lower face. From the right face. Left face. Cut a quarter from the right face and above. From the left and above. From the left and below.*

PROBLEM 4. FIG. 90. — *Directly below the eye, draw a sphere and from in front and above cut a quarter. Cut an eighth. Cut a quarter from in front. From in front and below. Cut an eighth from in front.*

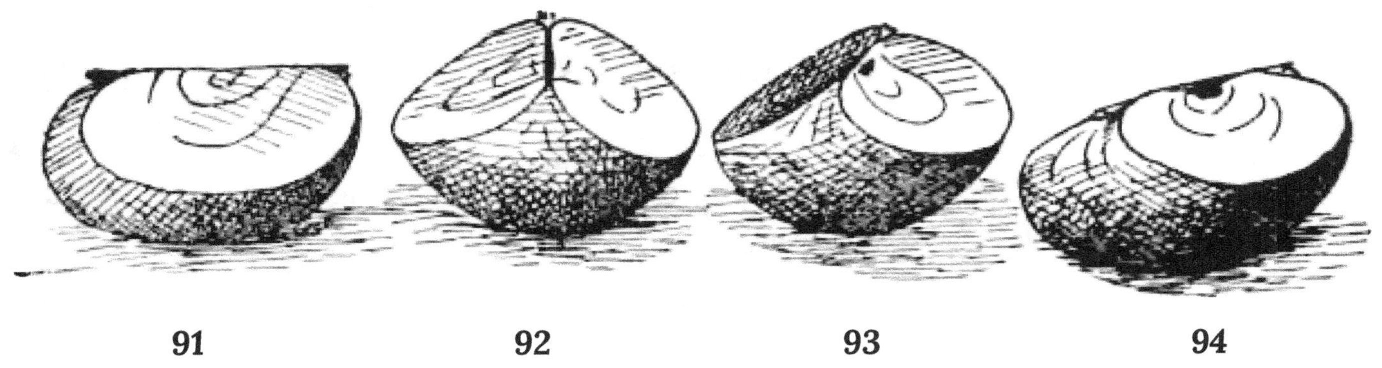

91   92   93   94

FIGURES 91 – 96 are some simple applications of the quarter and three-quarters spheres.

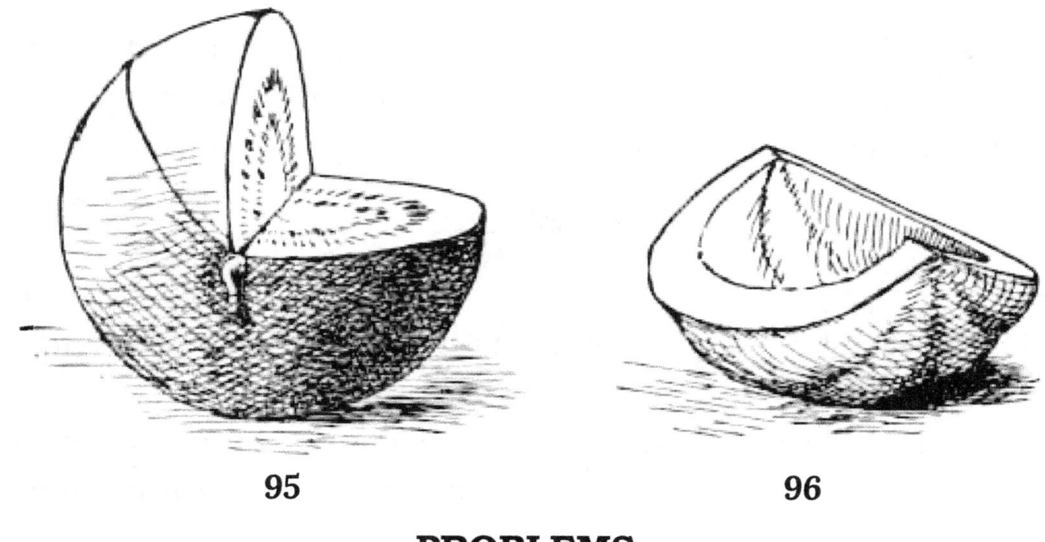

95   96

PROBLEMS.

Problem 1. — *Draw an apple quarter in a horizontal position below the eye. Receding. Vertical.*

PROBLEM 2. FIG. 95. — *Draw a watermelon below and at the left of the eye and at the right and above cut out a receding quarter. At the left and above. Above. At the right. At the left.*

Problem 3. — *Draw a melon below the eye and from in front cut out a horizontal eighth. A quarter.*

Problem 4. — *Draw Fig. 96 on the blackboard.*

DRAWING THE PRISM.

These general directions are to show how to draw objects containing oblique lines and having the general shape of a triangular prism.

The process is much the same as in drawing the cube.

Directions.[37]

37   Edge or edges and small letters will refer to the real object, and line or lines and large letters to corresponding parts in the drawing the same as in drawing the cube.

200

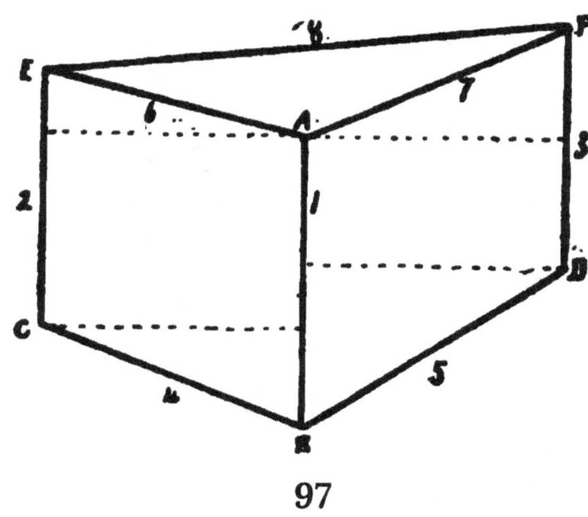

(1) Place the prism below the eye as in Fig. 97. (2) The unit of measure[38] is the nearest vertical edge which may be drawn as long as the height of the prism is to be. (3) Draw the unit of measure which is line 1. (4) To find line 2, compare the length of *edge* 1 with the horizontal distance between edges 1 and 2 and make the same comparison in the drawing with line 1. Not knowing the length of line 1, simply draw an indefinite vertical line. (5) Find and draw line 3 in the same manner. (6) To find corner C, pass the pencil horizontally through corner c and note where the pencil crosses edge 1. Mark this point on line 1 and from it draw a light horizontal line. Where this line crosses line 2, it will mark corner C. (7) Draw line 4. (8) Find corner D and draw line 5 in the same manner. (9) To find corner E, draw through corner A a light horizontal line to line 2. Pass the pencil horizontally through corner a and note how far corner e is above it. Mark this distance on line 2 above the light horizontal line and it will give corner E. Draw line 6. (10) Find corner F and draw line 7 in the same manner. (11) Draw line 8. Lines 6 and 7 are parallel; that is, they converge to the same point with lines 3 and 5.

38   Any vertical or horizontal line may be used as the unit of measure. These directions relate to all vertical prisms.

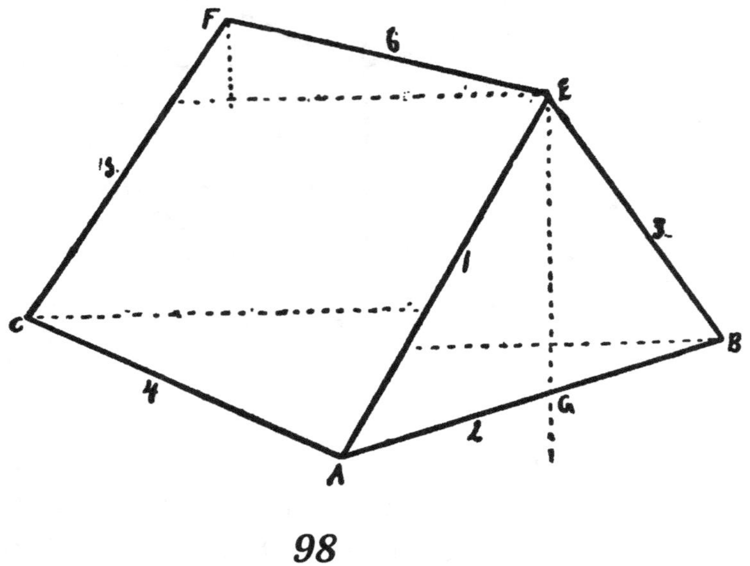

98

Draw the vertical prism in various positions above and below the level of the eye.

How to draw the triangular prism when all the edges are receding.

(1) Place the prism as in Fig. 98. (2) Choose a point to represent corner E and from it draw a light indefinite vertical line. (3) Pass the pencil vertically through corner e and note how far corner a is at the left of it. Mark this point in the drawing the required distance at the left of the vertical line for corner A. Draw line 1. (4) To find corner B, pass the pencil horizontally through corner b and note where it crosses edge 1. Mark this point on line 1 and from it draw a light, indefinite, horizontal line. Place corner B in this line as near as possible and draw lines 2 and 3. (5) The position of corners A and B may now be proven by using the distance eg as a unit of measure and making corresponding measurements in the drawing with EG. (6) To find corner C, pass the pencil horizontally through corner c and note where it crosses edge 1. Mark this point on line 1 and from it take an indefinite horizontal line. Compare the distance eg with the

distance from line 1 and the horizontal line to corner C and make the same comparison in the drawing with EG. Draw line 4. (7) To find corner F, draw a light, indefinite, horizontal line from E. Compare eg with the distance from e to a point even with corner f, and at the same time note how far corner f is above the pencil and make the same comparison in the drawing with EG and mark corner F. (8) Draw lines 5 and 6.

Problem 1. — *Draw a triangular prism below the level of the eye.*

Problem 2. — *Draw a triangular prism above the level of the eye.*

Problem 3. — *Draw a triangular prism on a level with the eye.*

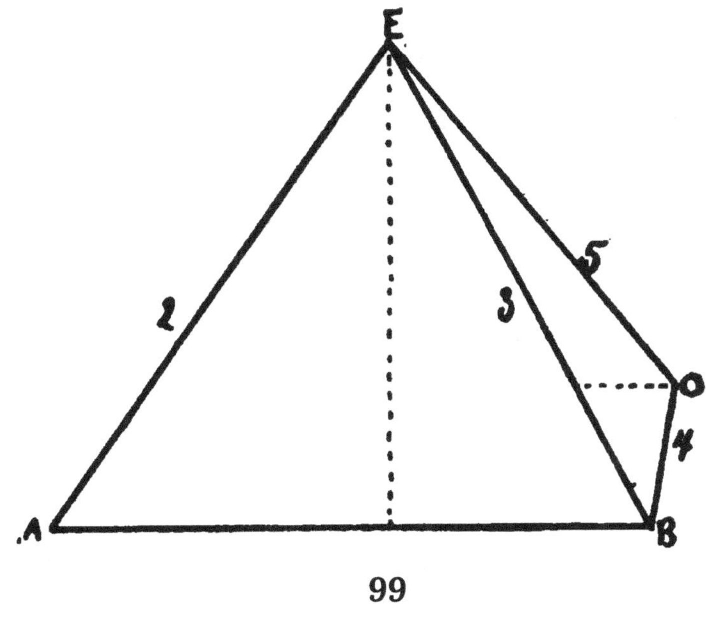

DRAWING THE PYRAMID.

When the pyramid contains a horizontal line, it may be drawn as follows:

(1) Place the pyramid as in Fig. 99. (2) Draw the nearest horizontal line AB for the unit of measure. (3) To find the apex E, pass the pencil vertically through e and note where the pencil

crosses edge 1. Mark this point on line 1 and from it draw an indefinite vertical line. The apex E will be in this line. (4) Compare the length of ab with the distance from edge 1 to the apex e and in the drawing make the same comparison with line 1. (5) Draw lines EA and EB. (6) To find corner C, pass the pencil horizontally through corner C and note where it crosses edge 3. Mark this point on line 3 and from it draw a light, indefinite, horizontal line. Corner C will be in this line. (7) Compare the length of edge 1 with the distance from edge 3 out to corner c and make the same comparison in the drawing with line 1. (8) Draw line EC.

Trust the eye and measure less and less with the pencil. The eye will become far more accurate than any measurement that can be made with the pencil.

Problem 1. — *Draw a pyramid similar to Fig. 99 above the eye.*

Problem 2. — *Draw a pyramid containing a horizontal line with the base on a level with the eye.*

Problem 3. — *Draw a pyramid containing a horizontal line below and slightly at the right of the eye.*

Problem 4. — *Draw a pyramid composed entirely of receding lines. (1) Below the level of the eye. (2) Above the level of the eye. (3) With the base on a level with the eye.*

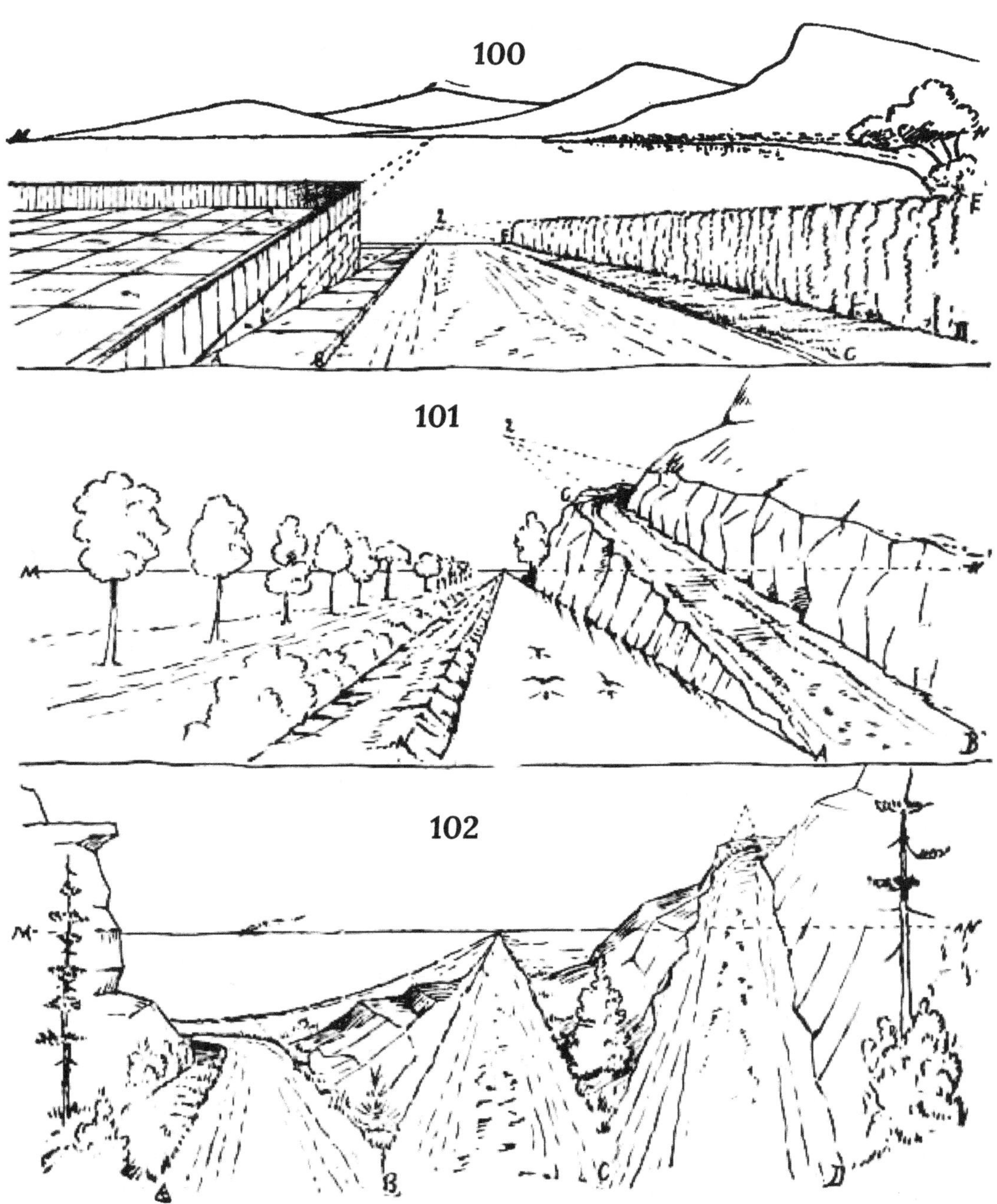

100
101
102

VANISHING POINTS.

All parallel receding lines converge at a point called its vanishing point (V.P.)

When the receding lines are parallel with the ground plane, they converge at a point in the H.L. In Figs. 15 - 19, the receding lines are parallel with the ground plane and therefore converge at a point in the H.L.

When the receding lines are not parallel with the ground plane, they converge at a point outside of the H.L. For example, in Fig. 100, the receding lines of the promenade on the left, being parallel with the ground plane, converge at a point in the H.L. But the receding lines of the sidewalk, road, and hedge, being at an angle with the ground plane, converge at a point outside of the H.L. As the lines run downhill, they converge at a point below the H.L.

In Fig. 101, the receding lines of the canal, being parallel with the ground plane, converge at a point in the H.L. But the receding lines of the road on the right, being at an angle with the ground plane, converge at a point outside of the H.L. As the lines run uphill, they converge at a point above the H.L.

In Fig. 102, there are three roads. The one on the right going uphill converges at a point above the H.L. The one on the left, going downhill, converges at a point below the H.L. The road in the middle is level and converges in the H.L.

To recapitulate:

There are two classes of receding lines. (1) Those that converge at the C. of V. (2) Those that converge outside of the C. of V.

Those that converge outside of the C. of V. may be divided into three classes. (1) Those that converge in the H.L. (2) Those that converge below the H.L. (3) Those that converge above the H.L.

Those that converge in the H.L. are said to be level, parallel with the ground plane; those converging below the H.L. run downhill; those that converge above the H.L. run uphill.

Receding lines are divided into three classes. (1) Horizontal receding lines which vanish at the C. of V. and are at right angles with the picture plane. (2) Oblique horizontal receding lines which vanish in the H.L. outside of the C. of V. (3) Oblique receding lines which vanish outside of the H.L.

Figure 100 may be drawn as follows:
(1) Draw the H.L. (2) Choose the C. of V. and draw the promenade on the left. (3) Choose V.P. 2 anywhere below the H.L. (4) Choose the points B, C, D, and E and from each draw a receding line to V.P. 2. (5) Choose the point F[39] for the end of the road and hedge. (6) Add the details.

Figure 101 may be drawn as follows:
(1) Draw the H.L. (2) Choose the C. of V. and draw the canal. (3) Choose the V.P. 2. (4) Choose the points A and B. and from each draw a receding line to V.P. 2. (5) Choose the point C and draw the road. (6) Add the details.

All the different classes of receding lines may be used in the same drawing and in drawing the same object. For example, in Fig. 104, the road begins level, runs downhill, uphill, then is level again.

Figure 103 shows the process of drawing Fig. 104, as follows:
(1) Draw the H.L. (2) Choose the C. of V. which we will call V.P. 1. (3) Choose the points A and B and from each draw a receding line to V.P. 1. (4) Choose the point C and draw the horizontal line CD. (5) Choose the V.P. 2 below the H.L. and to it draw a receding line from C and D. (6) Choose the point E and draw the horizontal line EF. (7) Choose the V.P. 3 above the H.L. and to it draw a receding line from E and F. (8) Choose the point G and draw the horizontal line GH. (9) From the points G and H draw a receding line to V.P. 1. (10) Draw the details.

Problem 1. — *Draw a road similar to Fig. 104, running downhill and then up to the C. of V.*

39   This point must be taken this side of the V.P.

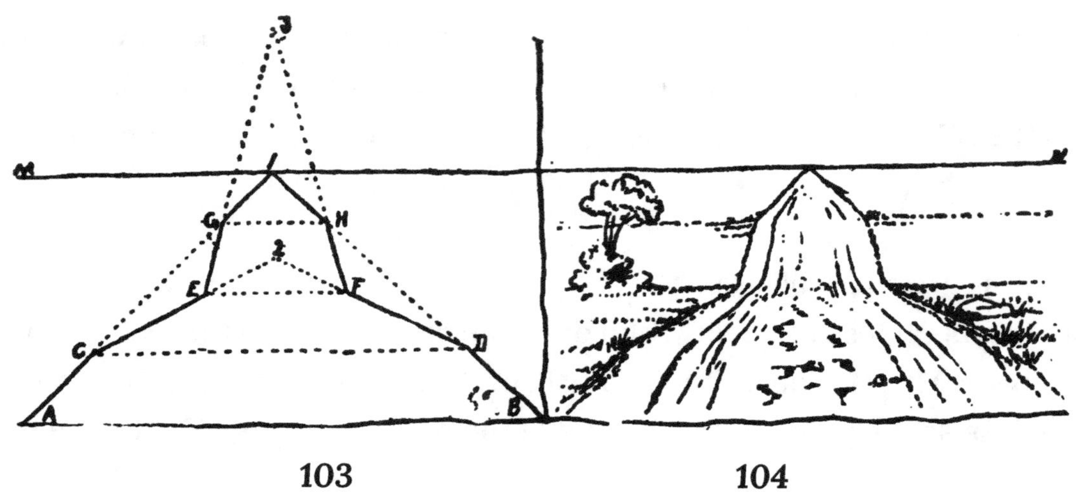

103

104

Problem 2. — Draw a road running uphill, then on a level to the C. of V.

Problem 3. — Draw a road similar to Fig. 104 on the blackboard.

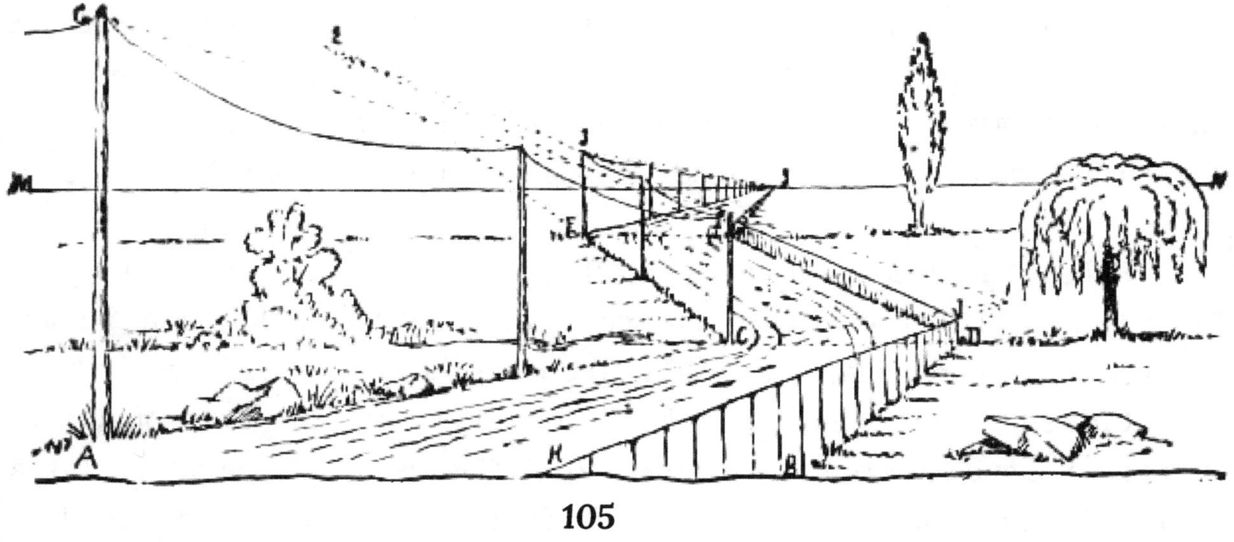

105

FIGURE 105 is similar to Fig. 104, except that there is a bend in the road which throws the V.P.s to one side. It is drawn as follows:

(1) Draw the H.L. (2) Choose the points A and B. (3) Choose the V.P. 1 and to it draw a receding

line from A and B. (4) Choose the point C and draw the horizontal line C D. (5) Choose the V.P. 2 and to it draw a receding line from C and D. (6) Choose the point E and draw the horizontal line EF. (7) Choose the V.P. 3 and to it draw a receding line from E and F. (8) In like manner choose the points G and H and draw the telegraph line and fence. (9) Draw the details.

Problem 1. — Draw Fig. 105 on the blackboard from memory.
Problem 2. — Substitute for the telegraph line in Fig. 105 aboard fence.
Problem 3. — Draw the willow tree in Fig. 105 on the blackboard.

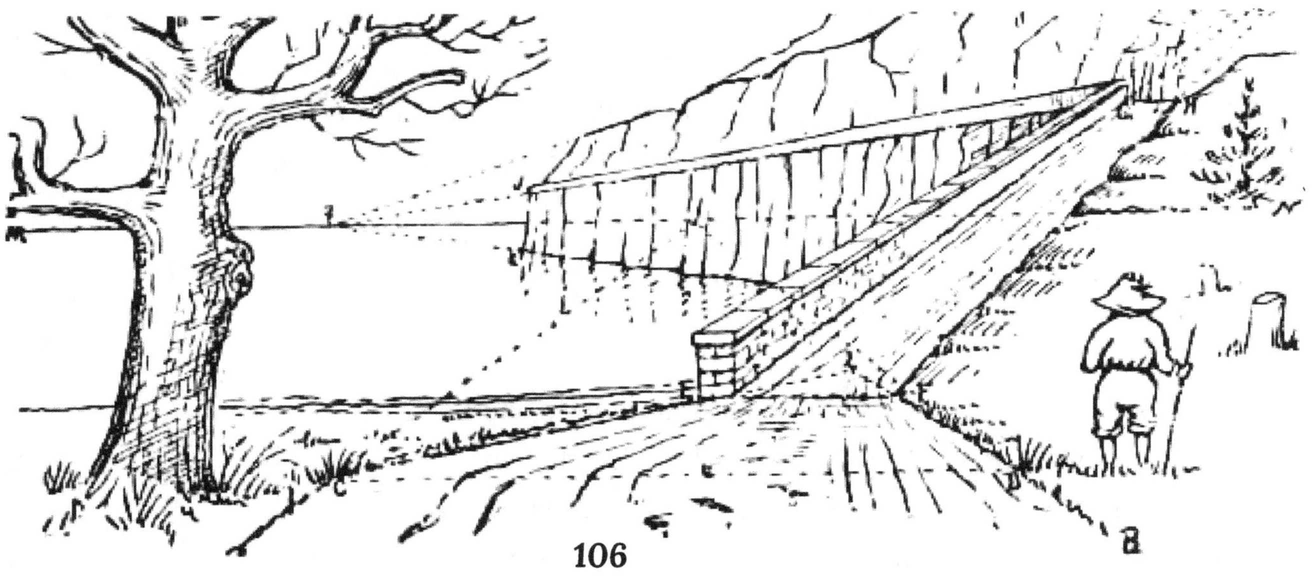

106

The road in Fig. 106 begins level, runs downhill, uphill, then is level again because it vanishes in the H.L.

Figure 106 may be drawn as follows:
(1) Draw the H.L. (2) Choose the V.P. 1 for the C. of V. (3) Choose the points A and B and from

each draw a receding line to V.P. 1. (4) Choose the point C and draw the horizontal line C.D. (5) Choose the V.P. 2 and to it draw a receding line from the points C and D. (6) Choose the point E and draw the horizontal line E.F. (7) Choose the V.P. 3 and to it draw a receding line from the points E and F. (8) Choose the point G and draw the horizontal line G.H. (9) From G draw a receding line to V.P. 4. (10) Choose the point J and draw J.K. (11) Through K from V.P. 4 draw a receding line. (12) Draw the wall alongside of the road. (13) Draw the details.

Problem 1. — Draw Fig. 106 on the blackboard from memory.
Problem 2. — Substitute in place of the middle road in Fig. 102 a railroad.
Problem 3. — Substitute in place of the telegraph line in Fig. 105 a row of trees.
Problem 4. — Place the shed in Fig. 41 on the bank of the canal in Fig. 101.
Problem 5. — Substitute the barn in Fig. 61 in place of the promenade in Fig. 100.

REVIEW QUESTIONS.

1. What class of objects is the triangular prism made the basis of?

2. What is the most prominent figure in the triangular prism?

3. In what three positions may the prism be studied?

4. What four classes of lines are used in drawing the triangular prism?

5. What three edges in the triangular prism are parallel?

6. Into what four parts is the vertical prism studied?

7. What classes of lines does the vertical prism containing a horizontal line have?

8. In Fig. 5 how is corner F found?

9. When a vertical prism contains a receding line, what classes of lines does it contain?

10. What is the base line?

11. What is the picture plane?

12. What is the ground plane?

13. What is the difference between the picture plane and ground plane?

14. Point to the picture plane in Fig. 18. The ground plane.

15. What is the central ray?

16. Why is not the central ray visible in the drawings? What point marks it?

17. How many central rays does each picture contain?

18. Do all parallel receding lines converge at a point?

19. What two classes of receding lines are there?

20. What receding lines converge at the C. of V.?

21. How many V.P.s may there be in a picture? How many C.s of V.?

22. In what four positions may the horizontal prism be studied?

23. When the horizontal prism rests on its base, what classes of lines are used when drawing it?

24. When the horizontal prism contains a vertical line, what classes of lines are used when drawing it?

25. In what four positions may the receding prism be studied?

26. When the base of the receding prism contains a horizontal line, what classes of lines does it contain?

27. When the receding prism contains a vertical line, what classes of lines are used when drawing it?

28. Where do receding lines parallel with the ground plane converge?

29. Where do receding lines converge that run downhill? That run uphill?

30. When are receding lines level?

31. When do receding lines converge at the C. of V.?

32. When do receding lines converge below the level of the eye? When above the level of the eye?

33. In Fig. 100 what part is level and what part runs downhill?

PART IV.

UNITY

It is natural for the untrained eye when drawing to see the details separately and not the whole form of which the details are a part.

It is easy to see the eyes, nose, mouth, or any particular part of the human head taken alone, but difficult to see these parts together as a unit, as a single form. Yet this power must be acquired before one can draw with ease and accuracy. We must gain the power of seeing objects as a whole, as a unit.

We often allow our knowledge to deceive our eyes. For example, when drawing a tree, our knowledge tells us that the foliage is composed of individual leaves, and using that knowledge to draw with, more than the eyes, we try to represent the individual leaves and, of course, fail. Unless very near to the tree, we cannot see the leaves separately but only the mass of leaves taken together. The whole is of more importance than the part, so it should be the aim to represent the tree as a whole, to draw the general shape as in Fig. 1 and then add the details as in Fig. 2. A great aid in seeing objects as a unit is to look through the half-closed eyes, making the object look blurred so that the details are eliminated and the mass is plainly seen.

All forms, however complicated they may be, are composed of simple forms or figures which, if recognized, will make the drawing of them comparatively simple and easy. As soon as we recognize figures we are acquainted with in complicated forms, they cease to a large extent to be complicated.

For example, the dog (Fig. 4) as he lies curled up asleep has an elliptical outline like Fig. 3. Without noticing the details at all, if this elliptical outline is drawn, it will give the general proportion to which the details may be added with little trouble. The ellipse gives the general proportion which is constantly before the eye and allows the mind to concentrate on the de-

1
2
3
4
5
6
7
8

tails; otherwise, the mind must perform the double duty of holding the general proportion and at the same time drawing the parts.

The bird's nest (Fig. 5) is simply a circle with an elliptical opening, and the three birds (Figs. 6, 7, and 8) are based on the circle, the body being a circle to which are added the head, tail, and legs.

The most common figures are the triangle, square, rectangle, circle, and ellipse. With observation and practice, the most complicated forms may wholly or in part be separated into these simple figures, which, when recognized, make the drawing of them comparatively easy.

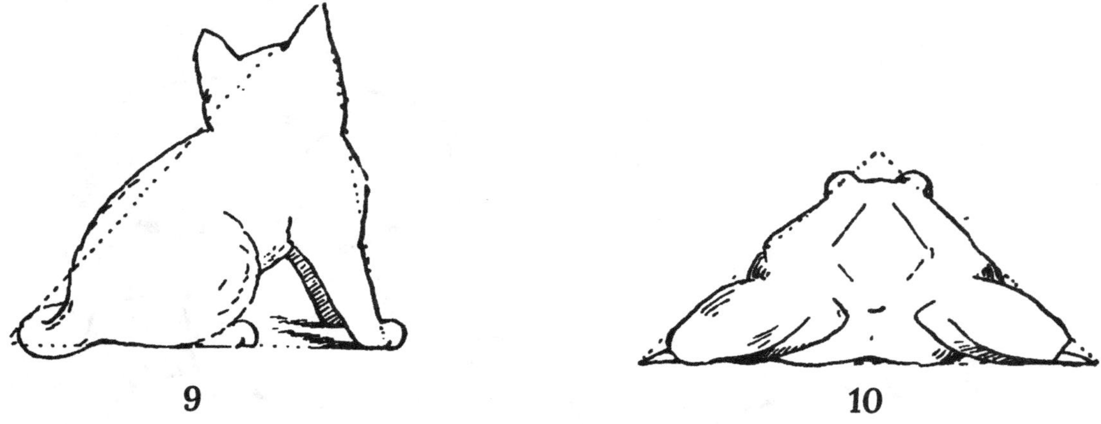

9

10

The kitten (Fig. 9) and the frog (Fig. 10) are triangular in shape.

11

12

The puppy (Fig. 11) and the bear (Fig. 12) are based on the rectangle.

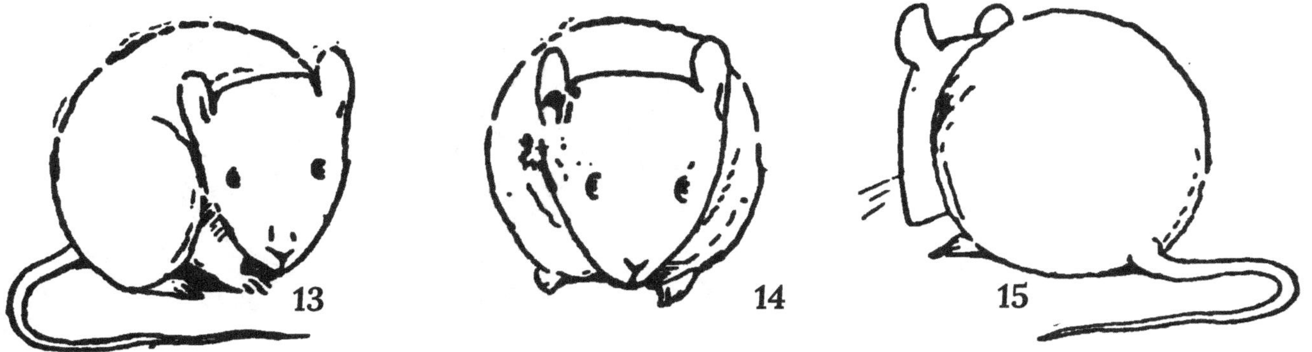

The three mice (Figs. 13, 14, and 15) are circular in form and the drawing of them is based on the circle.

The two hogs (Figs. 16 and 17) are based on the ellipse which is indicated by the dotted line.

Few would suspect that the human head could contain these simple figures, yet they are as common there as in other forms much more simple.

FIGURES 18, 19, AND 20 are triangular in shape. The face and hair of Fig. 18 are each triangular. The cap of Fig. 19 is rectangular and the collar of the coat triangular.

FIGURES 21, 22, AND 23 are each square or rectangular.

FIGURES 12 contains two rectangles and a circle. The square of which Fig. 23 is composed may be divided into two triangles.

FIGURES 24 is elliptical. Figs. 25 and 26 are based on the circle.

27

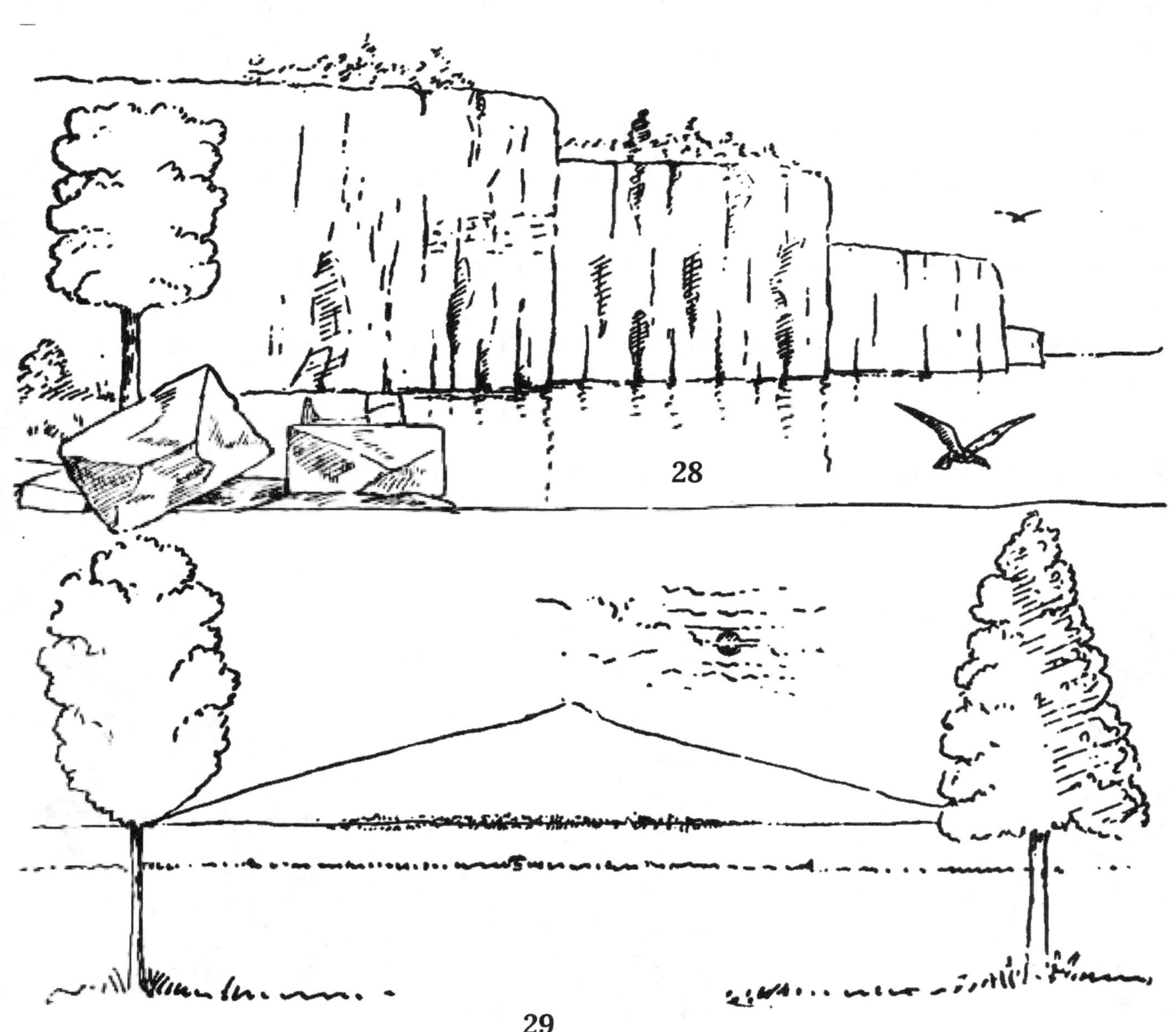

28

29

It is a little more difficult to recognize familiar figures in landscapes on account of the perspective deceiving the eye, but close observation will show them.

FIGURES 27 is composed of triangles. The water, the land, the tree-top, the bushes, wood pile, front, and roof of the cabin are each triangular in shape.

FIGURES 28, in the same manner, is made up of rectangles.

FIGURES 29 contains two triangles, one ellipse, and two rectangles.

These examples are to show how forms in nature are full of simple figures familiar to all. We can acquire the habit of seeing them by observation. Study the drawings in this book and point out these familiar figures. When walking along, notice the shape of the side of a building or any enclosed space, the shape of a leaf, plant, or flower, shrub or tree. Notice the form of a distant mountain, hill or plain, a wood, a field of grain, a meadow, or a clump of trees. Learn to group the form enclosed by lines, to see form by areas. This is more masterly than to see form line by line.

Cultivate habits of observation, and in a short time the power of seeing any number of objects as a unit will be acquired. Drawing will then receive a new light, become far more interesting and simple.

30
31
32
33
34
35

PROBLEMS.

Problem 1. — *Block in and draw Fig. 2.*

Problem 2. — *Block in and draw a maple tree from nature.*

Problem 3. — *Block in and draw Fig. 4. Draw it from memory on the blackboard.*

Problem 4. — *Block in and draw Figs. 5 and 6. Draw them from memory on the blackboard.*

Problem 5. — *Draw Fig. 7 and 8 on the same limb side by side.*

Problem 6. — *Block in and draw Fig. 9. Draw from memory on the blackboard.*

Problem 7. — *Block in and draw Fig. 10. Draw it from memory on the blackboard.*

Problem 8. — *Block in and draw Fig. 11. Fig. 12.*

Problem 9. — *Draw a circle and change it into Fig. 13. Into Fig. 14. Into Fig. 15.*

Problem 10. — *Draw an ellipse and change it into Fig. 16. Into Fig. 17.*

Problem 11. — *Block in and draw Fig. 18. Fig. 19. Fig. 20.*

Problem 12. — *Block in and draw Fig. 21. Fig. 22. Fig. 23.*

Problem 13. — *Draw an ellipse and change it into Fig. 24.*

Problem 14. — *Draw a circle and change it into Fig. 25.*

Problem 15. — *Block in and then draw Fig. 27. Draw it from memory on the blackboard.*

Problem 16. — *Block in and then draw Fig. 28.*

Problem 17. — *Block in and then draw Fig. 29.*

Problem 18. — *Draw two circles and change them into Fig. 30 and Fig. 31.*

Problem 19. — *Draw a circle and change it into Fig. 32. Draw Fig. 32 from memory on the blackboard.*

Problem 20. — *Block in and draw Fig. 33, using a circle as the basis of the body and head.*

Problem 21. — *Trace a circle in Figs. 34 and 35.*

Problem 22. — *Block in and draw Figs. 34 and 35.*

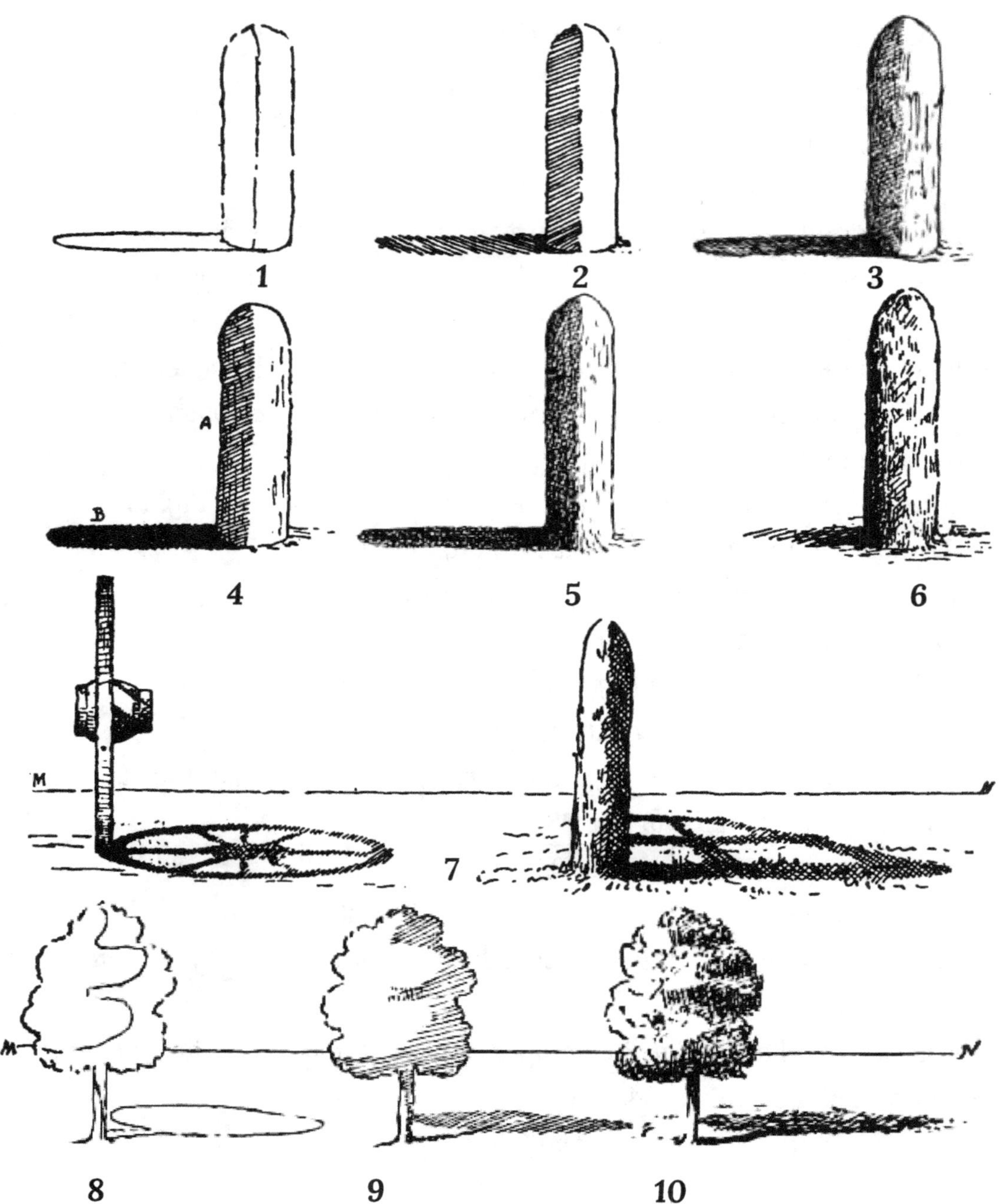

1
2
3
A
B
4
5
6
M
N
7
M
N
8
9
10

PART V.

LIGHT, SHADE, AND SHADOW

The primary effect of light, shade, and shadow is to give *relief, distinctness, solidity, and emphasis.*

Relief is the management of light, shade, and shadow so as to make an object stand out detached from the background. The jug (Fig. 12) seems to stand out from the wall back of it.

DISTINCTNESS *is the quality of being plainly seen.* The cube (Fig. 11) is much more plainly seen than it would be if simply drawn in outline. Fig. 3 shows more plainly than Fig. 1. The bear in Fig. 22 is more distinct than the trees beyond the cabin because he is shaded.

SOLIDITY *is having the appearance of substance, of being made of something.* Fig. 3 has the appearance of being more solid than Fig. 1. An object in simple outline has the appearance of solidity only in a limited degree. Draw Fig. 11 in outline and compare it with the shaded drawing of the same object, and this quality will be plainly seen.

EMPHASIS *in drawing is making an object or idea conspicuous.* Emphasis may be had by placing the object in such a light or shading it in such a manner as to attract the eye. The bear and the cabin in Fig. 22, by being shaded darker than the surrounding objects, are emphasized. The house in Fig. 21 is emphasized by being placed against the lighter sky beyond.

SHADES AND SHADOWS have no substance; they are simply the partial absence of light. But in drawing, they are treated as real objects as much so as solid forms.

SHADE is the dark part of an object, the part opposite the light, which is often called the shaded side. The shade is on the object and a part of it.

SHADOW is not a part of the object but is separate from it. It is caused by the object being in the path of the light, shutting it off and casting the shadow. In Fig. 4, A is in the shade and B is the shadow. In Fig. 11, the dark on the sides of the cube marked B and C are shades, and D is the shadow.

The process of shading is very simple; it is as follows:

PAPER. - Drawing paper should be used instead of common paper.

PENCILS. - A box containing four or more graded pencils should be used, though very good work may be done with only one pencil.

MODELS. - Plaster-of-Paris models are the best. If these cannot be procured, choose any light-colored box, free from markings or letters, and use it as a model.

DIRECTIONS. - Place the box, or a plaster-of-Paris cube, in such a manner that part will be in light and part in shade as in Fig. 11.

The highest light possible in the drawing will be the whiteness of the paper on which the drawing is made, and the lowest or deepest shade that can be made will be represented by the blackest mark that can be made with the softest pencil. These are the two extremes, beyond which it is impossible to go. Between these two extremes all the different shades are included.

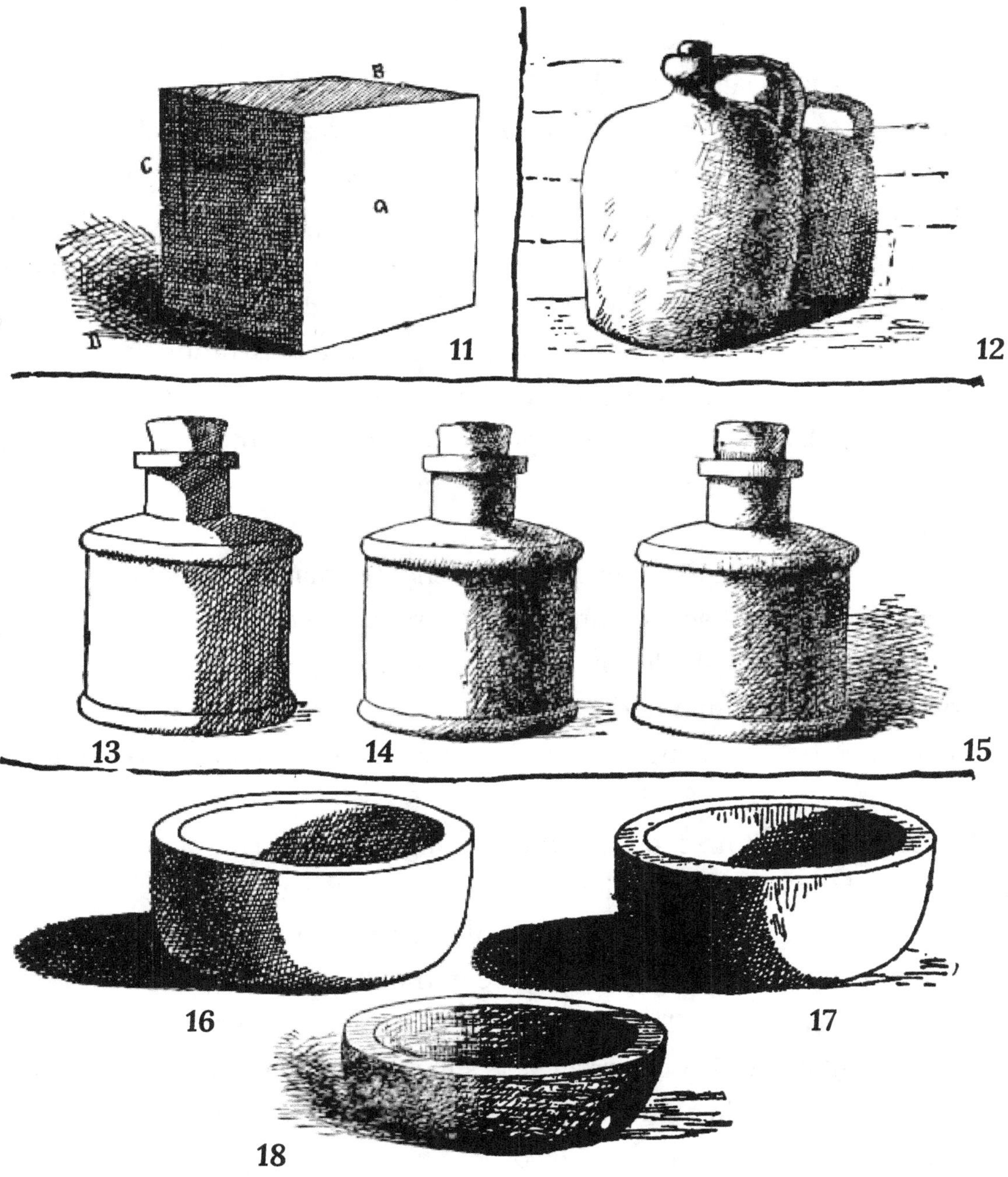

B
C
A
D
11
12
13
14
15
16
17
18

Make an outline of the box or cube. Look at the real box carefully and note the lightest side, and on the drawing mark this lightest side A. Note the side that is next darkest and mark it B. Mark the next darkest C, and so on until the darkest point is reached. These comparisons may be made much more accurately if, when looking at the object, the eyes are partly closed so as to see through the eyelashes. This will cause a blur that will eliminate the smaller details and give a better chance to judge the relative values of the broad masses of light and shade. Supposing, as in our illustration, we have found four grades of shading on the box. Let the lightest side, that which is most exposed to the light, marked A in the illustration, be represented by the white of the paper. Side B will be a grade darker and may be put on with the hard or medium pencil. Side C is still darker and may be put on with a grade softer pencil. The shadow D is still darker and may be made with a grade darker pencil. Reserve the softest pencil to shade the darkest places.

If only one pencil is used, the different grades of shading may be made by pressure on the pencil — light pressure for light shades, and stronger pressure for deeper or darker shades.

Usually, there are many more shades than are represented in the illustration, but the process is the same, however great the number.

It is best to practice on very simple objects at first, such as a cube, until some degree of accuracy is gained.

There will be a tendency at first to make the shading too light. This fault may be overcome by marking in a part of the deepest shading at first so that the two extremes of light and shade are before the eye to assist in judging the values of the remaining shades.

It is not necessary to make the light and shade in the drawing of the same brightness and depth that it is on the real object. This is usually impossible. It is only necessary to keep the *relative proportion* of light and shade correct. The sun is many times brighter than the whitest paper, and the deepest shades in nature are much darker than the blackest pencil. Yet both of these extremes may be represented truthfully on common white paper by keeping the relative proportion of light and shade correct.

There are three general grades of light in shading:

1. *Bright light.*

2. *Half light.*

3. *Diffused light.*

In bright light, the shades are comparatively light, and the shadows dark. Figs. 4, 16, and 19.

In half light, the shades and shadows are about equal in depth. Figs. 5, 17, and 12.

In diffused light, the shades and shadows are not defined; they are indefinite and blend together. Figs. 6 and 18.

Observe (1) that the shades in Figs. 4 and 16 are lighter than the shadows. (2) That the shades and shadows in Fig. 5 and 17 are about equal in depth. (3) That the shades in Figs. 6 and 18 are not defined but blend in together and that the shadows also are undefined.

FIGURE 11 is in bright light because the shade is lighter than the shadow. Fig. 19 is in bright light. Fig. 12 is in bright half light. Fig. 7 is in bright half light, and Fig. 3 is in the same light, and Fig. 23 is in partially diffused light, such as would be seen if the sun were partially obscured by light clouds or haze.

A diffused light is usually preferred to draw in for the reason that it does not contain strongly defined lines and edges and such strong contrasts of light and shade. It is also preferable because it is more at the command of the draughtsman and does not subject him to so many conditions but allows him to work out his ideas with freedom and delicacy.

But perhaps the bright and half lights are the best to begin shading in, as the shades and shadows can be easily seen and possess definite form.

The shade and shadow of the mass, or the object taken as a whole, is of more importance than

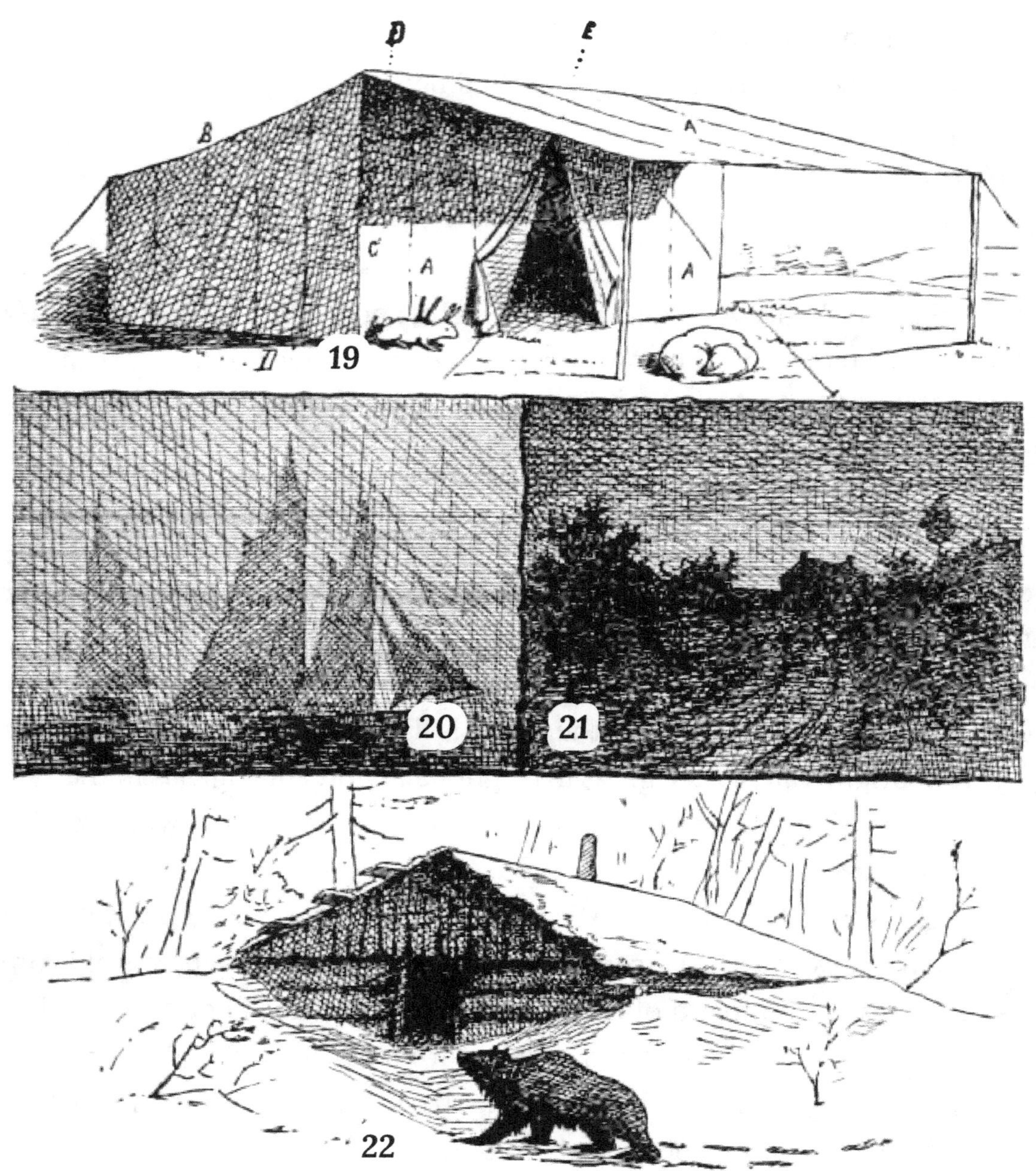

D
E
B
A
C
A
A
19
20
21
22

that of the details.

Figure 13 represents the mass shade, and Fig. 14 the detailed shade. In Fig. 13, no attention is given to the details at all. A broad flat shade is put over the shaded part as *dark as the lightest part of the shade*, and into this mass the shade of the details is drawn. Figs. 2 and 3 show the mass shade and the detailed shade plainly.

Observe in Fig. 25 that the whole bunch of grapes taken as a unit has a shade and a shadow of its own that does not belong to the individual grape. Observe in Fig. 26 that each individual grape has a shade of its own that does not belong to the whole bunch, and in Fig. 27 observe that each individual grape has a detailed shade of its own that does not belong to each grape as a whole. We must then look for (1) the shade and shadow of the whole, which will include the shadow of the parts; (2) the shade of the parts; (3) the shade of the details.

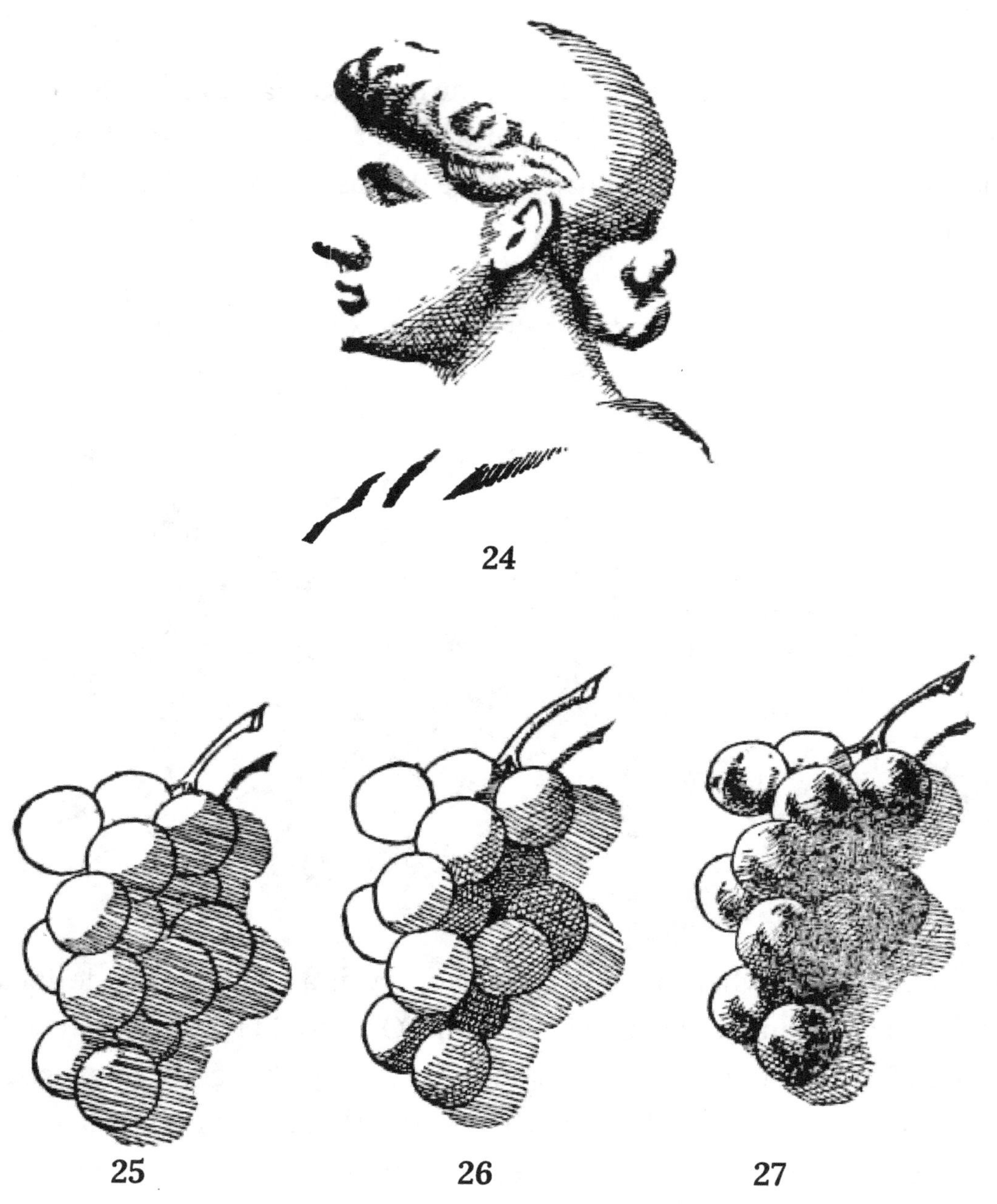

Place objects composed of a number of parts before you in the light, and study these three points carefully. A bunch of grapes, a pile of blocks, a group of fruit, a large flower are good examples to study. Observe a compact bush or tree, a distant wood, a group of buildings, or a pile of rubbish for the same points.

When shading round or curved surfaces, it is best to keep the light and shade separated as much as possible. After drawing the object in outline: (1) Carefully separate the light from the shade by means of a light line as in Fig. 1. (2) Place an even shade over the shaded part as dark as the lightest part of the shade as in Fig. 2. (3) Into this general mass-shade mark the deeper shades as in Fig. 3. Figs. 8, 9, and 10 express the same idea with a little more complicated object.

Always look for the broad masses of light and shade first, which are best seen through the half-closed eyes, and then the shade of the parts is comparatively easy to manage.

Care must be taken not to mistake color for shade. They are quite independent of each other and should not be confused. Close observation is usually sufficient to detect both.

Shades and shadows are opposite to the light that causes them.

In Figs. 3–6, the light comes from the right. In Fig. 7, from the left. In Fig. 29, from directly in front. In Fig. 30, directly back. In Fig. 31, from diagonally back, and in Fig. 32, diagonally in front. In Fig. 10, the light comes from diagonally in front.

A shadow is darkest nearest the shadow that casts it.

In very bright sunshine, this cannot be seen, as the shadow is the same throughout, but in half light, it can be readily seen.

In Fig. 7, notice that the shadow is darkest nearest the object that casts it. The shadow of the awning on the side of the tent in Fig. 19 is darkest where it joins the awning.

There is a saying that "an artist is not accountable for his light." To a certain extent, this is true, for so endless and multifarious are the changes it assumes that it seems to be entirely at the caprice of the draughtsman, but this should not be carried to the extremes of putting shades in impossible places or shadows where they do not belong. Nature does not do this, and she is the best authority. Still, there is no question but what much liberty may be taken with shades and shadows and great compass given to their utility.

A reflex light is light reflected into a shade or shadow.

The reflex light is usually caused by some surrounding object reflecting the light into the shade or shadow.

Round or cylindrical objects usually have a strong reflected light at the outer edge of the shaded side, the darkest part of the shade being removed nearer the center of the object. In Fig. 12, the light part of the shade between the darkest part and the shadow is the reflected light. It may be seen also in Figs. 14–17 and on the grapes in Fig. 27. The subject of reflex lights is a wide one and full of interest.

Other conditions being equal, the further an object is away, the lighter it becomes.

28

The point of rocks in Fig. 28 can be plainly seen, even to the crevices and details of the rocks, but across the lake, the wood is not only lighter in shade but the details are less marked and more massed together. The hill beyond is still lighter and the details less defined, while the mountains beyond are simply broad masses of shade with no visible details. Distance obliterates the details and broadens the masses.

Shadows are often used to show the shape of objects that cannot otherwise be seen.

In Fig. 7, the shape of the wheel is shown to be round by the shadow it casts on the ground, and the post is shown to be a fence directly in front of the eye by the shadow it casts on the ground at the right.

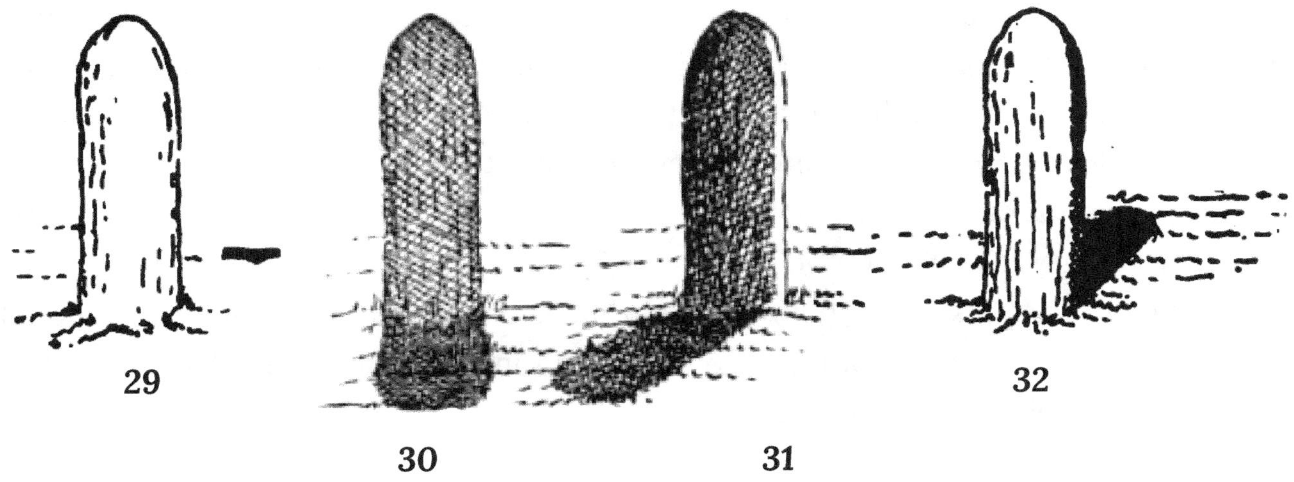

29

30

31

32

Strictly speaking, there is no outline in nature.

That which we commonly call outline is the dividing line between two shades, the ending of one shade and the beginning of another. Fig. 19 contains no outline; the shade alone is represented, and that suggests the outline. The distant hills and mountains in Fig. 28 have no outline but simply one shade ending and another beginning. Observe in nature how the fields, hills, woods, etc., are merely patches of shade and color that end more or less abruptly.

Fog, haze, smoke, and storms obscure distance, shade, shadow, and details.

These all have a tendency to make objects of the same shade. Fig. 20 represents a fog. Observe that there is no distance and that the vessels show very little, if any, detail.

Darkness and clouds obliterate shadows and cast an even shade over all objects.

In cloudy weather, there is very little detailed shade and shadow because a shade is cast over everything alike. Compare Figs. 20 and 21 representing fog and darkness; in one, the distance is obscured, and in the other, it is not. The fog covers the light; the darkness is merely the absence of it.

No more should be put in the drawing than is essential to complete the idea to be expressed.

Parts that are not necessary to complete the idea should be suppressed or omitted. In Fig. 22, attention is to be drawn to the end of the shanty and to the bear in the foreground. This is done by placing them in the most conspicuous place in the picture, which is at or near the center, and by making them the darkest part of the picture. The trees beyond the shanty are suppressed by leaving them in outline so they will not attract attention.

All of the illustrations in this chapter are emphasized by omitting all surrounding objects but those necessary to complete the idea.

It is useless to begin shading before the outline is completed or to think any amount of shading will make a correct drawing out of a poor outline. He who cannot represent form by outline will not be able to do so by light and shade.

HOW TO STUDY SHADE AND SHADOW.

Choose for models a cube, a cylinder, and a sphere, also several blocks similar to Fig. 4, about four inches long.

Study the models (1) in bright light, (2) in half light, (3) in diffused light.

Bright light is direct sunlight.

Half light is when the sun is partly obscured by haze, light clouds, or by a screen made of cotton sheeting.

Diffused light is the light of an ordinary room or of a cloudy day.

Place one of the blocks in a bright light on a plain light surface and draw it (1) with the light coming from the right as in Fig. 4, (2) with the light coming from the left as in Fig. 7, (3) with the light shining directly on the block as in Fig. 29, (4) with the block between you and the light as in Fig. 30, (5) with the light coming from diagonally back as in Fig. 31, (6) with the light coming over the left shoulder as in Fig. 32, (7) with the light coming over the right shoulder. Study the cube, the cylinder, and the sphere in the same manner.

Observe how the shadows increase in length from morning till noon and from noon till evening.

Study the same models in diffused light.

Study reflex light on the cylinder and sphere in both bright and diffused light. Reflex light may be modified by using a sheet of white paper for a reflector to reflect light into the shade.

Study the mass shade and the detailed shade of a pile of blocks.

EASY PROBLEMS.

Problem 1. — (1) Draw Fig. 1. (2) Add to it the mass shade as in Fig. 2. (3) Add the detailed shade as in Fig. 3.

Problem 2. — (1) Draw Fig. 1. (2) Shade it in bright light as in Fig. 4. (2) Change it to half light as in Fig. 5. (3) Shade it in diffused light as in Fig. 6.

Problem 3. — (1) Draw Fig. 4 with the light coming from the left as in Fig. 7. (2) With the light coming from the right as in Fig. 3. (3) With the light shining directly on the post as in Fig. 29. (4) With the post between you and the light as in Fig. 30. (5) With the light coming from diagonally back as in Fig. 31. (6) With the light coming from diagonally in front as in Fig. 32.

Problem 4. — (1) Draw Fig. 8. (2) Add to it the mass shade as in Fig. 9. (3) Add the detailed shade as in Fig. 10. (4) Draw and shade in like manner from nature a maple tree. (5) A chestnut tree. (6) A bush.

Problem 5. — Draw and shade a round disk in bright light with the edge toward you and with the light coming from the left as in Fig. 7.

Problem 6. — Shade Fig. 12 with the light coming from the right.

Problem 7. — Draw and shade Fig. 16 on the blackboard with white crayon.

Problem 8. — Shade Fig. 19 with the light coming from the left.

Problem 9. — Draw and shade Fig. 19, Fig. 20, Fig. 21, Fig. 22.

Problem 10. — Draw and shade Fig. 23. Shade Fig. 23 in bright sunlight.

Problem 11. — Draw and shade Fig. 24.

Problem 12. — (1) Draw Fig. 25 and add the mass shade. (2) The shade of the parts. (3) The shade of the details.

Problem 13. — Draw and shade Fig. 28.

REVIEW QUESTIONS.

1. What is the primary effect of light, shade, and shadow on an object?

2. What is relief in drawing? Distinctness? Solidity? Emphasis?

3. How may an object be emphasized?

4. Do shades and shadows have substance? What are they?

5. What is a shade? A shadow?

6. What is the difference between a shade and a shadow?

7. Point out the shade in Fig. 19. The shadows.

8. What kind of objects should be chosen to shade from at first?

9. What is the highest light possible when shading on paper? The deepest dark?

10. What are the two extremes in shading?

11. Describe the process of shading.

12. How many grades of light and shade in Fig. 11? Fig. 19?

13. How may the masses be clearly seen when there are many details?

14. How may the tendency of making shades too light be overcome?

15. How may brightest sunlight and deepest shade be represented?

16. Name the three general grades of light.

17. Which is the darkest in bright light, the shade or the shadow? In half light?

18. What is the chief characteristic of diffused light?

19. Is Fig. 3 in bright, half, or diffused light? Fig. 6? Fig. 5? Fig. 13? Fig. 12? Fig. 19? Fig. 14? Fig. 30?

20. What light is best for a beginning student to draw in?

21. What light is usually preferred by the draughtsman? Why?

22. Which is of the most importance: the mass shade or the shade of the details?

23. How dark may the mass shade be made?

24. Should the light and shade be kept separate when shading round objects? How separated?

25. What shade should we look for first? Second? Third?

26. Where is a shadow the darkest?

27. What is the characteristic of the shadow in bright sunlight?

28. Is an artist accountable for his light?

29. May much liberty be taken with shades and shadows?

30. What is a reflected light?

31. Point out the reflected light in Fig. 12. Fig. 15. Fig. 17. Fig. 27.

32. What does distance do to shades?

33. How many grades of shade in Fig. 28?

34. How are shadows sometimes used to show the shape of an object?

35. How is it that there is no outline in nature?

36. What effect have fog, haze, smoke, and storms on an object?

37. What effect have darkness and clouds on an object?

38. Which is the most opaque: fog or darkness? Which is darker?

39. What should be put in a picture?

40. Is it right to omit any part of a drawing?

41. Will nice shading correct the outline of a drawing?

42. When is there no shade or shadow?

43. Where is the darkest point of the shading on a cylinder?

44. How could the dog in Fig. 19 be emphasized?

45. What does Fig. 1 teach? Fig. 2? Fig. 3? Fig. 4? Fig. 5? Fig. 6? Fig. 7? Fig. 8? Fig. 19? Fig. 12? Fig. 11?

46. What does Fig. 18 teach? Figs. 16, 17, and 18? Figs. 25, 26, and 27?

47. What does Fig. 22 teach? Fig. 24? Fig. 28?

REFLECTIONS.

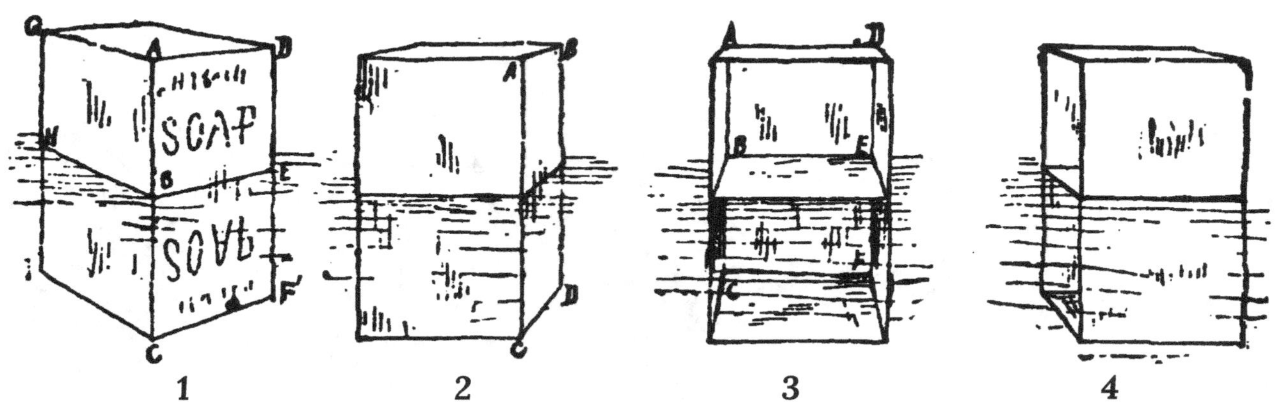

All surfaces reflect light to a greater or lesser degree, but only polished surfaces reflect images. In nature, water is the great reflector. So prominent is this characteristic of water that it is difficult to represent it in a picture without reflections.

Perfectly still water is a mirror and reflects images as accurately from its surfaces as a glass mirror; so we will begin our study of reflections by substituting a mirror for real water.

Place a mirror horizontally on the table before you. Place on the mirror a cube or box as in Fig. 1 and observe: (1) That the reflection is an inverted image of the box and looks very much as if there were two boxes, one above another. (2) That corners C and F are the reflections of the corners A, D, and C, and that A B is equal to B C, D E to E F, and G H to H I. (3) That the top face of the box can be seen but not in the reflection. (4) That the receding lines of both box and reflection vanish at the same point. This may be seen plainly in Figs. 2, 3, and 4. (5) In Fig. 2 that the receding line C D slants more than the line reflected A B, the same as if it were a real box. (6) In Fig. 3 that the distances A B and D E are equal to B C and E F, and that the part of the inside of the box that does not show in the real box shows in the reflection.

The reflection may be drawn and the same rules followed as in drawing the real box.

(1) Place a box on the mirror and draw it as in Fig. 1. (2) Place it below and at the left of the eye as in Fig. 2. (3) Below the eye as in Fig. 3. (4) Below and at the right of the eye as in Fig. 4. (5) Place an object on top of the box and draw it.

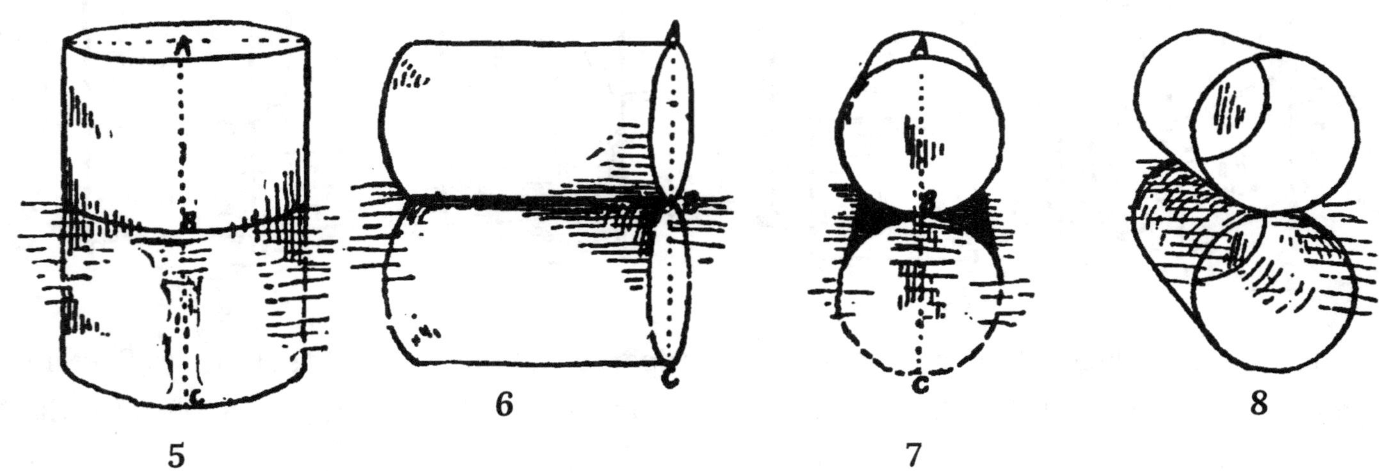

Place a vertical cylinder on the mirror as in Fig. 5 and observe: (1) That the top face of the real cylinder can be seen but not in the reflection. (2) That the distances A B and B C are equal. (3) That the curved line through C curves more than the one through B and that the curved line through B curves more than the one through A. (4) In Fig. 6 that the reflection of the horizontal cylinder is the same as the cylinder itself (Fig. 6 is represented as being at the left and on a level with the eye). (5) In Figs. 7 and 8 that the receding lines of both cylinders and reflections vanish at the same point. (1) Place a vertical cylinder on the mirror and draw it. (2) Place a horizontal cylinder on the mirror and draw it at the left and below the eye. (3) Below the eye. (4) At the right and below the eye. (5) Place a receding cylinder on the mirror at the right and below the eye and draw it. (6) Below the eye. (7) Below and at the left of the eye.

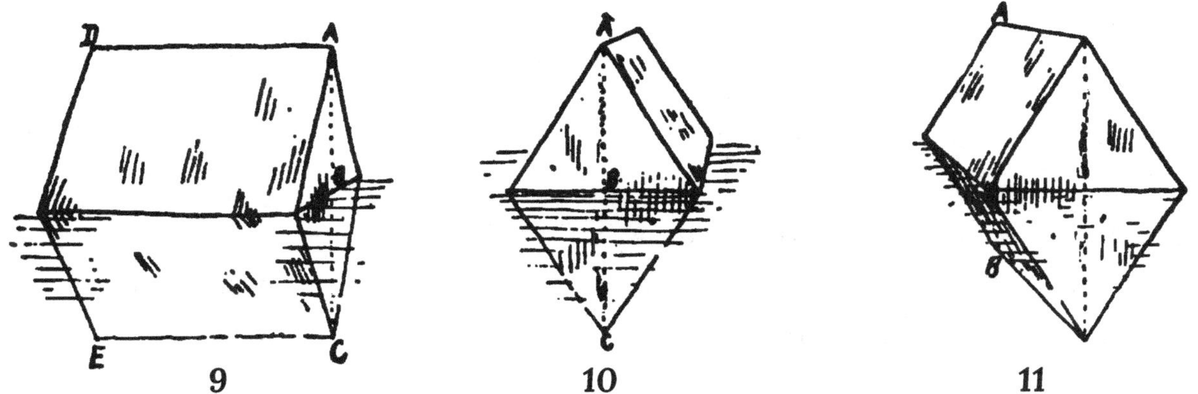

9   10   11

Place a horizontal, triangular prism similar to Fig. 9 on the mirror and observe: (1) That the distance A B is equal to B C. (2) That the point E is directly below the point D. (3) In Fig. 10 that one side shows in the prism, but not in the reflection. (4) In Fig. 11 that the reflected side is more narrow than the side reflected. (5) That the point B is directly below the point A. (6) That the receding lines in Figs. 10 and 11 of both prisms and reflections vanish at the same point.

(1) Place a horizontal, triangular prism on the mirror and draw it below and at the left of the eye. (2) Below and at the right of the eye. (3) Below the eye. (4) Place a receding triangular prism on the mirror and draw it below and at the left of the eye. (5) Below and at the right of the eye. (6) Draw a vertical triangular prism on the mirror.

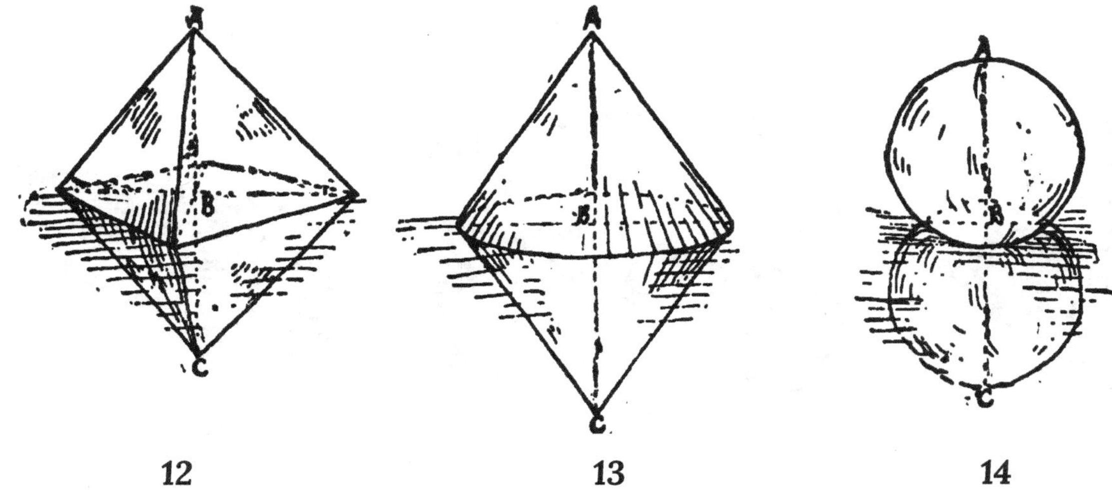

12   13   14

Place a pyramid, a cone, and a sphere on the mirror as in Figs. 12, 13, and 14 and observe: (1) That in each the distance A B is equal to B C. (2) That the points A B and C are in the same vertical line.

(1) Place a pyramid on the mirror and draw it. (2) A cone. (3) A sphere. (4) Place a sphere on a cube and draw them. (5) Place a sphere on a vertical cylinder and draw them. (6) Place a cone on a vertical cylinder and draw them.

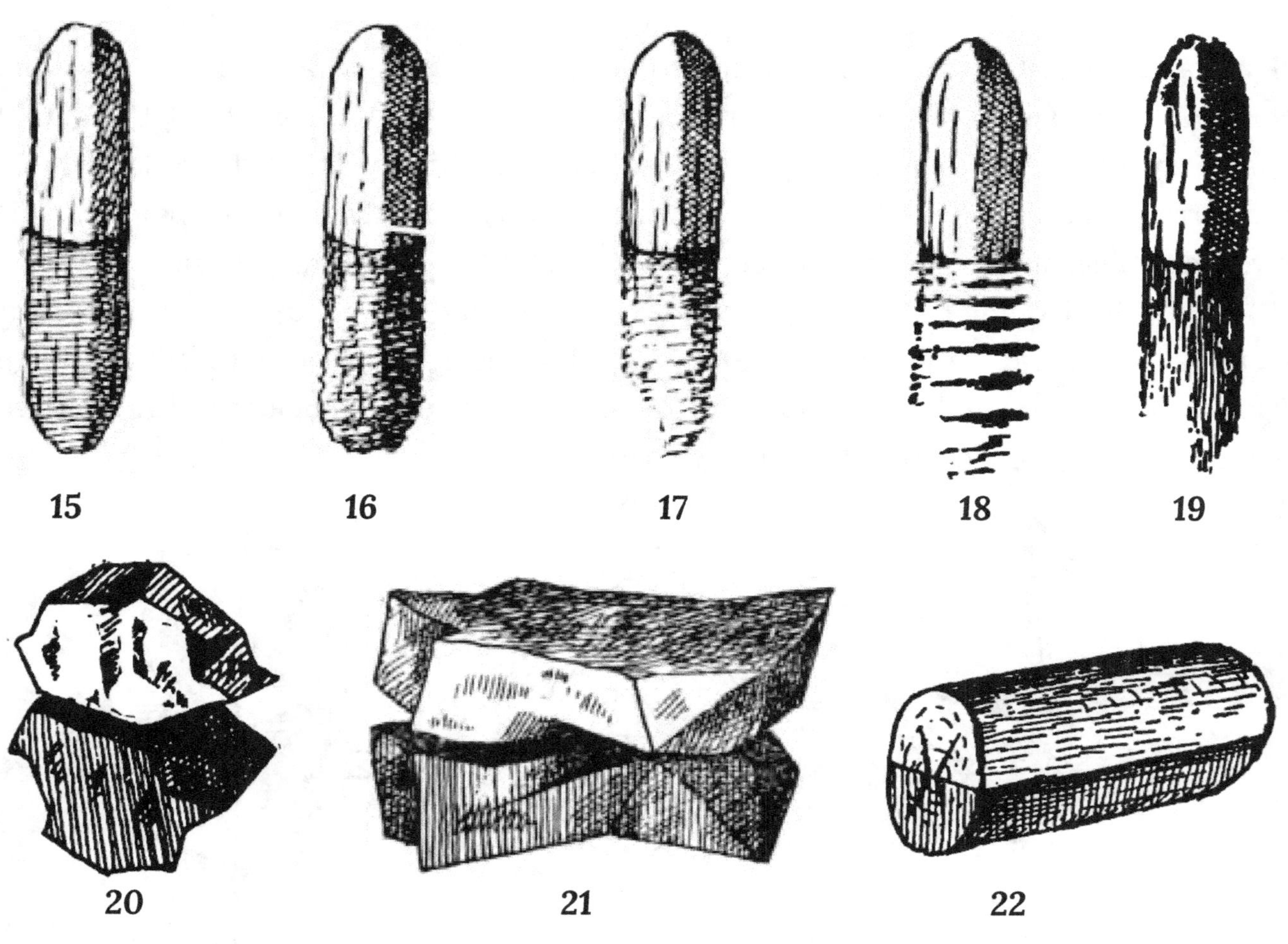

15 16 17 18 19

20 21 22

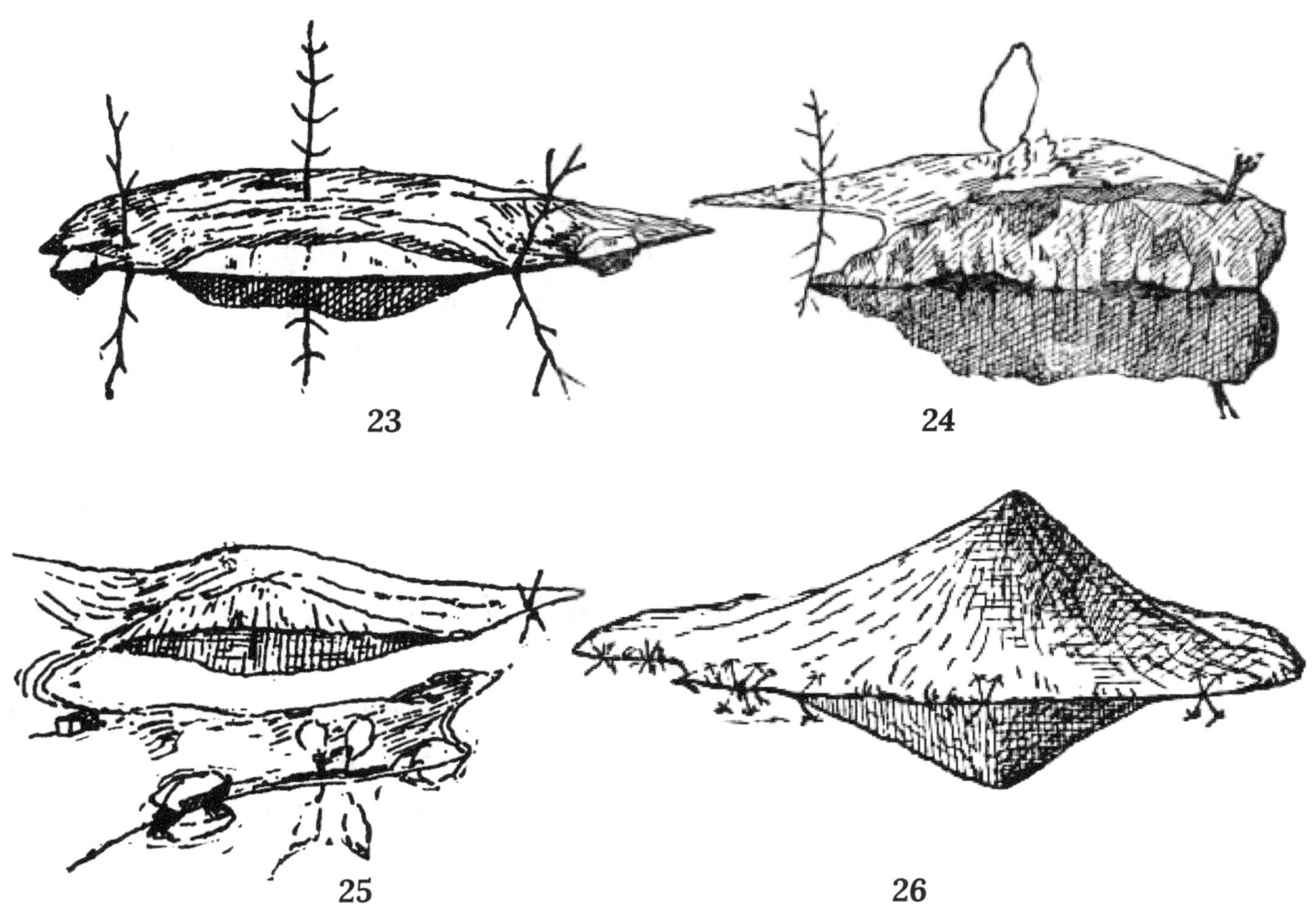

23

24

25

26

Figs. 20–26 are objects laid on the mirror and drawn.

Figs. 20 and 21 are bits of stone with their reflections in the mirror. In a picture, objects are large or small by comparison with familiar objects. As there is no familiar object to compare the stones with, they look like large boulders when in reality the bits of stone that they were drawn from were of the same size as the drawings.

Fig. 22 is a half-cylinder.

Fig. 23 is a handful of corn-meal laid on the surface of the mirror and brushed in the shape of an island. The trees are small twigs stuck in the corn-meal.

Fig. 24 is a small stone with the corn-meal brushed up against it so as to form an island with a cliff or bluff on one side.

Fig. 25 represents a point of land with a bay or lagoon extending into it.

Fig. 26 represents a volcanic island, also made with corn-meal.

Observe in all of these illustrations that the reflection is between you and the object reflected.

Place the following and similar objects on the mirror and draw them: pieces of stone, a cork, pieces of crayon, a half-cylinder, a spool, some twigs, a rubber eraser, a thimble, etc.

Place on the mirror a handful of sand or corn-meal and brush it into the form of an island, using small twigs for trees and bits of stone for boulders, bluffs, etc. Represent in the island a bay, a lake, a valley, a hill, and a mountain. Make a round island, a long island, an irregular island, etc.

Reflections are as varied as the conditions under which they are seen. When the water is perfectly still, an exact inverted image of the object is given as in Figs. 15 and 36. When the water is slightly in motion, the motion will be imparted to the reflection as in Figs. 16, 27, 28, 29, 30, and 31.

When the water is still more in motion, the reflection is often partly obliterated as in Figs. 17, 29, and 32.

When the water is covered with smooth ripples, the top of each little wavelet catches the reflection as in Fig. 18 or Fig. 33. Reflections from hard polished surfaces do not have that lateral motion given by the water when slightly in motion, but the reflection is hard like that in Figs. 18, 34, and 35.

27

Observe in Fig. 27: (1) That each point on the steps is as far above the surface of the water as the reflection of that point seems below the surface. (2) That the shadow on the wall is reflected the same as the solid parts. (3) That the receding lines of the reflection go to the same point as the receding lines of the solid parts.

When the surface of the water is disturbed by wind, the reflection of distant objects, such as the hills and islands in Fig. 32, cannot be seen at all, and the reflection of objects in the foreground is strongest the nearer they are to the object reflected. Notice in Fig. 29 the reflections of the bush, cracks in the rocks, and the deer, how they are strongest where they begin and gradually become fainter as the distance increases.

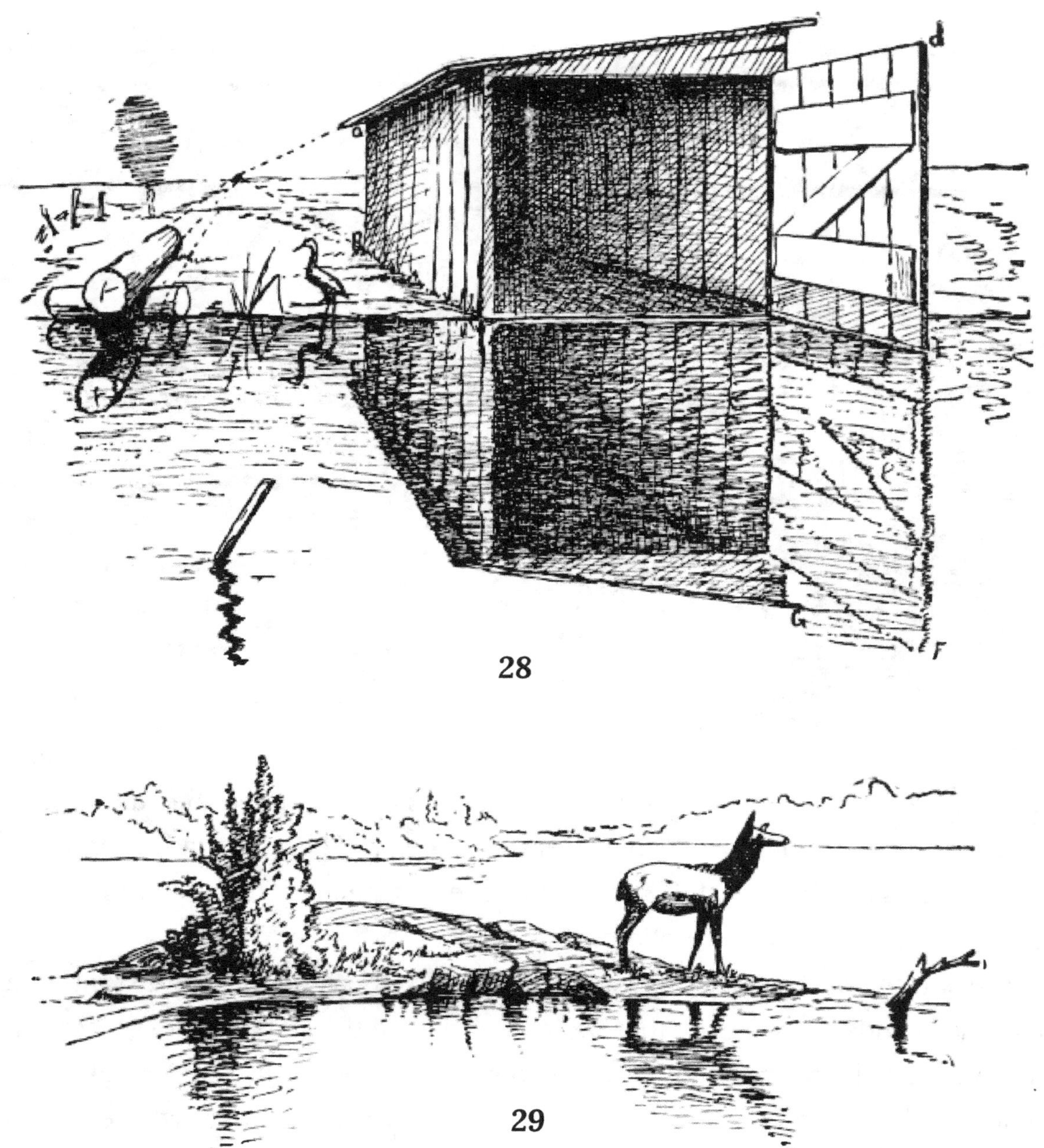

28

29

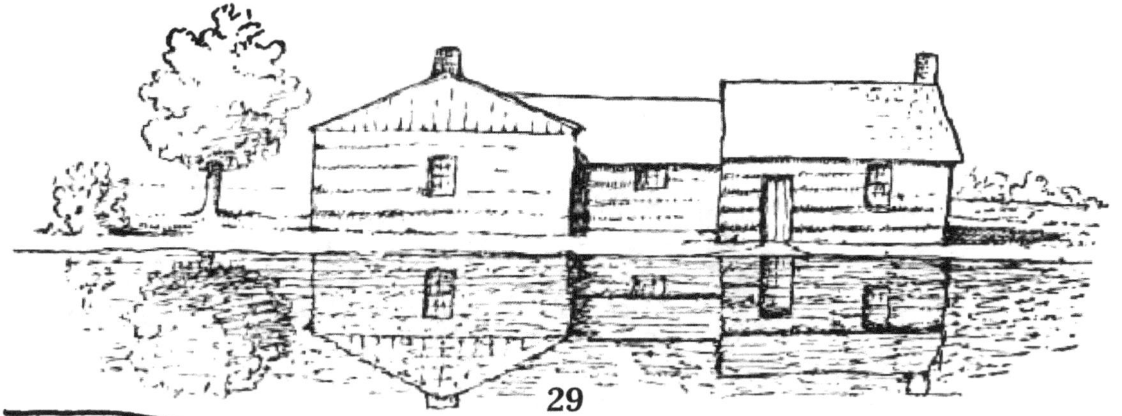

29

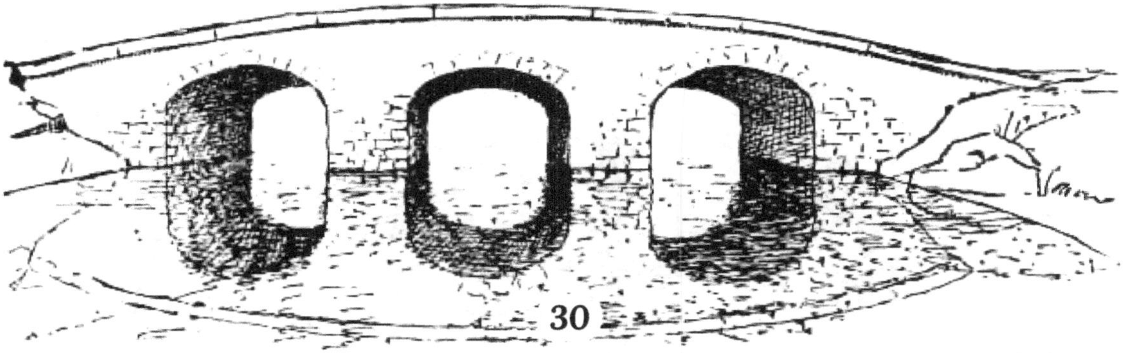

30

31

33
34
35
36

EASY PROBLEMS.

Problem 1. — Draw on the blackboard a box and its reflection.

Problem 2. — Draw on the blackboard a horizontal cylinder and its reflection. A vertical cylinder. A receding cylinder.

Problem 3. — Draw on the blackboard a horizontal, triangular prism and its reflection. A receding triangular prism. A vertical triangular prism.

Problem 4. — Draw on the blackboard a pyramid and its reflection. A cone. A sphere.

Problem 5. — Draw on the blackboard a post and its reflection as seen in a mirror. As seen in the water slightly in motion. As seen in water on which there are ripples. As seen in a polished surface.

Problem 6. — Copy Fig. 27 and then draw it on the blackboard. The same with Fig. 28. Fig. 29. Fig. 30. Fig. 31. Fig. 32.

Problem 7. — Draw a half-cylinder and its reflection on the blackboard. A spool. A stone. A tree.

Problem 8. — Draw Fig. 31 with a reflection similar to Fig. 18.

Problem 9. — Draw Fig. 32 with a reflection similar to Fig. 32.

REVIEW QUESTIONS.

1. What surfaces reflect light? Images?

2. What is the great reflector in nature?

3. What may be used as a substitute for still water when studying reflections?

4. How do perfect reflections differ from the object reflected?

5. What part of the box in Fig. 1 can be seen that cannot be seen in the reflection? In Fig. 3?

In Fig. 4?

6. How can the C. of V. be found in Figs. 2, 3, and 4? For Figs. 10 and 11?

7. Which will slant more, the receding lines of the box or its reflection?

8. Find the C. of V. in Figs. 7 and 8.

9. Which is the darker, the object or its reflection?

10. What are Figs. 20 and 21 to represent?

11. What is Fig. 23 composed of? Fig. 24?

12. How can a small stone be made to look like a large boulder in a picture?

13. Where is the reflection of an object found?

14. What is the difference between a reflection and a shadow?

15. Can a shadow be reflected? Point to a reflected shadow in Fig. 27.

16. How may islands, hills, etc., be formed on the mirror?

17. How may trees and rocks be represented on the surface of the mirror?

18. What effect has water in motion on a reflection? What effect have ripples?

19. What effect has a hard, polished surface on the reflection?

20. Does water always reflect images? When does it not?

21. What lesson may be learned from Fig. 27? Fig. 28? Fig. 29? Fig. 31? Fig. 32?